"HOW DARE YOU DISCUSS MY PERSONAL LIFE WITH OUR DAUGHTER? WHAT I DO IS NONE OF YOUR BUSINESS, WILL TYLER!"

"Anything that affects Erin is my business. And that includes the men you bring into her life."

His arrogance shoved Tori over the brink. Her hand flashed upward. He made no move to stop her as she slapped the side of his face, so hard that the sound of it cracked like a pistol shot in the room. The impact stung her palm and hurt her wrist. Pain brought tears to her eyes.

Will stood like stone. Only his eyes reacted to her blow, narrowing, darkening. Then his hands moved up to rest on her shoulders, their weight anchoring her in place. His gaze drilled into hers.

"Damn it to hell, woman, I should've left you in that truck to freeze!" he muttered.

In a swift, sure movement, he bent and captured her mouth with his.

Don't miss any of Janet Dailey's bestsellers

ALWAYS WITH LOVE *** AMERICAN DESTINY ***
AMERICAN DREAMS *** BANNON BROTHERS:
HONOR *** BANNON BROTHERS: TRIUMPH ***
BANNON BROTHERS: TRUST *** BECAUSE OF YOU
*** BRING THE RING *** CALDER PROMISE ***
CALDER STORM *** CAN'T SAY GOODBYE ***
CHRISTMAS IN COWBOY COUNTRY ***
CHRISTMAS ON MY MIND *** CLOSE TO YOU ***
A COWBOY UNDER MY CHRISTMAS TREE ***
CRAZY IN LOVE *** DANCE WITH ME ***
EVERYTHING *** EVE'S CHRISTMAS *** FOREVER
*** GOING MY WAY *** GREEN CALDER GRASS
*** HAPPILY EVER AFTER *** HAPPY HOLIDAYS
*** HEIRESS *** IT TAKES TWO *** LET'S BE
JOLLY *** LONE CALDER STAR *** LONG, TALL
CHRISTMAS *** LOVER MAN *** MAN OF MINE
*** MASQUERADE *** MAYBE THIS CHRISTMAS
*** MERRY CHRISTMAS, COWBOY *** MISTLETOE
AND MOLLY *** RANCH DRESSING *** RIVALS ***
SANTA IN A STETSON *** SANTA IN MONTANA ***
SCROOGE WORE SPURS *** SEARCHING FOR
SANTA *** SHIFTING CALDER WIND ***
SOMETHING MORE *** STEALING KISSES ***
SUNRISE CANYON *** TANGLED VINES *** TEXAS
FIERCE *** TEXAS KISS *** TEXAS TALL ***
TEXAS TOUGH *** TEXAS TRUE *** THAT LOVING
FEELING *** TO SANTA WITH LOVE *** TRY TO
RESIST ME *** WEARING WHITE *** WHEN YOU
KISS ME *** WITH THIS KISS *** YES, I DO ***
YOU'RE STILL THE ONE

Published by Kensington Publishing Corporation

TEXAS
TALL

JANET
DAILEY

ZEBRA BOOKS
KENSINGTON PUBLISHING CORP.
http://www.kensingtonbooks.com

ZEBRA BOOKS are published by

Kensington Publishing Corp.
119 West 40th Street
New York, NY 10018

First Kensington Books Hardcover Printing: September 2016
First Zebra Books Mass-Market Paperback Printing: July 2017
ISBN-13: 978-1-4201-3378-3
ISBN-10: 1-4201-3378-0

eISBN-13: 978-1-4201-3379-0
eISBN-10: 1-4201-3379-9

10 9 8 7 6 5 4 3 2 1

Printed in the United States of America

With gratitude to Elizabeth Lane, without whom this book would not have been written.

CHAPTER 1

The first November chill had painted the Rimrock Ranch with a golden brush. From the glint of sunrise on the high escarpment to the sweep of yellow grass across the plain, from the fading willows along the creek to the bursts of saffron, where the cottonwoods grew, the land was the color of Spanish gold—the gold that, legend whispered, lay hidden in a canyon on the border of the ranch.

By day, flocks of migrating birds swept southward. Meadowlarks settled on the pastures and brightened the air with their calls. Ducks, geese, and sandhill cranes traced elegant V formations across the autumn sky. By night the stars were diamond sharp, the harvest moon ripe and mellow above the horizon.

A man with an easy mind would have savored the season's rich beauty. But Will Tyler's mind was far from easy. Wherever he looked, what he saw was not so much beauty as trouble.

The grass was weak, still recovering from the summer drought and the raging wildfire that had charred the lower pastures. Even if the winter turned out to be mild, would there be enough to feed the calves and breeding stock he needed to sustain the ranch? Or, with finances strained to the breaking point, would he be forced to buy more hay at a cutthroat price for the cattle he'd kept after selling off most of his herd?

Will had counted on the auction of Sky Fletcher's superbly trained colts to shore up the ranch's funds. But the drought-impoverished Texas ranchers, who would have scrambled to buy the lot, were, like Will, too cash-strapped to pay. Only a few young horses had been sold, and those at cut-rate prices.

Worries gnawed at Will as he drove his twelve-year-old daughter, Erin, home to the ranch for the weekend. While school was in session, the girl lived in Blanco Springs with her mother, Will's ex-wife, Tori. But her weekends and summers were Will's. These days Erin, who loved the ranch, was the only bright spot in his life.

Will drove his pickup carefully, with the headlights on high beam. It was late, almost eleven, and the narrow, two-lane road from town was unfenced here, with a meager shoulder and steep barrow pits on either side. Deer, coyotes, even cattle and horses, had been known to wander onto the asphalt at night and cause serious accidents. He would've brought Erin home before dark, but she'd gone to a friend's house for a birthday party. She'd phoned him when it was over and he'd picked her up there.

Erin had turned on the pickup's radio. The local country music station added a twanging underbeat to the thrum of the truck's engine.

"So what's new with you?" Will asked, breaking the relaxed silence between them. "Anything happening at school? Got a boyfriend yet?"

The boyfriend question was an ongoing joke between

them. At two months shy of thirteen, Erin was more interested in horses than in boys. And Will would've run off any boy who got within a dozen yards of his daughter.

"Not yet. But Mom might have one. She's got a date tonight."

A knot jerked tight in the pit of Will's stomach. He and Tori had been divorced for eight years, but some part of him still claimed her. The marriage may have been a disaster, but they'd made Erin together—the best thing they'd ever done.

"You don't say?" He feigned a casualness he didn't feel. "Who's the lucky man?"

"His name's Drew Middleton. He's the new principal at the high school."

The knot pulled tighter. "What's he like?"

"He's okay. Seems nice enough."

"Think it's serious?"

"Maybe. Mom hasn't dated anybody in a long time."

"Uh-huh." Will swallowed hard. If Tori had found a man she wanted to date, that was her business. She deserved to be happy. But damn it all, he didn't have to like it.

With Erin at the ranch, Tori would have the house to herself for two nights. The thought of what could be going on there was enough to make Will grind his teeth. *Drew Middleton.* The name tasted like sawdust in his mouth. He'd never met the man, but he already wanted to punch him.

Will had paid scant attention to the radio, but when the signal for an emergency news bulletin came on, it caught his attention. "Turn that up," he told Erin.

The voice came through a crackle of static: *"The sheriff's office is asking for your help in tracking down a man who held up the convenience store in Blanco Springs, took cash, and shot a clerk. The suspect fled on a motorcycle going north. He's described as a white male in his thirties, wearing a black leather jacket and a black motorcycle helmet. He is armed and dangerous. If you see him, call nine-one-one."*

"Hey!" Erin exclaimed as the music came back on. "What if that guy's out here, on this road? What would we do if we saw him?"

"I'd keep driving and let you make the call," Will said. "Somebody like that, with a gun, I wouldn't take a chance on playing hero, especially with you along."

"But what if—" Her words ended in a yelp as the pickup's right front wheel slammed into something solid and stopped dead. Only her seat belt kept her from flying into the dashboard.

Will switched off the key, cursing under his breath. He wasn't sure what he'd hit. It hadn't felt like an animal, but just in case, he pulled his loaded .38 Smith and Wesson revolver from under the driver's seat. If he'd struck some unlucky creature, he'd want to put it out of its misery—or defend himself if it had any fight left.

He found a flashlight in the console. "Stay put," he told Erin as he opened his door. "Whatever happens, don't get out."

Climbing to the ground, he closed the door behind him and turned on the flashlight. The night air was chilly through his denim jacket, the full moon veiled by drifting clouds. The distant wail of a coyote echoed across the sage flats as Will walked around to the passenger side of the truck.

The pickup had come to rest at a cockeyed angle, probably blown a tire, which he'd need to change. In the beam of the flashlight, he could see what he'd hit. It was the engine block for some kind of vehicle, most likely fallen off the back of a flatbed because the fool driver hadn't bothered to tie it down. Heavy and solid, its edges were sharp enough to puncture a tire, which was just what had happened. If he hadn't been distracted by the announcement on the radio, he might have seen it in time to stop.

Erin rolled down the window. "What is it?" she asked. "Is it an animal?"

"No, just a big, nasty chunk of metal. But I'll have to change the tire."

"Can I help? I can hold the light for you."

"No, just stay put. I'll be fine."

He'd stuck the .38 in his belt and was walking around to get the spare and the jack when he saw it—a single headlight approaching fast down the long, straight road from the direction of town, maybe half a mile away. It looked like a motorcycle, sounded like one, too.

Will turned off the flashlight and laid it on the ground. One hand drew the weapon out of his belt. "Close the window, lock the doors, and get down," he ordered Erin. He caught the flash of her frightened eyes as she obeyed. He'd probably scared her for nothing, but he couldn't take any chances.

The motorcycle was slowing down. Maybe the rider was just some Good Samaritan wanting to help. But Will couldn't lay odds on that. He might be safer inside the truck, but that could expose Erin to more danger. Right now, his daughter's safety was the only thing that mattered.

A few yards ahead of the truck, the motorcycle pulled onto the shoulder and stopped. The rider swung off his machine. He wore a black leather jacket with a dark helmet, the visor pulled down to obscure his face. His right hand held a small pistol with the look of a cheap Saturday-night special. He had to be the robber. Will waited in the shadows, gripping the .38, as the man approached and spoke.

"What the hell happened here? We were supposed to meet down by the crossroad." His whiny-pitched voice sounded vaguely Eastern, and strangely familiar. "Never mind, I got the package on the bike. Show me the money, and we're good."

Will stepped into the moonlight, his pistol leveled at the man's chest. "Hands where I can see them, mister. Now, nice and slow, drop your weapon. Then kick it over here toward me."

"Shit, you're not—" The motorcyclist froze in surprise. He dropped the gun on the ground. As he kicked it toward Will, his hand flashed. Suddenly there was a knife in it. As his arm flexed for the throw, Will pulled the trigger. The .38 roared, striking the man squarely in the chest. He toppled backward, dead by the time he hit the ground.

Will stared down at the bleeding body, cursing out loud. He'd never meant to kill the stupid jackass, but he'd had little choice, especially with Erin to protect.

"Daddy?" Erin had rolled down the window partway. Her voice sounded thin and scared. "Are you all right?"

"I'm fine, honey. Close the window and stay in the truck. Don't try to look. I'll come around." Leaving the body where it lay, he circled behind the truck to the driver's side. Once inside, he reached across the console and gathered his daughter in his arms. She clung to him, trembling.

Will felt shaken, too, when he thought about what he'd just done. His younger brother, Beau, who'd been an army sniper in Iraq, had never revealed how many kills he'd made. But for Will, this was a first. He'd never taken a human life before. Now, even though he'd killed a criminal in self-defense, the thought sickened him.

Erin pulled away as he released her. She'd be all right, Will told himself. She was strong, like Tori. "You need to call the sheriff, Daddy," she said.

"I know. But first I'm going to call your mother."

Will reached for the cell phone in his pocket. As an afterthought, he climbed out of the truck again and closed the door. His conversation with Tori could easily get emotional. It might be better not to have Erin listening.

His legs felt unsteady. Leaning against the side of the cab, he scrolled to Tori's number and pressed the call button. The phone rang, once, then again. Maybe she'd turned it off, the better to enjoy her new boyfriend. But no, it wouldn't be like Tori to do that, not even on a date. She had clients who needed her. More important, she had a daughter.

Will was waiting for his ex-wife's voice message to come on when she picked up. "Will?" He could sense her tension. "What is it? Is Erin all right?"

"Erin's fine," Will said. "But I need you to come and get her. There was an . . . incident on the way to the ranch. The truck's stuck on the road with a blown tire, and I can't leave."

"An *incident,* you say? What happened, Will? What are you not telling me?"

"I'll explain later. Erin said you had a date. Hell, bring him along if you want. I don't care. Whatever you're doing, just drop it and get here. Now."

"I'm on my way. Tell Erin I'm coming." She ended the call without saying good-bye.

Will waited a couple of minutes, then called 911. The night dispatcher who answered his call was a woman whose voice he recognized.

"Carly, this is Will Tyler," he said. "Tell the sheriff he can stop looking for that convenience store robber on the motorcycle. I just shot him."

"Is he dead?"

"As a doornail. I need somebody to come, pronto."

"Where are you?" There was an odd note to her voice.

"About ten miles out of town, on the road to my ranch. My pickup's got a blown tire."

"I hear you. Stay in your truck and don't touch anything. Somebody will be right there."

She hesitated, as if weighing her next words. "There's something you need to know, Will. Whoever you shot, it wasn't the robber. That man was picked up a few minutes ago, headed for the freeway on his motorcycle. The cash was on him, along with the gun and some cigarettes he took. They're bringing him in now."

"I can drive you if you want, Tori." Drew Middleton straightened his tie. Tall and slender, with hazel eyes and light brown hair, he was appealing enough to make Tori wonder if there was a chance for something real between them.

"Not a good idea." She dropped the cell phone back in her purse and reached for the door latch of Drew's Honda Accord. "You've never met my ex, but I can guarantee you that tonight wouldn't be the best time."

"Is everything all right?"

"Erin's all right, evidently. Whatever else is going on, that's Will's problem."

"Hang on. I can at least open your door and walk you to the porch."

Tori waited while he climbed out of the car and came around to the passenger side. Drew had taken her to a seafood dinner and a show in Lubbock. They'd made it back to her driveway for a few minutes of pleasurable front-seat necking. Just as she'd begun to wonder whether she should invite him in, her phone had rung.

Stiletto heels clicking, she strode up the front walk and turned for a quick kiss on the porch. "Gotta go," she said. "Thanks for a very nice evening."

"I'll call you, okay?"

"Sure." She let herself in and raced to grab her fleece-lined ranch jacket out of the hall closet. No time to change out of her dressy black sheath. If Erin needed her, she would get there as fast as she could.

Minutes later, she was in her station wagon, roaring down Main Street, past the Shop Mart, the drugstore, and the Blue Coyote bar, on her way out of town.

Standing outside the pickup, Will gazed down the road at the distant headlights. He hoped to hell it was Tori. He wanted Erin gone before the law showed up. The girl had witnessed next to nothing, and she didn't need to be upset by the ugliness of a crime scene investigation. If the sheriff needed to question her, he could do it tomorrow, at home.

The dispatcher had warned him against touching anything. But Will had taken the liberty of dragging an old blanket out of the truck's backseat and laying it over the dead man's corpse. If he'd just contaminated the evidence, too bad. He didn't need Erin seeing the body, or Tori, either.

He'd thought about phoning Beau, or even Sky, at the ranch, then changed his mind. His brothers had enough on their plates without his adding to the pile. This was his own mess. He would clean it up by himself.

But one question continued to chew on him. If the bastard he'd killed wasn't the robber, who the devil was he?

The headlights were coming closer—a low vehicle going like a bat out of hell. That would be Tori, all right. The truck's hazard lights were blinking. She should be able to see them. But just to make sure, he turned on the flashlight and waved it. Seconds later, the station wagon screeched to a gravel-spitting halt behind the truck.

Tori piled out of the driver's side. Under her open canvas coat, Will could see that she was dressed to kill— tight black dress, dangling earrings, honey-blond hair flowing loose, the way he'd always liked it. And she was wearing those high heels that made her long legs look extra sexy.

All for another man.

But he couldn't let that get to him now. What mattered was that she'd come as soon as she could.

"What's going on? Where's Erin?" Her gaze surveyed the tilted truck. At least, from the driver's side of the cab, she couldn't see the body.

"We hit something and punctured a tire. Erin can tell you more in the car." He opened the driver's-side door of the truck and swung his daughter to the ground. "Just get her out of here, Tori. You can take her to the ranch or home with you. I want her gone by the time the sheriff gets here."

"I'll take her home." Tori caught sight of the motorcycle parked ahead of the truck. "Whose bike is that? Why's the sheriff coming?"

"I'd just gotten out of the truck when that motorcycle

pulled up. The man had a pistol and a knife. I had to shoot him."

"Thank God you had a gun." Wide-eyed, Tori clutched her daughter close. After taking a moment to compose herself, she spoke. "Are you in trouble, Will? Do you need me to stay as your lawyer?"

"I'll be fine. There's no way it could've been anything but self-defense." Will glanced down the road and saw the flicker of approaching red lights. "Just take Erin and go. She doesn't need to be part of this. I'll call you later."

Tori needed no more urging. She raced with Erin to her car, backed away from the truck and turned for home. Will stood watching her taillights as she drove past the oncoming sheriff's vehicle and the ambulance. No one tried to stop her.

Moments later, Blanco County sheriff Abner Sweeney pulled up in his tan SUV. A deputy rode beside him in the passenger seat. The ambulance parked behind him.

Sweeney, a short, pugnacious redhead whose manner had become even cockier since winning the recent election, climbed out of the vehicle. Trailed by his deputy, he stalked up to where Will stood.

"So where's the body, Tyler?" he demanded.

"Around there." Will nodded to the other side of the truck. "I covered him out of common decency, but I didn't touch anything else. I admit to shooting the man, but I fired in self-defense."

"How can I be sure of that?" Sweeney's chin jutted as he glowered up at Will's imposing height. His hand rested on the butt of his pistol.

"You'll see his gun on the ground and the knife still in his right hand," Will said. "And you won't find my prints on anything."

"Did you check his pulse to make sure he was dead?"

"Didn't have to. A thirty-eight blows a mighty big hole, especially at close range. And I know *dead* when I see it."

Two more deputies had come out of the ambulance with an evidence kit, a stretcher, and a folded body bag. After donning latex gloves, they peeled back the blanket to reveal the dead man sprawled in the headlights of Will's truck. His helmet was still in place. Blood from an ugly chest wound had soaked the shirt beneath his leather jacket. One deputy began taking photos of the scene with a small camera, the flash making little bursts of light. Another checked the motorcycle, pulling a packet of white powder from one of the panniers.

Sheriff Sweeney frowned at the body, then turned back to Will. "He's deceased, all right. Suppose you tell me what happened."

Will related the story to the best of his recollection. He hadn't wanted to mention that Erin was with him, but realized that it might come to light later. Better to come clean now than be caught in a lie.

"So your daughter was a witness. Where is she?" Sweeney demanded.

"I called her mother to come get her. And she wasn't really a witness. I ordered her down on the floor when the bastard showed up. She didn't see anything."

"So why would you send her away? Is there some reason you don't want me to question her?" The sheriff's eyes narrowed, as if he suspected some dark, hidden secret.

"You have children, Sweeney. Would you put your young daughter through something like this? If you need to talk to Erin, you can do it tomorrow—with her mother present."

"I'll do that." Sweeney ruminated a moment, maybe remembering that Tori was a lawyer. Abruptly he changed his tack. "You say you'd gotten out to change a flat tire. So what were you doing with a gun?"

The little man seemed determined to prove some kind of wrongdoing. Will's nerves were screaming, but he forced himself to answer calmly. "I already told you. I'd hit something on the road, and I took the gun because I thought it might be an animal. It wasn't, but when the motorcyclist showed up with weapons, I used that gun to protect my daughter."

"And you thought the man was the robber we were after?"

"Yes, until I called the dispatcher. By then, he was already dead."

"Did you look at his face? Maybe raise that visor on his helmet?"

"I told you, I knew better than to touch him."

"Then what do you say we have a look? Maybe somebody here will recognize him." Sweeney turned toward the dead man. By now, the deputies were gathering up the evidence, preparing to bag the body and lift it onto the stretcher. One of them had already taken Will's .38.

The sheriff wasn't wearing gloves. He motioned for one of the deputies to remove the helmet.

As the visor came up and the helmet was lifted free, Will's pulse lurched. He exhaled, his breath whistling through his teeth.

The sheriff's shoulders sagged as if he'd been gut kicked. "God and Jesus," he muttered.

There could be no mistaking the swarthy features and the shaved head with its black Maori tattoos. The man Will had shot dead was Nick Tomescu, the brother of Stella Rawlins, who owned the Blue Coyote.

CHAPTER 2

Slumped on a stool in the darkened bar, Stella Rawlins crushed the butt of her last Marlboro in the overflowing ashtray. Her head ached, and her feet throbbed in their cherry-red high-heeled cowgirl boots. Beneath the black silk blouse she wore, her 38DD bra had chafed a raw line around her ribs. It was well after midnight and the Blue Coyote had been closed for an hour. But she didn't want to leave until her brother Nick showed up—and he was seriously overdue.

Worry chewed at her. What if something had gone wrong? What if he'd screwed up and gotten himself arrested?

True, Nicky wasn't the smartest rooster in the coop. But even he should've been able to carry out the simple errand she'd sent him on—drive to the spot where the road cut off to the burned-out Prescott place, look for a dark blue pickup truck, give the driver the package, take the money, and bring it back to her at the bar. It was a no-brainer. So what could've happened to him?

She ran a nervous hand through her dyed red hair. If

something had gone wrong, Stella knew she'd blame herself. She'd looked after her younger half brother since he was a toddler. While their pretty, alcoholic mother had flitted from man to man, Stella had always been there for him. Last year, when he'd fled New Jersey after informing on the Romanian mob to beat a drug charge, she'd given him shelter here in Blanco Springs and hired him as her bartender and bouncer. Surprisingly, he'd been good at his job.

Maybe she shouldn't have risked him tonight. Nicky had never been quite right in the head. Behind his tough biker façade was a shy, almost childlike man, who became flustered if things didn't go as expected. She didn't dare trust him with anything more complicated than running a few drugs, maybe not even that.

What she needed was a new ally who could think on his feet, somebody she could count on to follow her orders while she kept her own hands clean. But such people tended not to last. Former sheriff Hoyt Axelrod, Slade Haskell, and Sky Fletcher's young cousin, Lute, were all dead, tripped up by their own failings. The last and smartest candidate for the job, Lute's sister, Marie, had betrayed her, killed the hit man Stella had hired to take her out, and vanished without a trace. *Good riddance,* Stella thought. Still, it made her nervous, knowing the woman was out there somewhere, itching for revenge.

Finding the right person would take time. And right now, Nicky, her only living kin, was all she had.

A light rap on the bar's front door broke into her musings. For a split second she hoped it might be Nicky. But she would've heard his bike as he rode up, and he would've come in the back. This was somebody else.

"We're closed," she shouted, not bothering to get up.

"Stella, it's Abner." The familiar, nasal voice came through the thin wooden door. "I saw your car outside. Let me in, I need to talk to you."

Stella got up to unlock the door. The sheriff was a friend. They'd done each other a few favors, but she didn't own him like she'd owned Hoyt Axelrod. Abner valued his job too much to break the law by taking bribes. And, although Stella hadn't lost her powers of seduction, Abner was faithful to his wife, a dumpy woman who seemed to be perpetually pregnant.

Still, if he'd arrested her brother tonight, chances were she could talk him into letting Nicky off.

Wincing with each step, she made her way to the door and opened it. Abner plodded into the bar, moving as if his feet were weighted with cement. At the table nearest the door, he stopped and pulled out a chair. "Sit down," he said. "Trust me, you don't want to hear this standing up."

Stella closed the door and took a seat. Talons of cold dread clutched her heart. Even before she heard the news, Abner's grave expression intimated what it would be. But when the words came, she still wasn't prepared to hear them.

"Your brother's dead, Stella," he said. "We got the call about eleven-thirty and found his body, along with his bike, about ten miles up the north road."

She went cold. Nicky was the one person on this miserable earth she truly cared about. She tried to tell herself that Abner's news was a mistake. But she knew better. Now the only thing she could do was extricate herself from the mess. Even as grief and shock slammed her, Stella's survival instincts kicked in. As far as the law was concerned, she knew nothing about her brother's activities.

She forced herself to respond. "The north road? But what was Nicky doing out there, so late at night?"

"We found a packet of cocaine on the bike," Abner said. "I'm guessing he was on his way to make a drug deal."

"Oh, Lord, no!" Stella shook her head in mock disbelief. "I warned him to stay away from dealing drugs. If only he'd listened to me, he could still be alive." She dabbed at her eyes. "Do you know how it happened?"

She waited for Abner to collect his thoughts. Maybe the drug deal had gone bad and the customer had pulled a gun. Or maybe Nicky's bike had been hit by some fool drunken cowboy. However Nicky had died, she'd have to face the truth and deal with it. "Tell me," she said.

"He was shot," Abner said. "A thirty-eight bullet through the heart at close range. At least you can go forward knowing he didn't suffer."

Stella's jaw tightened, holding back a cry of rage. Whoever had pulled that trigger was going to pay. "Who did it?" she demanded. "Who murdered my brother?"

"It was Will Tyler."

"Will Tyler." Stella uttered the name like a curse. Of all the families in Blanco County, she hated the Tylers most. It was as if they held themselves above ordinary people, like damned royalty. And now, she had even more reason to hate them. The head of the clan had murdered her darling Nicky.

"Tyler claimed it was self-defense," the sheriff said. "According to him, his pickup blew a tire. While he was outside the truck, the motorcycle came up the road and pulled off. The rider had a helmet on, visor down, and he was packing a pistol. Tyler assumed he was the biker who'd robbed the convenience store. He drew his thirty-eight and ordered the man to drop his gun. Your brother did, but then he pulled a knife. That was when Tyler shot him. He swore he didn't know it was Nick, not till we showed up and took the helmet off."

"But Tyler did admit to shooting Nicky."

Abner nodded. "No doubt about that."

"And you believe his story?" Stella felt the anger boiling up in her. She glared at the sheriff, her eyes narrowing to catlike slits.

"No reason not to. Nick's gun was on the ground. The knife was still in his hand. And Tyler said he'd had his little girl in the truck. Protecting her would've made his trigger finger extra jumpy."

"So you haven't arrested him?"

"He hasn't been charged. There'll be an inquest. But unless some new bit of evidence turns up—"

"I see." Stella could imagine, now, what had happened. Nicky had been told to look for a dark blue pickup. On the way he'd spotted Will Tyler's dark vehicle with a flat tire and assumed it was his buyer. He'd stopped to make contact, and Tyler had drawn his pistol. When poor Nicky panicked, Tyler had killed him.

And the Tylers, every last one of them, were going to pay.

Stella's hand flashed across the table and seized the sheriff's wrist. Her red-lacquered nails dug into his flesh.

"Listen to me, Abner," she hissed. "I know you want to keep your job. You may not have broken the law, but you've skated the edge a few times, and I know enough to hurt you. I want Will Tyler prosecuted, hear? If you can't find a reason to bring him in, invent one. Plant evidence if you have to—whatever it takes. The bastard murdered my brother. He's going to pay—in blood!"

*   *   *

It was barely dawn when Will gave up on sleep. Gritty-eyed and restless, he dragged on his clothes, started the coffeemaker in the kitchen, and wandered out onto the front porch of the rambling stone ranch house. It was still dark, the air chilly, the clouds tinged with pewter above the rolling prairie to the east. The high escarpment, which backed the ranch on the west, lay deep in shadow, its craggy buttes and turrets still awaiting the first touch of light.

The windmill next to the barn creaked as it turned in the faint breeze. There was no other sound at this hour, not even the chorus of birdcalls that would signal the start of a new day. Everything was quiet. *Too damned quiet,* Will thought. He wanted to shatter the silence with the foulest curses his mouth could form. But it wouldn't help him feel any better. And it sure as hell wouldn't change what had happened last night.

His black pickup was parked next to the porch, where he'd left it, with the ruined tire in the bed and the spare on the right front wheel. By the time he'd finished being fingerprinted, checked for gunshot residue, and grilled by Abner Sweeney, it had been almost midnight. After the lawmen had left, he'd changed the tire and driven home to a silent house, with nobody awake to meet him.

Drawn by the smell of fresh coffee, he returned to the kitchen, poured himself a cup, and took it back outside. As he stood at the porch rail, sipping and trying to focus his thoughts, a voice from behind startled him.

"Say, Will, that coffee smells mighty good. I could use a cup, myself."

Jasper Platt, the Rimrock's retired foreman, had come up onto the porch in Will's absence. He sat in one of the chairs, with the ranch's black-and-white Border collie at his feet. White-haired now, and too arthritic to ride, Jasper shared a duplex with horse boss, Sky Fletcher, behind the main house.

"Sure." Will strode back into the house and was back a moment later with a second cup of steaming black coffee.

"Thanks." Jasper reached for the cup, blew away the steam, and took a careful sip. "Heard you come in last night. You got in mighty late. Did you find yourself a lady friend in town?"

"Lord, I wish I had." Will pulled up another chair and sat next to the old man. Maybe talking things out would make him feel better. "I drove into Blanco to pick up Erin," he said.

"Mighty late for that little gal to be out. Is she here?"

"No, she's with Tori. Something . . . happened on the way back."

Jasper glanced off the side of the porch, which was high enough to give him a view into the truck bed. "Judgin' from the shape of that tire, what happened was bad," he observed.

"The tire was the least of it." Will drew a painful breath. "I had to shoot a man last night, Jasper. I killed him."

The old man listened, frowning and nodding, as Will related the night's events. "So who the hell was it?" he asked as Will neared the end of the story.

"Somebody I would never have shot if I'd known who he was. It was Stella Rawlins's brother, Nick."

"The dude with the tattooed head? Lord Almighty!" Jasper swore. "I wouldn't want to be you when Stella hears about that. The woman will be out for your blood."

Will gave him a grim nod. "There's that. And then there's my conscience. What if I killed an innocent man, Jasper? I've seen Nick in town. The man looked mean enough, but I always had the feeling he was scared of his own shadow. If I'd known it was him, I'd have figured the knife was a bluff and talked him into putting it down. Damn it, I can't say I ever wanted to find out how it felt to take a human life."

"You had Erin in the truck. You'd have done anything to keep her safe." Jasper scratched the dog's ears. "I never killed a body myself, but I was along when your dad shot a couple of rustlers that were makin' off with his cows. Bull was a dead shot. Plugged 'em both, right out of the saddle and left 'em in the dust."

"And knowing my father, I'm sure he wouldn't have batted an eye over it," Will said. "All my life I wanted to be just like him. As a kid I learned to walk like him, talk like him. Later on, I made the decisions I thought he'd make. But I could never be half as tough. I don't think any man could be as tough as Bull Tyler was."

"It wasn't like Bull to mention it, but he was always proud of you," Jasper said. "He would've been proud of you last night, doin' what it took to protect your little girl. You didn't ask my advice, but I'll offer it, anyway. You did what you had to. So put this ugly business behind you and move on."

Will set his cup on the porch, rose, and walked to the rail. The Rimrock was stirring to life, the aromas of coffee and bacon wafting from the bunkhouse kitchen. Soon the hands would be setting out for morning chores. Sky Fletcher's steel-blue pickup was already parked outside the horse barn. These days he was spending most of his nights in Blanco with his fiancée, Lauren Prescott. But Sky, Bull's secret son by a Comanche woman, could always be counted on to show up early for work.

In some ways—all the good ways—Sky was almost as much like Bull as Will was. But Will's younger brother,

Beau, was cut from a different bolt of cloth. His clashes with Bull had driven him away from the ranch for eleven years. Now, as foreman, he was perpetually butting heads with his brother. Some things, Will mused, never changed.

By now, the blinding edge of the sun had risen above the eastern horizon. The yellowed grasslands glimmered with early frost that would melt away as the day warmed. A raven rose from a tall cedar, flapped its wings and soared into the dawn.

A quarter mile to the southeast, four red brick bungalows, built to house the married hands and their families, were set back from the road in a neat line. Beau, with his pregnant bride, Natalie, had moved into one of them while they waited for their new home to be finished. The newlyweds could've easily stayed in the ranch house with Will. There was plenty of room, and Will would have welcomed them. But someone had warned Natalie that moving into the big house would be a sure way to doom their marriage.

Will had no doubt that *someone* was Tori.

He and Tori had been wildly in love when they'd married. But here on the ranch, their marriage had degenerated into a tug-of-war between Tori and Bull, with Will caught in the middle. Things had gone from bad to worse until the awful week that had torn them apart for good.

Had Tori been trying to save her friend Natalie from the same fate?

As if the thought could summon her, Will saw Tori's brown station wagon approaching up the long gravel drive. His spirits lightened as he glimpsed Erin in the passenger seat. He was glad Tori had brought her. Having his daughter here would go a long way toward salvaging the weekend.

As the station wagon pulled up to the house and stopped, Erin climbed out the door and bounded up the steps to give Will a quick hug. Will fought the urge just to hold her tight and not let go. He'd been so scared for her last night. But it wouldn't help to let her know that. Just let her be happy. Let everything be normal.

"Can I go see Tesoro?" she asked.

"Sure. Sky should be in the barn. Make sure he's close by." Erin's beloved palomino foal was almost six months old. By now, he'd reached 85 percent of his mature height, but only half his mature weight. He was all legs and spunk. Erin had worked with Sky to train and gentle him, but the spirited young colt was big enough to be rambunctious. Will worried about his precious daughter being hurt by an accidental kick or shove.

He watched her race across the yard to the barn, all sunshine. But as she stepped out of the vehicle, her mother's expression cast a shadow over the morning. Tori wasn't happy, and Will was about to find out why.

She looked up at him, where he stood on the porch. "We need to talk, Will," she said.

Jasper took his cue. "I think I hear Bernice in the kitchen," he said, pushing to his feet. "Maybe I'll go see what she's fixin' for breakfast."

As he headed inside, the dog at his heels, Tori came up onto the porch. She was dressed in jeans and a dark green sweater, her long, honey-blond hair brushed back from a face that was freshly washed and bare of the makeup she usually wore. Seeing her like that reminded Will of mornings on the ranch, waking up and seeing that beautiful, unadorned face on the pillow beside him. But why was he thinking about that now—especially since the new man in her life might already be seeing her in the same way.

"Want some coffee?" he asked her, determined to be civil.

"No thanks." She took the chair where Jasper had been sitting.

"Thanks for bringing Erin," he said.

"She wanted to see her foal. Then I'm taking her back to town with me."

"You can't do that." Will's nerves, already raw, caused him to snap at her. "I get her on weekends, Tori. We signed the damned papers."

"I know." She was maddeningly calm. "But Erin's welfare comes first. And after what happened last night, I don't think she's ready to be out here with you."

"What's the problem?" Will glanced toward the barn, where Erin had already disappeared. "I saw her. I talked with her. She seemed right as rain."

Tori's jaw tightened. "Will, you killed a man last night. Erin saw it happen."

The shock hit Will like a lightning bolt. His first reaction was denial. "No. She was down on the floor of the truck. Honest to God, Tori, I made her get down so he wouldn't see her."

"Erin's twelve years old. How could she not look? She told me what she saw."

"But she seemed fine this morning. Was she upset?"

"Last night? Very. She's putting on an act for you today."

"Lord." Will raked a hand through his hair. "To have her see me pull that trigger, see that man die—I wouldn't have done that to Erin for the world!"

"There's more." Tori was sitting straight on the edge of

her chair, hands clasped on her knees. "Abner Sweeney called me after we got home last night. He wants to question her today. According to him, you swore she didn't see anything."

"That's right. What did you tell him?"

"Nothing. I'm guessing her account will back up yours. We certainly can't ask Erin to lie. But you sent her away last night before the sheriff got there. And you claimed she hadn't seen the shooting. By the wrong people, that could be interpreted as obstruction of justice."

"*Justice!*" Will exploded out of his chair. "What *justice?* I killed the man in self-defense!"

A thought line deepened between Tori's eyebrows. "That's one way of looking at it. But you shot a man who'd just surrendered his gun, a man who hadn't yet attacked you with his knife. In a different light, that could be construed as manslaughter, or worse."

The implication made Will's gut clench. He paced to the top of the porch steps and turned back to face his ex-wife. "Did Abner tell you the man was somebody we knew?"

Tori shook her head as if to say, *How could this mess get any worse?*

"It was Stella Rawlins's brother, Nick."

"The bartender." It wasn't a question. Tori's face had gone pale. "Will, you know what that woman's capable of. The rumor is, she's got mob connections. And even without them, she could hurt you. Worse, she could hurt Erin."

"Or even you—anything to make me suffer for killing her brother." Will allowed himself a deep breath. He'd taken enough hits this morning. It was time to take charge of the situation. "For now, this is what we're going to do.

Erin will be safer here on the ranch than in town with you. We can call the teacher and arrange for her to do her schoolwork on the computer. If you're concerned about leaving her, you can stay here, too. Beau's old room's available, and except when you need to be in court, you can do most of your work from the ranch office."

She started to protest. "Blast it, Will, you can't just dictate—"

He cut her off. "Why not? If you think Erin needs you, what's wrong with your staying here? Are you afraid it might interfere with your love life?"

Tori's blistering glare told Will he'd overstepped. But at least the issue was in the open now. He braced himself as she rose, quivering with fury. "You don't own me anymore, Will Tyler," she said. "I've tried to keep our relationship civil because of Erin, but my so-called love life is none of your business!"

"Erin says he's the high school principal." Will had nothing to lose by pushing her a little further.

"That's right!" she snapped. "He's attractive, smart, decent, and, unlike you, he doesn't try to run my life. That's all I'm going to tell you. And don't you dare grill Erin about him! I won't have you putting her in the middle!"

"Agreed," Will said. "But speaking of Erin, there's one thing I need you to do. Call Abner and tell him that if he wants to talk to her, he can do it here, with both of us present."

"Fine." Turning away from him, she took her cell phone out of her purse and exchanged a few terse words before ending the call. "Abner will be here in an hour," she said in her crisp, neutral lawyer voice. "He'll want to talk with you as well."

"No problem, I don't have a thing to hide." Will tried to sound more confident than he felt. "Can I have my attorney present?"

"You're shameless." Tori shook her head, but Will knew there was no way she wouldn't be involved.

"How about some breakfast, you two?" Bernice, Jasper's widowed sister, had been the Tylers' cook and housekeeper since Will's boyhood. With his family gone from the house, Will did for himself most mornings. But when Erin was here, or when Beau or Sky dropped by, she enjoyed whipping up a feast of bacon, eggs, potatoes, and pancakes, with coffee for the grown-ups and cocoa for Erin.

From the back porch came the sound of Jasper ringing the iron triangle to call Erin from the barn. Maybe Sky would come, too, though he showed up for breakfast less often now that he was engaged and building a home for his bride on the 100 prime acres Bull had left him. The half-Comanche horse trainer was a very private man. He hadn't known he was Bull's son until Jasper had told him, and he still kept it quiet. He wasn't even aware that Will had guessed the secret. Will planned to let him know when the time was right, maybe on his wedding day.

They sat around the cozy kitchen table—Jasper, Will, Tori, and Erin, with one chair saved for Bernice and another, with the place set, for anybody who happened by. Bernice was just setting the platters of food on the table when the back door opened and Beau stepped in.

"Smells good." He was grinning, his face ruddy from the morning chill. "Hope you saved me a place."

"Right there." Will nodded toward the empty chair. "How's Natalie this morning?"

"Still asleep, I hope." Beau pulled out the chair, sat down, and began filling his plate. "She was up past mid-

night, tending a sick mare over at the Johnson place. With
the baby on the way, she needs more rest than she's getting." He glanced across the table at Will. "Hey, I saw
you on the news this morning, brother. It seems you've
become a local celebrity, gunning down a drug dealer in
the night. Maybe they'll send that hot Mindi Thacker out
from the TV station to interview you."

Will groaned. It was typical of his younger brother to
turn a crisis into a joke. Today it rankled him, even
though he knew that whatever happened, Beau would
have his back. "It's not funny," he growled. "Tori just filled
me in on the legal implications. And Abner Sweeney's on
his way out here now to ask more questions. You're welcome to sit in."

"Maybe I'll do that. Especially if Abner still sees me
as a cross between James Bond and Elliot Ness." Beau's
past career as a DEA agent had impressed the sheriff,
who still called him to discuss the occasional drug case.

"I'm guessing I don't have to tell you anything else."
Will's subtle nod toward Erin was a signal that he didn't
want to say more in front of his daughter.

"It was on the news." Beau speared a pancake with his
fork. "Bernice, I swear your breakfasts just keep getting
better. It's lucky for us some gentleman hasn't come
courting and stolen you away from us."

Accustomed to his banter, Bernice shook her head.
"Beau Tyler, you could sweet-talk a skunk, and I'd pay to
see you try it."

Laughter drifted around the breakfast table. In the past
Will had treasured mornings like this, with the people he
cared about gathered in the warmth of the kitchen. It was
sad how rarely it happened these days. In no time at all,
with Erin growing up, Bernice and Jasper getting old,

Tori making new choices, and Beau, as well as Sky, involved in starting new families, these times would be gone forever.

Where would he be by then?

If the worst happened and he ended up on trial, he could be looking at the world through prison bars.

CHAPTER 3

"**Y**ou say you couldn't tell who the man was, Erin?"
Abner Sweeney checked his antiquated cassette recorder, to make sure it was still working, and put it back on the coffee table. A bead of sweat trickled down the side of his neck. He was under orders from Stella to find something—anything—that might incriminate Will Tyler in her brother's death. So far, this poised twelve-year-old girl wasn't giving it to him.

"He was wearing a helmet that covered his eyes," she said. "I could sort of see his mouth, but not really because it was dark. I thought he was the robber we heard about on the radio. I'm pretty sure my dad did, too."

"Did the man say anything?"

"I couldn't hear. The window was closed."

"I see." Abner nodded, vaguely aware that he had to pee. It tended to happen when he was nervous, and he was nervous now. Not so much because of the girl, but because of her lawyer mother, sitting to one side, watching him the way a cougar would watch a sheep, ready to pounce at the first misstep. At least he'd managed to keep

Will out of the room by insisting he had to question him and his daughter separately.

"Let me ask you something else, Erin. Did either of your parents tell you how to answer my questions?"

"Yes. They told me to tell the truth."

"Then tell me the truth now. Did you see the knife?"

"Yes."

"Where was it?" Abner tried to ignore the urges of his bladder. Maybe he needed to have his prostate checked. He was getting to that age.

"Where was the knife, Erin?" he asked again.

"In the man's hand."

"What did he do with it? Here, show me with this." He handed her the ballpoint pen from his pocket.

"He put his arm back like this." She demonstrated, bringing the pen up and back, as if about to throw it.

"Did he throw it, or even start to?"

"No. That was when my dad shot him."

"You're sure of that?"

"Yes."

"Thank you, Erin." And that, Abner told himself as he switched off the recorder, was as good as he was going to get.

Tori gave Erin a hug and sent her out of the den, where the interview had taken place. "Go see if Bernice needs any help," she said. "I'll be right here if you need me."

Tori thought that Will would've been proud of their daughter, but one thing troubled her. When Erin indicated that the dead man hadn't moved the knife forward to throw it, the sheriff's bland expression had undergone a subtle change—a narrowing of the eyes, a tightening of the lips. As a courtroom lawyer, she'd learned to read people, and she didn't like what she'd seen.

Should she tell Will, or would that just worry him? She put the question aside as Will walked into the den, so tall and strong, and so totally in command that his presence seemed to fill the room. She didn't have to be here, Tori reminded herself. They'd been divorced for eight years, and she was doing her best to move on. Meeting Drew had given her hope that she really *could* move on.

Will's domineering ways had always made her a little crazy. Today was just one more reminder of that. But Will had gotten into this mess protecting their daughter. For that, she owed him.

The sheriff had excused himself to rush down the hall to the guest bathroom, giving Tori a moment alone with Will. He walked over to the armchair, where she sat perched on the edge; his broad-shouldered frame loomed above her. "How did Erin do?" he asked.

"She did us proud. Calm and cool, spoke right up— more than a match for the likes of Abner Sweeney."

A smile twitched at one corner of his grimly set mouth. "At least we did one thing right, didn't we?"

"We did." *And we did most other things wrong—my open defiance, Will's siding with his father, and the last thing, the darkest thing, when he accused me of something that didn't happen. Will never apologized; and I never forgave him.*

"Will, let's get started." The sheriff bustled back into the den, took his seat, and turned on the recorder. Will sat down at the end of the sectional leather sofa. "I hope you won't mind if I record your testimony. There's going to be an inquest, and I want to make sure your version of what happened is accurate."

Will shrugged. "Fine. It won't be any different from what you heard last night. Tell me when to start."

Tori listened while Will related the same story he'd told her. Abner stopped him from time to time to ask questions. Tori could tell the sheriff was probing for any detail that might conflict with what Erin had said. It was almost as if he was trying to build a case against Will. What she didn't understand was *why*. There was no bad blood between the sheriff and the Tylers. And Abner was no longer running for the election he'd just won. What was driving him?

Partway through the session, Beau wandered into the den, took a seat, and leaned forward to listen. Only when Will had finished his story, which matched Erin's, did he speak up.

"Sheriff, according to Will, the man said something about a package and money. The newscast I saw mentioned that the deputies found cocaine on his bike. Can we assume that Nick Tomescu was on his way to a drug deal, and that he mistook Will for his customer?"

Abner looked flustered. "We can't assume anything," he said.

"Did you question his sister?"

"I did. Stella was grieving, of course. She said she didn't know anything about her brother's activities. I'm inclined to believe her."

"Of course." Beau rolled his eyes in Tori's direction. She responded with a subtle shake of her head. Stella Rawlins would never admit to being involved in anything. And she appeared to have the sheriff wrapped around her little finger.

Restless as a bull in the bucking chute, Will rose to his feet. "Are we finished, Sheriff? I need to get to work."

"Just one more thing, Will," the sheriff said. "Last night you told me you'd sent your daughter away because she hadn't seen anything. That turned out to be untrue. Do you have anything to add in defense of your statement?"

Tori's eyes were on Will—his tightened jaw, his narrowed eyes. She knew that look all too well. It was the look of a man who'd had enough. As he drew in his breath, she braced for the explosion.

Will exhaled, holding himself in check. "I'm done here," he said. "Ask my lawyer."

With that, he strode out of the room. Tori heard the closing of the front door—not quite a slam—and the roar of his pickup as he sped away. She guessed he'd be headed somewhere out of reach, maybe up to the summer pastures on the caprock to check the grass and mend the fences. That had been his way when they were married— in any kind of emotional crisis, Will would simply walk away and disappear into his work.

Abner was staring after him, slack-jawed. Tori rose, speaking into the silence. "Sheriff, I believe you already know the answer to your question. Will didn't know that Erin had seen the shooting until I told him this morning. You've no call to read anything else into the situation. Agreed?"

"Well, yes, I suppose so." Abner stood, turned off the recorder, and stuffed it into his imitation-leather briefcase. "I guess we really are done here."

"You said there'd be an inquest." Beau had risen as well. "Can you give us some idea what's involved and how long it'll take?"

"My best guess is ten days to several weeks. We'll need to get the coroner's report and schedule the judge. If the judge wants to impanel a jury, that'll take more time."

"A jury? Why, for God's sake?" Beau demanded.

"To decide whether Will should be charged and tried—most likely for manslaughter."

With that exit line, Abner picked up his briefcase and keys, and headed out the front door.

That evening, after a long, restless afternoon, Tori stood at the porch rail and watched the last rays of the setting sun fade behind the escarpment. The canyons lay deep in purple shadow, the high buttes above them still bathed in velvety mauve light. Quail called from the cedars along the foothills. Horses, their nostrils testing the wind, nickered and snorted in the paddock. The evening breeze carried the smell of dust and an ominous chill, a warning, perhaps, that the first norther of the season was already sweeping down the distant plain.

She glanced at the luminous dial of her watch. Drew had planned to pick her up two hours from now for an eight o'clock movie and late-night pizza. Either she would need to go home, change, and be there when he arrived, or call now and cancel their date.

The question was, should she stay here with Erin? Her daughter had seemed fine today, but last night she'd had trouble sleeping. Tori had ended up putting an old Disney movie in the DVD player and watching it with her until her head drooped and her eyes closed. If Erin was still traumatized tonight, Tori didn't want to leave her, not even with Will. At times like this, a child needed her mother.

And Will—did he need her, too?

But that couldn't be allowed to matter. Will was his own man, and she was no longer his wife. It made sense that she'd agreed to be his lawyer. But that was where she had to draw the line. Sympathy wasn't part of the bargain.

So, if she canceled her date and stayed here, would that be sending Will the wrong message?

A brisk November wind whistled across the porch. Tori shivered beneath her light wool sweater. Either way, it was time to make a decision.

She was about to go back inside when she felt a warm weight settle on her shoulders. As the smells of sage, wood smoke, and horses enfolded her, she recognized Will's fleece-lined range coat and the strong hands that had wrapped it around her.

"Can't have you freezing out here, can we?" Will's husky baritone rumbled in her ear. He stood behind her, his hands on her shoulders, his breath stirring her hair. A long-forgotten thread of heat uncurled in the depths of her body, recalling the sensual passion that had created Erin and the other baby, the one she'd lost. In those early years their lovemaking had been good. More than good—until the end, when even love hadn't been enough.

Tori closed her eyes, an ache rising in her throat. "You weren't here for supper," she said. "Where've you been?"

"Working. Riding. Thinking. Whatever the hell a man does at a time like this. By the time Abner finished with me, I wasn't fit company for you or anybody else." His hands lingered on her shoulders. "How's Erin?"

"Fine. When I last checked, she was doing her homework in the dining room." The old memory tugged at her, standing in the ranch kitchen, feeling the brush of his stubbled whiskers on the back of her neck . . . She felt the heat rising, her body warming. Even after eight years apart, she wasn't immune to Will's raw masculinity.

But there was only one sensible choice here, and Tori

forced herself to make it. "I hope you can keep Erin company awhile," she said. "I was about to leave. I have a date tonight."

His hands dropped from her shoulders. He took a step backward, widening the space between them. "You had a date last night," he said.

"Yes, I know." Turning, she slipped off his coat and thrust it toward him. "My plan is to drive back here afterward, with a bag packed for a night or two. How long I stay here will depend on how Erin is doing. If we agree that she's better off on the ranch for now, I'll call the school on Monday and arrange for her lessons. But you can't keep *me* here, Will. I'm not a prisoner. I have a life."

Stony-faced, Will took the coat. "But will that life be safe? Damn it, Tori—"

"I'll be just fine. And for heaven's sake, don't wait up for me. I'm not sixteen anymore." Sweeping past him, Tori strode into the house to get her purse and say good night to Erin. Was Will more concerned about her safety or about her being with another man? Either way, she couldn't let his problems dictate her life. She was going on a date with Drew Middleton, and, by heaven, she was going to have a good time.

The grandfather clock in the front hall struck the hour of twelve. Will counted the chimes from his bed, where he lay on his back, staring up into the darkness. Midnight, and Tori still hadn't come back from her so-called date. She was out there somewhere with some goody-two-shoes bastard who held the power to change all their lives—Tori's, Erin's, and his own. Will had never met

Drew Middleton. If he ever did—and it was bound to happen sooner or later—it would take all his restraint to keep from punching the man in the face.

Damn it, Middleton didn't belong in the picture. He didn't have a clue about Tori, didn't even know her. He hadn't watched her grow up, changing from a coltish youngster who tore around the ranch with Beau and Natalie to a stunning woman, returning home with a brand-new law degree. Her beauty had knocked Will's socks off back then. It still did.

It wasn't Drew Middleton who'd driven Tori to the Lubbock hospital in a blue norther the night Erin was born. It wasn't Middleton who'd walked the floor with Erin when she had the croup. And it sure as hell wasn't Middleton who'd held Tori in his arms while she sobbed over the loss of their second baby, five months into her pregnancy.

The man was an outsider. He didn't belong in Tori's world or in Erin's. Why couldn't Tori see that?

Twelve-fifteen. Was Tori in Middleton's arms right now, or maybe even in his bed?

Stop it! Will forced the image from his mind. It was time he quit agonizing over his ex-wife and opened his eyes to the reality that was staring him in the face. He had every right to be concerned about Tori's safety. But her romantic life was her own business. The two of them shared a much-loved child. For Erin's sake, he and Tori kept their connection, talking and meeting often, even sharing Sunday dinners on the ranch. But that didn't make her *his*. Whether he liked it or not, she hadn't been *his* in a very long time.

A faint sound shocked him to full alertness—a smooth engine gearing down as it approached the house. Will sat

up, ears straining in the darkness. Tori's aging wagon had
a distinctive rumble and a squeak in the chassis. He
would know the sound of it anywhere. But this vehicle
was almost silent, more like a late-model high-end sedan.

Tires crunched on gravel as it pulled up to the porch.
Will was already grabbing for his clothes, yanking them
on, shoving his bare feet into his boots. Was it a highway
patrol car, its driver coming to tell him that Tori had been
in some horrible accident? Or could it be one of Stella's
minions sneaking up to the house to do some damage?

Heart pumping adrenaline, he opened the top drawer
in the nightstand and took out the pistol he kept there. By
the time he reached the living room, the sound of the engine had stopped. Headlights were shining through the
front window. Whoever it was, at least they weren't trying to sneak up on the place. But this could still mean bad
news.

Now Will could hear footsteps and voices—one of
them a man's, one of them Tori's. At least she sounded all
right—more than all right. She was laughing. He stepped
back into the shadows of the hallway—not wanting to be
seen, but too curious to turn away and go back to bed.
Why would Middleton—if that's who it was—be bringing her here? Why hadn't she driven herself? Was he
about to meet his ex-wife's new boyfriend?

The parked car's headlights shone blindingly bright
through the plate glass window. As Will's eyes adjusted
to the glare, he could make out a silhouette on the porch—
two people, one taller, locked in a passionate kiss. His
pulse slammed.

Don't look, you damnfool idiot! Go back to bed! Will
chastised himself. But he was rooted to the spot, fighting
emotions he had no right to feel as the silhouette sepa-

rated and became two people, the taller one leaving. An instant later, Tori's key turned in the lock. She stepped into the darkened living room.

Will backed into the shadows, but not soon enough. Tori must've heard him, or sensed he was there.

"Will?" Clutching her overnight bag, she stood outlined in the open doorway. Her hair fluttered in the night breeze. "Is that you?"

He stepped out of the shadows. Her breath caught in a low gasp. "Good grief, don't tell me that's a gun in your hand! Who were you planning to shoot?"

"This isn't anything to joke about, Tori. I heard a strange car. I thought it might be a prowler."

She closed the door and locked it behind her. "I told you not to wait up for me. If you'd been asleep, you wouldn't have heard the car."

"I'm not exactly sleeping well lately," Will growled. "Where's your wagon?"

"Dead in my driveway. Bad starter, I think. Drew drove me here."

"Too bad he didn't stick around for an introduction. After seeing how he said good night to you, I wouldn't have minded meeting him."

Her chin went up in defiance. "Stop badgering me, Will. I'm tired. I'm going to bed."

He stood his ground, his silence asking the unspoken question that hung between them.

Tori's patience snapped. "For your information, I haven't slept with the man. If I decide to—which I might—that will be none of your business, Will Tyler. Now get out of my way. I want to check on Erin. Then I'm going to sleep."

Ignoring the knot in his gut, Will stepped aside to let her get by. Part of him ached to crush her in his arms, sweep her off to his bed, and stake his claim on her all over again. But the time when that might have happened was long past. Tori would never be his again.

As they passed in the entrance to the hallway, something awakened and cried out in him. He reached out and caught her cheek with his hand, lightly cupping her face, lifting it to the pale light that filtered from the front window. The pupils of her eyes were large and dark, her lips moistly swollen. He ached to bend close, to brush those lips with his, but she pulled back with a sharp little breath, shook her head, and fled down the hall toward Erin's room.

The next day was Sunday. Although the Tylers weren't big on church attendance, Sunday dinner on the Rimrock was an honored tradition. It was a time when the family, and those who counted as family, gathered around the dining-room table in relative peace to celebrate their blessings.

Lauren Prescott raised her bowed head after Jasper droned the usual grace over the food. She'd been included since the past summer, when her old family home had gone up in flames and Sky had asked her to marry him. The Tylers always welcomed her, but even after more than three months of being engaged to Sky, she still felt like an interloper.

As family and friends helped themselves to roast beef, potatoes and gravy, salad, and fresh hot rolls, Lauren's gaze drifted around the table. Beau, seated across from her with his wife, had been her friend and champion since last spring when he'd hired her accounting skills for the ranch. But Natalie, petite and dark-eyed, her pregnancy beginning to show, was so busy with her veterinary practice and her new marriage that Lauren had scarcely gotten to know her.

Tori had become Lauren's friend after helping her find an apartment in town. But Tori, in her own way, was also an outsider here. Today the tension hung heavy between her and Will. Something was going on between them. It showed in the way they avoided each other's eyes, the way they spoke not to each other but to their daughter.

Flanked by her parents, Erin basked in the love of everyone at the table. She might not realize it, but Will's daughter was the glue that held the ranch family together, the bond that brought them here and made them—for this brief time—one.

Bernice sat closest to the kitchen. She'd always been kind and friendly. But her brother, Jasper, had never warmed to Lauren—and Lauren understood why. For three generations the Tylers and the Prescotts had been bitter enemies. Jasper remembered every wrong, every misdeed, every dispute, from the beginning. *Trust a skunk before you trust a Prescott,* he was known to say, though not to Lauren's face.

Bull Tyler and Ferguson Prescott, Lauren's grandfather, had started the feud. Both men were dead now, but the animosity remained. When Lauren's father, the late congressman Garn Prescott, had died this summer, Jasper had refused to attend the burial service. Though he'd been at the graveside, Will, too, had had his own issues with the congressman. Now, as the only living descendant of Ferg Prescott and his son, Garn, Lauren carried a heavy burden of past family sins. Only time would tell what that burden would cost her.

She felt the light press of a hand on her knee. Seated next to her, Sky gave her his secret smile. She reached under the edge of the tablecloth and brushed the back of his hand in a furtive caress. Her history and Sky's were intertwined in ways neither of them could have imagined when they'd first met. That hidden bond made her love him all the more. She could hardly wait to become his wife. Maybe then they could start anew and put the old family scandals to rest.

"How's the new house coming along, Sky?" It was Beau who asked the question. "I've meant to ride over and take a look now that the fall roundup's done."

"The outside's finished," Sky said, "as well as the plumbing, heating, and wiring. Once the Sheetrock's up and prepped, I can turn Lauren loose on the inside."

"I'll be in decorator heaven!" Lauren said. "We'll have a big housewarming when it's done!"

Sky had wanted to build his bride an entire house with his own hands, but his responsibilities on the Rimrock had made that impractical. Under his supervision, the crew he'd hired to put in a well and septic tank, run the power line and construct the log house, with its broad, covered front porch, was doing a fine job. The place wouldn't be big and sprawling like the Tyler home, but with Lauren dipping into her inheritance to decorate the rustic interior, it would be beautifully finished and comfortably furnished.

Will had been uncharacteristically quiet throughout the meal. Sky had told Lauren about the shooting of Stella Rawlins's brother and the possible consequences. No wonder Will looked so troubled. Lauren could sympathize with him. Stella, she suspected, had ruined her father's reputation and contributed to his death. As always there was no proof against her, but if rumors were true, the woman was as dangerous as a coiled rattlesnake. And now she'd be out to avenge her brother by hurting Will any way she could—starting with the law.

* * *

Will walked into the room that served as the Rimrock office and closed the door behind him. He usually looked forward to Sunday dinners, but today's meal had been an ordeal of silence and small talk, with everyone avoiding the one topic that was on their minds—the shooting and what was going to happen next.

Will had excused himself at the end of the meal, muttering something about the need to use the office computer; but the truth was, he'd just wanted to be alone and think things out. Until yesterday he'd felt certain that he'd acted in self-defense, and any case against him would be dismissed. But yesterday's senseless grilling from Abner had changed his mind.

For whatever reason, the sneaky little toad was out to get him.

Sitting, he switched on the computer and brought up a search engine. He spent the next half hour reading up on Texas law, the inquest process, and the precedents for charges that could stem from an incident like the one he'd been involved in. What he found wasn't encouraging. By pulling the trigger a split second too soon, he might have left himself vulnerable.

With a muttered curse he switched off the machine. Most of what he'd read, he could've learned from Tori. But now that she had a new man in her life, he couldn't expect her to drop everything and come running whenever he needed her. And unless her help involved protecting Erin, he had too much pride to ask.

A new man in her life.

The thought deepened the dark hollow Will felt inside. He and Tori were past history, but even now, the thought of Drew Middleton, or any man, taking her away was like having the earth slide out from under his feet. Tori was a beautiful woman, and sooner or later, this was bound to happen. But why the hell did it have to happen now?

Swiveling the chair, he gazed up at the leather-framed sepia-toned photograph on the wall. Bull Tyler had refused to sit for a painted portrait, like the one of his wife that hung above the sideboard in the dining room. But years ago, when he'd been featured in a magazine article about Texas ranching, he'd agreed to be photographed.

The picture, taken when Bull was fifty, showed a handsome, vigorous man in his prime. Dressed in a corduroy jacket, plaid shirt, and leather bolo, and sporting a well-trimmed moustache, he emanated authority. His piercing gaze, from under thick, dark eyebrows, challenged any comer to take him on.

In the last years of his life, after the riding accident that paralyzed his legs, Bull had ruled the ranch family from his wheelchair. But there was no trace of any weakness in this photograph. This was the way Will had chosen to remember his father—powerful, dynamic, and always in charge.

That memory would haunt every decision Will had ever made.

What would you do in my place, Dad? Will gazed up at the blunt, chiseled features as if waiting for an answer. But why ask when he knew what the answer would be? Bull Tyler would have told everybody to go to hell, turned his back, and then walked away.

Maybe for Bull, that would've worked, but not these days. The law had too much power. Will would fight the possible charges with every resource he had. But he'd be a fool not to see the cold reality that was staring him in the face. He'd killed a man—the wrong man. If things went badly, he could find himself spending time behind bars.

Starting now, he needed to get his priorities in order—beginning with his family and the ranch.

Abner had told Beau that scheduling and carrying out the inquest would take several weeks. After that, there'd be a trial—or not, depending on the outcome. Either way, Will would have some free time before any decision was made—time to tie up loose ends and put some things right.

One task nagged him every time he looked at his father's proud face. It was the land—the precious canyon parcel with the spring and the rumored Spanish gold—that Bull had sold to his hated neighbor, Ferg Prescott, for the sum of $1.

Except for that small piece of land, less than an acre, no part of the Rimrock had ever been sold. For the sake of family pride, if nothing else, Will knew he had to get it back.

Last spring he'd made Garn Prescott, Ferg's son, a generous offer for it. The congressman had refused to sell, blaming some deathbed promise to his father. But things had changed since then. Garn was dead.

Now the land belonged to Lauren.

CHAPTER 4

William stepped out of the office and walked down the hall to the living room. He'd hoped Lauren and Sky would still be here; but except for the hum of the dishwasher in the kitchen and the steady ticktock of the grandfather clock in the entry, the house was quiet. Nobody appeared to be around, not even Erin.

Mildly puzzled, he walked out onto the porch. He discovered Jasper in his customary chair, a Corona in his hand and the dog sprawled at his feet.

"Awfully quiet in there," Will said. "Where is everybody?"

Jasper took a swig of his beer, flecks of foam clinging to his upper lip. "Bernice is napping. Beau and Natalie went home. The others piled into Sky's pickup, and he drove 'em over to see the new house."

"Did they say when they'd be back?" Will glanced off the porch and saw Lauren's vintage black Corvette parked on the gravel. At least she hadn't left for town.

"Don't reckon they'll be long. Not that much to see." His wise, pale eyes studied Will. "So you're thinking about getting that canyon parcel back, are you?"

"Am I that easy to read?"

The old man chuckled. "I've known you since you were in diapers, Will Tyler. You come out here looking all wrought up, you ask where everybody is, and then you check for the Prescott girl's car. Doesn't take much to figure that one out."

"It's been on my mind since Garn died," Will said. "But with Lauren still mourning her father, it didn't seem fitting to ask her about it. Now . . ." Will gazed into the blue distance, where two vultures circled on the updrafts. Some people believed that the ugly black birds were a portent of evil. Will had never held with that old superstition, and he wasn't about to start believing it now. "I'm trying to get some things done before the inquest wraps up. Hopefully, it'll come to nothing, but you never know. If I have to go away for a while . . ."

"Don't even talk like that," Jasper said. "When the girl marries Sky, the land will at least be back in the family."

"But not the way it should be. I want a signed, recorded deed giving that land back to the Rimrock. And I won't settle for less."

"It might not be that easy. For all you know, that land could've gone with the rest of the Prescott Ranch when Garn sold out to the syndicate."

"No, I checked with the county recorder," Will said. "The old deed's still valid, made out to Ferguson Prescott and his heirs in perpetuity. The property's Lauren's to sell."

"If she's willing to sell it. She's a Prescott, after all. Stubborn devils, Ferg and his boy. Garn's daughter won't be no different." Jasper took another swig of his Corona. Something in the old man's look told Will he knew more than he was telling. But Jasper was full of secrets, most of which he would probably take to his grave.

For now, there was no time to pry any more out of him. Sky's steel-blue pickup had come over the last rise, trailing a plume of dust as it bounced across the burned-over flatland toward the house. Will waited as the truck pulled up to the porch; he was pondering what he could say to influence Lauren. *How much does she know about the land?* he wondered. *How much had her father told her—and Sky?*

Tori and Erin climbed out of the rear seat. Instead of coming up onto the porch, Erin was tugging her mother toward the paddock, where the colts were romping in the afternoon sunlight. Even from a distance Tesoro's hide gleamed like gold, making it easy to spot him among his darker-coated playmates. In a way it was too bad Erin was so smitten with her young colt. The sale of such an animal would give the ranch a much-needed influx of cash. But no amount of money was worth breaking his daughter's heart.

Lauren waited for Sky to come around the truck and open the passenger door before she climbed to the ground. Sky's fiancée was a stunner, with a model's rangy figure, coppery eyes, and an unruly mane of auburn hair. Reared with wealth, she was accustomed to the best. For Sky, a man of secure but modest means, keeping her happy would be a challenge. But the two of them did seem deeply in love. Will envied them that.

Will came down the steps to meet her and invite her inside for a talk. He meant to offer her a fair price for the land, but there was always the chance she wouldn't agree to sell. If she dug in her heels and refused, he might have a fight on his hands, with Sky siding against him. But there was no way he was backing down. One way or another, he would make the stolen land—and there was no other way to think of it—part of the Rimrock once more.

* * *

Sky settled himself in the leather armchair by the fireplace, a safe distance from the sofa, where Will had invited Lauren to sit. He knew exactly what was on Will's mind. The surprise was that his half brother had waited this long to bring it up.

Sky had shown Lauren the disputed land early on and told her what little he knew about it. He understood how much Will wanted that small parcel back where it belonged. But the decision to sell, or not to sell, would be Lauren's, and he would support her choice. Knowing what was coming, he'd already made that clear to her. Right now, he was nothing more than an interested observer.

"Something to drink?" Will was still on his feet. "A beer? Some wine?"

"No, thank you," Lauren declined, as did Sky.

Will lowered his tall frame to the edge of the sofa, looking ill at ease as he turned toward Lauren. "Something tells me you already know what I want to talk to you about," he said.

"Yes, and I'm familiar with the circumstances," Lauren replied. Sky had to admire her quiet poise.

Will cleared his throat. "I offered Garn a fair price for that parcel of land when he was running for reelection. But he told me he'd promised his father not to sell it. I take it you aren't bound by the same promise."

"I don't even remember my grandfather. I was a toddler when my parents divorced, and my mother took me back to Maryland. So, no. I'm not bound by anything," Lauren said. "The syndicate owns the original ranch, including the land where the house was before it burned. But that little parcel wasn't included. According to my dad's lawyer, it's mine now." She gave Will a knowing smile. "But something tells me you're already aware of that."

Will shifted on the sofa. "Then let's get right down to business," he said. "I'm prepared to offer you the same price as I offered your father. I can give you the check today, and you can sign the deed over in town tomorrow." He waited, the expectant silence broken only by the ticking clock, as Lauren took her time. At last she spoke.

"I don't need your money, Will. As a U.S. congressman my father had excellent life insurance, as well as insurance on the house and my grandfather's antique-car collection. I'm the sole beneficiary."

An expression of cold astonishment flashed across Will's face. Sky had nothing but respect for his secret half brother, but it tickled him to see Will put down so handily by a woman. *My woman,* he thought.

"I've never owned a piece of land before," Lauren said. "I'm not saying I won't sell it eventually. But I want to get to know it first—to explore it and learn more about its history. Maybe then—"

"You know that story about the hidden Spanish gold is nothing but bunk!" Will snapped.

"I know that my grandfather searched every inch of the land and never found it. But this isn't about the gold." Lauren gave Will a few seconds to stew over what she'd said. "I don't want to sell it yet, but here's what I will do. I'll free up the spring so your cattle will have water in the bigger canyon below. And when I sell it to you—*if* I sell it, which I won't promise—the price will be exactly what my grandfather paid Bull for it. One dollar."

Right then, Sky would have given anything for a camera to photograph Will's face. He looked as if he'd been smacked with a wet fish. But it didn't take long for Will to recover.

"You can stop grinning now, Sky," he growled. "You're the one who'll be living with this woman. Think about that!" Rising, he extended his hand to Lauren. He'd gained some concessions, but he still didn't look happy. "Given a choice, I'd rather pay the money and buy that land now," he said. "I'll try to be patient. But my father won't rest easy in his grave till this is settled."

"I'll keep that in mind," Lauren said. "I'm sorry I never knew your father. From what I've heard about him, he must've been quite a man."

"He was," Will said. "He was more than a man. He was a force."

He still is. Sky kept his silence. But he knew Lauren had meant those words for him, as well as for Will.

Stella's feet, in their high-heeled red cowgirl boots, throbbed after a night of tending bar in the Blue Coyote. When Will Tyler had fired a bullet through Nicky's innocent heart, she'd not only lost a brother, she'd lost a damned good bartender. She would mourn him for a long time to come. But for now, she'd channeled her grief into rage. Tyler would pay for what he'd done. Before she was finished with them, his whole family would pay.

So far, she'd left his punishment to Abner and the law. But she couldn't depend on the legal system to give her justice, let alone vengeance. She could always use her Dallas connection to call in a hit on the man. But that would be expensive. It would also be too fast and too easy to give her the satisfaction she craved. She wanted to see Will Tyler squirm. She wanted to see him suffer.

Stella had planned to close the Blue Coyote at ten, as she usually did on Sunday nights, but the sad-eyed cowboy in the corner booth, nursing his can of Dos Equis beer, showed no inclination to leave.

She might have given him a gentle nudge out the door, but Stella had recognized the lanky young man. She'd seen him come in a few times with the crew from the Rimrock. Last spring, early on, he'd given Lute Fletcher a few rides to town in his old rust bucket of a pickup. The kid didn't look like much, but it wouldn't hurt to learn more about him.

What was his name? She searched her memory and found it. Ralph, that's what one of the men had called him. She'd make an effort to remember and use it.

Slipping an old Hank Williams CD in the boom box, she turned the volume down low. Then she popped the tab on a fresh beer, sidled over to the booth, and took the seat across from him.

"That beer of yours must be getting stale, Ralph," she said, smiling. "Here, have a cold one on the house."

"Thanks." He accepted the can with a shy smile. He looked young, barely twenty-one, Stella guessed. His eyes were light brown, and his mud colored hair wanted cutting. The hand that clasped the beer can was nicked and calloused, the fingernails streaked with embedded dirt.

"You look sadder than a hound dog pup, cowboy," she said in her folksiest manner. "If there's anything you need to get off your chest, I'm a good listener."

The melancholy strains of "Your Cheatin' Heart" drifted through the darkened bar. The young cowhand sipped the cold beer, maybe weighing the wisdom of sharing his troubles. After a long moment's hesitation, he sighed. "It's my wife, Vonda," he said. "We had to get married this summer on account of she was in a family way. Mostly it's okay, bein' married. My boss, Will Tyler, let us move into one of the little family houses on the ranch. It's nice enough, and the rent's a lot cheaper than livin' in town, but . . ."

He tipped the can to his lips, his Adam's apple quivering as he swallowed. "It's always about the damned money!" The words exploded out of him. "Will pays as good as most ranchers around here, and we got insurance for when the baby comes, thank God. But that ain't enough for Vonda. She wants to move to town, where she can hang out with her friends. She wants fancy clothes and her own cell phone and her own car to cat around in. She wants a big-screen TV and all kinds of furniture and gadgets for the baby."

He raked his hand through his unruly hair. "Lord, I work my ass off, but cowboyin' don't pay all that much. Tonight, when I tried to tell her how it was, Vonda threw me out. She says I'm not gettin' any you-know-what till I can figure out a way for her to have what she wants."

"How old is Vonda?" Stella asked.

"Sixteen. Just a kid. If I hadn't married her when she got pregnant, her folks woulda thrown me in jail, her daddy bein' sheriff and all. Even then, they threw her out and won't have nothin' to do with us."

Something clicked in Stella's head. So this downtrodden cowboy was Abner's son-in-law. Interesting. She gave him a sympathetic look. "I'm guessing you haven't done any bartending."

"Nope. But I'm right sorry about you losing your brother, Miss Stella. Damn shame what happened." He brightened. "Say, maybe you could teach me bartendin'."

"I'm afraid I need someone with experience." Stella rose and smoothed out her tight denim skirt. "But if you'd like to earn a little extra money, I could use some help around the place—cleaning up, fixing things, maybe running a few errands."

"Heck, I can do all that stuff!" He was grinning now, as eager as a puppy. "Just let me know what you need."

"I'll think on it, Ralph. Check back with me the next time you're in town. Right now, it's time to finish your beer and go home to that little wife of yours. With luck, she'll be feeling lonesome by now."

As she closed the bar, Stella watched the taillights on the rattletrap truck fade toward the highway. Ralph might not be the sharpest tack in the barrel, but he was desperate for cash, eager to please, and in the right place to be of use. Given time and a little coaching, he could turn out to be helpful.

How loyal to the Tylers was he? But that wouldn't matter. Get him hooked on the money, get him to cross the line, and then threaten him with exposure. With a wife, and a baby on the way, the kid would do anything she asked him to do.

But Ralph couldn't put Will Tyler in prison. She couldn't even count on Abner to do that. Fortunately, a couple of months ago, an ace had fallen into her hands—an ace she would put into play first thing tomorrow.

After her late-night encounter with Will, Tori hadn't looked forward to spending Sunday night at the ranch. She could've ridden back to town with Lauren or borrowed a spare vehicle from the ranch, but she was still worried about leaving her daughter. Erin had appeared calm and cheerful all weekend, doing her homework and spending time with her beloved colt. But she'd witnessed something no child should have to see. During Abner

Sweeney's interrogation she'd seemed almost too composed, her recollection of the shooting almost too clear. Tori suspected Erin was keeping her emotions bottled up inside, where they could fester if not given a chance to heal.

So here Tori was, curled on her side in Beau's former bed, fervently willing sleep to come. But it wasn't happening—not while her memory kept replaying last night's explosive clash with her ex-husband—the accusations, the anger . . .

And the hunger in Will's eyes when he cupped my cheek with his hand.

For Erin's sake, she and Will had maintained a truce over the years, masking their raw wounds with a layer of polite tolerance. Last night had stripped that layer away.

With a sigh of frustration, Tori turned over and punched her pillow into shape. Why did this have to happen now, when she'd finally met a man who could promise her the secure, stable life she'd always wanted?

Drew was kind, romantic, and thoughtful. More important, he gave her respect and treated her as an equal. With Will, the sex had been amazing. But out of bed he'd treated her more like a possession than a companion. Worse, he'd backed his father, who'd insisted that she abandon her law practice to stay home, mind the house, and breed a tribe of little Tylers. She'd tried that. But the miscarriage and the hemorrhaging that followed had come so close to killing her that it had been necessary for the doctor to perform a partial hysterectomy. She'd given Will one perfect daughter. But Bull had never forgiven her for not having sons.

The grandfather clock, brought here from Savannah by Will's mother, chimed one. With an inward groan Tori shifted in the bed and closed her eyes. She was finally beginning to drift when a cry shattered the darkness.

The sound had come from Erin's room.

Tori bolted out of bed, stumbling over her shoes, where she'd left them on the rug. Still in her silk nightgown, she plunged down the hall. Erin's door was open, the darkness inside broken by a shaft of moonlight falling through the window, lending enough light for Tori to find her way.

"Erin?" She could see her daughter now, sitting up in a nest of covers. Sinking onto the bed beside her, Tori gathered her close. Erin was trembling. Her breath came in little hiccupping sobs.

"It's all right. I'm here, sweetheart." Tori stroked the tangled silk of her hair. "What is it? Did something frighten you?"

"B-bad dream," Erin stammered. "So awful."

"Erin?" Will had turned on the hall light. Clad in the old Indian-blanket patterned flannel robe Tori had given him for their first Christmas together, he stood in the doorway. "What's the matter, honey? Are you all right?"

"She's fine." Tori clutched her child closer. "Just a nightmare, that's all."

Will walked into the room and sat down on Erin's opposite side. "We're right here, girl." His throat was still thick from sleep. "You're safe."

Still shaking, Erin freed her arms to wrap around both her parents. They held each other, the three of them, in a tight, awkward circle. Tori could feel Will's warmth, feel the tension in his clasp. Whatever forces had separated them, they would unite in a heartbeat to protect their precious daughter.

"Talking might make you feel better, Erin," Tori said. "Tell us about your dream."

Erin swallowed hard. "There was this man—a man in a motorcycle helmet. He came in the front door with a gun. I heard him and came out of my room. I had a gun, too, right in my hand. I shot him. He fell down . . ." She sucked in air, as if struggling to breathe. "His helmet fell off, and it was you, Daddy. It was you I shot!" She broke into fresh sobs.

"No, don't cry, honey." Will's arms tightened around her. "It was just a dream. I'm fine. We're all fine."

Erin pulled free, gazing up at Will with big, frightened eyes. "Daddy, are they going to put you in jail for shooting that man?"

The partial light from the hall etched black lines of anguish on Will's face. When he spoke, his manner was confident. "Not much chance of that. I fired in self-defense, and I've got the best lawyer in Texas to help me prove it. So go back to sleep, and don't worry your pretty head about it. Hear?"

She hesitated, then nodded. "Okay. I'll try. But could you and Mom stay here for just a little while, till I fall asleep?"

"Sure." Will's eyes flickered toward Tori. "We'll stay as long as you need us." As Erin snuggled into the covers once more, he pulled a chair close to the bedside and sat down.

Tori rose, walked around to the other side and slipped under the coverlet next to her daughter. One arm lay across Erin's shoulders, cradling her close. "Go to sleep," she whispered. "It's all right. You're safe. We're here with you."

Tori closed her eyes. But she could only pretend to sleep. She was sharply aware of Will's presence next to the bed, the sound of his breathing, the shifting of his weight on the chair. Her ex-husband was tough like his father, with the stubborn resolve and mental stamina to see him through any crisis. If he was worried about the outcome of the shooting—as he must be—he would keep it to himself and soldier on. But what about his tender-hearted young daughter? Erin's nightmare had shown just how deeply affected she was. How would she cope if Will was put on trial, or was even convicted?

As Will's attorney, Tori realized, it would be up to her to save her ex-husband—and in doing so, to save their daughter. Whatever else was on her agenda, it would have to be set aside, including her personal life. Only this case could be allowed to matter.

The dimmed light from the hall cast Will's long shadow across the bed. Nestled in that shadow lay his slumbering daughter and the woman who'd walked out on him eight years ago, changing his life forever.

When they were married, he'd loved watching Tori sleep. But those days were long over. They'd ended when she'd returned from her father's funeral in Florida, madder than a wet wildcat and ready to serve him with divorce papers. She'd stayed in the guest room long enough to find a place in town, and never shared his bed again.

His eyes traced the contours of Tori's face—the chiseled bones, the creamy, golden skin. He could tell by the tautness of her breathing that she was only pretending to sleep. But seeing her with her eyes closed, one arm cradling their daughter, deepened the empty space inside him.

He'd wanted to be a good husband. But so many pressures—the ranch, his father, her need for a career, and finally his own jealousy—had driven a wedge between them. That wedge was still in place, and Tori's new love interest was driving it even deeper.

As a man with a man's needs, Will hadn't remained celibate since the divorce. He'd had brief relationships, a few one-night stands and a few so-called arrangements with women who didn't expect more than an occasional romp between the sheets. None of the women had lasted. None of them had been Tori. But maybe that was just as well. As Tori herself had pointed out, he was married to his ranch—too much competition for any woman to handle, even her.

Still, she looked so desirable with her eyes closed, her soft lips parted, and her hair flowing over the pillow like spilled honey. Overcome by a sudden impulse, he reached out and brushed a fingertip along a silky tendril. He wouldn't do more. The river of hurt between them was too wide and too deep to be bridged by a touch.

Her eyes flew open. She gazed up at him in the darkness, her expression guarded.

"Erin's asleep," Will whispered. "Go back to bed and get some decent rest. I'll stay here awhile."

She eased away from her daughter and sat up, looking uncertain.

"Come on." Will walked around the bed and offered his hand. Sliding her feet to the floor, she took it, allowing him to pull her up without disturbing Erin. Her palm was warm and soft, but he could sense the tension in her fingers before he released them. Her mauve silk nightgown clung to her slender curves, outlining her small, perfect breasts and shadowing the V at the top of her thighs.

Despite his resolve Will felt the heat surge through his body. His sex rose to a jutting erection beneath the old

flannel robe he'd thrown on when he heard Erin. He
tugged the ends of the sash to make sure the robe wouldn't
fall open and humiliate him. He slept in the raw, something Tori would doubtless remember. She might also remember how easily he became aroused. Right now, the
urge to have her—to sweep her up and carry her down the
hall to his room, fling her on the bed and lose himself between those long, silky legs—was driving him crazy. But
the timing was all wrong. The last thing he wanted was to
make a fool of himself with the one woman who could
bring him down.

Side by side they moved past the bed and out into the
dimly lit hall, where they could talk without waking their
daughter. Will forced himself to keep his eyes on her
face. Tori was no fool. If his gaze wandered to her body
in that sexy nightgown, she would be aware of it.

"It's all right," she said. "I can stay with her until
morning."

"No, get some rest," he told her. "You've got a busy
day ahead, and I'm not sleeping worth a dang, anyway. If
you need to go back to town in the morning, you can bor-
row that spare red truck. But for now, I hope you'll leave
Erin here. After what happened tonight, I don't think
she's ready to go back to school."

"For once, I agree with you," she said. "I'll talk to the
school tomorrow. Whatever happens, Erin's welfare
comes first. Agreed?"

"Agreed. *Whatever happens.*" Dark possibilities played
like a slide show through Will's mind. *How will it feel,* he
wondered, *hearing prison doors slam shut, knowing I'll be
an old man by the time they open again for me?*

Tori must've sensed his anxiety. She turned toward
him, a softness in her eyes. One hand reached up to brush
the collar of his worn flannel bathrobe. "I can't believe

you're still wearing this old thing," she said. "It even smells the way I remember."

Will felt his chest constrict. She was so close to him, like a butterfly that would take wing if he so much as breathed. He forced a smile. "So how does it smell to you?"

"Like a man. Sweaty and tired from an honest day's work. Like you."

"Maybe I should toss it in the laundry more often." Will mouthed the words, scarcely aware of what he was saying. She smelled like the gardenia-scented bath soap she'd always favored, the same aroma that used to swim in his senses when he buried his face between her breasts. Right now, he wanted to drown himself in her and never come up for air.

Her hand lingered on the collar of his robe. Was it an invitation? A tease? Or just a gesture she had to know how much he wanted her. Did she want him, too?

Will ached to kiss her, to clasp her in his arms and let his hungering hands feel every curve and hollow of her through the thin silk. But that wasn't going to happen. He and Tori had built a cautious trust over the years. They'd made unspoken rules, drawn lines that were not to be crossed. To cross those lines, to shatter that trust now, when he needed her help, could be the worst mistake of his life.

Summoning the last of his resolve, he lifted her hand from his robe and brushed a kiss across her palm. "Get some rest," he whispered. "Good night, Tori."

Releasing her hand, he turned and walked back into Erin's room.

CHAPTER 5

Blanco County prosecutor Clay Drummond was a man at the top of his game. He'd run unopposed in the recent election, standing on his record of toughness, high conviction rate, and absolute incorruptibility. Now at fifty-three, stocky and muscular as a bulldog, with iron-gray hair and a face chiseled in determination, he was setting his sights on higher office—maybe Texas attorney general, if the party would back him. Meanwhile, he had a job to do; and his future depended on his doing it well.

Abner Sweeney's report was waiting on his desk when he arrived Tuesday morning, after a three-day weekend of bird hunting at a friend's cabin. Preoccupied with other concerns, he barely gave the two-page typed report a glance—until two names jumped out at him. The first was *Nikolas Tomescu*. The second was *Will Tyler.*

Drummond scanned the report, then read it again, his pulse pounding like a prizefighter's before a title match. News of the shooting must've been all over the media, but he hadn't read a paper or glanced at TV all weekend. Until now, he'd been unaware of what had happened. But whatever had gone down, he needed to take charge of it—ASAP.

This wouldn't be the first time he'd dealt with the Tylers. Last spring he'd constructed an ironclad case for first-degree murder against the second Tyler brother, Beau. He'd assumed the conviction would be a slam dunk. But then, before the trial, the real killer had been exposed. Beau Tyler had gone free, cleared of all charges—and Drummond had been left with a pile of useless evidence and egg on his face.

This time it was Will Tyler, the respected head of the family, who'd run afoul of the law. There'd been no charges filed and no arrest made, pending the inquest. But Abner seemed to think he had enough on Tyler to charge the boss of the Rimrock with manslaughter, or even second-degree murder.

Drummond had no special quarrel with the Tylers. As far as he knew, neither did Abner. But he liked to win. And the press from a high-profile case like this one could jump-start a man's political rise. Both he and the sheriff had personal reasons to find Will Tyler guilty.

As for the victim, Nikolas Tomescu . . .

In the silence Drummond became aware that beneath his fresh white shirt, his body had broken out in a cold sweat. There was a lot more at stake here than just winning. It was as if everything that truly mattered was about to be laid on the line.

In this small community he was admired and envied. He had plenty of money, thanks to his wife's inheritance. He had a perfect family, a respected career, and a promising future. But two months ago, in a weak moment, he'd made one stupid mistake—a mistake that could cost him his marriage, his children, his career, and even his freedom.

Drummond glanced at the list of missed calls on his office phone. One number appeared three times. No messages, but he didn't need any.

It was time to give the devil her due.

He reached for his desk phone, then changed his mind. He took his cell out of his pocket and punched in the number.

"What the hell took you so long?" The husky female voice was unmistakable. "I called you three times, and you never called back."

"I was off the grid," he said. "Got home from a hunt late last night. I just heard about your brother."

"You could at least say you were sorry. Nicky was all the family I had. All I want now is to see Will Tyler pay for what he did—behind bars."

"So do I. That's why I called you. I'd like to make a deal."

"A deal?" She gave a derisive snort. "You're not exactly the one holding the cards, Mr. Prosecutor."

"I know. And I plan to do my job. But I'll work even harder for you if there's something in it for me."

"I'm listening."

A bead of sweat trickled down Drummond's temple. "I want that surveillance tape, Stella, and your promise that there are no copies. I want this whole mess over and done with."

She had the gall to laugh. "How about this deal? If you don't put Will Tyler away, I'll turn the tape over to the press. When you get out of jail, you'll be lucky to get a job cleaning toilets."

Drummond had tried to remain calm and cool, but his anger now boiled over. "If I go down, I'll take you with me. Procuring an underage girl. How's that for a charge?"

"Oh, but there was no procuring. I hired the girl as a

waitress. And I had no idea she was underage. She even showed me a fake driver's license. When she fessed up later that she was just sixteen, I showed her the door. I'm guessing she left town. Taking her upstairs was *your* idea, not mine. Even if it can't be proved she was underage, that surveillance camera caught you with your tidy whities down. Either way, I'd say you were in big trouble."

Drummond could imagine the smirk on her painted face. He swore under his breath. If he thought he could get away with it, he'd be tempted to find the woman and strangle her with his bare hands.

"I'm counting on you. Keep me posted." She ended the call on a maddeningly cheerful note.

Drummond could feel a headache coming on. The pounding grew worse as he recalled how he'd gotten into this mess. His wife, Louise, could be a real bitch when she was in a bad mood. Last August, after one of their nastiest late-night fights, he'd driven to the Blue Coyote for a drink. By the time he'd downed enough Scotch to cloud his judgment, the perky little waitress had begun looking pretty good to him. Friendly and willing, she'd met him out back on her break, took his money, and led him up the stairs. It was only afterward, as he was pulling up his pants, he'd noticed the surveillance camera mounted in a high corner, well out of reach.

Stella had probably paid the girl to target him. Whether she had or not, he was at her mercy now.

The voice of Glenda, the receptionist, startled him out of his thoughts. "Mr. Drummond, Ms. Tyler is here to see you."

Drummond's shoulders sagged. At any other time he'd have been happy to see his former law partner. But Tori Tyler couldn't have picked a more awkward time to show up—especially if she was here to talk about her ex-husband's case.

"Send her in." Drummond straightened his bolo tie and arranged his features in a welcoming smile. Maybe he could at least learn a thing or two from her.

He heard the familiar *click* of her high heels on the tile floor. An instant later, the door opened and Tori strode into his office. Dressed in tailored slacks, a white silk blouse, and a suede blazer, she took his breath away. She'd always had this effect on him. But even back when she was his junior law partner, and going through a divorce, he'd known better than to lay a hand on her.

The fact that he'd been half in love with the lady for years made his present situation even more painful.

"Hello, Clay." She gave him a friendly smile, but she looked frayed. Drummond knew her well enough to sense that she was worried. And he could pretty well guess why. Will Tyler was her daughter's father—and anything that affected her little girl affected Tori.

He rose, extending his hand. "How've you been, Tori?"

Her handshake was cool and cautious. She'd be representing her ex, of course. She and Drummond had faced each other in court countless times over the years, but this time it would be personal.

"I've been better," she said. "Family crisis, as you're no doubt aware."

"I just read Abner's report," Drummond said. "Sit down. Tell me what's on your mind."

She took the straight-backed chair that faced his desk and pulled it closer. "It's just . . ." She hesitated, very unlike the confident Tori he knew. "It's Abner," she said. "Will shot that man in self-defense. No question. But when Abner came out to the ranch on Saturday, to interrogate Erin and Will, he seemed to have a personal agenda. He was slanting his questions, making it look like Will had shot a man who was no threat to him."

"Nick Tomescu. He was a tough-looking brute, all right. But Abner's report says he had no history of violence."

"I'm aware of that. But it was late at night. The man had a helmet on. And Will had just heard the radio alert on the biker who'd robbed the convenience store. He thought he was facing a criminal who'd already shot one person." She shook her head, more emotional than Drummond had ever seen her. "What if it *had* been the robber? He could've killed Will and found Erin in the truck. Anything could've happened."

"According to this report, the man had surrendered his gun."

"But he had a knife, raised to throw. Clay, this case should never go to trial. It was self-defense, pure and simple."

Drummond exhaled, feeling for her but mindful of his own dilemma. "For now, that will be up to the judge at the inquest. If the ruling is self-defense, Will's trouble will be over." *But mine will just be starting,* he thought.

"I heard there might be a jury," Tori said.

"So did I. But evidently that's not going to happen."

"You've probably guessed that I'll be representing Will." Tori had pulled herself together, speaking calmly now. "I'm doing it because he's Erin's father, and she needs him. But even more important, Will is innocent."

Drummond nodded his understanding. "What can I really do for you, Tori? The last thing I want is to hurt you and your daughter."

"You can find out what's driving Abner and why he'd

be so determined to punish a man for doing what any father would."

Maybe Stella's got something on Abner, too, Drummond thought. *But I'll be damned if I'm going to ask him.* "I'll look into it," he lied. "If I learn anything, I'll call you."

"Thanks." She stood. "You've always been a friend, Clay. I know you have a job to do. But I hope you'll at least keep me informed—and, of course, share any new evidence with me as the attorney for the defense."

He watched her walk out, admiring her leggy stride and the way her slacks clung to her shapely hips. Tori was a magnificent woman and a longtime friend. She'd made a good case for her ex-husband's innocence. But given what Drummond was facing, none of that could be allowed to matter. Whatever happened, he had to save himself from ruin. He had to make sure Will Tyler went to prison.

A cold wind almost blasted Tori off her feet as she stepped out of the county building. Autumn-bright leaves were flying off their branches in a storm of reds and golds. To the northwest, muddy-looking clouds were roiling in over the caprock. The forecasted norther was moving in fast.

Clutching her blazer around her, Tori raced across the parking lot to the old red pickup she'd borrowed from the ranch while her wagon was in the shop. Flinging herself into the driver's seat, she grabbed for the door, which the wind had blown open, and yanked it shut.

For a moment she sat still, catching her breath and thinking about her meeting with Clay Drummond. In the nearly six years she'd worked as Clay's law partner, he'd never been anything but honest and fair with her. She

knew his wife, Louise, and his three children—one in
college now, the other two in high school. She'd even had
dinner in their home. Even though they were on opposite
sides of the legal process now, she'd always believed she
could trust the man. But today he'd seemed uncomfortable, as if he couldn't wait for her to leave. When she'd
argued in favor of Will's innocence, she could've sworn
she'd seen the man squirm. What was even more disqui-
eting, he'd kept breaking eye contact while she was talking to him, which wasn't like Clay at all.

Something wasn't right. And she owed it to her client—
to Will—to find out what it was.

Will.

How many times had she relived that encounter in the
hall outside Erin's room? If she'd made one more move,
where would she be right now? She'd seen the hunger in
Will's eyes and felt the heat rising between them. The
urge to reach down and touch the sash on his old bathrobe
had been almost overpowering. One tug at the loose knot
would have been enough to push them over the edge. But
Will had saved them both. He had kissed her hand and
walked away, leaving her weak-kneed and quivering in
her silk nightgown.

Time to put the whole incident out of her mind and get
on with her day. It wouldn't happen again. She wouldn't
give it a chance. Neither, evidently, would Will.

She was fishing her keys out of her purse when her
cell phone rang. It was Drew. "Hi," she said, welcoming
the diversion. "Aren't you supposed to be in school, Mr.
Middleton?"

He chuckled. "Even the principal needs a recess break.
How about you? Are you working?"

"Sort of. I've been laying some groundwork for Will's
defense, in case he needs it."

"Can't he get himself another lawyer for that?"

"Not one who'll work for free. Since he's Erin's father, and since she was a witness, I really do have to be involved. It's family business."

There was a beat of silence. "All right," he said. "But I confess I'd feel more secure if you weren't so chummy with your ex."

"We're not *chummy*. We have a daughter, who means the world to both of us. If it weren't for Erin, I'd probably never speak to him again."

"*Ouch!*" Drew's laugh sounded forced. "Sorry, that's not why I called. Just wondering if you were free for a movie tonight."

She hesitated, checking her mental to-do list.

"I need to see you, Tori," he said. "Besides, you could use a fun chick flick with popcorn and some good old-fashioned back-row snuggling."

"Isn't the back row where your students sit to make out?"

"At least they won't be sitting behind us. Is that a yes?"

She relented. "Sure. My house, seven-thirty?"

"Let's make it seven. We can get pizza before the movie."

"Fine. Seven. See you then." She ended the call. At least she'd have something to take her mind off Will's troubles tonight. Drew had a way of relaxing her, making her laugh. He never confronted her or made unreasonable demands the way Will had done when they were married. And Will would never offer to watch a chick flick just because he thought she'd enjoy it.

Drew is a gem, Tori told herself. If she didn't grab him fast, some other woman would.

As she started the truck, a gust blasted a shower of

leaves onto the windshield. Tori turned on the wipers to clear them away. She'd planned to drive to the ranch tonight to brief Will on the case and check on Erin. But given her date with Drew and the chance of a storm moving in, it made more sense to spend the night in town—which brought up the question of what would happen when Drew drove her home.

He'd said he needed to see her. Did that mean he wanted to take their relationship to a new level? Was she ready for that? Tori wasn't a prude. The one brief fling she'd had when she was still reeling from the divorce had been doomed from the start. And she'd never been one for casual sleeping around. She'd come to believe that love, or at least emotional intimacy, should be there before sex happened. Had she reached that point with Drew?

What would he do if she hadn't?

During her musings she'd let the truck idle too low and killed the engine. Shifting down, she started it again and pulled out of the parking spot. Her station wagon was still waiting for the arrival of a new starter. Maybe it was time she began shopping for a new vehicle, something that wouldn't strand her somewhere at night or break down in bad weather. The next time she saw Will, maybe she'd ask him for some suggestions.

Will again. Damn.

Muttering under her breath, Tori ground the pickup's aging gears and roared out of the parking lot.

After lunch—a beef sandwich eaten off the kitchen counter—Will chose a sturdy paint gelding from the long barn, saddled it, and took the trail up to the back pastures. The windy weather wasn't the best for riding, but he'd wanted to check the stock and the fences before the coming storm. At least that was his excuse.

He didn't really need to go. He'd put Beau in charge of readying the pastures and the cattle for bad weather, and, much as Will was tempted, he'd learned better than to show up and try to supervise. Beau knew his job, and any interference from his big brother would only rile his temper. Will had resolved to keep his distance, but he wanted to get out of the house and see things for himself.

The events of the past few days had left him shaken and out of sorts. He felt the need to ride the ranch alone, to see the land and see himself as part of it. With so much uncertainty hanging over him, he needed a reminder of who he was, why he was here, and what he was fighting for.

Collar raised against the wind, Stetson jammed on and tied under his chin, he rode across the fire-scarred flat and up toward the edge of the foothills. The stiff breeze whipped waves across the yellow grassland and battered his sheepskin coat. A pair of ravens soared on the windy swells, tumbling as if in play.

In the pastures red-coated Hereford cattle clustered with their backs to the wind. After the summer drought and the fire that had followed, Will had sold off most of his steers at a loss. The animals that remained were breeding stock—prime cows and bulls and last spring's half-grown calves—his best hope for the next season. If he could keep them fed and healthy over the winter, he'd have a good start on next summer's herd. But if the coming winter turned harsh, the price of extra hay and the calorie-rich cottonseed cake known as "cow candy" could bankrupt him.

In the distance he could see Beau's crew with the flatbed

truck, setting up stacks of baled hay to serve as extra wind breaks for the cattle. Two generations ago, when Bull's father, Williston Tyler, had cleared the land for pasture, he'd had the foresight to leave clumps of cedar growing in place. Last summer's wildfire had destroyed many of the scrubby evergreens. A few stands had been spared, but if the storm turned out to be a bad one, the trees wouldn't be enough. Cold would be the worst danger. The cattle were still growing their long winter coats. They'd been given extra feed to strengthen their resistance, and heaters had been installed to keep their water tanks from freezing over. But the worry wouldn't ease till this early storm had passed.

Last summer, after the drought and the fire, he and Beau had taken out a hundred-thousand-dollar short-term bank loan, secured by some acreage, to tide the ranch over for a few months, pending the sale of the steers and Sky's colts. But the cattle had sold low; and with other Texas ranches in as much trouble as the Rimrock, few of their owners had cash to spend on new horses.

At the first of the year, the loan, along with the interest, would be due. If they could talk the bank into an extension, they had a chance of pulling through. Otherwise, they'd have no choice except to lose the land or sell it—a solution that would make Bull Tyler turn over in his grave.

As if spurred by the thought, he headed the horse uphill toward the escarpment. A forty-minute ride brought him to the mouth of a narrow box canyon with high, red sandstone walls. Sheltered from the wind, it was a mystical place. Soft red sand covered the floor. On the side where a sheer cliff rose straight up, a panorama of Native American petroglyphs—wild animals, warriors, mythic spirits, and many, many horses—paraded across the sandstone face, telling silent stories of a past that would never live again.

Will dismounted, tethered the horse, and walked up the canyon, enjoying the peace of the place. But someone had been here recently. For the space of a breath, Will felt the warning prickle at the back of his neck. Then he relaxed as he recognized the prints of Sky's worn soles and Lauren's narrow designer boots. This, he knew, was one of their favorite places.

Near the spot where Will stood, mesquite bushes screened a small, steep side canyon—the disputed canyon that his father had sold to Ferg Prescott years ago for a dollar. The last time Will had been here, the stream in its bed had been dammed at the top. Barbed wire had blocked the entrance with a sign reading, *PROPERTY OF PRESCOTT RANCH*. But as Will pushed his way through the brush, he realized something had changed. The barbed wire and the sign were gone. Water trickled down the rocks, the sound of it music to a rancher's ears.

Lauren had kept her word. But the parcel was still in Prescott hands, and she had nothing to gain by selling it. Will was doing his best to be patient, but with the threat of jail hanging over him, he needed to get the matter settled. Whatever happened next, he owed it to his father's memory to make the Rimrock Ranch whole again.

Will returned to the ranch house, hung up his coat and, hearing voices, found Jasper and Erin at the kitchen table, drinking cocoa with marshmallows. "You look like you could use some thawin' out," Jasper said. "Pan's still hot on the stove. Help yourself to what's left."

"Thanks." Will emptied the steaming cocoa into a mug, skipping the marshmallows, which were too sweet for his taste.

"Daddy, can I go out and see Tesoro?" Erin asked. "Sky's out there. I just saw him drive up."

"Have you finished your schoolwork?"

She grinned. "All done."

"Fine, then. But put on a coat. It's brisk out there."

Erin raced to get her coat. The front door opened and closed as she left the house. Will took a cautious sip of hot cocoa and settled back in his chair. He'd hoped to catch the old man alone for a quiet talk.

"I rode out to the petroglyph canyon today," he said. "Lauren promised me Sunday that she'd free up the water in that little side canyon. It's been done. The fence and the sign are gone, too."

Jasper's gaze narrowed beneath his grizzled brows. "But the gal hasn't budged on selling you back that land, has she?"

"She asked for more time. I'm trying to be patient and give her some rope." Will studied the man who'd been more of a father to him than Bull Tyler ever had. "You don't like her much, do you?"

Jasper's scowl deepened. "She seems nice enough, all right. And she makes Sky smile, which takes some doin'. But she's Garn Prescott's daughter and Ol' Ferg's granddaughter, and they was both rotten, no-good skunks! I'll never trust a Prescott as long as I live!"

Will shook his head. "Well, I hope you change your mind, Jasper. When Lauren marries Sky, she'll be family."

"She'll still be a Prescott. I'll wait to pass judgment."

"Speaking of Old Ferg," Will said, changing the subject, "I've always wondered why my dad sold him that little canyon—and for just a dollar. You've been with our family longer than anybody on the ranch, even me. I know there are stories Bull never wanted told. But he's gone, and I need to know. Are you ready to tell me?"

"Maybe." Jasper's mouth tightened as if holding back the secret. Will waited, giving the old man a moment to ponder. When Jasper cleared his throat, Will braced for what he was about to hear.

"This was after your mother was killed in that wreck, you understand," Jasper began. "Bull loved his wife. He mourned her till the day he died. But there was another woman he loved, too. He sold the land because of her— and to protect you and Beau."

Will nodded, knowing better than to speak.

"I'm telling secrets I swore not to tell," Jasper said. "But since I might not be long for this world, maybe it's time you heard. Bull got the woman pregnant. She knew she couldn't expect him to marry her, so she went home to her people in Oklahoma. She left a letter meant for Bull, but Ferg Prescott got his thievin' hands on it first. There were things in that letter that could've dirtied Bull's reputation, if they came out, and hurt his children down the line.

"The blackmailing bastard offered Bull the letter in exchange for selling him that piece of land." Jasper pushed to his feet, a signal that the story was done. "So now you know. That's just one reason why I don't trust the Prescotts, and there are plenty of others."

"What about the woman?" Will asked, already guessing the answer.

"Bull sent a man to find her and give her money for the baby. But he never saw her again."

"She was Sky's mother, wasn't she? Does Sky know?"

"He does. I told him. And I reckon he's told Lauren." Jasper hobbled toward the kitchen door.

"One more thing," Will said. "What about the Spanish gold? Is there anything to that old rumor?"

Pausing in the open doorway, Jasper turned and gave Will a dark glance. "I've told you enough," he said. "That's a story for another time—if I ever choose to tell it."

Being with Drew was just the diversion Tori needed. Tonight's date—pizza, cokes at the Burger Shack, and a silly romantic movie—had made her feel seventeen again. They walked out of the theater arm in arm.

Now what?

Wind blasted them as they walked down the block to his sleek gray Honda. "You've got school tomorrow. It's probably past your bedtime." Tori managed a nervous laugh. "I sound like I'm talking to Erin, don't I?"

He ushered her to his car and opened the door, the perfect gentleman. "Actually, I'm not quite ready to turn in. How about a nice, grown-up beer at the Blue Coyote? We can wind down and talk a little. Sound good?"

"Sure," Tori answered, hesitant but wanting to please him. She liked Drew, liked him a lot. But was she ready for what he might be leading up to?

They drove the few blocks to the last corner in town, where the cheap neon sign cast a blueish glow over the customers who wandered in and out. Late on a weeknight, the place wasn't crowded. The big-screen TV above the bar was turned off, the classic country music muted and mellow with a throbbing underbeat.

Drew guided Tori to a quiet corner booth, his hand warm and possessive on the small of her back. They took their seats and ordered two Coronas from the tired-looking blond waitress. The girl came right back with their drinks.

She looked too young to be working in a bar, but nobody seemed to care.

Tori studied him across the table. He was a handsome man, with regular features and light brown hair that almost matched his good-natured eyes. He wore a brown cashmere sweater under his fleece-lined wool jacket. Flawless conservative style.

"I had fun tonight," she said. "Thanks for talking me into this."

He reached across the table and captured her hand. "I'm hoping the night might get even better," he said. "I'm falling hard for you, Tori. But before I crash and burn, I need to know where we're headed. Are we ready for the 'My place or yours' question?"

Tori had sensed what was coming, but his words had still caught her off balance. Scrambling for a reply that would put him off, without driving him away, she averted her gaze for a moment and glanced around the room.

In the shadowed space behind the bar, a figure stood, holding a glass and a towel—a woman with a buxom figure and flame-red hair. Everybody knew who she was, of course. But what startled Tori was that Stella Rawlins was looking straight at her, those green eyes blazing with pure, murderous hatred.

CHAPTER 6

Chilled by Stella's look, Tori shifted position, turning inward in the booth. Seated at an angle, she could no longer see the woman behind the bar. But she still felt the prickling awareness of those eyes, like a spider crawling up her back.

For the first time, she realized how wise Will had been to insist on keeping Erin safe at the ranch. Stella Rawlins was capable of anything, and now her hatred was focused on the Tylers.

As Will's ex-wife and his lawyer, was she in danger, too? Maybe. But she refused to let that make a difference. She had her life and her work, and nobody, not even Stella, was going to intimidate her.

"Tori?" Drew's polite voice broke into her thoughts. "Did I say the wrong thing?"

She pulled her attention back to him, choosing her words with care. "No, you said the perfect thing, Drew. I appreciate your honesty. I like you a lot—more than *a lot*. I like the way you make me feel and the way you always seem to be here for me." She licked her lips, a nervous gesture. "When you kiss me, I feel all the right tingles.

But I hope you'll be patient a little longer. Right now, while I'm under so much stress, isn't a good time to be swept into something new—not even if it's something wonderful."

Had she been tactful enough? He looked disappointed. But he managed a smile. "If you're under stress, I can think of a great remedy," he joked. "But I understand—at least I'm trying to. Since I happen to think you're a woman worth waiting for, I'll try to be patient. But don't expect me to wait forever, Tori."

"I know better than that. Just a little more time, that's all I'm asking." She nodded toward her half-emptied glass. "I think I'd better leave the rest. Too much beer has an unflattering effect on me."

"Ready to go, then?" Fishing out his wallet, he left a couple of bills on the table. Then he rose, gave Tori his hand, and ushered her outside. The wind had risen to a howl. It whipped Tori's coat around her body as they walked to the car. The air carried the earthy scent of a coming storm. She filled her lungs with it, breathing away the stale, smoky odors of the Blue Coyote and the memory of those hate-filled eyes, watching her from the shadows.

They drove back to her house, saying little. *It isn't too late to reverse course and invite him in,* Tori reminded herself. She had little doubt that Drew would be a good lover, tender and considerate. But tonight she would be jittery, nervous, and torn by doubts. No, this wasn't a good time. When it happened—*if* it happened—she wanted to be ready.

He pulled the car into her driveway, walked her to the front door, and gave her a lingering kiss. "Think about what I said," he murmured as she unlocked the door. "Call me if you change your mind."

From the open doorway, she watched his big, sleek car glide out of the driveway. As the taillights vanished down the street, she closed the door behind her and switched on a lamp. The house was quiet. Safe, she thought, unless one of Stella's minions was hiding in a closet, ready to jump out at her. Maybe she should have invited Drew inside. At least she wouldn't have been here alone.

Laughing at her own fear, she walked through the split-level house, turning on the lights. Nothing. She was being silly. All the same, she was glad Erin was safe on the Rimrock with Will.

She paused, thinking of her daughter. When she'd brought Erin to the ranch on Saturday, she hadn't planned on leaving her there. Most of the clothes Erin liked, along with spare underthings, sanitary pads, schoolbooks, and other necessities, were here. Tori had already packed a suitcase for her and planned to take it when she drove to the ranch tomorrow. But with a storm moving in, the roads might be better tonight. She glanced at her watch. It was barely ten-thirty, not too late to change clothes, make the twenty-mile drive to the ranch, and stay the night in Beau's old room.

Fifteen minutes later, dressed in her jeans and her warm ranch coat, she was driving down Main Street, headed out of town. After she passed the last streetlight, the night was pitch-black, darkened by the clouds that had poured in over the caprock to fill the sky. Wind battered the old pickup, threatening to blow it off the road. Tori's fingers cramped on the wheel as she struggled to hold it steady.

She'd been driving about ten minutes when the storm broke in full fury. Lightning streaked across the sky. A fusillade of marble-sized hailstones blasted the vehicle with a clattering roar, covering the road in an instant.

Worried but calm, Tori geared down and turned on the wipers. She'd driven in bad storms before. She'd be fine.

The windshield had fogged over. Remembering too late that the truck had no air-conditioning to clear the glass, she punched the defroster button and cleared a spot with her hand. Her headlights showed nothing but white. She was driving blind. But she'd traveled this road hundreds of times over the years. The ranch turnoff couldn't be more than a few minutes ahead. She didn't dare pull off the road and wait. The storm could get even worse, stranding her. She had to get to the house.

The truck crept forward through the swirling whiteness. Hailstorms tended to pass with the storm front, giving way to rain or sleet. Surely, this one would stop in the next few minutes. If anyone in the house had left a light on, she'd be able to see it in the distance and find the gravel lane that turned off the main road. Maybe she should call. But her purse, with her phone in it, was out of easy reach. If she braked to find it, she could kill the engine or skid on the ice-slicked road.

She pushed on, minute after tension-fraught minute, inching forward with the defroster on full blast. By now, she knew she'd missed the turnoff to the lane. But the road's steep edges gave her no room to turn around without the risk of sliding off and getting stuck. What she needed was a wide spot or, better yet, a side road to a ranch or farm where she could drive in, back out, and make the turn.

The hail had given way to a driving, icy sleet that froze on the surface of the road. As the whiteout cleared to a dark gray, Tori could make out the road's shoulder in the headlights. Just ahead, a rutted lane cut off to the right, probably leading to a farm—just what she'd been looking for. Tapping the brake, she eased the wheel into a careful right turn. So far, so good. But she'd only gone a few feet down the cutoff when she realized her mistake. The farm road sloped at a sharp angle from the high shoulder of the road. Under these icy conditions, its steep surface could be too slippery for the truck to back out.

She stopped the vehicle, pulled the hand brake, and shifted into neutral, with the engine still idling. Surely, the old pickup would have four-wheel drive. Tori searched on and under the dashboard, but couldn't find any way to switch it over. All she could do was try to back out.

With a muttered prayer she shifted into reverse, released the hand brake, and floored the gas pedal. The engine roared. The worn tires spun on the slick ice. But the truck didn't move.

She slumped over the wheel, collecting her thoughts. The only option left was to keep going down the farm road and hope it led to someplace where she could find shelter.

Taking a deep breath, she drove slowly forward. Beyond the reach of the truck's headlights, the road descended into a black fog. Between the storm and the clouded windshield, Tori was driving almost blind. She didn't see the electric wire fence and the bulky forms of cattle on the far side of it until she was about to crash into it.

Swallowing a scream, she slammed her foot on the brake. The truck fishtailed and skidded to a stop, inches from the fence.

The engine had died. Shaking, Tori turned off the ignition and pulled the hand brake. She couldn't go forward; she couldn't back up; she'd be a fool to get out of the truck in the storm. She wasn't going anywhere. It was time to find her phone and call for help.

She'd tossed her purse into the backseat with Erin's suitcase. Hooking the strap with her finger, she dragged the purse into the front and fished out her cell phone. The display screen showed a low-battery signal. Tori muttered an unladylike curse. She usually plugged in the phone when she went to bed, but it was too late for that now, and she'd left her car charger in her station wagon.

If I could just reach one person . . .

Mentally crossing her fingers, she scrolled to Will's number and pressed *call*. Her heart sank as she counted the rings. No answer. When his voice message came on, she spoke rapidly. "Will, I'm stuck off the road in the storm, somewhere past—"

She broke off in midsentence. Her phone had gone dark.

Will had gone to bed early in the hope of getting some needed rest. But between the storm outside and the worry demons in his head, sleep was impossible. Around ten-thirty, he rolled out of bed, dressed, and took a moment to look in on Erin. Then, shrugging into his sheepskin coat, he went out to his truck.

Icy sleet spattered the pickup as he drove the back roads of the Rimrock, using his powerful spotlight to check every fence, every pasture where the cattle were gathered. Not that he could do much if any of them were in trouble. That would have to wait for daylight. But every animal was precious. In terms of hard cash, the death of any cow, calf, or steer would mean a two-thousand-dollar loss to the ranch.

The crews had done all they could to protect the cattle against cold and wind. But in an open pasture, there wasn't much that could be done about lightning. As a boy Will had seen what one lightning strike could do to a closely packed herd. The memory of those charred, swollen bodies would haunt his nightmares for the rest of his life.

There'd been lightning strikes, dangerously close, as the storm front moved through. Dawn would tell if the lightning had done any damage. Tonight there was nothing he could do.

He was turning around to go back to the house when the spotlight caught a movement along the fence. Driving closer, Will saw that one of the spring calves, probably panicked by the storm, had run headlong into the fence and become caught in the wire. Unless it was cut loose, the young animal wouldn't last till morning. Turning up his collar, Will climbed out in the icy downpour and hauled his toolbox out of the back of the truck. He got a rope as well. If the six-hundred-pound calf tried to fight him, he'd need a way to control it. Maybe he ought to call the bunkhouse for some help. But he remembered then that he'd left his cell phone on the nightstand by the bed. He was on his own.

Fortunately for him, the calf had worn itself out struggling and didn't put up much resistance. Still, it took Will a good twenty minutes, working in the glare of the headlights, to cut through the tangle of wire and free the calf, which loped off bawling for its mother. By then, his hands were numb inside his soaked, half-frozen leather gloves. His teeth were chattering, his clothes clammy against his chilled skin.

He took time to close the hole in the fence and put away his tools. Then he piled into the truck, turned up the heater, and headed back to the house.

At least he wouldn't have to worry about Tori tonight. She'd phoned Erin that afternoon, saying she had a date that night and planned to drive out to the ranch in the morning. She was probably snuggled in a warm bed with that fancy new man of hers right now. Well, why the hell not? Tori was a free woman. She could damn well sleep with anybody she wanted. What was it to him? Right now, all he wanted was a hot shower and a few hours of decent rest before first light.

He'd made it to his bedroom and was peeling his wet clothes off his shivering body when he remembered his cell phone. Reflexively, he reached for it. He'd been out of the house for more than an hour. Tired as he was, on a night like this, he needed to check for messages.

There was only one. Will's throat jerked tight as he heard Tori's frightened voice, cutting off before she could tell him where she was, if she even knew. The fool woman must've decided to come tonight, after all. And she'd been caught in the storm, driving blind in that old truck with its worn tires. Lord, she could be anywhere. He checked the time on the message. She must've called soon after he'd left the house. Wherever she was, she'd been there for at least an hour.

Will grabbed for dry clothes and pulled them on in urgent haste. Somewhere out there, in the storm, lost and cold and scared, Tori was waiting for him to find her.

The cab of the rusty pickup was frigid inside. Shivering beneath her midweight coat, Tori searched the backseat for some kind of blanket or even an old spare jacket. But the truck had been left clean. She found nothing.

She was tempted to start the engine and turn on the heater, but the gas tank was almost empty—and in this old vehicle, there was the worry of an exhaust leak filling the cab with deadly carbon monoxide. Likewise, if she left the lights on, the truck might be easier to spot. But if no one came by, she could run the battery so low that the truck wouldn't start.

She checked the luminous dial on her watch. It was after midnight. She'd been stuck here more than an hour. There was no way to know if Will had gotten her message, or if anybody was out looking for her.

Maybe she should have called Drew instead. Sensible fellow that he was, he would probably have called the highway patrol. The troopers would have found her by now. She'd be safe and warm somewhere.

But Will? If she'd reached him at all, the man would be out driving the roads in the storm, growing more frustrated and annoyed by the minute. If he found her, she could expect an angry chewing-out all the way back to the ranch for putting herself in danger. She imagined his Bull Tyler voice, as she'd always called it, dressing her down as if she were a misbehaving child.

But even that would be better than *not* being found.

Teeth chattering, she pulled her coat tighter. If she'd accepted Drew's polite proposition, the evening would have ended very differently. Maybe she'd been wrong to refuse. She liked Drew a lot, and he was great husband material—good-looking, kind, stable, and great with children. She knew several attractive women in town who'd likely jump at the chance to sleep with him. Was she a fool to risk losing a man who could give her a happy life because she wasn't ready to do the same?

A layer of ice had formed on the outside of the truck. Tori could no longer see through the windows. If Will had missed her phone call, nobody would be looking for her. She could be here all night.

How much cold could a body stand before hypothermia set in? she wondered. Was it possible to freeze inside a closed vehicle like this one?

Drained by cold and fatigue, she yawned. What she wouldn't give right now for a warm bed —with or without Drew Middleton in it. Drew wouldn't have had much luck tonight. All she'd want to do was sleep.

Tori's eyelids were drooping. Her head sagged, then jerked up again. She mustn't sleep. She needed to stay alert, to move, to stay warm. But she was so tired, too tired to keep herself from drifting. She slumped over the steering wheel.

Find me . . . Please find me, Will . . .

She jerked awake with a startled gasp. Something—or someone—was banging hard on the outside of the truck. Ice shattered as the heavy hammer broke through, splintering the safety glass on the side window. Through the fog in her mind, a voice, hoarse with strain, shouted her name. *Will's voice.*

Seconds later, he'd freed the door and yanked it open. In the glare of headlights, he looked like a wild man, red-eyed and unshaven, his woolen cap askew on his head, his coat crusted with ice. As she stirred and sat up, he lowered his arms and, for a moment, simply stared at her.

"What the hell, Tori?" he said.

Tori didn't even try to respond. She tried to climb down from the driver's seat, but her cramped legs buckled beneath her. She fell out of the truck into his arms. He was cold, his bare hands icy, his stubbled chin rough against her forehead. His arms held her painfully tight, their strength almost crushing her.

"Fool woman!" he muttered. "Come on!"

Scooping her up, he carried her to his pickup, which was parked on the asphalt road with its lights on. The engine was idling. She could feel the heater's blessed warmth as he shoved her onto the seat. "Erin's suitcase . . ." she muttered. "My purse. Get them."

Slamming the door, he vanished down the slope, into the dark. In a moment he was back, climbing into the driver's seat and tossing her things, along with the hammer, into the space behind. From somewhere, he pulled out a moth-eaten blanket and thrust it toward her. It was dusty and smelled like the dog, but it was warm. Tori laid it over her legs as he geared down. The truck roared up the road. Within a quarter mile was a farm gate with a wide, level area to turn around. Only when they were headed back toward the ranch did he speak again.

"Damn it, Tori, you could've died out there! You missed the turnoff to the ranch lane by a couple of miles. What were you thinking?"

"I couldn't see. I was lost."

"At least you could've let somebody know you were on your way—even Erin or Bernice."

"It was late."

"Then maybe you should've waited till morning. Three hundred head of cattle to worry about, and I spend half the night chasing all over creation after one muleheaded woman! Do you know how long it took me to find you?"

"Stop browbeating me, Will. We aren't married anymore."

"Then why didn't you call your fancy new boyfriend to come and find you?"

"Right about now, I'm asking myself the same question." Tori glanced sideways at his angry profile, square jaw set, strong hands clamped on the steering wheel. Will would always be Will—stubborn, hard-charging, and determined to be right. He was the most maddening man she'd ever known. Yet, when she'd found herself in danger, he was the one she'd called.

He drove in brooding silence now, turning the truck

up the long gravel lane to the house. *Sad,* Tori thought, *how things can change.* Fourteen years ago, when she became Will's bride, she thought she'd found heaven on earth. What a naïve child she'd been. She hadn't stood a chance against Bull's domination, Will's duty to the ranch, and, finally, his senseless jealousy over an older man's attentions—a man she could barely abide. That jealousy had struck the final blow to their crumbling marriage.

But all those things were in the past. Now it was only their daughter who kept them tied into some semblance of a family.

"How's Erin?" she asked as he pulled up to the house.

"Fine. She was asleep when I left."

"I saw Stella Rawlins tonight, in the Blue Coyote," Tori said. "The way she looked at me—it gave me the shivers. I realized then that Erin needed to be here with you, out of harm's way."

He reached behind the seat to get Erin's suitcase and hand Tori her purse. "I don't want you messing with the woman. Don't even go into that bar."

"I was safe enough. Drew and I stopped by there for a beer. We didn't stay long."

Tori's legs were still unsteady, the ground slick with ice. She gripped Will's arm as he helped her up the steps, across the porch, and into the dark entryway of the house. He was like a rock beside her, solid and cold.

Releasing her, he closed the door behind them. "Can *Drew*—" He spoke the name contemptuously. "Can he protect you? Does he carry a gun?"

"I don't know. I never thought to ask."

"Well, *you're* going to carry one, at least till this nasty business is over. I have a nine-millimeter Kel-Tec that's small enough to fit in your purse, but mean enough to blow a hole in anybody who threatens you. I'll get it for you in the morning." He set Erin's suitcase on the floor, shed his coat, then tossed it over the rack in the hall. "Who knows, maybe *Drew* could use some protecting, too. According to Erin, he's a mild-mannered type."

Something in Tori snapped. With a sharp intake of breath, she spun to face him. "How . . . dare . . . you?" She kept her voice low, but every word was charged with fury. "How dare you discuss my personal life with our daughter? What I do is none of your business, Will Tyler!"

"Anything that affects Erin is my business. And that includes the men you bring into her life."

His arrogance shoved Tori over the brink. Her hand flashed upward. He made no move to stop her as she slapped the side of his face—so hard that the sound of it cracked like a pistol shot in the room. The impact stung her palm and hurt her wrist. Pain brought tears to her eyes.

Will stood like stone. Only his eyes reacted to her blow, narrowing, darkening. Then his hands moved up to rest on her shoulders, their weight anchoring her in place. His gaze drilled into hers.

"Damn it to hell, woman, I should've left you in that truck to freeze!" he muttered.

In a swift, sure movement, he bent and captured her mouth with his.

Will's crushing kiss went through Tori like a lightning bolt—a flash of heat that melded all the hurt, all the anger, all the loneliness of the past eight years, into one burning rush of need. For the space of a heartbeat, she resisted. Then, with a whimper, her lips parted. Her body softened against his hard planes. Her fingers raked his thick, damp hair, pulling him down to deepen the kiss. He groaned, his hands sliding down over her curves in an act of pure possession, pulling her in closer.

"We . . . mustn't do this . . ." Tori's faint murmur of

protest vanished into darkness as if the words had never been spoken. She was shivering with cold. So was he. They clung together, craving warmth, craving intimacy, both of them aware they were careening toward disaster, and knowing that they'd already gone too far to stop.

He swept her down the hall, pausing for the barest instant at Erin's door to make sure their daughter was asleep. Then, in the next moment, they were in his room, ripping off clothes, leaving garments where they fell on the rug, before they tumbled, naked and shivering, into each other's arms and into his bed.

"You're cold." He reached for the down comforter and pulled it over them.

"So are you." She ran her hands over his big, rugged body, remembering every line and hollow, every nick and scar. Only one scar was new—the short, deep gash along his outer thigh where he'd been bitten by a huge rattler last spring and nearly died. That was part of him now, and part of her memory.

Even the way his erection curved slightly to the left was as she remembered, as was the low growl, from deep in his throat, as he mounted between her willing legs and pushed deep, filling the dark, needing place inside her like a man coming home after a long time gone. No foreplay was needed. She'd been ready for him from the moment of that first soul-shattering kiss.

They made love like two dance partners, separated by years, who still recalled the steps. But the music had changed to a throbbing, hunger-driven beat, pounding in its urgency, savage in its demands. Tori stifled a cry against his shoulder as she climaxed, clenching around him in spasms that rocked her to the core. An instant later, he moaned and shuddered, filling her with the warm flood of his release.

For a moment he lay still, his breath easing out in a long exhalation. Then he moved off her, rolled over, and, without a word, sank into exhausted sleep.

That, too, was very much as Tori remembered. Some things never changed.

She slid out of bed and pattered into the bathroom. Will's old flannel robe hung on a hook behind the door. Tori wrapped it around her and walked back to stand beside the bed, gazing down at the man who lay sprawled in sleep like a tired child. Overcome by tenderness and dismay, she shook her head.

Heaven save her, what had she done?

CHAPTER 7

William woke to silence at 4:15 a.m. Tori was gone from his bedroom, along with her clothes. No surprise there. She probably hadn't wanted to face waking up next to him. And she definitely wouldn't have wanted Erin to discover her in his bed.

He'd needed her last night. Something told him she'd needed him, too—for the first time in eight long years. But he'd be a fool to think their wild encounter had been anything more than a one-night stand. Knowing Tori, he believed she was already beating herself up with regrets. Unless he missed his guess, today would be back to business as usual, with both of them pretending nothing had happened.

Put it aside, he told himself. Right now, he had more urgent concerns than his ex-wife. The morning stillness told him the norther had passed, leaving bitter cold in its wake. There was nothing to do but get up and deal with the damage.

He rolled out of bed and flipped the light switch. Nothing happened. There were probably lines down between here and Blanco, which meant no heat, no coffee, even, till the power crews got out this way. There was nothing to do but get dressed in the dark, go outside, and face the dawn.

He pulled on layers of clothing—thermal underwear, a wool shirt, and a down vest to wear under his coat. Thick wool socks went under his winter boots. In the living room he took a moment to light the fire that was already laid in the fireplace and check the wood box for more logs and kindling. That done, he added his coat, his thick wool cap, and his leather gloves.

He was about to step outside when Tori walked in from the hall. She was wrapped in Will's old flannel robe, her hair tousled from sleep. The memory of her ripe mouth and eager body rose in his mind. He forced it away.

"It's early," she said. "Is everything all right?"

"That's what I'm about to find out. You might as well get some sleep while the place warms up." He turned to go, but her voice stopped him.

"Will, about last night. We need to forget it ever happened."

He'd expected this from her. Still, it stung. "It's already forgotten," he said. "And don't worry, I'm not going to say anything to your new boyfriend."

Before she could respond, he walked out the door and closed it behind him. On the porch what met his eyes confirmed his worst fears.

In the east the sky was paling to gray. The grim dawn cast enough light to reveal the ice-glazed nightmare the storm had left behind. Frozen sleet coated the roads and buildings. Its weight had bowed the willows to the ground and broken branches off the tall cottonwoods. Worst of all, Will knew from experience, the frozen pastureland would offer no forage for the cold, hungry cattle.

The bunkhouse was already stirring. No lights there, either, but smoke was curling from the chimney. All hands would be needed to get hay to the pastures, to de-ice and refill the watering tanks, and aid the distressed cattle. Will could see where Sky had parked his truck with the headlights on in the open doorway of the long barn. Once he'd made sure the horses were all right, he would join the crews in the pastures.

Beau's Jeep was coming down from the east pasture, its familiar headlights bouncing along the rough road. Will watched as it came nearer, apprehension a dark coil in the pit of his stomach. The news would be bad, his in-stincts told him—as if any news this morning could be good. He braced his emotions as the Jeep rounded the last curve and rocketed into the yard.

Beau braked the jeep to a halt and climbed out. Red-eyed and unshaven, he looked as if he'd barely slept. Will came down the icy steps to meet him. "Bad?" he asked, meeting his brother's eyes.

Beau nodded, his mouth pressed into a tight line. When he spoke, his voice cracked like an old man's. "More than bad. Lightning strike. I counted seventeen dead around the burnt spot in the pasture. Hope to God there aren't more, but we won't know for sure till the sun's up."

Will's knees had gone weak. He braced a supporting hand on the Jeep's warm hood. "Damn," he muttered. "That's all we need to push us over the edge."

Behind him, the front door opened and closed. Tori had come out onto the front porch. Her gaze took in the frozen landscape and the stricken faces of the two men at the bottom of the steps. "What is it?" she asked. "What's happened?"

Beau gave her the news. She'd been a ranch wife long enough to know what it meant. No dramatics, just bear up and move on. She shook her head. "I'm sorry. If there's anything I can do—"

"Just make sure Erin's all right, and keep her inside today." Squaring his shoulders, Will turned back to Beau. "Let's get the men together. We've got a herd to save."

The two brothers climbed into Beau's Jeep and headed toward the bunkhouse, tires crunching on the icy ground.

Heartsick, Tori watched them go. The death of that many prime cattle would mean disaster for the future of the ranch. The cows and heifers, many of them pregnant, were the backbone of next year's herd, the spring calves a promise of profit next fall. And the two pedigreed Hereford stud bulls, if either was lost, would cost a small fortune to replace.

Will was tough, like his father. He hid his emotions behind a stoic mask. But Tori knew he was devastated. Last night's losses, coupled with the summer's drought and fire, would put the ranch's survival in serious peril. Couple that with the legal charges hanging over him, and Will would be staggering under his invisible burdens.

Until the moment she'd stepped outside this morning, Tori had been preoccupied with what had happened last night in Will's bed. How could she have dropped her guard that way? What, if anything, would Will expect going forward? And how would it affect her growing relationship with Drew?

Now, compared to the morning's disaster, last night was no more than a pebble in her shoe, to be cast aside and forgotten. Like the storm had done, it had come and gone. There was nothing to do but put it behind her and move on.

But Will's hidden anguish tore at her heart. There was nothing she could do about the problems with the ranch. But as his lawyer it was up to her to see that he didn't pay for killing Nikolas Tomescu. Whatever it took, she couldn't let him down. She would question Erin, question Abner and his deputies, inspect the crime scene, scour every legal book she could find for a precedent. She would fight for Will's innocence with everything she had. He had killed in defense of their daughter, and she wouldn't give up until he was cleared of all blame.

Ralph Jackson slumped on a barstool in the Blue Coyote, so tired he could barely drink the free Tecate that Stella had shoved in front of him. At ten on a Thursday night, most of the customers had cleared out. The others would soon be gone, too. Nobody was paying any heed to the scruffy cowhand hunched over his beer.

"Cowboy, you look like you just got drug through a manure pit behind a mule." Stella studied him across the bar. Her silk blouse was so tight over her ample bosom that Ralph could see the outline of her nipples. He averted his gaze, reminding himself that the woman was old enough to be his mother.

"Been workin' my ass off all week for those damn Tylers," Ralph said. "Diggin' trenches with the backhoe and shovin' in those stinkin' dead cows. Hell, I oughta get double pay for a dirty job like that."

"But you don't, do you?" Stella clucked sympathetically. "How many cattle did they lose?"

"Nigh onto twenty, most of 'em hit by lightning. And I was on the crew that got to bury 'em."

"Poor boy."

For some reason she looked pleased. *But that's natural,* she thought, remembering that Will Tyler had gunned down her brother.

A week had passed since the storm. Now, as was typical for Texas, the weather was warming again, and the ice had melted. The work of keeping the cattle fed had eased off some. But taking care of cows was dirty work. When he tried to get close to Vonda, she complained that he smelled like a corral. And there was always the money, which never seemed to be enough.

"How's your wife?" Stella asked.

Ralph sighed. "Vonda's mad at me again. She wants to go to the beauty shop in town and get herself some of them fake fingernails. When I told her we didn't have the money, she threw a hissy fit. Locked me out of the bedroom and told me not to come back till I had it."

"Does she know you've been working for me?"

"Yeah. She's all for it, as long as I'm bringin' in extra cash." He looked up at her. "So, have you got any cleanin' up or fixin' to do around here? I don't need much, just enough for Vonda's nails."

"Couldn't her family give you any help? I'd think her father's sheriff job would pay well enough."

"Hell no!" Ralph's fist clenched around the cold can. "Vonda's folks kicked her out when she got pregnant. They won't have nothin' to do with us. I know Abner Sweeney was voted sheriff, but not by me. I can't stand the little turd."

Stella ran a towel over a damp spot on the bar. The last customer had left. Now Ralph was alone with her. "The work around here's pretty well been done," she said. "But how'd you like to make two hundred dollars?"

"I'd like that a lot." Ralph was already counting the

money in his head. He'd give Vonda fifty for the beauty shop and keep the rest for himself. He'd been wanting a new pair of boots, but if he bought them, Vonda would know he'd kept money back. Maybe he could just save it up for something big later on, like a new four-wheel ATV or the down payment on a better truck. "What do I have to do for that?" he asked.

"Not much. Just deliver a package, collect the cash from the customer, and bring it back to me."

Ralph wasn't too dumb to figure out what would be in the package. But as long as he didn't know for sure, and as long as nobody got hurt, what was the harm in it? "Sure," he said. "No problem."

"Fine. Come into the back office. I'll give you some directions—and a few rules. We'll see how this goes."

Ralph followed her, noticing how she limped, as if her red high-heeled boots were hurting her feet. He remembered how a friend of his, Lute Fletcher, had done some work for Stella. Lute had become greedy, gotten in too deep, and ended up dead. But Ralph wasn't like Lute. He knew the limits. Just a little job here and there, when he needed spare cash. That's all he'd do. He could walk away anytime he wanted.

Clay Drummond didn't bother to get up when the sheriff walked into his office. He had scant respect for the annoying little man whose visits always left him in a bad mood. And this morning, Clay was in a bad mood already. Stella had just given him another of her so-called reminder calls, hinting at what could happen if he failed to put Will Tyler away for shooting her brother. Now, as if the day could only get worse, here was Abner in his face.

"You got the notice about the inquest, right?" Abner took a seat opposite Clay's desk.

"I did," Clay said. "It'll be just you, me, the judge, the coroner, and any witnesses we want to call in."

"What about Tori?"

"She can be there if she wants, but only to listen. And Will won't be there at all. The inquest isn't a trial. Its purpose is to examine the evidence and, based on that, determine whether a suspect should be charged and tried. You'll be a witness, of course, and maybe one or two of your deputies."

Abner quite possibly knew all this, Clay thought. But he enjoyed treating the little man as if he were an ignorant bumpkin.

"What about the little girl?" Abner asked. "She saw the whole thing."

"I spoke with Tori on the phone. She doesn't want her daughter put through having to testify. We agreed that, for now, the interview you taped will be enough."

"Well, I want you to know, Drummond, that I plan to do my job. And I expect you to do yours. Those Tylers have always thought themselves a cut above everybody else. It does a body good to see one of 'em go down and face justice like us ordinary folks." Abner took a tissue from a box on the desk and blew his nose. "Do you think we can get Will for murder?"

Abner was like an attack dog straining at the leash. Earlier, Clay had wondered whether Stella was pulling the sheriff's strings, as well as his own. Now he was convinced of it.

"Murder?" Clay shook his head. "Not likely. We'd have to prove malice, and there's no evidence of that. The inquest will be looking at self-defense versus manslaughter, which carries a sentence of two to twenty years in Texas."

Abner smirked. "Even the minimum would take Will Tyler down a peg. What've we got to prove?"

Clay leaned back in his chair. "Tomescu had already surrendered his gun when Will shot him. As I see it, the case hinges on the knife, and whether a reasonable man would see it as a threat. If so, that would argue for self-defense."

"It wasn't much of a knife," Abner said. "Just a little switchblade. Even if Tomescu had thrown it, it wouldn't have done much damage."

"But throwing it could've wounded Will or maybe distracted him long enough for Tomescu to grab his gun back and use it. That's what the defense will argue if this goes to trial. Like I say, it's a fine line."

Abner's face lit. "What if Tomescu hadn't tried to throw the knife at all? What if Will put it in his hand *after* the man was shot dead?"

"Wouldn't the knife have Will's prints on it if he'd done that?"

"Not if he'd wiped it clean and used a handkerchief or something to put it in the dead man's hand."

Clay frowned. Evidence tampering was a crime, but if Abner was willing to try, it was no skin off his nose. "Could have happened," he said. "What else can you think of?"

"Will's a cool-headed shot. He could've wounded the man instead of blasting him through the chest. Ever see what a thirty-eight can do to a body at point-blank range?" Abner stood. "Will Tyler deserves to pay for what he did. And it's up to us to see that he does."

With that parting line, the sheriff marched out of Clay's office and closed the door with a *click*. Clay opened his desk drawer, took out a bottle of Lortab, and gulped one down with the last of his morning coffee. Abner Sweeney was a jackass, but at least they were on the same side. And discussing Will Tyler's case with him had clarified Clay's own concerns about the upcoming inquest. Will Tyler was one of Blanco County's leading citizens. He was respected, even liked by most of the people who knew him. Given the evidence, and the mitigating circumstances, there was a good chance the judge would rule against pressing charges.

Will would walk free, and Stella Rawlins would be out for blood.

Clay liked being county attorney, especially with the prospect of moving on to something bigger. He liked being a respected member of the community and having the kind of family life people admired. If Stella released that security footage, everything he'd worked for would be gone—his job, his marriage, his children, and his future. He'd be lucky to stay out of jail. One way or another, he needed to get that tape and destroy it. Until then, he'd have no choice but to do what she wanted.

And what she wanted was for Will Tyler to go to prison.

The physical evidence alone wouldn't be enough to send the case to trial. Neither would the coroner's findings nor even the testimony of the witnesses. That left the judge.

Apart from the juvenile court, there were just three judges in Blanco County. Clay knew them all—decent men, but human, with human failings. They had their weaknesses, and Clay knew how to use them—a small favor with implied repayment, a concession in some unrelated matter, or just a damned good argument. It was something he did well.

And it wasn't as if an inquest was a life-or-death mat
ter. Any room for doubt would be enough to justify sending a case to trial—a trial that could be delayed by weeks,
even months, buying him more time to deal with Stella.

Feeling better, Clay picked up the phone and buzzed
the receptionist at the front desk. "Glenda, could you find
out which judge is on the Tyler inquest and get him on
the phone for me? Thanks."

Lauren had never been an early riser. But sharing a
bed with Sky was changing that. When he spent nights
with her in town, he was usually gone by first light. If she
wanted any morning time with him, she had to get up,
too. Now that she was getting used to it, she'd come to
enjoy the peace of early dawn and the beauty of the sunrise that came with it. But waking to full alertness at such
an ungodly hour was still a challenge.

This morning, ten days after the terrible ice storm, she
woke to the aromas of bacon and fresh coffee. Flinging
aside the covers, she pulled on her quilted silk robe and
pattered into her apartment-sized kitchen. Sky, dressed
and ready for the day, was standing at the stove, scrambling eggs. He glanced around with a heart-melting grin.
"Good morning, sleepyhead," he said.

"You're fixing me breakfast?"

"I'm fixing *us* breakfast. Sit down."

She sank onto a chair, blinking herself awake as he
passed her a cup of steaming coffee, bitter and black, the
way he liked it. Lauren added cream and sugar before
tasting hers. Through the kitchen window she could see
the barest glint of morning. The weather had cleared and
warmed in the past week, but the autumn colors were
gone, the grass brown, the trees bare and broken.

"How can I learn to be a good ranch wife if you spoil me like this?" she joked.

"There'll be plenty of time for that." He set two loaded plates on the table and popped two slices of bread out of the toaster. "Eat up," he said.

"If I eat all this, I'll get fat."

"All the more for me to love."

Laughing, she filled her fork. This was the Sky Fletcher few people knew—laughing, teasing, affectionate, and happy. Opening himself to her as he did was the best gift she could have asked for.

"Aren't you going to work this morning?" she asked.

"Soon. There's plenty to do, and I want to be there for Will, in case he needs anything. The inquest is scheduled for this morning. He's putting on a brave face, but if the decision is to charge him, he's going to take it hard."

"How soon will he know?"

"Tori will be at the inquest. She'll call him as soon as it's over. Lord, I hope it's good news. The ranch has enough trouble as it is. We don't need a trial. We need Will."

"How's Erin taking all this?"

"She's one brave kid—doesn't want her dad to know how scared she is. But I think Will's even more worried for her than he is for himself."

"He would be." Lauren sipped her coffee. "Lately I've been thinking about that piece of canyon land Will wants to buy from me. I know it would please him to get it back. It might even take his mind off his troubles for a little while."

"You'd sell it to him for that reason? It's a nice idea, Lauren, but I thought you wanted time to explore the place while it's yours."

"I do," Lauren said. "So why not do it soon? The weather's supposed to be mild for the next couple of weeks. You and I could take Erin with us and spend some time exploring. Or if you can't get off work, I could just take Erin. We could pack a picnic lunch, make it fun for her. When we've explored to our heart's content, then I'll sell the land to Will for a dollar, as I promised I would. That land has been a sore spot between our families since before you were born. It's time we put an end to it and made peace."

Sky reached across the table and clasped her hand. "That's a great idea, and I love you for thinking of it. Do you want me to bring it up to Will, or would you rather wait and do it yourself?"

"Let me do it," Lauren said. "I could use a few points with the ranch family—especially with Jasper."

Finished with his breakfast, Sky rose. "Don't worry about Jasper. He's a prickly old bird, but he'll come around. Nobody could resist you for long."

"Don't count on his coming around anytime soon. Not as long as my last name's Prescott."

"Don't worry, I've got a plan to fix that." He strode to her side of the table, lifted her to her feet, and gathered her close for a lingering kiss. As her body molded to his through the silk robe, Lauren felt the warm stirrings of desire. It would be tempting to coax him back to bed and make him late for work. But Sky wasn't a man to be coaxed into shirking his duties, not even by a warm and willing woman. Maybe that was one of the reasons she loved him so much.

"I'll call you when I know about the inquest," he said.

"Thanks. I'll be waiting to hear."

She kissed him at the door; then she walked to the window to watch his truck drive away. She was far luckier than she deserved to be, Lauren thought. She had her

health, her career as an accountant, all the money she
needed, and the love of a wonderful man. It didn't seem
right that someone as fair, honest, and good as Will Tyler
should be surrounded by problems—a ranch that was
sinking into a financial quagmire, a possible prison sentence, and a failed marriage to a woman he clearly still
loved.

What had happened to drive Will and Tori apart? Will
had never talked about it in Lauren's hearing. Tori, although she was Lauren's friend, had never shared the story
of her marriage and how it had ended. Lauren told herself
that it was a private matter—as such things should be.

Still, she couldn't help wanting to know—in part because she wanted to avoid similar mistakes, but mostly
because she cared deeply about these two people and
their lovely young daughter. They'd become part of her
life—her future family. She wanted to understand them.

Lauren turned away from the window and began clearing away the breakfast dishes. She would give anything
to help Sky's half brother and his loved ones through
their troubles. But for now, there was nothing she could
do but hope and wait.

Beau found Will in the stallion barn, cleaning out stalls
with a shovel and a broom. He was going at it with a fury
that Beau understood all too well. Last spring, Beau had
been the one facing trial. Things had turned out all right,
but he knew how his brother must be feeling.

"Hey." Beau leaned against a partition, trying to look
casual. "We pay teenage boys to do that job. You're the
boss, not a stable hand."

Will gave him a glance, then went back to shoveling.
"What am I supposed to do, sit on the porch with Jasper

and wait for the call? Hell, I might as well make myself useful."

"You'll get through this, Will," Beau said. "I know that sounds like a stupid thing to say, but I've been in your shoes. You're a tough man—even tougher than you think you are."

"Don't be so sure of that." Will straightened, bracing the point of the shovel blade on the floor of the barn. "Wait till you have your own child. Then you'll understand. I'm not afraid of prison. I could survive a few years if it came to that. And I know you'd take care of the ranch. But the idea of leaving Erin, having her grow up without me, with the shame of a father behind bars—that's the worst. And if her mother marries that prissy school principal, knowing he'd be raising Erin in my place . . . Lord, that's what I can't even stand to think about."

"But that's not going to happen," Beau said. "You're innocent. The bastard had a knife up to throw at you. You killed him in self-defense."

Will muttered a curse. "Didn't you learn anything in the DEA? It's not about guilt or innocence, damn it, it's about politics! Both Abner and Clay Drummond are counting on a lot of press from this case. Throw Stella into the mix, and anything could happen. They'd see me hang if they could get away with it!"

The jangle of a cell phone startled both men into silence. Mouth tightening, Will reached for the phone in his vest pocket.

"Relax, it's not yours. It's mine." Beau pulled out his phone and took the call. Will tensed, like a man about to receive a blow, as his brother answered, then turned away.

"Yes," Beau was saying. "He's right here, Tori. Yes, I'll tell him." He ended the call.

"She called *you?*" Will faced him, bristling.

"She thought it might be easier for me to tell you face-to-face," Beau said. "The case is going to trial. Abner's on his way out here to arrest you."

"Call Abner." Will was stone-faced. "Tell him I'll be driving into town. I won't have my daughter seeing me led away in handcuffs."

"I'll call him," Beau said. "But I'll be driving you."

"No need for that," Will said. "This is my problem, not yours."

Beau put a hand on his brother's shoulder. "It's our family's problem. And you're not going through it alone."

CHAPTER 8

Tori waited in the rear entryway to the county build-ing, which housed the sheriff's department and the jail. Flanked by an armed deputy, Abner Sweeney stood beside her. His freckled face wore a self-satisfied smirk. A set of handcuffs dangled from his plump fist. He swung them back and forth, humming under his breath, a maddening sound.

"I can't imagine you're going to need those cuffs," Tori said. "Will's coming in on his own. He's not going to run away or attack you. You'd be safer putting them on *me*."

She was only half joking. Right now, it was all she could do to keep from punching the obnoxious little man in the mouth.

He chuckled. "I always did like your sense of humor, Tori. But the cuffs are part of the arrest process. They let the suspect know who's in charge."

The suspect? Will? Tori was still struggling to accept the unthinkable. The judge's decision had left her reeling, her confidence shaken to the core. How could this be happening?

She steeled herself as Beau's Jeep pulled up to the curb. Inside, she might be falling apart, but she couldn't let Abner know that—or Will. Especially Will.

The inquest had raised her hopes at first. As the evidence was presented, she'd felt sure that the conclusion would be self-defense. But at the last moment, the judge, a man Tori had known and trusted for years, had expressed his doubts and called for a trial. Stunned, Tori had looked around for Clay as the room emptied, hoping he might give her some explanation. But the county prosecutor had already left.

Will climbed out of the Jeep. Without waiting for Beau, who'd driven him, he strode up to the jail entrance and through the automatic doorway. Head high, face expressionless, he appeared proud and unafraid. But Tori knew what he must be feeling. His eyes didn't even flicker toward her as the sheriff cuffed his wrists and read him his rights. That done, the deputy led him back to booking, to be searched, fingerprinted, photographed, and humiliated. The sheriff followed, leaving Tori in the entryway.

Beau had come in through the outside door. As Tori turned and saw him—the friend who'd been there since her childhood—something broke inside her. A sob caught in her throat. She began to shake, as if the earth were breaking apart under her feet.

Beau reached her in two long strides and gathered her close. Holding her gently but firmly, he spoke. "It'll be all right. We can get him out tomorrow, after his bail hearing."

"I'm his lawyer. I know that." Her voice wavered. "But I'm scared, Beau. What if I can't do this? What if I let him down and he goes to prison? Maybe Will should hire somebody else."

"You won't let him down." He eased her away, holding her at arm's length. "When it comes to protecting people you care about, you're a tigress, Tori. Will may not be your husband any longer, but he's Erin's father. You won't just be fighting for him—you'll be fighting for her, for our whole family!"

"But what if I fail? What if I lose? The judge in there had every reason to rule in Will's favor. But in the end he went the other way. Something like that could happen again, and it would kill Will. It would kill Erin."

"That's why we have juries," he said. "Will shot that man in the belief that he was saving himself and Erin. Your job is to help those jurors see the truth." His grip tightened on her shoulders. "I've known you most of my life, Tori. You always had your eye on the prize. I've never known you to doubt yourself."

He was getting to her, as only Beau knew how. But the uncertainty was still there. "I've never had so much depending on me—or so much to lose," she said.

"You still love him, don't you?"

Beau's question caught Tori off guard, but she managed a quick recovery. "That's a low blow if I ever heard one," she said.

"You didn't answer my question. Do you still love him?"

The night of the storm flashed through her mind—Will's crushing arms, his kisses, their bodies seeking each other in desperate need. But that hadn't been love. It hadn't even been close.

"I care for him, of course," she said. "He's Erin's father, after all. But right now, that can't be allowed to matter. Will is my client. That's how I need to think of him."

He let her go with a quick hug. "You'll do us all proud, lady," he said. "And when Will's cleared, we'll have a big celebration. For now, let's both get back to the ranch. This'll be a tough day for Erin. She's going to need us."

Leaving her, he headed out to his Jeep. Tori watched him drive away. Beau had given her a good pep talk. But she'd known him since kindergarten and she'd recognized the look in his eyes.

Beau was as scared as she was.

Abner strolled down the hall to the row of holding cells, where Will Tyler had been taken after the booking procedure. He'd phoned Stella right after the inquest. She'd been pleased as punch. Abner was pleased, too. Putting a Tyler behind bars was no small accomplishment.

Abner and Will Tyler went back a long way. In school Will had been everything Abner wasn't—popular, smart, admired, and rich, at least by Blanco standards. He'd held class offices, gotten the best grades, and dated the prettiest girls, while Abner, a pudgy nobody, had been ignored. Will had never been unkind to the lonely boy. Like the other popular students, he'd simply treated Abner as if he didn't exist.

Abner had always envied the Tyler men—their power, their self-confidence, their brazen masculinity. Over the years that envy had fermented to hatred. He'd watched from behind the one-way glass as Will was strip-searched, dressed in an orange jumpsuit, and photographed face-on and in profile. It was satisfying to see a proud man like Will brought down to the level of a common criminal. It would be even more satisfying to see him behind bars.

The cells were walled on three sides, with bars open to the hallway. Each cell was designed to hold two men, but today most of them were empty. Will would be alone.

As Abner neared the cell, a nervous prickle stole up his spine. Watching Will from behind mirrored glass was one thing. Facing him, even through iron bars, was another.

Stopping next to the wall, just short of the cell, he took a careful peek around the corner. Will was stretched out on the lower bunk, his long legs crossed, his arms supporting the back of his head. His eyes were closed.

Was he asleep? Not likely, Abner surmised, stepping in front of the bars. He was faking it, as if to show his captors how little this humiliating process had affected him.

Even in the ill-fitting orange jumpsuit, which was inches too short in the legs, Will made an impressive figure—like a sleeping lion, relaxed but alert, and still dangerous.

Maybe this was a bad idea, coming here without a deputy along. Abner inched back toward the wall, intent on leaving. But just then, Will opened his eyes. His left eyebrow slid upward. For the space of a long breath, nothing else moved. Then he spoke.

"Do you need something, Sheriff, or did you just come by to gloat?"

Abner drew himself up. "You've no call to say that, Will. It was the judge who put you in here, not me. I'm just doing my job."

"Well, do it somewhere else. I may have to be here, but I don't have to listen to you whine and make excuses. If you've got anything to say that's worth hearing, call my lawyer." Will rolled over in the bunk, giving Abner a view of his orange-clad back.

Seething, Abner stalked back up the hall, toward the booking area. With a few well-chosen words, Will had cut him down yet again, making him feel like a small, powerless nobody. And the arrogant bastard had done it lying down in a jail cell.

Abner's prostate was acting up again today—or maybe it was just stress. He stopped by the men's room to relieve himself. A glance in the mirror confirmed what he knew: He was fat and homely, with a dowdy wife, a house full of kids, and a sixteen-year-old daughter who was about to make him a grandfather at forty. He was undereducated, underpaid, and would likely never advance beyond his present job. The confrontation with Will had brought it all home.

But this fight wasn't over. Will wouldn't be so high-and-mighty once he'd been locked up in the state prison for a few years; and Abner was determined to put him there. Whatever it took, whatever he had to do, the sheriff vowed, he would break Will Tyler and bring him to his knees.

Clay got the call from Stella as he was leaving work. Her timing was so spot-on that he suspected the woman was somewhere in the parking lot, watching him from her car. "I take it you've heard the news," he said.

"More or less. But I wouldn't mind hearing your take on the story."

"We lucked out with the judge. But getting a jury to convict him won't be that easy. The evidence that Will Tyler shot your brother in self-defense was pretty persuasive, especially the taped interview with his daughter."

"Well, now, that's your problem, isn't it, Mr. Prosecutor?" Her tone made Clay want to wrap his hands around her neck and shake her till it snapped. "Tell me about the evidence," she said.

"No surprises. There was the knife, the two guns involved, Will's flashlight, Nick's helmet, and the packet of cocaine that the deputy found on the bike. The fact that Nick was probably dealing won't help our side any."

She sighed. "Oh, Lordy, I told him to stay away from that awful stuff. If only he'd listened to me."

Her performance was an act, Clay knew. Stella had her fingers in plenty of dirty pies, including illegal drugs. But trying to prove it would be like slitting his own throat.

"What about the witnesses?" she asked.

"Again, no surprises. Abner, the coroner, one deputy, the tape of the girl, and parts of Will's taped interview."

"But nothing that would cast doubt on his story?"

"Not really. That's why everybody was surprised by the judge's decision."

Not quite everybody, Clay knew. Convincing the judge that justice would be best served by a trial had involved some advance persuasion on his part, along with a bottle of very expensive Scotch. A bit unethical? Maybe, but it was how smart lawyers worked the system.

"Well, Clay, it sounds to me like you've got homework to do."

He imagined her licking her chops like a hungry cat. "Any suggestions?"

"You're a smart man. You'll figure something out. You'd better." She let the implication hang.

"I want that tape when this is over, Stella. You'll owe me that much if I win."

She chuckled. "We'll see about that. Ask me again when Will Tyler's on his way to prison."

She ended the call, leaving Clay standing by his car, cursing silently at his cell phone. The day was brisk, but he could smell the sweat under his suit jacket.

The trial date wouldn't be set until the bail hearing

tomorrow. But the court's docket wasn't crowded. A manslaughter case shouldn't take more than a few weeks, a month at most, to schedule and prepare. Meanwhile, as Stella had said, he had homework to do.

When it came to threats, the woman wasn't bluffing. If rumors were to be believed, she'd already taken down one powerful man who'd failed to deliver—the late congressman Garn Prescott. If Will Tyler went free, Clay knew she wouldn't hesitate to do the same to him.

He started the car and pulled out of the parking lot, thinking as he drove. Every defense, even a solid one, had its weak spots, and Clay prided himself on being able to find them. This time he would need to be at his sharpest and most ruthless. His career, his family, and perhaps his freedom would be hanging in the balance.

The evidence was straightforward and had been seen by everyone involved. Not much room for manipulation there. He'd have some leeway with jury selection, but Tori would have to approve any juror he chose. Regarding the witnesses, most of them appeared to be favorable to the defense—except for Abner.

Clay remembered their meeting in his office before the inquest. The sheriff had seemed almost as anxious as Clay was to get a conviction. Either Stella had something on him, or he just plain hated Will Tyler. Maybe both.

Abner could be the key to winning this case, especially if he could be manipulated into twisting a few facts. Much as Clay disliked the pompous little toad, maybe it was time to give some thought to an alliance.

The next morning Will, dressed in a suit Tori had delivered to the jail, appeared before the judge. The proceedings took no more than a few minutes. Bail was set at

$15,000, the trial scheduled for early next month. Beau posted the bond with the clerk, and Will was released to go home.

Beau drove him back to the Rimrock in the Jeep, with Tori following in her station wagon. Will had been gone less than twenty-four hours. But the man returning was no longer the man who'd left the ranch yesterday. Will had experienced rage, shame, and humiliation in a way he'd never known before. And he'd been slapped with the cold possibility of losing all he held dear.

As the Jeep turned off the highway and up the long, straight road to the ranch, he gazed out the window at the autumn landscape. The ice storm had drained the rich gold from the grass and stripped the leaves from the cottonwoods and willows. But there was a stark beauty in the pale sweep of the plain, with the russet cliffs of the escarpment jutting against the November sky. Where the creek ran, the leafless willows hung deep bloodred, a slash of crimson against the ecru skin of the land.

Off to the right, the alkali lake, where Jasper liked to hunt wild turkey, had dried to a glittering white smear. Patches of blackened earth and the skeletons of burnt cedar trees marked where the worst of last summer's fire had burned. But the land was already healing. Next spring the grass would grow and the fire-scarred cottonwoods would leaf out. Bright patches of Indian-blanket gaillardias, Tahoka daisies, blue dayflowers, and blooming cacti would dot the prairie with color, and life would go on, as it always did. Beau and Natalie's son would be born. Sky and Lauren would marry and begin their family. Erin would grow into graceful young womanhood.

Would he be here to see it? But with his fate in the balance, Will knew better than to think that far ahead. For the next few weeks, he would live for each day. He would take Jasper bird hunting. He would ride and play chess with Erin, work the stock with Beau and Sky. He would fill his eyes with the sight of Tori and his ears with the sound of her voice. But he would not forget where he'd been or what lay ahead.

Like ammunition for a coming war, he would store up his anger, his outrage, and his hatred of the corrupt justice system that had allowed this to happen. If the trial went the wrong way, he would need it all to fuel his strength.

Erin was waiting on the front porch when the Jeep pulled up and stopped. As Will climbed out of the passenger side, she flew down the steps and flung herself into his arms. She was growing long and lean like her mother. Her hair smelled of hay and horses. She didn't speak, but he could tell from the slight jerk of her breathing that she was holding back sobs. With her involvement as a witness in his case, there'd been no way to shield her from what was going on. She knew what her family was facing, and she was handling it with remarkable courage. Will couldn't have been more proud of her.

"I love you, Daddy," she whispered.

A lump rose in Will's throat. As he hugged his daughter close, it was as if he could feel the slow breaking of his heart.

Parked next to the Jeep, Tori watched as Erin greeted her father and led him into the house, followed by Beau. This was an emotional time that had little to do with her. She would give them a few minutes before she went inside to join them for lunch.

Will was her client now. The man she'd loved, married, and divorced, the man who'd given her Erin, the man who'd swept her away in an explosion of need on the night of the storm—that man couldn't be allowed to matter now. Emotion would only cloud her ability to defend him.

Once more, applying cold logic, she asked herself the forbidden question—the one she'd been asking, answering, and rethinking all the way on the drive from town to the ranch.

If the unthinkable happened and Will went to prison, what would be best for Erin?

Will's daughter loved being on the ranch, especially her time with Tesoro. She loved the house, loved her room, and loved spending time with Bernice and Jasper. To take that away from her would be cruel. But with Will gone, there'd be no reason to keep the big house open. Bernice could retire and move into Sky's half of the duplex, next to Jasper. Beau and Natalie would have their own home. So would Sky and Lauren. Erin would be welcome to visit, but nothing would be the same. The Sunday dinners around the dining-room table, the long talks with Jasper on the porch, playing in the paddock with Tesoro, watching sports on the big-screen TV with the men of the family, and helping Bernice in the kitchen—all these things would be gone for her.

Erin wouldn't just be losing her father's presence. She'd be losing her whole happy, secure world.

But enough, why agonize over something that hadn't happened—and wasn't going to happen? She was going to win Will's case and set him free, Tori told herself. Failure wasn't an option. The stakes were too high for that.

She was getting out of the car to go into the house when her cell phone rang. She glanced at the display. The caller was Drew.

"Hi," she said, "I was just thinking about you—good thoughts."

He laughed. "Nice to know. I was thinking about you, too. Extremely good thoughts. What are you up to today?"

"I'm at the ranch. Some business with Will's case."

She sensed the slight hesitation. "Oh? How's that going?"

"I can't discuss the details. Lawyer-client privilege. But the trial's four weeks off, and it's shaping up to be a fight. I'll have my work cut out for me."

"I take it that means you're going to be busy."

"I am. I'm counting on you to help keep me sane."

She meant what she'd just said. If she let him, Drew would provide an oasis of calm amid the craziness of the upcoming trial. Besides, she needed to give him some encouragement. Otherwise, he could be gone. Distracted as she was right now, she wasn't ready to lose him. When her life slowed down enough to make future plans, she wanted him there.

"I can do more than that, but not over the phone. Are you free for steak and lobster in Lubbock tonight?"

Was she? Tori had work to do, but she'd already come to the decision to make time for him. "That sounds wonderful," she said.

"Seven o'clock? I'll pick you up. And I loved that black dress on you the last time."

"I'll wear it again, just for you. And seven is fine. Gotta go." Tori ended the call, thinking about the need to structure her life into separate compartments—Will's trial, Will's family, Erin as her daughter, Erin as a witness, and her time out with Drew. If she tried to deal with everything at once, she'd be on the fast track to a meltdown.

In the house she found Will, Beau, Bernice, Jasper, and Erin seated around the kitchen table, eating a lunch of grilled cheese sandwiches, baked beans, and potato salad. Tori grabbed a Diet Coke from the fridge and slipped into the empty chair. As if by mutual agreement, they were laughing and exchanging small talk, putting Will's trouble on hold for now.

"Lauren's taking me on a treasure hunt tomorrow," Erin announced. "We're packing a picnic and going up the canyon to look for the Spanish gold."

"Well, don't get your hopes up about findin' it," Jasper said. "That tale about the Spaniards hidin' their treasure before the Comanches killed 'em all is nothin' but a made-up story."

"Well, who made it up?" Erin demanded. "That's what I'd like to know."

"Can't say for sure," Jasper said. "The story's been goin' around since before my time. But I know that Lauren's granddad Ferg Prescott searched every inch of that little canyon—dug it all up by his self and never found a thing."

"Is that why he bought the canyon from Grandpa Bull? Just so he could look for the treasure?"

"You'd have to ask Old Ferg that question. And he's long gone to his grave."

"Well, maybe he didn't look hard enough or dig deep enough. If the treasure's there, we're going to find it!"

Tori listened, enjoying the exchange. It was a relief to be talking about something besides Will's case. Even Will was getting involved in the conversation.

"You know the canyon belongs to Lauren now," he said. "Anything you find will be hers."

"No," Erin protested. "Lauren promised me if we find the treasure, we'll share it with everybody, even Jasper and Bernice."

"Now that's right nice of her," Jasper said. "'Specially

for a Prescott. But I'm not holdin' my breath till you two make us all rich."

"It's not the treasure that matters, Erin," Tori said. "The important thing is that you and Lauren have a fun adventure. I hope you thanked her for inviting you."

"I did." Erin helped herself to another sandwich. "Sky was going to come, too, but he's got work, so it'll be just us girls. Why don't you come with us, Mom? I know it would be fine with Lauren."

"I'm afraid it'll be a workday for me, too," Tori said. "Go and have a wonderful time."

Disappointment shadowed Erin's face. Then she brightened. "The Vegas rodeo finals are on TV tonight. You could stay and watch with Dad and me."

Guilt was like a cold stab between Tori's ribs. "Sorry, sweetheart, but I've got work in town this afternoon. And tonight I've got plans."

Tori's gaze shifted toward Will. He didn't speak, but his expression had darkened. No doubt he'd guessed what those plans were. Tori could imagine what he was thinking. Here he was, facing a life-changing ordeal, and she was running off to go on a date with another man.

Tori looked away, refusing to acknowledge his silent message. As Will's lawyer, she would give her all to win his case and save him. But she wasn't his wife anymore—and the fact that she'd slept with him in a weak moment didn't give him ownership. If she let him, Will would drown her with his need to be in control. That had happened in the past, but it wasn't going to happen again. She had a private life, and tonight she needed a break.

"Say, Will." Beau came to her rescue. "I could use your advice on where to move the cattle next. Maybe this afternoon we could saddle up and ride out to check the grass in the empty pastures."

"Sounds fine to me," Will said.

"Can I come, too?" Erin asked.

Will gave her a fatherly frown. "Is your schoolwork done?"

"I finished it before you got here."

"Okay, you can ride along on old Belle. And tonight we can make popcorn and watch the rodeo finals, just you and me, unless Jasper wants to join us." The look he gave Tori said it all. They were still a family; and at a time like this, it was wrong for her to be away.

But Tori wasn't about to let Will push her guilt buttons. She was going out with Drew tonight and, by damn, she was going to have a good time.

CHAPTER 9

Tori and Drew lingered over their dessert wine, enjoying the panorama of the city, the glow of candles, and the tinkle of piano blues from the adjoining bar. The steak and lobster had been well-prepared, the atmosphere romantic, the conversation easy.

Tori gazed at the man across the table, grateful that, without being asked, he'd avoided all mention of the upcoming trial. He was, at all times, tactful, soft-spoken, and kind. And he was handsome enough to break hearts in his tweed blazer, dark shirt, and tie—not a bolo, but a real silk tie. With the candlelight sharpening the planes of his face, he could have stepped out of a PBS Edwardian drama.

She found herself imagining Will in this upscale dinner club—his big, rugged presence overpowering the intimate space, his restless nature demanding that they finish the meal and get back to the ranch to check on the cattle. He'd be more at home at a barbecue, where he could fill his plate and grab a beer, eat at his own pace, socialize or not, and leave when he was good and ready, with no apologies.

But why was she thinking about Will tonight?

"A penny for your thoughts." Drew's hand slid across the table to capture hers.

"I was thinking how much I needed this break tonight." It wasn't quite true, but close enough. "Thank you, Drew."

"My pleasure. I know how much you must have on your mind."

That's the right thing to say, at the right time, she thought. "What I've got on my mind right now is you," she said.

"I hope you mean that." His hand tightened on hers, smooth palm, no calluses; but then, he was an educator, not a rancher. "I know I agreed to keep things platonic till the trial's over. But if I'm going to wait, I need to know what I'm waiting for." He cleared his throat. "Not to get too personal, but for a woman who's been divorced eight years, you're pretty involved with your ex."

"It's because of Erin. She loves her father and she loves the ranch. My staying involved gives her a sense of family."

"So what if things were to come together for us, and I was in the picture full-time? Would that mean a sort of ménage à trois, with you running back and forth between two men?"

It wasn't so much his question that surprised Tori as his timing. "Certainly not! Things would have to change. Erin's growing up. She could handle a different arrangement."

"But could Will? Why hasn't he remarried? Is he still in love with you?"

His question rocked her, but only for the instant it took to come up with an answer. "Will *is* married. He's married to his ranch. No woman on earth could compete with that."

He gave her hand a reassuring squeeze. "I think I'm

beginning to get the picture. Not that I want to pry, but I could be more understanding if I knew what split you apart."

Tori gave him the *Reader's Digest* condensed version of her story—how Will had put his father and the ranch ahead of his marriage, how Bull had disapproved of her working, and how things had gone from bad to worse after her miscarriage and partial hysterectomy.

"So you can't have more children?"

"Not the regular way." *Will that be a problem for him?* Tori wondered. However Drew might feel about having a family, it couldn't be helped. At least she wouldn't have to worry about telling him later. "My father-in-law wanted a houseful of strapping grandsons. He never forgave me for not being able to produce them."

"And Will?"

"Will adored Erin from the first moment he saw her. He'd wanted more children, of course, but when they didn't come, he lavished all his love on her. She was enough." Tori realized her voice had gone tender.

"So what finally happened between you?" Drew asked.

"That's another story. We could be here awhile."

"I'm listening." His thumb stroked the back of her hand, raising a tingle of awareness.

"First off, you have to know that I grew up in Blanco Springs. My father was a county judge."

"So the law's in your blood." He gave her a smile.

"Something like that. While I was away at law school, he retired and moved with my mother to Florida. I came home to Blanco and married Will. Five years later, with the marriage already crumbling, my father died of a heart attack.

"When I got the word, I took Erin and caught the next flight to Florida. Will was too busy with his father and the ranch to leave right then, but he promised to be there in time for the funeral." Tori paused. She'd told him enough. The rest was better left alone.

"Let me guess," he said. "Will didn't show up for your father's funeral."

"That's right. I stayed two weeks to settle things and be with my mother. He never showed up, and I never lived with him again."

And never slept with him—until the night of the blizzard. But that lapse in judgment was best buried and forgotten.

There was more to the story—like the reason why Will hadn't come to Florida, or so much as called her during the two weeks she was away. But even after eight years, that memory was a raw wound. And the truth—that the deathblow to the marriage had been struck by Will's jealousy and distrust—was too painful to share.

She gave Drew an easy laugh. "Next time we'll talk about you," she said.

"There's not much to talk about." He signed the bill the waiter had left on the table and rose to help her with her chair. "I grew up in Omaha, one older sister. Graduated from college with a master's in educational administration. Worked here and there. Came to Blanco for a change of scene—or maybe to find the right woman. What do you think? Have I found her?"

"That remains to be seen." She snuggled into her coat as he settled it around her shoulders and offered her his arm as they walked to the car. She was tired and she'd drunk a little too much wine. But she had to credit Drew for a pleasant, relaxing date.

It was almost eleven when he pulled up to her house and walked her to her door and gave her a long, slow goodnight kiss. "I won't invite myself to come in," he said.

"But not because I don't want to. You must look lovely in your sleep."

"Thanks for understanding," she said. "I need to start work on Will's case tomorrow, and I'm going to need a clear head. Besides, you've got school, Mr. Middleton."

"Sleep tight, Tori." He feathered a second kiss across her lips and turned away. As she opened her door, he trotted out to his car and climbed inside.

Tori watched him drive away. Their date had been rewarding, she thought. They'd gotten to know each other without crossing any lines. Maybe she'd revealed too much of herself, but Drew had been a good listener and a perfect gentleman. She wanted the chance to know the man better. But preparing for Will's trial had to come first. For the next few weeks, nothing else could be allowed to matter.

She could only hope Drew would have the patience to wait.

By ten the next morning, the weather had warmed enough to feel comfortable. Wearing hats and jackets and packing a lunch, a flashlight, and a small shovel, Lauren and Erin mounted up and took the trail that wound through the foothills into the deep canyons. The turquoise sky was winter-bright, dazzling above the time-sculpted towers of the escarpment. A quail, perched atop a stunted cedar, scolded them as they rode past. The earth smelled rich and clean.

They rode side by side, laughing and chatting. Lauren was glad she'd decided to take the girl exploring today. After Will's night in jail, Erin had become more and more worried about her father. A day of treasure hunting in the canyon would provide a welcome diversion.

Lauren, too, had felt the need to explore the sliver of land that had caused so much contention between the Prescotts and the Tylers. She'd been there with Sky when they'd freed up the spring and taken out the barbed-wire fence. But he'd been in a hurry that day so they hadn't stayed long. Today she wasn't expecting to find Spanish treasure; but before selling the land back to the Rimrock, she wanted to at least take a closer look. With winter coming, this brief warm spell might be her last chance.

By the time they reached the petroglyph canyon, they were both hungry. They tethered the horses near the canyon mouth, where the animals could graze and drink from the spring. Then they spread a cloth on the sand at the foot of the decorated cliff and feasted on Bernice's homemade bacon sandwiches, topped off with oatmeal cookies and canned root beer.

"Jasper says we won't find any treasure because it's just a story," Erin said. "But what if it's really there? Do you think it might be?"

"My grandfather never found it," Lauren said. "But what do *you* think?"

Erin nibbled her oatmeal cookie. "Sky always tells me the best way to handle a horse is to think like the horse. Maybe if we want to find the Spanish gold, we should think like the Spaniards. You know, pretend we're trapped in the canyon and the Comanches are closing in, and we have to hide our treasure fast."

"That's a very clever idea," Lauren said. "What do you say we clean up our picnic and try it? You're in charge."

They packed the remains of their lunch, put on work gloves, and gathered up the tools they'd brought. Erin led the way up the box canyon's narrow, steep entrance to the small clearing on higher, more level ground.

Putting down their tools, they surveyed the spot. On the left, a wall of broken rock rose fifty feet above their heads. Fallen boulders and scree lay thick along its base. Willows, on their right, overhung the spring that trickled down into the lower canyon; behind the spring a high bank of crumbling earth sloped upward, then crested and dipped toward pastureland now owned by the syndicate that had bought out the Prescott Ranch.

The ground under their feet was hard-packed sand and gravel, dotted with tussocks of weedy grass. Almost thirty years had passed since Ferg Prescott had dug for buried treasure here and left empty-handed. The canyon looked as if it hadn't been touched since.

Glancing around her, Lauren experienced a strange unease. She'd never known herself to have psychic gifts, but instinct whispered that something dark had happened here—something evil, best left alone.

Erin, however, was all grins and excitement. Asking her to leave, based on a whim of imagination, would be cruel, Lauren decided. For now, she would play along. But she'd keep an eye out for the first sign of trouble.

Erin's gaze traveled up the crumbling cliff. "This is cool!" she exclaimed. "If there's treasure here, maybe the two of us together will be smart enough to find it! Now let's think. We're Spaniards, we've got a chest full of treasure, and the Comanches are coming after us. What do we do?"

"We need to get away." Lauren joined in the game. "But gold is heavy and hard to carry. We'll have a better chance of escape if we hide it now and come back for it later."

"Right." Erin glanced around. "So what do we do with it?"

"We could bury it," Lauren suggested.

Erin thought a moment, then shook her head. "We're in a hurry. Digging a hole in hard ground takes time. And we might not even have a shovel. Besides, we'd have to camouflage the hole when we were finished. That would take time, too. What else could we do?"

"Drop it into the spring?"

"Too easy to see. And if the treasure's in a wooden chest or a leather bag of some kind, the water could ruin it and scatter the gold. What else?"

"Let's look around." Lauren was enjoying the harmless fun. Maybe the unease she'd felt earlier had been nothing more than her imagination. "If the Spaniards were here at all, it would've been two or three hundred years ago, maybe even longer. Any hiding place would have changed on the surface."

"Maybe." Erin made a slow visual circle of the clearing, muttering half to herself. "We're on the run. We have to hide the treasure someplace fast, someplace safe and dry, where nobody will see it."

A curious raven launched itself from the cliff top, circled, and glided down to perch on a nearby boulder. Unafraid, it studied the visitors with intelligent black eyes. Erin froze, staring at it. "The rocks," she said. "We'd hide the treasure in the rocks. It's the only place that makes sense."

The idea made sense to Lauren, too. But over the years tons of rock would have broken loose and crashed down the cliff to shatter at the bottom. The layer of scree piled along the cliff base was at least five feet thick. If any treasure had been buried in the rocks, it would be buried deep.

"Can you imagine how much rock must've fallen down here since the time of the Spaniards?" Lauren asked. "You and I could never dig through it all. If there's more loose rock up on that high wall, it could even be dangerous. Maybe we should just take Jasper at his word and go home."

"Not yet." As the raven flapped away, Erin stood her ground, gazing at the fallen scree. "I read this in a detective book once. When a lot of rocks fall by themselves, they usually land together—you can see it if you know what to look for. And when you look up, the rocks should match where they came from, and match each other. If not, that's a sign the rocks have been moved. I'm looking for a place where the rocks have been moved."

Lauren suppressed the urge to argue. She'd never seen this stubborn side of Erin before. The girl was definitely her father's daughter. And she was so excited, so determined to find what she was looking for. As long as it made her happy, it wouldn't hurt to play the game a little longer.

"There." Erin pointed. "Right there. Look."

Not far from the steep trail that led down into the petroglyph canyon, rocks were piled against the foot of the cliff. Lauren wouldn't have noticed on her own, but the rocks did indeed look as if they'd been moved there. The way they were stacked wasn't how they'd have landed if they'd fallen naturally. And not only did they not match each other, they didn't match the cliff face above them, where they would have broken off.

Erin was beside herself. "There's got to be something behind those rocks! Come on! Let's get them out of the way!"

"Wait!" Lauren held her back. "Let me make sure it's safe." She scanned the cliff face where it rose above the rock pile. It looked solid enough. To make doubly sure, she flung a fist-sized rock at the cliff. The rock bounced off and clattered to the ground, but nothing else moved.

"All right, we'll try it," she said, wishing they'd brought hard hats. "But if you hear something break loose, jump back fast."

The sandstone rocks were heavy, but not massive. None of them would have been too large for a strong man to lift into place. Lauren and Erin, however, had to struggle. They started at the top of the pile, loosening the rocks and rolling them off to one side or the other. It was slow going, but Erin's enthusiasm kept them at it.

"I told you we'd find it," she said. "The treasure's got to be here. It's just got to be!"

Lauren kept her silence. By now, she was certain the girl would be disappointed. If these rocks had been piled up centuries ago by treasure-hiding Spaniards, the exposed surfaces would be uniformly weathered, dotted with lichens and overgrown by native plants. These rocks were still clean, meaning they probably hadn't been here more than a few decades. Whatever lay behind them would likely have been hidden, not by Spaniards, but by Lauren's own grandfather Ferguson Prescott.

Beau got the phone call as he and Will were riding back to the ranch in Will's pickup. They'd spent much of the morning checking the pasturelands. The past summer's fire had burned most of the grass to the ground. By early fall new grass had sprouted, painting the land with promise. But the ice storm had left it brittle, brown, and stunted. There was no way the cattle would survive the winter without extra feed.

After lunch they'd driven up onto the caprock to buy hay from a farmer they knew. The man was fair and honest, but the price of hay had skyrocketed all over Texas. Will's stomach had clenched as he heard the final amount.

But, knowing it had to be done, he'd taken out his pen and scrawled the check. The huge, rolled hay bales would be delivered two days from now.

They were headed back down the winding road to the ranch when Beau's phone rang. Mired in his own gloom, Will didn't pay the call much attention at first. Only when he heard Beau arguing did he start to listen.

"This can't be your final decision," Beau was saying. "Look, we've always paid our bills. I can bring in some collateral. Just a few more months, that's all we're asking—"

He broke off with a curse as the call ended. "The bank's declined to extend our loan," he said. "I tried, but they know you'll be going to trial, and they don't want to take a chance. *Damn them!*"

Will felt surprisingly calm, but maybe he was just numb. "I was expecting something like this," he said. "Getting arrested doesn't exactly raise a man's standing with the bank."

"So what can we do about it?" Beau demanded.

"For now, not much. We've already cut expenses to the bone. When the loan comes due, if we can't pay, we'll have no choice except to lose the land. The only alternative would be to sell it first. The syndicate's got money, and I'm guessing they'd be happy to add some Rimrock land to their spread, especially if they could pin us to the wall and get it for a bargain."

"The syndicate!" Beau swore. "They'd gobble up the whole damned county if they could. Dad would turn over in his grave."

"He'd turn a lot faster if we went under and lost the ranch. This is about survival—especially if I end up doing prison time."

"Don't even think about that," Beau said.

"I have to think about it. If it happens, I want to leave the Rimrock in manageable shape."

"You think I can't handle the ranch alone?"

"Let's not even go there."

They drove in tense silence for a mile before Beau spoke again. "Hey, maybe Erin and Lauren will find the Spanish treasure and share enough money to bail us out. Wouldn't that be something?"

"Dream on, little brother." With a bitter chuckle Will rounded the last bend in the road and set a straight course for home.

Erin and Lauren had cleared about three feet off the top of the rock pile. Lauren was getting tired. Her back and shoulders ached. She was going to be sore for a week.

She'd paused a moment to massage the small of her back, when Erin gave a shout.

"There's a hole back here! It looks like . . ." She shoved more rocks off the pile, then scrambled up the remaining heap for a closer look. "Lauren! It's a cave! Bring me the flashlight!"

"Get down!" Lauren caught her waist and dragged her back. "There could be anything in there!"

"Anything?" Erin was grinning. "Like Spanish gold?"

Lauren found the flashlight in the pack and switched it on. "Stay here while I check it out," she said.

Lauren crept up the pile of rocks. The prickling danger sense she'd felt earlier was screaming now. She'd never thought of herself as brave, but if anything came flying out of that cave, she'd want it to get past her before it got to Erin.

Peering over the top of the pile, she shone the faint light into the cave. The walls were uneven rock, the ceiling about five feet above the stone-littered floor, which appeared to drop off near the back of the cave. There was no sign of life, not even bats or spiderwebs. But something about the place gave Lauren cold chills—maybe it was the distinct, musky odor that lingered in the cave's stale air.

"What's in there?" Erin demanded.

"Nothing much, but go ahead and look." Lauren moved back and handed her the flashlight. "Remember, I said *look*. I didn't say *climb over.* You're not going in there."

Erin clambered up to the opening and shone the light into the cave. "Wow!" she muttered. "I can see all the way to that hole in the back. Maybe that's where they hid the treasure."

"Don't even think about it," Lauren said.

"Okay, for now. But let's move more rocks away. Then it'll be easier to see what's there."

They shoved the rocks to the sides until the pile was no higher than their knees. Lauren was hurting, but she couldn't help being curious. If they hadn't found Spanish gold, they'd at least discovered *something.* But her danger sense was still tingling. With most of the rock barrier gone, daylight lit the cave. They could see clearly all the way back to the dark opening in the floor. It was irregular in shape, like a jagged crack where the ancient rock had split and settled. At its widest point it was about two feet across.

Erin had picked up the flashlight. "Let's go see what's down there!"

"Wait!" Lauren handed her a rock. "Throw this down first. If we can hear it land—"

"Got it." Erin gave the stone an easy toss. It bounced off the edge and vanished down the dark crack. They could hear the faint clatter as it ricocheted off the sides, then silence. They glanced at each other. The hole was deep.

"Don't worry, I'm only going to look." Erin started forward.

"No—listen!" Lauren gripped her arm. *"Listen!"*

For the first few seconds, they could barely hear it—a faint, rattling buzz—one, then a second, then a chorus of sound that seemed to echo off the walls of the cave.

"Rattlesnakes," Erin said. "I know that sound. They've got a winter den down there."

Lauren's knees went weak. She'd always been terrified of snakes. "Let's get out of here!" she said, tugging Erin back.

Erin resisted. "We'll be all right. The snakes are down there to hibernate. As long as we don't bother them, they won't bother us."

"That's enough, Erin. We're going."

"The treasure could still be down there. I just want to look—"

"Not now! If you want to see what's down there, come back with Sky—"

"Did I hear my name mentioned?"

Sky had just come up the trail from the lower canyon. As he stepped into the clearing, Lauren's first impulse was to fling herself into his arms. But it was Erin who needed attention.

"What's going on?" As always, Sky was a man of few words.

"We found this secret cave!" Erin spoke up, talking fast. "There's a hole in the back, and I think the treasure might be down there, but Lauren won't let me look."

"For heaven's sake, Erin, it's a rattlesnake den!" Lauren said.

"What would you say to me taking a look?" Sky asked. "Don't worry, I know about snakes. I'll be careful."

Lauren remembered him telling her how Will had been bitten on the thigh by a Texas diamondback last spring and nearly died. "I wish you wouldn't," she said, knowing that Sky would do what he wanted.

He squeezed her shoulder. "It'll be fine. All right, Erin?"

"All right," Erin said, stepping aside for him. "But promise you'll tell me what you find."

"I promise." He pulled leather gloves from the pockets of his thick denim jacket and tugged them on. Erin handed him the flashlight. He frowned at the cheap dime-store item. "Don't you have anything stronger?"

"This was all we could find," Lauren said. "We didn't plan on needing it."

"Guess it'll have to do." He glanced around, picked up a stout piece of a broken branch, and, turning on the flashlight, ducked under the low ceiling of the cave.

Lauren kept her eyes on him. Sky had lived all his adult life on the Rimrock. Surely, he'd be experienced with snakes. But terror gripped her as he dropped to a crouch beside the hole and shone the light down into the opening. For a moment he moved the light around, probably making sure there were no snakes close enough to strike. Then he bent forward, peering into the darkness as if straining to see by the poor light. Lauren's heart crept into her throat as he lingered, looking down for what seemed like an eternity. At last he rose partway and, ducking to clear his head beneath the ceiling, stepped outside.

One look at his grim face told her something wasn't right.

"What did you see?" Erin was all eagerness.

"Mostly just snakes. Plenty of those. But no treasure. I could see all the way to the bottom, and it wasn't there. Sorry, Erin."

"Me too." Her face fell. Her shoulders slumped. "I was really hoping I could help my dad with the ranch. I've heard him and Uncle Beau talking. I know they're having money troubles."

"Oh, honey!" Lauren hugged the girl, her eyes misting. Glancing up, she met Sky's gaze. His jaw was set, his eyes guarded. She knew her man. He was troubled. And something told her it wasn't just about the ranch.

"You saw something else, didn't you?" she guessed. "What was it?"

He handed her the flashlight and pulled off his gloves. His gaze flickered toward Erin. He hesitated, as if weighing the wisdom of telling her, then decided to go ahead. "I saw bones," he said. "They looked like human bones."

CHAPTER 10

The door to Clay Drummond's office burst open. Tori strode in like an Amazon in full battle gear. Even dressed in jeans and a baggy sweatshirt, with her reading glasses perched atop her rumpled blond mane, she was spectacular, Clay thought. But he knew she hadn't barged in here to be admired.

Ignoring his invitation to take a seat, she loomed over his desk. One hand clutched a sheaf of papers, which she shoved in his face. "Take a look!" she said. "I've spent the past two days researching precedents for Will's case. Here's what I found—five similar cases in Texas alone to support a verdict of self-defense. Read them! This trial is a farce—a waste of time and taxpayer money!"

Clay took a deep breath, forcing himself to stay perfectly calm. "It wasn't my decision to try this case, Tori. It was the judge's. Will took an innocent man's life. My job is to prosecute him to the full extent of the law. That's what I intend to do."

Standing, arms akimbo, she braced her fists on her lovely hips. "How long did we work together, Clay? How many times since then have we faced each other in court?

I know how you like to win. But, as far as I'm aware, you've always done it honestly. This case feels different, almost as if somebody's got it in for Will. What's going on here?"

"As I told you, Tori, I'm just doing my job." He straightened the papers she'd flung at him. "By the way, there's been a new development. You'll get the official word in a couple of days, but as long as you're here, I may as well give you a heads-up. Abner and I have been reviewing the evidence, both physical and circumstantial. We're in agreement that, along with the present charges against Will, we should add obstruction of justice."

Tori went rigid. "*Obstruction?* Good Lord, Clay, how did the two of you come up with that?"

"Think about it," Clay said. "First, Will contaminated the crime scene by covering the dead man with a blanket from his truck. Since his DNA, and who knows what else, was already on the blanket, there'd be no way to tell if he'd touched the body."

"Will wouldn't have been thinking about that," Tori said. "His only intention was to keep Erin from seeing the man."

"Second," Clay continued, "Will sent a key eyewitness away from the crime scene before the sheriff arrived, giving her time to think about her testimony, maybe even change it, before her interview."

"Oh, good grief! Why don't you charge me, too?" Tori snapped. "I was the one who picked her up and drove her home. For heaven's sake, Clay, Erin's a child. She was scared and upset. Besides, Will had told her to get on the floor. He didn't know she'd witnessed anything until I told him the next day."

"I'm aware that Erin's a child, Tori. I also know the girl would say anything to help her father." He rose be hind his desk. The feeling that he had this beautiful, powerful woman at his mercy was strangely heady, almost erotic. "One more thing," he said. "Just so it won't be a surprise, we'll be calling your daughter as a witness—for the prosecution."

The afternoon sun was sinking toward the caprock by the time Sky returned with Erin and Lauren from their canyon adventure. Tired and hungry, they unsaddled their horses, rubbed them down, and put them away.

He glanced at Erin as they left the barn, wanting to make certain she was all right. She'd been quiet on the ride home—but then, none of them had felt like talking much. The discovery of the bones in the rattlesnake den had sobered them all. The flashlight had been too weak for a clear look. But Sky had known what he was seeing.

Maybe he should have kept quiet about the bones. They appeared to have been there a long time. And there could be no question of retrieving them from that deep, narrow space, especially with the snakes denned up for the winter. Leave the dead to lie—that would be sound advice. But there was something Sky had kept to himself—something that would compel him to go back to the cave with a stronger light for another look.

The sight of those fragile bones had touched him deeply. He wouldn't rest easy, Sky knew, until he'd learned more about how they'd come to be there. Light and distance may have fooled his eyes, but every instinct told him he'd been right.

He had looked down into that awful darkness and seen the remains of a child.

"Yum! I smell cinnamon rolls!" Erin's piping voice broke into his thoughts as they neared the house. "Bernice told me this morning she was going to make a big batch. Come on in and have some!"

"That sounds wonderful! I'm famished!" Lauren tugged Sky toward the kitchen, where Bernice had just finished icing a big pan of spicy, fresh-baked cinnamon rolls. Jasper sat at the table, waiting for his share.

Bernice greeted the three of them with a smile. "Something told me you'd come back hungry. You're just in time. Wash up and have a seat."

After a quick cleanup, they joined Jasper at the table. Armed with saucers and forks, they dug into the pan of warm, delicious rolls. Bernice poured glasses of cold milk, then sat down to eat with them. "So, did you find the Spanish gold?" she asked.

Lauren shook her head.

"Told ya, ya wouldn't," Jasper said. "See, it's just a story."

"We didn't find gold." Erin spoke between bites. "But we found a cave with a snake den at the bottom of a hole. Sky looked down there and saw some bones, didn't you, Sky?"

Jasper's fork dropped from his hand and clattered to his plate. "'Scuse me," he muttered, picking it up again. "Gettin' butterfingers in my old age."

"Do you know anything about a cave in that canyon, Jasper?" Lauren asked.

Jasper frowned, looking down at the table. "Seems like I recollect something about a cave. But I never went up that little canyon. Had no call to, 'specially after Bull sold it to Old Ferg."

"So you never heard anything about the bones?" Lauren persisted.

"Nope. Most likely just some old-time Injun that fell down there and died, rest his heathen soul."

Sky thought that Jasper looked distinctly uncomfortable. He'd bet his best saddle that the old man knew a lot more than he was saying. Maybe later, when they were alone, Jasper would tell him the truth. But before asking, Sky wanted to go back to the cave with a strong light and take another look at those bones.

"You goin' out again tonight, Ralphie?" Vonda looked up from dabbing black polish on her toenails, which she could barely reach over her bulging belly. Her voice, lately, had taken on a whine that grated on Ralph's nerves like the sound of a mewling cat. He could hardly wait to get out the door.

"Gotta go to work, baby," he said. "Stella don't pay much, but with a kid on the way, we can't make it without me workin' two jobs."

"But we don't have any fun since you started that job—not even in bed."

"That kind of stuff could be bad for the baby." Lord, he'd tried. But sex with Vonda these days was like pumping a beach ball. Some men claimed pregnancy made their wives sexier, but Ralph didn't buy it—especially now that he was getting some on the side.

"You're tired all the time. And I'm cooped up here in the house, just gettin' bigger and doin' nothin'! You haven't even took me to a movie since you started workin' for that woman," Vonda whined. "I thought bein' married would be fun, like a date that doesn't end. But it sucks! And bein' pregnant sucks worse! You got me this way, and you owe me better'n this!"

"Hell, I bought you those damn fake fingernails and gave you money for lunch with your friends. I even bought you a TV to watch while I'm gone."

"That old TV is crap! It's not even a flat screen!"

"Well, too bad. I'm doin' the best I can. Just deal with it, Vonda." Ralph walked out and slammed the door behind him.

As he drove his old pickup into town, he dragged on a cigarette to calm his nerves. Stella was expecting him at eleven for a delivery run, and she wouldn't stand for any slipups. He didn't want to risk riling her and getting fired. The money was too good for that.

Ralph thought about how he had stashed away $7,000 in a secret bank account. It was enough to buy a half-decent used truck. But if he showed up with it at home, Vonda would know he'd been holding out on her, and all hell would break loose. She might even be mad enough to phone her daddy and tell him about her husband's part-time job.

For now, he'd be smart just to leave the money in the bank and keep adding to it. He'd be damned if he was going to be stuck with whiny Vonda and a bawling brat for the rest of his life. When the time came to split, he could give her a little money, take the rest, and leave Blanco County for a new start somewhere. Vonda would be okay. Once her folks got a look at the kid, it would be just like in the movies. They'd take her back for sure.

Stella was just closing up when he pulled into the parking lot of the Blue Coyote. He went in the back way, as the last customers were leaving. Angie, the blond young waitress, was just wiping off the tables. She gave him a tired smile, and he knew he'd be welcome in her room when he finished his run. He'd have to give her some money, of course. But what the hell, Stella always paid him in cash, and he'd have plenty to spare.

With the front door locked, and Angie on her way upstairs, Stella ushered him down the hall to the storage room that doubled as her office. She looked tired, but then she always did, after a night of tending bar on her feet. Her lipstick was gone, and her black eyeliner had smudged into the creases around her eyes. His mother would be about her age, if she hadn't died of breast cancer, Ralph thought. But his mother had been a churchgoing woman, nothing like Stella.

"You were Lute Fletcher's friend, weren't you, Ralph?" The question came out of nowhere.

"Can't say we were real good friends. We worked together for the Tylers, and I gave him a few rides to town before he quit the ranch. Never saw much of him after that."

"You know what happened to him, don't you?"

"I know he's dead. Shot by that crooked sheriff."

"I had nothing to do with his getting shot," Stella said. "But Lute was in trouble before it happened. He got greedy. I gave him my trust, and he tried to steal from me. As for his sister, Marie—" She broke off, as if she'd tasted something bitter. "Did you know her? Now, *that* woman was a real she-devil."

"I never met Lute's sister," Ralph said, feeling a tad nervous. "But I'm not like Lute, ma'am. All I want is to earn whatever you pay me."

"Now that's what I like to hear." She gave him a feline smile. "I've got plans for you—plans that involve a lot more money than you're making now. But first you need to show me I can count on you. Understand?"

Ralph's mouth had gone dry. He nodded.

"Good. We'll talk more later. For now, here's your package. Instructions are in the bag. Now get going."

Ten minutes later, Ralph was on the road, with two packets of cocaine on the seat beside him, hidden under a wrapped cheeseburger in a take-out bag from the Burger

Shack. By now he knew the drill. Drive to an isolated spot on Blanco County's network of backroads. Wait for the customer to show up, turn over the package, collect the cash, and take it back to the Blue Coyote for Stella. After she'd given him his cut, he'd be free to go.

He never asked who the customers were, never even looked at their faces, if he could help it. Most of them, he suspected, were local users or small-time dealers who worked nearby cities like Lubbock and Wichita Falls. The less he knew about them, the better.

The source of Stella's drug supply remained a mystery as well. He'd heard rumors she had connections with a Mexican cartel and a powerful Dallas crime family. But these were only rumors. Stella Rawlins played her cards close to her ample chest. Nobody was in a position to accuse her of any crimes—including Ralph himself.

Ralph was startled from his musings by the flash of red and blue lights in his rearview mirror. His heart dropped like a buckshot quail as he pulled over to the side of the road, braked, and rolled down the window, praying he could bluff his way out of the situation.

The sheriff's vehicle parked behind him. The door opened and the officer climbed out. *Lord help me, it's Abner.*

"Hey, Ralph." The sheriff was just tall enough to peer in the window of the truck. His headlights illuminated the space behind him. "I recognized your old truck. D'you know you've got a taillight out?"

"No." Stomach clenching, Ralph forced himself to look his father-in-law in the eye. "Thanks. I'll get it fixed tomorrow."

Abner didn't budge. "What're you doing out here at this hour, anyway? Is Vonda all right?"

"She's fine. Just touchy, with the baby so close and all.

We had a spat tonight. Nothing serious, just this and that. I'm taking a drive to cool down and clear my head."

"Vonda was always a feisty one." Abner sounded as if he missed his daughter. "But you'd better be getting home to her. She could go into labor, and her all alone in that little house without a car."

"Yes, sir, I'll do that." Ralph started the engine.

"Oh, and be careful on these back roads at night," Abner added. "We've had some reports of illegal drug trade out this way. Run into those scum balls, and they'd just as soon shoot you as look at you."

"Thanks, I'll be careful. I'm going now." Ralph shifted into low and pressed the gas pedal.

"That's a good boy! Go home to your wife!" Abner slapped the fender of the truck as Ralph drove away. Ralph was shaking like a junkie in need of a fix. Running deliveries for Stella was such easy money and paid so well that he tended to forget how risky it could be. Get caught by the law, and you'd wind up in prison. A deal gone bad, or even a case of mistaken identity, and you could wind up dead, like Stella's bartender brother, who'd been shot by Will Tyler. Anything could go wrong out here.

But he didn't plan to stay in this business long, Ralph reminded himself. All he wanted was enough money to buy a decent vehicle, leave Blanco Springs—and Vonda— in his rearview mirror, and never look back. With the new, better-paying jobs Stella had mentioned, he should be able to get there even faster than he'd hoped.

Glancing in his side mirror, he saw the taillights of Abner's big, tan sheriff's vehicle vanishing down the dark road. He'd handled that encounter like a pro, Ralph told himself. Everything had gone fine. And if he played his cards right, things were bound to get even better. Nobody was going to suspect the sheriff's son-in-law of carrying drugs in his old rust bucket of a truck—not even the sheriff himself.

"Hello, Stella . . ."

The razor-sharp voice pulled Stella out of a deep sleep. The woman bending over her bed was tall, with ropy muscles and long black hair, which hung in strings over her ragged gray T-shirt. An ugly white scar slashed the left side of her lean Comanche face from her temple to the corner of her mouth. In her right hand she gripped a huge, gleaming kitchen knife. Laughing like a witch, she raised the knife high and brought it down in a swooping arc . . .

Stella woke with a gasp. Her heart was pounding, her body drenched in cold sweat. Jerking bolt upright in bed, she stared into the darkness. *It's all right,* she told herself. *I'm safe.* She'd been dreaming again, that was all.

Shaking, she glanced at the bedside clock. The luminous digits read three fifteen. Too early to get up and make coffee. But how could she go back to sleep after that god-awful nightmare? She should've known better than to mention Lute's sister, Marie Fletcher, to young Ralph. It was as if speaking the name had been enough to trigger the dream that had plagued her for months.

Stella had survived and thrived because of her ability to control people. But she'd never been able to control Marie. In fact, it almost had been the other way around. Using her married name, Marie Johnson, the woman had hired on as a waitress. But her real agenda had been to avenge her brother's death and take over Stella's operation. After Stella hired a Dallas hit man to take Marie out,

Marie had fled on her motorcycle, leaving the gunman to burn to death in his blazing car.

Marie was still out there somewhere, and Stella had no doubt that someday she'd be back for revenge.

Now that Nicky was dead, Stella had lost her only protector. She'd changed the locks on the Blue Coyote, bought extra fastenings for the doors and windows of her apartment, had an alarm installed on her Buick, and kept a gun within reach, even in the bathroom. But nothing could lock out her fear, or those blood-chilling dreams.

The bedroom was cool. Stella swung her feet to the floor; she reached for her Chinese silk robe and pulled it around her. At this hour there'd be nothing on the living-room TV but infomercials, shopping shows, and religious rants. But anything would be better than going back to sleep and waking up in the nightmare again, with Marie looming over her bed.

In the kitchen she took a cold beer from the fridge, popped the tab, carried it to the sofa, and switched on the TV. The pitch woman on the shopping channel was selling fake Navajo turquoise jewelry that was probably made in a Shanghai sweatshop. Stella stared blankly at the screen, her thoughts elsewhere. Maybe it was time to pull up stakes and leave the country. There were quiet places in Mexico where Marie would never find her. She had useful contacts there and enough money to last her for years. She'd be fine.

But she had unfinished business here in Blanco Springs. Will Tyler had murdered her brother, and she couldn't walk away until she'd seen the high-and-mighty son of a bitch pay for what he'd done. She'd been counting on the law to put him away, but the process was taking far too long. The trial was still two weeks away. Meanwhile, Will Tyler was out on bail and sitting pretty. She'd wanted him to *suffer,* and he was doing far too little of that. She was getting impatient. She wanted some action. Maybe it was time she took matters into her own hands.

With Slade Haskell and Hoyt Axelrod both dead, she was shorthanded when it came to taking vengeance. All she had was a friendly sheriff, a county prosecutor who was scared to death of her, and a willing but inexperienced young flunky. But she'd managed with less. There had to be something she could do.

It would have to look like an accident—one that couldn't be traced back to her. And it would have to be devastating, something that would strike at the very heart of the Tylers' ranch.

Stella lit a cigarette, inhaled, and blew a smoke ring up into the darkness. Whatever her plan turned out to be, she'd enjoy thinking about it for the rest of the night.

Tori drove up to the house, parked, and stepped out of the station wagon with her briefcase. Looking across the yard, she could see Will and Erin standing by the paddock fence, watching the spring-born foals romp in the late-November sunshine.

Something tightened around Tori's heart as her gaze took in the two of them. Erin was pointing toward her young palomino, exclaiming about something. Will was nodding, listening to every word, as if memorizing the sound of her voice.

With Thanksgiving three days away, and the trial scheduled for the following Wednesday, these precious days were all about family. No one at the ranch had expressed any doubt that Will would be acquitted; but everyone, including Will, seemed to be quietly preparing for the worst.

Days ago Tori had notarized a document giving Beau

power of attorney to sell Rimrock land without the need for Will's signature. Either way the trial went, with the hundred-thousand-dollar bank loan due with interest by January 1, they'd have to find a buyer for the land or lose it to the bank. There was no other way to pay the money off. These were dark days for the Rimrock. But at least this year, the ranch family could celebrate Thanksgiving Day together.

Tori was crossing the yard to join Will and Erin at the fence when her cell phone rang. It was Drew. She stopped to take the call.

"Hi," he said. "I was hoping I could catch you before I left for my sister's."

"Aren't you supposed to be in school today?" she asked.

"No, I decided to play hooky. Since I'll be driving to Omaha and back for the big day, I thought I'd take the whole week off. The assistant principal can ride herd on the students for a few days."

"Well, here's wishing you a great trip." Tori had neglected Drew for the past week. She hadn't meant to do that. But the coming trial and Will's other problems had drained her time and energy until there was nothing left for her so-called social life. "Sorry I've been so unavailable," she said. "I hope you'll let me make it up to you later."

"I plan to give you plenty of chances," he said. "But I want to leave you with one thought. I've stood back and been patient while you've dealt with the trial and the issues related to it. But once that trial is over, no matter how it turns out, you'll need to decide between me and Will. I'm falling in love with you, Tori, but I won't play second fiddle to another man. If you and I are going to

make this work, you'll need to be on board with me a
hundred percent. Understand?"

"I understand, Drew," Tori said. "You've been a saint
through all this, and I promise I won't keep you waiting
much longer."

"That's what I wanted to hear," he said. "I'll call you
when I'm back, and I'll see you again after the trial."

"Be safe," Tori said, and ended the call. Drew was the
perfect gentleman. She really did care for him and wanted
to see where their relationship might go. But why did he
have to add to the pressure on her now, at a time when
she was already a bundle of anxiety?

Slipping her phone back into her purse, she reached
the fence and took her place next to her daughter. Will ac-
knowledged her presence with a nod and a flicker of a
smile. He was putting on a brave face, but Tori knew the
thought of what lay ahead was tearing at his heart.

The foals, all legs at this stage, were romping in the
paddock, pushing, rearing, nipping, and galloping. It was
serious play, strengthening their young bodies and build
ing their survival skills, as well as their social skills with
other horses. It was possible to see which animals, even
at this young age, would be dominant later on.

"Look, Mom! Look at Tesoro!" Erin pointed to her
golden foal, racing ahead of the others. "See how fast he
is! And you can already tell he's the one in charge."

Tori took a moment to admire the beautiful young colt.
His palomino coat gleamed in the sunlight. His creamy
mane and tail fluttered in the breeze as he ran. Tesoro was
going to be a magnificent stallion. But Tori still worried
about her daughter owning and raising such an animal.
She'd urged Will to have Tesoro gelded for Erin's safety,
but it was a lost argument. Not to breed such a valuable

creature would be unthinkable, and Erin, who'd been promised the foal before he was born, would have no other.

"Maybe I didn't find the Spanish gold," Erin said, "but we have a golden treasure right here, don't we, Daddy?"

"We certainly do." Will squeezed her shoulders. Lauren had told Tori about Erin's wanting the Spanish gold to help save the ranch. Tori had resolved to wait and tell Will about that later. Right now, his emotions were raw enough.

Will glanced down at the briefcase in Tori's hand. "I see you've come on business," he said.

"I'm afraid so. I was hoping to go over some trial notes. If you're busy with Erin, it can wait."

"No, it's fine." Tori could tell he was weary of the whole business. "Let's get it over with. Erin, don't you have schoolwork to do?"

"A little. If I finish in time, can I go with you to check the herd?"

"We'll see."

They crossed the yard to the house, the three of them walking together with Erin in the middle. Once inside, Erin went to her room. Tori and Will settled themselves in the den with the paperwork on the coffee table between them. From the open ranch office across the hall, they could hear the sound of a ringing phone and Beau's muffled voice as he picked up the call. The closing door cut off whatever they might have heard of his conversation.

Tori found her reading glasses in her purse and slipped them on. She looked up to find Will watching her from his chair. His impossibly blue eyes were ringed in shadow. In all the years she'd known him, she'd never seen him look so tired.

"Are you all right, Will?" she asked gently.

"I'm fine, considering." He shifted in his chair, one hand reaching up to massage the back of his neck. "I'm just so damned weary of this whole mess, Tori. All I want is to have it over and done with. The crazy thing is, if I had that night to do over, I wouldn't have done any different. Whoever the bastard turned out to be, I couldn't take a chance on letting him get to Erin."

"And I'd have done the same in your place," Tori said. "Now let's get to this witness list the prosecution sent me, along with the names I've added, like the nine-one-one dispatcher on duty that night."

"Carly will vouch for me," Will said. "When I called in, I was sure I'd killed the robber."

"She should have a recording of the call. If I can play that, it'll be even more powerful than her testimony." Tori started at the top of the list. "Abner?"

Will shook his head. "I can't figure him out. I've known him since grade school and, in all that time, we've never exchanged an unfriendly word. But I could swear he's out to get me. If we can find out why and use it somehow on the stand—"

"Will." Beau had left the office and walked into the den. "I just got a phone call you need to know about."

Will sighed. "I don't suppose it was the bank calling to say they've changed their mind."

"No. It was Bob Stevens, the new syndicate manager for the Prescott Ranch. He had an interesting proposal."

"He wants to buy some land?"

"Not land. It seems Bob has a wealthy friend in San Antonio with a passion for palomino horses. They were talking, and Bob happened to mention that we had a palomino foal with a lot of promise. The man wants to fly out and look at Tesoro. He said that if the foal's everything he expects, he'll offer you seventy-five thousand for him. Throw in his mother, and he'll make it an even hundred thousand. That would be enough to pay off the bank loan and save the ranch."

Tori sat silent, her eyes on Will. She could imagine what was going through his mind. This was a way out, a way to keep the Rimrock intact and honor the family tradition that no part of it should be sold.

All he had to do was break his daughter's heart.

CHAPTER 11

Mouth set in a flat line, Will rose from the chair, walked out of the room and down the hall. He knew Beau was waiting for some kind of response, but he had none to give him. Right now, what drove him was the need to be alone.

Entering the ranch office, he closed the door behind him, raised the Venetian blind that shaded the wide window, and stood looking out across the ranch yard toward the barns, then to the paddock, where the foals were still romping. Even at a distance Tesoro's coat shone like a polished gold coin in the sunlight.

Beyond the paddock the rolling hills of the pastureland rose to meet the crags of the escarpment. In the pitiless blue sky, a lone vulture circled on outstretched wings.

Will had lived his entire life for the Rimrock. From the time he was old enough to shovel his first forkful of hay, he had taken care of the land and the animals. He had labored till his hands bled, sacrificed a college education and any chance he might've had to see the world—and he'd lost the only woman he'd ever loved when he'd been forced to choose between her and this ranch.

Now it had fallen to him again, the duty to keep the Rimrock whole—but not without another agonizing choice.

Selling Erin's beloved foal and the mare, plus some interest they could pay out of pocket, would clear them with the bank, keep their credit in good standing, and save the acreage that would otherwise be lost. But Erin would be heartbroken. She would never trust him again. Worse, she would learn from this that honor was an illusion, and any promise could be broken on a whim.

Turning away from the window, he studied his father's picture, where it hung on the wall. Even in the black-and-white photograph, Bull had the look of a man who never gave in, never gave up, and never stepped aside.

What would you have done, Dad? Will asked silently, as he often did when faced with a tough decision. *How would you have handled this in my place?*

But this time, Will realized, he already knew the answer. To the Bull Tyler whom Will remembered, the land had been more important than love and family, more important than life itself. A horse and a child's tears would have meant nothing to him. For all Will knew, Bull would have sold his entire family down the river for the sake of this ranch. In a way he almost had.

Gazing at that face, Will felt a sudden flash of understanding. All his life he'd tried to measure up to his father and had failed. And now he knew why.

I'm not you, Dad, he said, continuing the silent conversation. *I may look like you, maybe even talk and act like you sometimes. But I'm not you, and I'm not going to make the decision you would have made. I'm not going to destroy my daughter's happiness for a piece of earth that has no mind, no heart, and no memory. If you don't like it, fine. When I get there, we'll settle our differences in hell.*

Decision made, he opened the office door and walked back into the den. Beau was standing by the bar. He'd opened a beer from the miniature fridge. His grip tightened around the can as Will appeared. "Well?" he asked.

"Tesoro isn't mine to sell," Will said. "I promised him to Erin, and we're keeping him. So you can tell Bob's rich friend that the answer is no."

The can came down on the bar with a thud, splattering beer on the mahogany surface. "Are you crazy?" Beau demanded. "That foal is ranch property, and we can sell him if we have to. Erin can always choose another foal to raise and fuss over. But that palomino is the key to saving our land."

Will shook his head. "I can't believe this. You sound like Dad."

Beau's eyes flashed a startled look, but he swiftly recovered. "Well, you know what Dad would say if he was here."

"I do, and for once I don't agree with him. I won't betray Erin and see her hurt. You're about to have a child of your own. When you do, you'll understand."

"I can't believe this!" Beau stalked out of the den, crossed the hall into the office, and slammed the door behind him.

Tori had been so quiet that Will almost had forgotten she was there. Now she rose from the couch and walked toward him. Without a word she reached out and pulled him to her in a hug that couldn't be mistaken for anything but gratitude. "Thank you," she whispered. "For Erin and for me."

Will waited until she'd stepped back. "I need you to do something for me. As you know, if I go to prison, Beau will have power of attorney to sell ranch property. I need a separate document drawn up declaring Erin sole owner of her foal."

"I'll have it for you to sign tomorrow. But do you really think that's necessary?"

"I hope it won't be." Will didn't like going against his brother, but this needed to be done. "Beau means well. But his idea of what's right doesn't always match mine."

Tori nodded. "How much do you think we should tell Erin about this?"

"No more than we have to. The idea that Beau would've sold Tesoro to pay off the bank would just upset her. She's already got enough grief on her young shoulders. I just wish to God I could spare her this mess."

Will turned away, but she seized his wrist. Her grip was surprisingly strong as she yanked him back around to face her. "Listen to me, Will Tyler!" Her eyes blazed, passionate and falcon fierce. Her voice rasped with emotion. "We're going to beat this, do you hear? You're innocent of any wrongdoing. I'm going to prove it to the world, if I have to take on the whole damned justice system. So help me, I won't let you lose your freedom! I'll fight this to the last breath in my body!"

Her honest gaze burned into him, its heat pure enough to sear all pretense from his soul. He'd prided himself on having the strength to stand alone. But he'd never needed anybody the way he needed this woman.

Resistance crumbling, Will jerked her against him. His kiss was hard, hungry, and demanding. He felt the barest flicker of resistance before she caught fire in his arms. Her mouth went molten, tongue dancing tip to tip with his. Her arms clasped his neck. Her frenzied fingers tangled in his hair. Pressing tight against her, his arousal ached for release. Will cursed silently. Under different conditions he would've taken her on the sofa, on the floor, on the bar, anyplace he could get her under him. All he wanted was to push inside her and thrust until the tension and anxiety burst in one sweet explosion.

But there were people all around them. Beau was in the office. Erin was in her room. Bernice was probably in the kitchen. Any one of them could walk in without a warning.

Reluctantly he released her. They were both breathing hard. Tori's blouse was rumpled, her lips wet and swollen. Will's erection was still straining his jeans.

"Damn it, Tori," he muttered.

She shoved him away from her—shoved him hard. "Go," she said. "Just go."

Forcing himself to turn away, Will strode out of the den and headed for the front door.

Knees shaking, Tori tucked in her blouse, smoothed her hair, and slicked on some tinted lip balm. Will's kiss, and her own fevered response, had left her weak. What a time to rediscover that, under the tension, the bad memories, and the coldly controlled anger that kept them civil for Erin's sake, their old chemistry still sizzled.

The timing couldn't have been worse. Serving as Will's lawyer called for calm detachment and total focus on his case. It wasn't going to work if the two of them couldn't keep their hands off each other.

Tori knew better than to think this sudden compulsion to rip each other's clothes off was leading anywhere. Chalk it up to stress and hormones, nothing more. Will had been impossible when they were married, expecting her to kowtow to his father and be as dedicated to the ranch as he was. And a career woman with a mind of her own was probably the last thing Will had wanted in a wife. They were definitely *not* going to do that number again.

People didn't change—that was the bitter lesson Tori's failed marriage had taught her. Even so, today, when Will had refused to sell Erin's foal, she'd glimpsed the man she'd fallen in love with—the man she'd lost when he'd tried to turn himself into Bull Tyler.

And she could almost—under different conditions— have fallen in love with him all over again.

For most of the past week, Sky had planned to go back to the cave in the canyon. But work with the colts, running them through their training to keep them sharp, had kept him too busy to take time off. Still, he hadn't stopped thinking about what he'd found there. The memory of that small skeleton, barely glimpsed in the dark pit, had haunted him day and night. It was as if those lonely bones were calling to him, demanding . . . what? Recognition? Justice?

Today he'd made an effort to finish early. It was midafternoon when he saddled Quicksilver, the gray gelding that had become his favorite, and headed for the foothills. He'd thought about asking Lauren along, but that would have taken extra time, and she was busy with work in town.

Not that she'd have been eager to come. She'd fallen silent, visibly affected, after he'd told her about the bones. No sense exposing her, or Erin, to that dark place again.

He reached the petroglyph canyon with plenty of daylight to spare. Leaving the horse to graze by the spring, he climbed the steep, narrow trail to the clearing and the cave.

Everything was as he'd last seen it, the cave open, with rocks heaped on both sides of the entrance. Sky checked around for rattlesnakes, but, as expected, he didn't find any. By now, the frigid nights would have driven them underground to hibernate till spring. Most snake dens had multiple entrances and passageways. Even with the rocks blocking the cave, they'd have had no trouble coming and going.

Sky had worn gloves, armed himself with a pistol, and brought along the high-powered spotlight he kept in his truck. He didn't plan to kill any snakes unless they threatened him. This was their territory, after all, and he was the intruder. But he planned to be extremely careful.

The back of the cave lay deep in shadow. He switched on the spotlight and inspected the floor, walls, and ceiling. Nothing. Sky's Comanche grandfather had taught him a snake song. He sang it under his breath as he crouched on the edge of the hole—not for the snakes, which, as he'd since learned, couldn't hear, but to steady his own nerves.

The light shining down into the hole revealed nothing near the top, but Sky could see movement a dozen feet down, where a huge Texas diamondback slithered along a ledge. Was it close enough to strike him? He'd have to take that chance if he wanted to see the bones, which were a good twenty-five feet lower and could only be viewed by leaning in at an angle.

The snake wasn't coiled and didn't appear to be bothered by the light. Deciding to go ahead, Sky stretched out on his belly to anchor his weight and pushed his head and shoulders out over the opening. Gripping the spotlight with one gloved hand, he slanted the light toward the bottom of the hole.

At last he could see the bones. He'd been right about their size. They were small, definitely the bones of a child, maybe eight or nine years old. But that wasn't all. As Sky peered downward, he caught a glimpse of color. It looked like a fragment of red-plaid cloth—maybe a neckerchief or what was left of a collar, circling the neck bones. Moving the light lower, he saw something else that made him gasp. Lying across the small pelvic bone was what looked like a leather belt with a brass buckle. This was no old-time Indian, as Jasper had claimed. These bones were the remains of a young boy, dressed in the clothes of a modern-day white child.

The huge rattler raised its head and hissed. Startled, Sky jerked backward, dropping the spotlight. It fell, crashing against the sides of the pit to lie dark and broken somewhere below.

With a muttered curse, he scrambled to his feet. He was through looking. But he knew what he'd seen. Earlier, when he and Lauren had questioned Jasper about the bones, the old man had appeared nervous, as if he might be hiding something. When he got home, Sky was going to find him and demand the truth.

Those bones were on Lauren's land. She had a right to know their story.

"Count them if you want." Stella thrust the envelope into Ralph's hands. It was stuffed with bills, so heavy that Ralph could feel the heft of their weight. Opening the flap, he ruffled through them with his fingers. *Sweet Jesus, they're hundred-dollar bills!*

"Ten thousand dollars!" Stella snatched the envelope away. "All yours if you do the job I have in mind."

Ralph's head swam. With $10,000, plus what he'd put aside in the bank, he'd have enough money to buy a better truck and get out of town. He could put it all behind him— whiny Vonda and the baby he'd never wanted in the first place, his crappy job running cows for the Tylers, and the dangerous work he was doing for Stella. Those late-night deliveries paid beyond his wildest dreams, but Ralph was smart enough to know that if he didn't get out, he'd wind up in jail or dead, like Lute Fletcher.

"I won't have to kill anybody, will I?" he asked, hoping she'd think he was joking.

She laughed. "Nothing like that. Just a little property damage to the Tyler place."

Ralph hesitated. The Tylers were honest folks. In the three years he'd worked for them, they'd always treated him fairly. True, the work was hard, but they paid as well as any other ranch in the county; and the bunkhouse food, when he could still get it, was a lot better than Vonda's microwave cooking.

"Think about it." Stella patted his shoulder. "What do you owe those people? To them, you're nothing but a saddle bum they can work to death for slave wages. You can earn more in ten minutes than you'll earn busting your back for the Tylers in six months."

He was already thinking. Last week, in town, he'd found an eight-year-old Ford pickup in good condition. The owner was anxious to sell it and could probably be bargained down. Ralph could imagine himself driving that truck out of Blanco with new boots on his feet, money in his pocket, Vonda far behind him, and the whole damned country ahead.

He shrugged, trying not to appear too eager. "Guess I could do it," he said. "Tell me more."

Stella gave him a sly smile. "I'll tell you more when the time comes."

"And when'll that be?"

"Not long. Come by in a couple of days, and I'll give you the details."

"And the money?"

"A thousand now and the rest when you're done." Stella counted out ten bills, then put the envelope in a drawer of her metal army-surplus desk and locked it with the key she wore on a chain around her neck.

Ralph walked out with a smile on his face, $1,000 in his wallet and his head full of plans. He'd give Vonda a hundred just to keep her quiet, but there was no way he'd tell her about the rest. And he'd be smart not to tell Stella he was leaving. She wouldn't like that. It would be safest just to clean out his bank account, do the job, collect the cash, buy the truck, and get the hell out of Dodge. Run fast and far, where Stella, Vonda, Abner—and maybe the Tylers—would never know to look for him.

Plan in place, he climbed into his rusty old pickup and started home. The country oldies station he liked was playing "Take This Job and Shove It." Ralph turned the volume all the way up and sang along.

"So you went back and looked down that hole again." Jasper shook his head. "I wish you hadn't done that, Sky. All it'll do is dredge up old sins. Some things are best left alone."

The two men, dressed in warm jackets, sat on the shared porch of their duplex, sipping Mexican beer and relaxing at the end of a long day. The black-and-white Border collie was curled in his usual spot next to Jasper's feet. Above the escarpment a fiery sunset was fading to the deep indigo of twilight.

Sky closed his eyes for a moment, breathing in the aromas of wood smoke, horses, and the night's coming frost. "After I saw those bones, I knew I had to get a better look," he said. "Now I almost wish I hadn't."

Jasper reached down and scratched the dog behind the ears. "Like I said, some things are best left alone."

"It's too late for that," Sky said. "I saw what was left of a collar and a belt. It was a young boy down there—a boy who had a name and a story. I need to know what happened to him. So does Lauren. It's her land now." He turned to look straight at Jasper. "If you know the story—and something tells me you do—"

"Oh, hell," Jasper muttered, "I reckon I won't get any peace till I tell you. But once you hear the truth, you're liable to wish you'd left well enough alone."

"I'll take that chance," Sky said.

Jasper shifted in his chair, crumpling the empty beer can between his gnarled hands. "What happened up in that little canyon was before my time here. I didn't know about it myself till Bull told me a few months before he died. He made me swear not to tell, but since the ones involved are all in their graves, I reckon your knowing won't hurt none. And since you're plannin' to wed a Prescott, it might help you understand why Bull and Ferg hated each other like they did."

Sky settled back to listen. He'd hoped to have Lauren with him tonight, but she was home nursing a cold. Maybe that was just as well. The old man might talk more freely without her.

"Ferg and Bull weren't always enemies," Jasper said. "As boys the same age, on neighboring ranches, they grew up friends. When they weren't workin' to help their dads, they were tearin' around on their bikes and ponies, learnin' to rope, and playin' cowboys and Indians in the canyons. I reckon it was about as good a life as two boys can have—till somethin' happened."

Jasper sat silent for a moment, watching the dusky shadows creep across the yard. "Ferg had a younger brother—Cooper, that was his name. Cooper was a couple of years younger than Ferg. As Bull put it, he was slow in the head—I guess the way they say it now would be that he was mentally challenged.

"Cooper didn't have friends his own age, so whenever he could, he tagged after Ferg and Bull—not that the boys liked havin' him along. Kids that age can be pretty mean. I guess they teased him and played tricks on him. But Cooper just kept taggin' along like a puppy, probably not smart enough to figure out they didn't want him."

Jasper gave Sky a sharp glance. "I'm tryin' to tell this pretty much how Bull told it to me. One day—the boys would've been about eleven—they were playin' cowboys below the canyon, shootin' off their cap guns and throwin' their lassos. Cooper was with 'em, and Ferg got the idea to pretend the youngster was a cattle rustler they'd caught. They used a bandanna to tie his hands behind his back—something Cooper didn't mind. They'd done that to him before. I guess he was happy just for the attention.

"Then Ferg got a new idea. 'Hey, let's hang the thievin' varmint!' he said, and he made a loop with his rope."

Sky felt the horror uncoiling in his gut. He wanted to stop Jasper from telling the rest, but it was too late now. He needed to hear the story, all the way to the awful end he knew was coming.

"Ferg was a big, husky kid. He put the rope around Cooper's neck, tossed one end over a cottonwood limb, and hauled his little brother off the ground. Then he tied the other end to the roots of an old stump. Bull said he would've tried to stop him, but it was just a game, and he thought, for sure, Ferg would untie the rope in time. I'm guessing Ferg thought the same thing. They weren't bad kids. They just didn't know how far was *too* far."

Jasper shook his head and cleared the emotion from his throat. "When they realized what was happening, they tried to untie the rope from the stump, but the knot was tangled in the roots, and they didn't have a knife to cut it. By the time they finally got him down, Cooper was dead. The boys knew they were in big trouble, so they concocted a scheme. First they dragged the body up the canyon to the cave, untied his hands, and dropped him down that hole, right where you found him."

Sky swallowed the ache in his throat. Those little bones had a name now—Cooper Prescott, who would have been Lauren's great-uncle.

"Since Bull hadn't done enough to stop the hanging, and since he'd helped hide the body, he was guilty, too. The boys made a pact—cut their fingers and sealed it in blood—that they'd never tell what had really happened to Cooper. They made up a story for their folks that some Mexicans in an old car had grabbed the boy and kidnapped him. They even made up a license plate number. The authorities combed the state for those Mexicans. Course they never found 'em."

The old man fell silent again, his hand stroking the dog.

"I'm guessing there's more to the story," Sky said.

"The rest is about Bull and Ferg," Jasper said. "What happened with Cooper put an end to the friendship. For years afterward, Ferg was afraid that Bull would tell on him. He threatened Bull that if the story ever got out, he'd swear that Bull was the one who'd hanged Cooper. After all, who'd believe that Ferg would kill his own brother?"

"Bull never told, did he?"

"Not till he told me, a long time after Ferg was dead. I guess he wanted somebody to know the truth, in case the body was ever found."

"And what about the land?"

"That canyon was Tyler property. The Spanish-gold legend was around even then. Nobody put much stock in it, but Ferg was always afraid somebody would go lookin' for that gold and find Cooper's body. He wanted to own that little strip of land so he could keep people off it."

"And his chance came when Bull got involved with my mother." Incredibly, the fragments of Sky's family history were coming together.

"Yup. That's the part of the story you already know. Ferg blackmailed Bull into selling him the land."

"And when he was digging around up there, pretending to look for the gold, he was really covering the cave?"

"That's about the size of it." Jasper pushed himself to his feet, a sign that the conversation was winding down. "So," he said, "are you going to tell your future wife that she's the grandchild of a murderer?"

"Whether he was a murderer or just a crazy kid who went too far, I'm going to tell her everything," Sky said. "Lauren has the right to know."

Sky told the story to Lauren the next night, while they were nestled on the sofa in her apartment. He told it gently but carefully, leaving out nothing that Jasper had told him.

By the time he finished, tears were flowing down Lauren's cheeks. "That poor, innocent little boy! Oh, Sky!" She pressed her damp face into the hollow of his shoulder. "There must be something we can do! Can't we at least get those bones out so we can bury them in the family cemetery?"

"I've thought about that," Sky said. "But I don't think it's possible. The hole's jagged all the way down, and the bones are wedged deep. Even without the snakes there, nobody could get to them safely. And if we tried to lift them out with some kind of line, they'd be liable to break on the way up. The same with blasting out the hole. That little skeleton's been down there more than fifty years. It's bound to be fragile. As far as I can tell, the only way to preserve it is to leave it right where it is."

"Oh, I suppose you're right. But we've got to do something for the memory of that poor child." Sighing, she snuggled deeper into his arms. For a time they sat in silence, watching the moonrise through the dark window. At last she stirred.

"I just thought of a plan," she said.

"Want to tell me about it?" He was getting drowsy.

"Not yet. It'll take a little time, but if I start on it tomorrow . . ." She yawned. "I might need your help. If I do, I'll let you know."

"All right, my mysterious lady. I'll settle for knowing that you can do whatever you set your mind to."

With a lingering kiss they ended the discussion for the night.

CHAPTER 12

Ralph stood on his front stoop, smoking a Marlboro from the pack Stella had given him. The night breeze was cold, but even in his thin denim jacket, he barely felt the chill. Truth be told, he was too churned up to feel much of anything.

Through the closed door behind him, he could hear the blare of a TV reality show. Vonda liked the one where they locked hot men and women in a house and filmed them bitching at each other, or falling into bed. Stupid show, but that was Vonda for you.

At least he wouldn't have to put up with her much longer. All he needed to do was carry out Stella's orders, and he'd soon be on the road with plenty of cash in his pocket.

The cigarette had smoldered low enough to burn his fingers. With a muttered curse he dropped it on the porch, ground it out with his boot heel, and fished another one out of the pack in his pocket. His cheap lighter flared in the darkness as he lit it and inhaled the bittersweet smoke.

From where he stood, he could see the lights from the

big stone house where the Tylers lived like royalty, lording it over their land and their cattle and their underpaid shit-shoveling crew, like him. Tomorrow they'd be gathering in the house for Thanksgiving dinner. That was when he would carry out Stella's plan—the plan that would change everything.

Just thinking about what she wanted was enough to scare the spit out of him. But she'd given him another thousand-dollar payment with his marching orders tonight. Back out now and he could end up as dead as Lute Fletcher.

The job itself would be easy. The hard part would be making sure he wasn't seen. Get caught, and all bets were off. He'd, for sure, go to jail—unless Stella got to him first. He was just beginning to realize how dangerous the woman was.

He'd already withdrawn his savings—by now, almost $15,000—from the bank, and hidden the cash in his truck. As soon as he'd gotten full payment from Stella, and maybe bought that used truck he'd had his eye on, he'd be out of here.

He turned to go back inside, then paused, torn between need and fear. Maybe he'd be smart to forget the money and go tonight—just get in the old truck and drive. He was already in too deep with Stella. The little he knew about her operation was barely the tip of the iceberg, but it could be enough to damage her. If she knew he planned to leave, he wouldn't put it past her to make him disappear. All the money in the world wouldn't do him any good if he wasn't alive to spend it.

He'd taken two strides toward his truck, when he realized he'd left his keys on the kitchen table. Stopping in his tracks, he cursed. Vonda had been nagging him to stay home more. She would throw a hissy fit if he came in, got the keys, then tried to leave again.

He sighed, feeling trapped. But never mind, it might be better if he stayed, Ralph told himself. He needed the promised cash, and he couldn't afford to make Stella angry—not yet, at least. After he did the job tomorrow, he'd stick around long enough to make sure the Tylers didn't suspect him. Then he'd collect his pay, make nice with Stella, and wait for the first chance to make tracks.

The plan made sense, as long as he could make it work. Otherwise, if anything went wrong, he'd be a dead man.

Fear crawling along his nerves, Ralph turned around once more and walked back into the house.

Bundled in Bernice's knitted afghan, Tori stood at the porch rail. The evening breeze was cold. Clouds gusted across the sky, playing hide-and-seek with the waning crescent moon. The air smelled of snow, but the forecast was for a mild storm, not a killer like the last norther that had blasted the land with sleet, ice, and lightning.

From the glowing rooms behind her came the sound of a football game on TV, intermingled with whoops and cheers from the watchers—Will, Beau, Sky, Jasper, and Erin. The aroma of baking pies floated from the kitchen, mingling with the homey smells of popcorn and wood smoke. As usual, the Tyler Thanksgiving celebration had started the night before the holiday, with snacks and game watching. Tomorrow, for the first time, Natalie and Lauren would be joining them for the traditional turkey feast.

Tori had always looked forward to the fun, food, and family that was Thanksgiving on the Tylers' ranch. But this year would be bittersweet. Behind everyone's smiles and laughter was the awareness that this could be the last holiday when the entire ranch family would be together. Will's fate hung in the balance, awaiting the outcome of the trial in two weeks. Jasper and Bernice were getting old. Erin was growing up. And as for herself . . .

She brushed back a lock of windblown hair. Drew hadn't phoned her since leaving for Omaha on Monday. Was he giving her time and space to make up her mind about him? Or had the revelation that she couldn't have more children cooled his interest?

It surprised her how much she missed him. Drew was an island of stability in the sea of turmoil her life had become. She wasn't in love with him—not yet, at least. But she liked him. There were even times when she needed him.

"Here you are." Will had come out onto the porch, moving to stand beside her. He was wearing the plaid woolen shirt he'd worked in that day. It smelled of sagebrush, hay, horses, and his powerful male body. He stood with his hands on the rail, silent now, as if waiting for her to speak.

"How's the ball game?" she asked, making small talk.

"Fair. The Cowboys are up by two touchdowns. But I couldn't stay with it. Too much going on in my head."

"Are you all right?"

"Fine . . . considering."

Tori checked the urge to reach over and lay her hand on his. It might be a comfort, but they'd gone too far down that road already.

"There's something we need to talk about," he said.

"I'm listening." Tori felt the tension, like the sudden snap of a bowstring. Whatever Will was about to say, she sensed it wouldn't be easy to hear.

He cleared his throat. "If the trial goes badly, and I end up going to prison—"

"Don't say that!" She cut him off. "Don't even think it. It's not going to happen."

"Are you that sure of yourself, Tori?"

"I have to be. It's the only way I can do my job."

Will's throat moved, but he didn't reply. In the silence the mournful wail of a coyote echoed through the darkness.

"There are some things we *need* to think about," he said. "One of them is our daughter. Whatever happens, we'll want to make this as easy on her as we can."

There's no way any of this will be easy on Erin, Tori thought, but she held her tongue.

"If I go away—and it could be for years—there'll be no one in this house. Bernice wouldn't stay on. She's already talked about going to live with her sister. Jasper . . ." Will shrugged. "I'm guessing he'd stay put as long as he can, but he's getting old. He won't be around forever. Beau and Natalie will have their own place and their own family. So will Sky and Lauren."

He gazed across the shadowed yard toward the long horse barn. "This house has been home to Erin all her life. Her room, the animals, Jasper and Sky, even those Sunday dinners—I can't stand the thought of her losing all that, as well as losing her father."

"I know." Tori kept her voice low to hide the emotion. "I've had the same thoughts myself."

"If I go to prison, you'll need to move back here," he said. "I'll pay for a new vehicle, for you to drive to work and take Erin to school. The utilities and maintenance on the house will come out of the ranch budget. You can rent out your house in town or keep it for your office. That way, Erin will still have this place to call home."

Tori bit back a surge of annoyance. She knew Will was only thinking of Erin, but how like him it was to have everything planned out and expect her to fall in line. His idea made some sense, but why couldn't he have asked for her input, instead of just dumping the whole package in her lap?

"Can't this wait until we know the outcome of the trial?" she demanded. "You're innocent, Will, and you're making plans as if you're going to be found guilty."

He looked down at her, his eyes narrowing. "Maybe you believe in the justice system. But I don't trust it. I don't trust the judge. I don't trust the witnesses. I don't even trust the jury. Anything could happen in that courtroom. If it's the worst, I need to know that Erin will be all right—and Erin needs to know it, too."

The night wind had sharpened. Shivering, Tori pulled the afghan tighter around her shoulders. He was right about Erin. Their daughter needed to feel secure about what would happen if her father went to prison. But how could Will expect an instant answer? With so many uncertainties hanging over them, how could she make him a promise that might bind her to this place for years?

"If it's your boyfriend you're thinking about, we could work that out." Will's voice had gone flat and hard. "I don't have any claim on you. I know I can't ask you to live like a nun. If you wanted to get married again, I wouldn't stand in the way of letting him move in here for the duration."

Something jerked in Tori's chest. "Will—"

"This isn't about you and me, Tori. It's about Erin and what would be best for her."

"I know." Tori gazed down at his work-scarred hands, where they gripped the porch rail. For years she'd accused him of being just like his father. But Will was not Bull Tyler. She should have known that when he'd refused to sell Erin's beloved colt, even though the money would have paid off the bank loan. And now, for Erin's sake, he was even willing to let another man live in his family home, with the mother of his child. There was no way Bull would have been so selfless.

And Will was right. This wasn't about the two of them. It was about their daughter. But right now he needed to back off and stop pushing her.

"I get what you're saying, and I agree in principle," she said. "But that plan of yours is a lot to take in. I need time to think."

"How much time?"

"As much time as it takes." Tori was exhausted after a long day of preparing for the trial. Will's heart was in the right place, but his timing was way off. "You'll have my answer in the next few days. Right now, that's the best I can do."

"Do you plan to talk to Erin about this?" he asked.

"Maybe."

"And your boyfriend?"

"His name's Drew. And it's way too soon for that."

"I need this settled, Tori. Lord knows I need *something* settled."

"I understand. But I need time." Sensing a brewing storm between them, Tori moved toward the front door. "Now, if you'll excuse me, I promised Bernice I'd take the pies out of the oven. They should be done about now."

Before he could say any more, she quickened her steps and fled into the house, closing the door behind her. She sympathized with Will's worries, and she would do everything in her power to defend him. But right now, they were both on edge. The last thing they needed was a big, blowup fight.

* * *

Will lingered on the porch after Tori had gone, feeling the burn of cold wind on his face. The familiar sounds of night on the ranch drifted to his ears—the creak of the turning windmill, the shifting and nickering of horses in the barn, and the bawl of a calf in the lower pasture. Smoke, curling from the tall metal chimney on the bunkhouse, blended with the earthy smells of sage and manure.

Closing his eyes, Will filled his senses with memories of the only home he'd ever known. If things went badly at the trial and he ended up in prison, he would need these memories to keep him strong. But, Lord, how could he stand it, being cut off from everything and everyone he'd ever loved?

Tori was right—he needed to go on believing in his own innocence and the fairness of the American justice system. But the ugly knot in the pit of his stomach wouldn't go away. With so many twisted facts working against him, how could he expect to walk out of court a free man?

Tonight he'd pretty much given Tori permission to move her boyfriend into his house, feed him at their table, and sleep with him in their bed. Speaking the words had damn near killed him, but if that was the price of having Tori stay here with Erin, so be it. This was about his daughter's well-being, not his personal feelings. But the personal feelings were there, and they were too powerful to be denied.

Drew.

The name left a nasty taste in Will's mouth. He didn't even know the man, but the thought of Tori in Drew's arms was enough to rouse Will to a near-murderous rage. Even after eight years apart, he still tended to think of her as his woman—and that one wild encounter, the night of the storm, was seared like a brand into his memory. He'd been a fool to let her go—and damn it, *he wanted her back.*

If he made it through the trial with his freedom, by heaven, he was going to fight for her. *Drew* was going to have some serious competition.

But the reality was, if he was convicted and sentenced, all bets would be off. He couldn't ask Tori to wait for him, or to tie herself to the man he'd be after years behind bars.

"Are you all right, Daddy?" Erin had come out onto the porch to stand beside him.

"Fine, honey. Just getting some air. I thought you were watching the game."

"It's just a game. I don't care that much about it."

"What *do* you care about these days?"

"Important stuff, like you and Mom and the trial. I wish I knew what was going to happen."

"So do I." Will rested a hand on her shoulder. "You're a smart girl. I know better than to sugarcoat the situation for you. I'm just as scared as you are. But I can promise you two things. Whatever happens, you'll be all right, and I'll still love you."

Erin didn't answer. When he heard a little breathy sound, Will realized she was crying.

"It's all right." He pulled her against his side, thinking how fast she was growing up. If he went to prison, she could be a woman by the time he got out.

"I don't want you to go away, Daddy!" She wrapped her arms around his waist and held on tight.

"It's all right to cry, honey." He stroked her hair. "Just remember, we Tylers are a tough family. One way or another, we'll get through this."

"But if you go, what'll we do without you? Everybody counts on you to be the boss—Beau, Sky, Jasper, even Mom."

"Now I'd argue with that. You just mentioned the four

most contrary, mule-headed people I know!" Easing her
away from him, he used a gentle finger to lift her chin. Her
tear-streaked face almost broke his heart. "Now, what do
you say we go inside, give you a minute to wash up, then
sit down and watch the rest of the game?"

She gave him her best imitation of a smile. "Sure. And
let's have the best Thanksgiving ever tomorrow."

"That's my girl." Aching with pride, Will followed his
daughter into the house.

Stella scanned the dark parking lot before locking the
back door of the Blue Coyote. Out of habit her hand
reached for the 9 mm Glock she kept in her oversized purse.
It was after eleven, she was alone, and a lady couldn't be
too careful.

Her Buick was parked a dozen yards away, in a well-
lit spot. It hadn't escaped her that somebody, like Marie,
could wire a bomb to the ignition. But the big sedan had a
sensitive alarm system that would go off if anybody got
too close. An ambush from the shadows would be more
Marie's style. But the bitch would show herself first.
She'd want Stella to know she'd come back for her revenge.

As a precaution Stella keyed the remote to unlock the
doors and start the engine. No bomb. She climbed into
the driver's seat, locked the doors, and put the Buick in
gear. Her feet, in their red cowgirl boots, were killing her.
She couldn't wait to get home, pull them off, and soak in
a warm, sudsy bath.

Tomorrow the bar would be closed. Although she'd
never been much of a cook, she usually fixed a little
Thanksgiving dinner for herself and Nicky. This year,
with her brother gone, it wouldn't be worth the bother.

But if things went as planned, she'd be celebrating in a different way.

Could she depend on Ralph to do what she was paying him for? Up to now, he'd done as he was told. But this job would take some guts. She wouldn't put it past him to get cold feet, take the two-thousand-dollar payment she'd advanced him, and hit the road.

Either way, Ralph was a flunky who'd pretty much outlived his usefulness. He wasn't smart enough to justify keeping around, which meant he'd have to go. It was only a question of when and how.

With Hoyt Axelrod dead and Marie in the wind, she'd lost the only people she could count on to kill in cold blood. Getting rid of Ralph was hardly worth the cost of a hit man, but since she'd always had a rule against offing folks herself, that might be her only option. The fact that he was Abner's son-in-law called for extra caution. His death would not go unnoticed or uninvestigated.

But she was too tired to think about that now. Tomorrow, after she knew how Ralph's little errand had gone down, she could make her plans.

Turning onto a side street, she headed for the apartment complex where she lived. She was getting weary of Blanco Springs and this whole business. Now that Nicky was gone, maybe it was time she pulled up stakes and headed for Mexico, where she had the connections, and enough money stashed away, to set herself up for the rest of her life.

She was liking that idea more and more. But first, she had to settle the score for her brother's death. It would be easy enough to have Will Tyler killed. But she wanted him to suffer—to pay with his freedom, his resources, and all that he cherished. Only then would she feel satisfied. And only then would she feel free to leave.

The trial was a week away, but she was too impatient to wait. Payback for Nicky's loss would begin tomorrow, while the family was at dinner.

She would stay home and listen. When she heard the blare of sirens, she would know Ralph had carried out her orders.

Thanksgiving Day dawned bleak and overcast, with dry flakes of snow blowing on the wind. Even on a holiday there were chores to be done —the cattle and horses had to be fed and watered, the fences checked, the horse barns shoveled out, and the stalls laid with clean straw. All the hands pitched in, including the Tyler brothers and Sky.

Ralph showed up on time and joined the others. Today the men who lived in the bunkhouse would enjoy a nice Thanksgiving dinner and a free afternoon. Ralph couldn't help envying them. Vonda, who was too pregnant and tired to cook, would be heating a couple of frozen turkey dinners in the microwave. But what did it matter? Once he'd carried out Stella's orders, nobody was going to have a good holiday, especially the Tylers.

As he worked, busting the ice off the water troughs and scattering hay in the pastures, dread clawed at his gut. It wasn't too late. He could make some excuse, then walk to his truck and drive away. He had enough money stashed in a grocery bag under the seat to get him to some far part of the country, where he could rent an apartment and live frugally till he could find some kind of job.

Just go, he told himself.

But then he thought of the money and what Stella could do to him if he ran out on her. She had rumored connections with the kind of people who could find anybody, anywhere. If he wanted to live, he would have to do what she wanted.

By noon the work was done. The men were dismissed to go back to the bunkhouse or home to their families. Ralph had driven his truck the quarter mile from his bungalow to the ranch yard. Climbing into the cab, he lit a cigarette and watched Will, Beau, and Sky trail toward the house. *Rich bastards, those Tylers. They deserve what they're about to get.*

Stella had told him to make his move while the Tylers and the ranch hands were at dinner. That wasn't likely to happen for an hour or more. Meanwhile, he could hardly sit here and wait in plain sight. He had little choice except to go home, eat his microwaved Thanksgiving dinner with Vonda, then make an excuse to go back to the barn.

Starting up the truck, he drove home. He found Vonda lying on the couch with the TV blaring and the two dinners sitting on the counter, still frozen. He opened one, shoved it in the microwave, and set the timer.

"Want me to cook yours, too?" he asked her.

"Not now. I don't feel real hot. I've got a bellyache."

"Can I get you anything?"

She shook her head and closed her eyes. Ralph turned down the volume on the TV and waited for his dinner to heat. When it was ready, he ate it, standing up, off the counter. *So much for Thanksgiving,* he thought.

Tossing the plastic tray in the trash, he glanced at the clock on the stove. It was early yet, but he was getting anxious. He'd planned to go back to the barn on foot, less chance of being seen. Add a few more minutes to circle around the back way and, with luck, the timing should be about right.

"Where are you going?" Vonda demanded as he slipped on his denim jacket again.

"Just something I promised to check on. I won't be long." He started for the door.

Straining, she managed to sit up. "Do you have to go *now*? I feel—oh!" Her face froze in shock as wetness spread down the legs of her sweatpants. "Oh, Ralphie, I think my water just broke!"

Seized by a sick panic, Ralph paused in the doorway. Whatever was happening here, he had to do the job for Stella. If he didn't, she was liable to kill him.

"You can't go now!" Vonda wailed. "You need to drive me to the hospital! I'm going to have this baby!"

Damn! Ralph felt the cold sweat beading under his flannel shirt. But first babies took a long time, didn't they? He could still go and make it to the hospital, an hour away in Lubbock. He had to.

"This won't take long," he said. "Get ready. I'll take you as soon as I get back." As an afterthought he tossed her his cell phone. "If you need help before then, call nine-one-one."

Before she could say anything else, he was out the door.

Should he take the truck? It would get him there and back faster. But no, a vehicle could be spotted too easily, and everybody knew that old rust bucket by sight. Passing the truck, he broke into a run, cutting up the road, across the open ground and behind the outbuildings to the rear of the barn. There, aching from a stitch in his side, he slumped with his hands on his knees, fighting the urge to retch.

So far, he'd seen nobody outside. All to the good. The sooner he got this over with, the sooner he could get back to Vonda and drive her to the hospital.

He didn't want to see the baby. He didn't want to see anything that might have the power to hold him to this place. He would take Vonda to the emergency entrance, make sure she was in good hands, then report to Stella. Once he had the money, it would be *Good-bye, Blanco Springs*.

The long barn, which held the mares, their growing foals, and some of Sky's trained colts, was unlocked at the near end. Ralph slipped inside, closed the door behind him, and walked the long line of stalls toward the far end. Horses snorted as he passed. Some raised their heads and looked at him with their luminous dark eyes. Most of them were familiar. Some he'd even ridden to work the cattle. Ralph didn't love horses, but he liked some of these. Knowing what was about to happen, he kept his gaze lowered, avoiding eye contact with them.

A cart heaped with dry straw had been left at the barn's far end. Steeling his resolve, Ralph took out his lighter, clicked it, and held the flame to the straw. The dry fuel caught with a startling *whoosh*, so close that Ralph could feel it singe his eyebrows. He jumped back as the flames rose higher than his reach. The fire was burning faster and hotter than he'd expected. He had to get out of here.

The blazing cart was blocking the nearest door. The only way out was at the other end, where he'd come in. With the fire spreading to the roof supports, he raced between the stalls. He stumbled over a pitchfork and caught himself on his knees. Scrambling to his feet, he rushed on.

By now, the horses were going wild, screaming and rearing, lunging against the sides of their stalls. He wasn't crazy about horses, but these were all about to die horrible deaths, and it would be his doing.

As he raced past the stalls, Ralph began a frenzied grabbing at the gate latches, jerking open the ones that yielded easily. Horses, he knew, tended to panic and balk in a fire and had to be dragged out of burning buildings. But if any of them had the sense to run out, he would leave the door open. Maybe a few smart animals would make it. Stella couldn't be too mad about a few horses.

Besides, if he happened to get caught, he could always claim that he'd smelled smoke and had rushed into the barn to save the horses.

Just behind him a big bay mare burst out of a stall he'd unlatched. Shrieking in terror, she reared on her hindquarters, her hooves flailing the air.

Ralph glanced back just in time to see the massive, black, iron-shod hooves coming down toward him. Then something slammed his head, and the world exploded into blackness.

CHAPTER 13

Tori closed her eyes and did her best to listen as Jasper's mumbled grace droned on. This Thanksgiving dinner was a poignant celebration, a blessed pause in the frenetic pace of their lives, when worries and differences were put aside. Everyone around the table seemed resolved to make the most of the day. For now, at least, they were together; and even in the face of change, they were still very much a family.

The prayer ended, eyes opened. Hands reached out to pass around platters and bowls of carved turkey, dressing, hot rolls, potatoes, and gravy. That was when the dog, who had been napping on the porch, began a frantic barking.

Bernice, who was facing the window, was first to see the smoke. "Lord help us!" she cried. "The barn's on fire!"

In a flash they were all on their feet, overturning chairs in their haste to get outside. "Somebody call nine-one-one!" Will shouted, racing for the front door with Beau behind him. Lauren already had her phone out and was making the call.

"Tesoro! He's in his stall!" Squirming out of Tori's clasp, Erin streaked headlong out the door, passing Beau on the front porch.

"Beau, get her! She mustn't go out there!" Tori fought her way through the melee of chairs and shifting bodies. By the time she caught up with Beau in the yard, he'd grabbed Erin and was holding her while she struggled to get free and run to the barn. "Tesoro . . . ," she sobbed. "I've got to save him!"

"I'll get Tesoro, I promise," Beau was saying. "Now calm down and stay here with your mother. That's an order."

After passing her off to Tori, Beau wheeled away and joined Will in the race across the yard. Holding her daughter tight, Tori glanced around for Sky. He was nowhere to be seen. But she knew where he must be. In his quiet way he would have slipped out the back at once and been first to reach the burning barn. By now, he'd be inside, fighting to rescue the horses he loved like his children. And, because she knew the man, she was sure he wouldn't abandon any animal, not even for his own safety.

Lauren had come out onto the porch. One look at her pale face confirmed that she knew it, too.

The men who'd stayed for the holiday came pounding out of the bunkhouse to help. Shouting, Will directed them to hook up the hoses and start spraying inside the barn. After the damage from the past summer's wildfire, the barn's shingled roof had been replaced with steel panels. But it was the older, lower part of the barn that was burning now, flaming upward from the inside. If the temperature got hot enough, and the supports weak enough, the whole building would collapse.

Breathing through their neckerchiefs, men were dragging hoses, soaking feed sacks, filling buckets, rushing in and out of the barn. The scene brought back the memory of the wildfire that had nearly destroyed the ranch a season ago. That fire had been far bigger, sweeping through the tinder-dry scrub, consuming everything in its path. But then, at least, they'd had time to prepare and evacuate the stock. This blaze had started with no warning at all.

The garden-sized hoses were far too small, the water stream barely enough to wet down the stalls, let alone fight the fire. If the fire engine, with its big tank, didn't get here soon, the barn would be lost, along with many of the precious animals.

The first few horses had emerged. Faces covered with wet feed sacks, they were coughing and struggling against the men who gripped their halters. Tori recognized Belle, the aging bay mare, among them, and Lauren's powerful black gelding, Storm Cloud. But there was no flash of Tesoro's golden coat. She clasped her daughter tighter. "Remember, Beau promised to save him," she whispered, adding her own silent prayer.

Beau was still outside. He soaked his clothes at the pump, masked his face with a neckerchief, and charged into the billowing smoke, carrying a bucket.

Natalie, who had been on a call that morning, had driven here in the big white SUV she used for her veterinary work. Burdened only a little by her bulging belly, she rushed to her vehicle. Lauren stood at the top of the porch steps, wide-eyed with fear but clearly anxious to help. "Come on!" Natalie shouted to her. "I'll need extra hands!"

Lauren sprinted down the steps and piled into the passenger seat. In the next instant they were roaring toward the barn, flying over the bumpy ground. It would be Natalie's job to treat any horses injured in the fire—or to put them down if they couldn't be saved.

Smoke was pouring out of the barn in thick, murky clouds. Even at a safe distance, Tori could smell it, even taste it when she licked her parched lips. She could feel the searing heat and see tongues of fire licking under the metal roof. The blaze appeared to be burning upward from the rear of the barn. That might give the horses near the front a better chance to get out, but how could anybody, man or beast, survive in that inferno? It would be tragic enough losing horses to the fire. But human lives . . . no, that was unthinkable.

More horses, driven from behind, exploded out of the barn to scatter and mill in the yard. One of the men had opened the paddock gate and was trying to drive them inside, but the horses were too fear-crazed to be herded. They would have to be rounded up later.

"There's Beau!" Erin shouted, waving as a figure emerged from the smoke with a grip on two struggling animals. "He's got Tesoro—and Lupita!"

Tears of relief welled in Tori's eyes, but she could see that something was wrong. The mare looked all right, but Tesoro was favoring one side, his head hanging low. Even from here, she could tell the colt was in pain.

And something else was wrong, Tori realized. Her last sight of Will had been when the men were hooking up the hoses. She could see Beau, leading Tesoro over to Natalie's SUV, but she couldn't see Will's red-plaid shirt anywhere. Fear crawled up her throat. Was he inside the blazing barn?

"Tesoro's hurt!" Erin fought to pull away, but Tori kept a firm grip on her daughter.

"It's all right. See, Natalie and Lauren have got him now. They'll take care of him. Having you there would just be one more worry." She glanced back toward the house. "Jasper and Bernice are on the porch with the dog.

Stay there and watch with them. I'll go find out what's happening." She released her daughter with a gentle shove toward the porch. "Go!"

Tori forced herself to wait until Erin had reached the steps. Then, giving in to her fear, she spun away and raced headlong for the barn. Smoke swirled around her, the acrid scent filling her nostrils and lungs, burning her eyes. Men were manning the hoses and leading more horses to safety. She could see Beau in the doorway of the barn, shouting directions. But there was no sign of Will.

She hadn't seen Sky, either. Would she find them both safe on the far side of the barn, maybe hidden from sight by the heavy smoke? Or could they be inside, maybe trapped, maybe even dead? With a prayer on her lips, she ran on. There was little she could do to help. She only knew that if Will was in danger, she had to be there.

Will had gone searching for Sky. Deep in the barn he found him. He was standing in a half-charred stall, soothing a fear-maddened chestnut mare with burns on her back—one of the last three horses left in the barn.

To Will, Sky looked like a man who'd just stepped out of hell—there was a wet bandanna plastered to his face; hair and clothes singed; his ungloved hands blistered by the sparks that exploded from the burning beams overhead. The eyes that turned and glanced at Will were bloodred from the smoke. He looked like a soldier in combat, ready to drop from exhaustion.

By now, the hose crew had wet down the stalls and the straw inside, making it a little safer to get the horses out. However, the fire had taken an upward path, and there wasn't enough water pressure to reach the wooden rafters and beams that supported the barn's metal roof. They were on fire now; and when they burned through, the whole structure would collapse. Will cursed his lack of foresight. After the summer fire it had been his cost-driven decision to replace only the roof and not the old structure of the barn beneath. Now he was paying the price.

Reaching Sky, Will grabbed his arm. "For God's sake, man, let's get out of here!"

Sky shook his head. "After the horses."

Will was aware of what Sky had been doing. He'd taken his stand in the most dangerous part of the barn, calming terrified animals, covering their faces with wet sacking, urging them out of their stalls and forward, to where other hands could lead them to safety. But the roof couldn't hold up much longer, and neither could Sky.

"We need to get the hell out of here!" Will shouted, pointing to the blazing rafters. But he knew he was wasting his breath. Sky would not go until every animal was safe. The only thing Will could do was to help him.

He didn't have Sky's natural touch with horses, but he opened the nearest stall. Dodging frantic hooves, he grabbed the young gelding's halter at the throatlatch and flung a dripping sack over the animal's face. Yelling, swearing, and yanking on the halter, he dragged the horse out of its stall, turning it toward the far entrance. After more prodding and cursing, he finally got the animal to where one of the cowhands was waiting to seize its halter and hurry it outside.

Will's lungs were already burning from the smoke. How much worse off must Sky be? With his unfailing gentleness, Sky urged the chestnut mare out of her stall and led her partway toward the far door, where one of the men waited to take her. Now only one horse remained, a big paint gelding, wild with terror. It was screaming and kicking, refusing to be led. Will glanced up at the blazing beams overhead. Tugging at Sky's arm, he pointed upward. Sky shook his head. "You can go!"

Will's gaze met Sky's. "No way. I'm not leaving without you! Let's get this horse out."

With Sky calming the horse, they managed to work their way on either side of its head, fling the last of the wet sacks over its face, and lead it out of the stall. When Will peered down the long row of stalls, through the blur of smoke, no one was there to take the horse.

Suddenly he saw why. The roof panels were buckling in the heat. Any second now, they would come crashing down. With a shout he yanked the cover off the big paint's eyes and gave its rump a resounding smack. The horse bolted toward the light at the far end of the barn and disappeared outside.

Will and Sky were now racing for their lives, pounding through choking smoke and searing heat. But they'd already delayed too long. With fragments of breaking, burning timbers raining on them, they heard the awful groan of warping, sliding metal. They were no more than twenty yards from safety, but it was too late to get out. They could only dive for any cover they could find.

As the roof panels sagged and came crashing down, the last sound to reach their ears was the faint wail of sirens.

Tori and Lauren waited next to the emergency vehicles, supporting each other in silence as the firemen hosed down the barn's wreckage and began clearing it away. The barn was a total loss, but the horses, now rounded up and herded into the paddock, had survived the fire with minor burns and a gash to Tesoro's shoulder, which would heal. The ranch hands who'd come running to help were safely accounted for, as well as Beau. Only two men were known to be missing—Sky and Will.

With rakes, shovels, crowbars, and gloved hands, Beau and the hired men were helping the fire crew lift away the bent roof panels and other debris. The ruined barn looked as if it had been bombed. In some places the charred walls of the barn and the heavy-timbered framework of the stalls were still standing. In other places the rubble was as flat as if crushed by a giant hammer. The work was painstakingly slow. One wrong move could crush or stab a survivor who might be trapped alive beneath the rubble.

Natalie, who'd been repacking supplies in her SUV, broke away and hurried forward, cell phone in her hand. "I just got a call from the nine-one-one dispatcher," she said. "That poor little girl who's married to Ralph Jackson is about to have her baby. Her husband's gone off somewhere, she's all alone, and the nearest doctor's in Lubbock. I'm going over there to see what I can do. If I need more help, I'll let you know."

Her eyes met Tori's in silent understanding. The ambulance and paramedics had arrived with the fire department; but if Will or Sky—or both—were found alive, here was where the more urgent need would be. If Natalie ended up having to deliver a baby, it wouldn't be the first time.

With a final comment—"Keep me posted"—she sprang into her vehicle, gunned the engine, and roared off toward the distant row of bungalows. Tori turned her gaze back to the grim search of the wreckage. She could feel Lauren, close beside her, trembling. Neither of them spoke. There was nothing to say. They were two strong women preparing themselves for the worst.

One of the firemen gave a shout. "There's a body under here!"

Tori's heart dropped. She felt Lauren's hand creep into hers as more men hurried to pull away the debris. Beau was the first one to recognize the dead man. He spoke in a flat voice.

"He's got blond hair, and I remember that shirt from this morning. That's Ralph Jackson."

Tori's knees went weak. She braced, willing herself to stand. Beside her, Lauren gasped. "It's his wife who's having a baby! We need to let Natalie know."

Not trusting her voice, Tori found the number on her cell and handed it to Lauren to make the call. This time it hadn't been Will or Sky the men had found. But the search was far from over.

She averted her eyes as the paramedics lifted away the body and zipped it into a black bag, though a glimpse told her that the man hadn't been badly burned. She'd barely known him, but the tragedy, and the fear that this was only the beginning, hit hard and deep.

Looking across the yard, Tori could see Erin standing on the porch with Jasper and Bernice. She was staying where she'd been told to stay, but she was straining against the rail, trying to see what was happening. Tori ached to go to her daughter, take her in her arms, and assure her that everything would be all right. But she couldn't do that yet—not when Erin's loving, secure world might have already come crashing down in the inferno of the burning barn.

"Quiet!" It was Beau who'd shouted. "Listen—I think I heard something!"

In the silence of straining ears that followed, Tori could hear nothing but Lauren's breathing and the pounding of her own heart. Maybe Beau had only heard the shift of cooling metal, or the sound of a trapped, injured animal that would need to be put down.

Or a man, terribly burned . . . She forced the thought away.

"Over here!" One of the men pointed toward a spot near the barn's entrance where the debris was piled high against a standing wall. "Listen, there it is again! Something's moving!"

Tori, who was farther away, held her breath, but she could hear nothing. She could only wait with Lauren, in an agony of undeniable hope, as each piece of wreckage was carefully lifted away.

Then there was a shout. "They're here! They're alive, both of them!"

Tori's knees buckled. She heard a sob from Lauren as two ghostly-looking men, singed, ragged, and coated with soot and ash, emerged from the rubble. Will was on his feet, stumbling through the debris. Sky, barely conscious, had to be supported between Beau and one of the paramedics.

Will's smoke-reddened eyes narrowed as he took in the scene around him. "Damn it, don't just stand there gawking!" he barked, gesturing toward Sky. "Get this man some oxygen!"

He needn't have spoken. The paramedics were already easing Sky onto a stretcher and clapping an oxygen mask over his face. But Will's take-charge manner was enough to show Tori that the man she knew so well was back.

Lauren had rushed to be near Sky, staying close as he was carried toward the waiting ambulance. As they loaded him, Tori heard her arguing with the paramedic.

The young man was insisting that she couldn't ride along because they had to take Will, too. But so far, Will showed no sign of wanting to go.

Tori gazed at Will through the clouds of settling ash. Her eyes misted as she thought of how close she'd come to losing him. She checked the impulse to stumble through the debris and fling her arms around his neck. Will had never been big on emotional drama, especially not in front of others. But he had to know how much it meant for her to see him safe.

For a slow beat of time, their gazes held. He cleared his throat. "Tell Erin I'm all right," he said.

"I'll tell her." The calm words masked a storm of emotions Tori had never expected to feel again. Heaven help her, she'd never stopped loving this gruff, stubborn, impossible man. But would love ever be enough to heal the hurt between them?

One paramedic stepped close. "Mr. Tyler, we're waiting. You need to come with us in the ambulance."

"The hell I do," Will growled. "My damned barn just burned down. I can't leave now."

"Don't be stubborn, Will," Beau said. "You've got some nasty burns, and you've inhaled a lot of smoke. You need to get checked by a doctor. I'll keep an eye on things till you get back."

"For once, do as you're told," Tori said. "If you ride with Sky in the ambulance, you can keep an eye on him. I'll follow in my car with Lauren. After you've been checked out, I'll drive you home."

Will's grime-coated features creased in a scowl. "Looks like I'm outgunned," he muttered. "All right, but this better not take long." He strode to the ambulance and climbed inside the back without help.

A press van had just pulled up to the barn. Will gave the reporters a contemptuous look before the doors closed behind him and the emergency vehicle, siren wailing, sped off toward the highway.

Natalie wrapped the baby boy in a clean blanket and placed him in the arms of his sixteen-year-old mother. The birth, thank heaven, had been an easy one. The baby was healthy, and the mother was doing fine. But knowing what she knew, Natalie could hardly go off and leave them alone.

Vonda gazed down at her son as if she couldn't believe he was real. Her fingertip brushed the small, perfect features, the little nub of a nose, the baby hands with their long fingers and tiny nails.

"He's a beautiful boy," Natalie said. "What are you going to name him?"

"Ralph, after his father. We talked about that." Her eyes welled with emotional tears. "Where's Ralphie? He's supposed to be here! Why hasn't he come home?"

Natalie had to look away. She'd received both messages Lauren had left on her phone—one saying that Will and Sky were alive, the other letting her know that Ralph Jackson had died in the fire. But how could she break the news to this poor girl? Vonda needed to hear it from someone she trusted. She needed her family to support her and soften the blow.

"Since he isn't here, why don't I call your parents?" Natalie offered. "They'll want to know you're all right, and they'll want to see their grandchild."

"No!" Vonda turned against the pillow, clutching her baby. "My folks kicked me out when I got pregnant. Mom said she wouldn't stand for having a sinner in the family! Ralphie's all I've got! Please, just find him for me!"

Heartsick, Natalie murmured an excuse and walked out onto the stoop with her cell phone. She knew the girl's parents, of course, not that she had much liking for either of them. Vonda's father, Sheriff Abner Sweeney, had been involved in last spring's case against Beau. He'd also been the one to question and arrest Will. Her mother, Bethel, was a staunch, Bible-thumping church-goer who'd birthed eight children, most of them girls. Vonda, her firstborn, had been the first to rebel and go astray. Natalie suspected she might not be the last.

But that was neither here nor there. As Natalie scrolled down the names on her cell phone, she could only hope that Abner and Bethel had enough Christian charity in their hearts to forgive the child who had nowhere else to turn.

The only phone number she had was the sheriff's. By now, he probably knew about the fire, and might even know that Ralph was dead. But unless she could reach him, Abner Sweeney wouldn't know that he'd just become a grandfather.

He answered on the first ring. "What is it, Natalie? I'm on my way to a fire at the Tyler place. Goin' by what I heard on dispatch, it might've been dee-liberately set. D'you think Will Tyler would be desperate enough to burn his own barn for the insurance?"

With effort Natalie held her temper in check. "The fire is out. And I was with Will, in the house, when it started. We were about to eat Thanksgiving dinner."

"Oh." The sheriff sounded disappointed. "So what was it you wanted? Can it wait, or is it an emergency?"

"It's an emergency—yours. Your son-in-law is dead, and your daughter just had her baby, a little boy."

She heard the squeal of brakes as he pulled off the road. "Say again?"

"Ralph died in the fire. I'm here with Vonda at their bungalow. She and the baby are fine, but she doesn't know about her husband yet. You and your wife need to get here. You need to be the ones to give her the news and take care of her."

There was a beat of silence. "I'll come as soon as I can. But I don't know about Bethel. She can be a hard woman once she makes up her mind."

"Bring her! I don't care if you have to hog-tie her to do it! This poor little girl needs her mother!"

Natalie ended the call.

Lights flashing and siren blaring, the ambulance barreled up the highway toward Lubbock. Will, riding in the back with Sky, had insisted on sitting up. Aside from minor burns, a raw throat, and smarting eyes, he felt fine. As he'd told the husky young paramedic, anybody who thought they could make him lie down was welcome to try. Since no one had challenged him, he'd taken a seat on the bench, where he could be close enough to look after Sky, and to talk to him.

Sky was awake. The oxygen was helping to revive him, but he was looking pretty rough. His scalp and face were pocked with burns where sparks had showered down from the blazing timbers. His hands had been burned as well, and his denim shirt was little more than scorched tatters. The burns would heal, but Will was more worried about Sky's lungs. There'd been enough oxygen in the burning barn to keep him alive, but he'd inhaled a dangerous amount of smoke. There'd be enough damage to keep him on humidified oxygen for a few days, at least. Maybe longer if there were complications.

Sky had saved every last animal in the barn and damn near died doing it. He seemed unaware of what a loss his death would have been to the ranch. But Will knew. This stubborn half-Comanche was as much a part of the Rimrock as the earth, the grass, the water, and all the living things that called it home. He was Bull Tyler's blood son, Will's own half brother. And yet he asked for no praise, no recognition of any kind except the freedom to care for what he loved.

Sky stirred and made a low sound. His eyes were open above the edge of the oxygen mask that covered his nose and mouth. He gazed up at Will as if he wanted to speak.

"Take it easy, brother," Will said. "You need to keep still and just breathe."

Brother? Sky's singed eyebrows twitched in an unspoken question.

"You heard me. I've been waiting for the best time to tell you I knew. I guess that time's now."

How? Another question expressed by a look.

"Jasper told me. But I knew before that—maybe even before you did. You've got Bull's eyes and some of his mannerisms, and you're almost as mule-headed as he was. I suspected the truth for a long time, but when you got shot last spring, and Beau and I had to give you our AB-negative blood, the same type as Bull's, that cinched it. I knew you were a Tyler."

And Beau?

"I'm guessing Beau hasn't given it much thought. But I could be wrong. I take it you've told Lauren."

Sky's head moved on the pillow, a slight nod.

"Well, we'll leave it at that," Will said as the ambulance swung into the hospital parking lot. "Just rest and get better. Tori's bringing Lauren with her. They should be along soon."

The back of the ambulance opened to glaring afternoon sunlight. Paramedics laid Sky's stretcher on a gurney and whisked him through the doors of the emergency entrance. An orderly brought out a wheelchair for Will. He waved it away and kept walking, following his brother until someone pulled him aside.

CHAPTER 14

Tori had stopped by the house long enough to grab her purse and keys, and to let Erin, Jasper, and Bernice know that Will and Sky were safe. Now, with Lauren buckled into the passenger seat, she was breaking speed limits on the highway to Lubbock.

"You didn't have to drive me," Lauren said. "I could've taken my own car."

Tori swung her station wagon past a lumbering hay truck. "You're too upset to drive," she said. "Besides, I told Will I'd be there to take him home—that is, if the hospital doesn't keep him overnight. You're welcome to come with us or stay there with Sky. If you stay, somebody can pick you up in the morning."

"You're pretty upset yourself. I can tell by the way you're driving." Lauren gazed ahead at the yellowed plain and the road that sliced across it in a straight black line to the horizon. "Were you as scared as I was?"

"Scared enough," Tori said. Days like today were part of ranch life. Lauren would learn that, if she hadn't learned already.

"Those damned horses!" Lauren muttered. "I love

horses, too, but Sky almost died for them today—and they aren't even his. How am I supposed to wrap my mind around that?"

"Horses are like family to Sky," Tori said. "If he cares for them so passionately, think how he'll be with his real family—you and your children. He'll do anything to provide for you and keep you safe."

Lauren fell silent for a moment. "I'm pregnant, Tori," she said.

"Oh—" Tori released her death grip on the steering wheel long enough to reach over and squeeze her friend's hand. "Does Sky know?"

"I just found out, myself." She shook her head. "Maybe, today, it was just as well Sky didn't know. I keep asking myself, what if he'd had to make a choice between saving the horses and being there for his child—and he'd still chosen those damned horses?"

"Thinking like that will only muddy the water," Tori said. "Believe me, I know. If I hadn't convinced myself that Will loved the Rimrock more than he loved me, maybe we'd still be married."

Lauren was quiet for a few moments, as if pondering what she'd just heard. "What happened with you and Will, Tori?" she asked. "Seeing how you always seem to be there for each other, I can't help wondering what went wrong."

Tori sighed. "Maybe it's time I told you. You sound as if you need to hear this."

As the miles sped by, Tori told her the story—how Bull had tried to dominate the marriage and how Will had been caught in the conflict between his wife and his father. "After I lost the baby and found out I couldn't have more children, Bull treated me like a failure," she said. "I begged Will to find us another place to live. But after

Bull's accident, that was out of the question. Will needed to be there to oversee his father's care and run the ranch."

"Why didn't you leave on your own?"

"I could have. But I still loved Will, and we both adored Erin. So I hung on . . . until I couldn't hang on any longer."

Tori began the final chapter—how her father had died in Florida and Will had been too busy to join her for the funeral.

"And that was the final blow? That he wouldn't be there for you?"

"Not quite." This was the hard part—the part she hadn't told Drew or even Natalie. But Lauren needed to hear it all. "There was a man," she said, "a longtime friend of my father's. He was widowed and made no bones about being attracted to me, but I wasn't the least bit interested. He was just a friend, and barely that.

"When he heard about my father's death, he flew down from Washington, D.C., and did his best to be kind and helpful. Yes, maybe he was a little too friendly, but without Will there, I needed some support. My mother was a wreck, so I had to make a lot of the arrangements. I truly appreciated his help.

"Two days before the funeral, Will changed his mind and decided to come. He phoned the house to let me know. My mother took the call and told him I'd gone to lunch with this man. She went on and on about how helpful he'd been and how much I'd appreciated his being there. Will hung up the phone and went ballistic."

Tori turned onto the street that led to the hospital. "When I didn't hear from him for the next three days, I gave him a call. He ripped me up one side and down the other—pretty much accused me of having an affair, which couldn't have been further from the truth. That was when I knew it was over. I came home two weeks later with divorce papers. End of story."

Tori pulled into the hospital parking lot. How trivial it all sounded in the retelling—two proud, stubborn people who'd had a misunderstanding and couldn't forgive each other. But at the time it hadn't been trivial at all. It had been like the end of the world.

"And the man?" Lauren spoke as if she already knew. "Who was he?"

Tori pulled into a parking spot, turned off the engine, and unfastened her seat belt. "Congressman Garn Prescott, of course—your father."

After Natalie's phone call Sheriff Abner Sweeney had driven back to town to pick up his wife. Bethel sat beside him now, her plump body rigid, her narrow-lipped mouth fixed in a straight line. She'd agreed to go with Abner. But he could sense her inner struggle. She had cast her daughter out for her sin. Now righteous judgment warred with compassion and motherly love.

Bethel, a preacher's only daughter, had grown up with her father's ironclad values. She'd raised her children as she had been raised, never dreaming that she'd one day be faced with an agonizing choice like this one.

"So Vonda and the baby are all right?" she asked Abner for perhaps the third time.

"That's what Natalie told me."

"But she doesn't know her husband's dead?"

"That's what I understand. Natalie said it was our place to tell her."

"You tell her, then. You're used to doing things like that."

"Fine, I'll tell her. But you need to be there." Abner

was already wondering how Ralph had died. Natalie hadn't offered any details. Had Vonda's husband perished fighting the blaze? Or . . . but no, that didn't make sense. Why on earth would Ralph set fire to his employer's barn—especially if he couldn't make it out of the barn in time to save his own life?

Ralph's pickup sat in the graveled driveway, in front of Natalie's SUV. The old rust bucket wasn't fit for anything but scrap. He could sell it and give Vonda the money toward a decent car. Lord knows, she was going to need it.

Strange that Ralph wouldn't have driven to fight the fire. Covering the distance on foot would have wasted precious minutes. Had somebody else picked him up? Or had he walked to the barn before the fire started?

For now, those questions would have to wait. Abner had a job to do, but he was also a father. His helpless, grieving daughter needed him, and he would be there for her.

Natalie came out onto the stoop as they pulled up. She hadn't been friendly to Abner since that mess with Beau last spring. But at least she'd come when Vonda needed help.

"Your daughter and the baby seem fine," she said before they could speak. "But just to be sure, you'll want to get them checked out by a real doctor, at the hospital."

"Thank you," Abner said. "I've been wondering about Ralph. How did he—"

"They found his body after the fire was out. That's all I know."

"And they don't know what started it?"

"You'll have to ask the fire crew. Right now, your daughter needs you—and I need to go." She strode out to her vehicle. By the time she drove away, Bethel had already hurried inside. Abner followcd her.

Vonda, looking so young and scared that it almost broke his heart, was sitting up in bed, clutching her baby in her arms. She was wearing a clean nightgown, and the sheets looked as if they'd been changed. But his daughter's face was pale, her hair plastered in damp strings around her face. She was gazing down at her infant son, as if she had no idea what to do with him.

Bethel was bustling around the room, straightening this and that, avoiding eye contact with her daughter. His wife would come around, Abner thought. It just might take some time.

"Hello, Daddy." Vonda managed a wan smile. "Would you like to hold my baby? His name is Ralph—Ralph Junior."

Abner took his grandson and cradled him close. The pink, puckered face, flattened nose, and tiny, waving hands tugged at his heartstrings—a familiar ache that felt strangely sweet.

Abner knew he wasn't the best man in the world. He'd skated the edge of dishonesty more times than he liked to think about. But he loved his family. The instant bond with this little boy was like the closing of a lock. Whatever happened, he vowed, he would protect this child and see that he and his mother never wanted for anything. He'd been wrong about a lot of things, like letting Bethel banish their daughter. But nothing could be more right than the fierce love he felt for this small, new life. In every way it made him want to be a better man.

Vonda looked up at him. "Daddy, where's Ralphie? He's supposed to be here."

Abner shook his head, knowing he had to face the hurt in her eyes.

"Has something happened to him?" Her voice broke. "Is that why you and Mama are here?" Her gaze widened as the truth struck her. "No!" she whispered. Then her voice broke into a keening wail. "No! Please, God, not Ralphie! No! *No!*"

"It's all right, honey." Bethel leaned over the bed to gather her daughter in her arms. "It was God's will, to pay for your sin and bring you back to us. We're here now. We'll take care of you."

Abner and Bethel had agreed it would be wise to take Vonda and the baby to the hospital. While Bethel got her ready to go, Abner stepped out onto the stoop and called in a pair of his deputies to investigate the fire. He would follow up on his own, later in the day. The blaze at the Tyler place was too well-timed to be an accident. He would bet money there was arson involved, maybe murder as well. And the key to it all could be his late son-in-law.

Abner had never thought much of Ralph Jackson. The boy was short on brains and ambition, and he hadn't made much effort to keep Vonda happy. But at least, with the Tylers, he'd had a secure job and a place to live. It didn't make sense that he'd risk it all by setting fire to the barn.

Maybe somebody else had set the fire and Ralph had caught them in the act. That could be reason enough to get him killed—but that theory would have to wait for the coroner's report. Abner was no Sherlock Holmes. But along with his experience and the reading he'd done, he knew how crime solving worked. If he could put this case to bed, it would raise his standing with the county government and the voters. Maybe, then, Clay Drummond would stop treating him like a damned stooge.

Bethel was taking her time getting Vonda ready for the hospital trip. *Probably a lot of emotion going on.* Abner was getting restless, when his gaze fell on Ralph's old truck. As long as he was here, just standing around, it wouldn't hurt to check it out.

He pulled a pair of latex gloves from the box he kept in his SUV, tugged them on, and walked over to the truck.

The driver's-side door was unlocked. No sign of the keys, but Ralph could've had them in his pocket. The floor was littered with empty Dos Equis beer cans and Snickers wrappers. Mummified French fries, cookie crumbs, and empty ketchup packets were lodged in the crease below the seat backs.

In the unlocked glove box, Abner found some gas receipts and a yellowed copy of the truck registration. Underneath these was a half-empty pack of condoms. *No surprise there. Vonda's better off without the cheating bastard.* But there was nothing here that might link Ralph to the fire in the barn.

Abner was about to climb out of the truck, when he saw that his shoelace was undone. Bending down to tie it, he noticed a crumpled plastic Shop Mart bag stuffed way back under the driver's seat. It was probably just more trash, but he'd be remiss to leave it.

With some stretching and grunting, he reached it, caught the corner, and gave a pull. He'd expected it to be empty, but the bag had a surprising heft to it. After dragging it free of the seat, he sat up, took a breath, and untied the knotted handles to look inside.

Abner's stomach lurched. Cold sweat beaded under his uniform. The bag was stuffed with cash—*lots* of cash, most of it in hundred-dollar bills.

Lauren sat on a folding chair next to Sky's hospital bed, listening to the labored sound of his breathing.

Lightly sedated, Sky was veiled by a misted oxygen tent. Fluid dripped into an IV tube connected to his wrist. A beeping monitor above the bed tracked his pulse and blood pressure, as well as his oxygen level, which had been fearfully low at first, but was beginning to rise.

She yearned to put her arms around him, or at least hold his gel-bandaged hands. But that, she knew, would only cause him more pain. The doctor had said he would live. Sky was young and strong, he'd told her. His vitals were good, considering what he'd been through. His second-degree burns should heal in a few weeks. But he'd inhaled enough smoke to damage his lungs—that was the real worry. Another minute in that burning barn would have killed him.

She gazed down at the modest diamond engagement ring on her finger—the ring she hadn't taken off in the three months since Sky had placed it there. She'd accepted his proposal without a moment's hesitation. But now she had to face reality and ask herself the hard question. Could she really do this—open herself to heartbreak again?

Mike, her first fiancé, had jumped off a bridge and drowned. Her father had died of a heart attack after shooting himself. Now she'd fallen in love with a man who took reckless chances for others, heedless of his own safety.

Lauren had heard how, last spring, Sky had been shot trying to save his worthless young cousin Lute. And in last summer's wildfire, he'd risked death, refusing to leave the ranch until every last animal was evacuated. This was Sky's way, throwing himself in the path of deadly danger for the sake of any living creature that needed him.

She needed him, damn it, especially now. But today in

that blazing barn, his mind wouldn't have been on their losing each other. And even if he'd known about the baby, he wouldn't have been thinking about their unborn child. All his intent had been focused on rescuing his beloved horses.

What would she do the next time something happened? And, ranch life being what it was, there would no doubt be a next time. How could she go on living if she lost him?

Lauren's agitated fingers toyed with her ring, twisting it, sliding it up past her knuckle, then back into place. *I can take it off right now,* she told herself. She could leave it on the side table and walk out of his life—move far away from here and never tell him about the baby. She had enough money to go anywhere she wanted. How hard could it be? Sky was the center of her world—but did she love him enough to face the prospect of losing him?

Settling back against the hard chair, she thought about Tori and Will and the forces that had driven them apart. Their divorce had been a bitter one. But Lauren could sense the fierce undercurrent of love that still flowed between them. How would things be different if, that one last time, they'd swallowed their pride and forgiven each other? Would they and their daughter be a happy family now?

What if she couldn't forgive Sky for the terrible risk he'd taken? What if she were to give up and walk away? Could she live with that decision for the rest of her life?

Rising, she gazed down at the man she loved to the roots of her soul. Sky Fletcher was who he was, and she knew better than to believe he would change, even for her.

Knowing what she knew, could she find the courage to build a future with this man?

With effort he opened his eyes, gazing up at her through the transparent oxygen tent. His cracked lips moved, forming her name.

"Lauren . . ."

She couldn't hear his voice, but it was enough. Her hand reached out to press his shoulder. "I'm here," she whispered, knowing it was true. She was his, and she was here to stay.

Will had been checked over, treated for minor burns, and released; but he'd refused to leave the hospital until Sky was stabilized and in the ICU, with Lauren watching over him. "I'll be back first thing tomorrow," he'd told the doctors. "Call me if he needs anything."

As they walked out to the parking lot, Tori keeping pace with his long strides, the depth of his concern prompted her to voice something she'd suspected for years.

"Sky's your brother, isn't he?"

"Right now, that doesn't make much difference," Will said. "I'd be just as worried either way."

"But he is, isn't he? I've always wondered. He's as much like Bull as you are, only in different ways."

Without answering, Will moved ahead of her and opened the passenger-side door of her station wagon. "Give me your keys and get in," he said. "I'm driving."

"Is that wise?"

"Keys." He held out his hand. With a sigh Tori opened her purse and handed him her keys. Regarding Will, she'd long since learned to choose her battles. This was no time for a useless argument.

He drove like he was angry—not at her, but at the horrific circumstances of the day. A treasured family holiday had been ruined, but that was the least of it. He'd also lost the barn on the brink of winter, with a storm due in, any day. Even if the insurance would pay much of the rebuilding cost, he couldn't buy time. He couldn't buy back the life of the man who'd died in the fire or the weeks Sky would need to heal from the trauma that almost killed him.

And he couldn't delay the trial, now less than a week away, with a possible outcome that could separate him from everything, and everyone, he'd ever loved.

Tori's gaze traced his defiant profile, lingering on the twitching muscle in his cheek. She knew Will, and she knew how much he was hurting. Part of her yearned to wrap him in her arms and tell him everything would be all right. But that would be a lie—the last thing Will would want to hear.

It was all up to her, Tori realized. If she could win an acquittal for Will, he would find a way to fight through and save the ranch. If she lost, the entire burden of the ranch, the barn, and the money problems would fall on Beau. In his own way Beau was as strong as Will. But he'd left once, years ago, after having it out with Bull. If things got bad enough, she wouldn't put it past him to throw up his hands, take Natalie and their baby, and return to his government job in the East.

"I got a call from Natalie," she said, feeling the need to break the uneasy silence. "Ralph Jackson's wife had a baby boy. Abner and his wife showed up and took them both to the hospital."

Will exhaled, easing his grip on the wheel. "It's a good thing they stepped up. I'll have Beau look into our insurance. Since her husband died in the fire, that should be worth something for the poor girl."

"How do you think the fire started?" Tori asked.

"Damned if I know. Everybody was supposed to be at dinner then. Nobody would've been in the barn."

"So when did Ralph go in? Did you see him outside fighting the fire?"

"No, but I was busy. He could've been anywhere. Maybe he was helping Sky get the horses out. When Sky's up to talking, I'll ask him."

"Maybe the fire was set, and whoever did it murdered Ralph. What do you think of that theory?"

"It's possible, I guess. There'll be an investigation and a coroner's report. Maybe after that, we'll have a better idea of what happened." Will lapsed into silence. Tori could imagine what he was thinking. By the time the investigation was finished, he could be far from home, looking at the world through prison bars.

Tori's memory shifted back to the night—barely remembered until now—when she and Drew had stopped off at the Blue Coyote for a late-night beer. She remembered glancing around to meet those absinthe eyes, and how their hate-filled gaze had made her skin crawl.

"It had to be Stella," she said. "Who else would despise you and your family enough to do this?"

"You could be right." Will's tone was carefully neutral. "But Stella wouldn't come on the ranch and set the fire herself. If she wanted it done, she'd pay or blackmail somebody else to do it. And she'd make damned sure nothing could be traced to her." He shot Tori a stern glance. "Leave it to the law for now. Trying to figure out who set the fire won't undo the damage. Besides, you've got more urgent things to deal with."

Yes, the trial. She couldn't forget that. Not when the worry was keeping her awake nights. She had a good case. Given the true facts, no reasonable jury would convict

Will. But something told her she'd be playing against a
stacked deck. Clay Drummond always liked to win, but
this time he seemed determined to the point of desperation. Something, Tori sensed, was very, very wrong.

Stella turned off the nightly news and poured herself a
glass of the finest Kentucky bourbon money could buy.
She'd ended the holiday with three wins in her column—
Will Tyler's barn burned to cinders, Sky Fletcher injured,
and Ralph Jackson dead.

When she'd heard the sirens around one-thirty, she'd
figured Ralph must've done his job, but she'd spent an
uneasy afternoon wondering what the chances were that
the fool would get caught and turn on her to save his own
skin. She'd asked herself, again and again, whether she'd
risked too much to strike at her enemy. Ralph was a weak
link. However the day went down, he would have to go.
It was just a matter of how and when.

Hours had passed as she waited for Ralph to call her
and demand the rest of the cash she'd promised him.
When no call came, she'd imagined the worst—that he'd
been caught and arrested.

After packing a valise, to have ready in case of a needed
getaway, she'd glued herself to the radio and TV for any
word about the fire. Not until the six o'clock news had she
learned that the fire was out, and that one man had died in
the blaze, presumably trying to save the horses. The owners of the ranch were unavailable for comment, but the
deceased ranch hand, Ralph Jackson, was being remembered as a hero.

A hero! What a joke! Stella grinned as she took another
sip of expensive bourbon. It wasn't often that fate played
into her hands. That it had happened today was a cause

for celebration. But she wasn't finished, not by a long shot. First thing tomorrow she would call Abner and make sure he took advantage of every chance to give the Tylers more trouble.

She could only hope Will's trial would go as well as the barn fire had. She could hardly wait to see Nicky's killer behind bars.

It was 1:15 a.m. when Sheriff Abner Sweeney parked behind the county vehicle lot, procured the keys to the department's tow truck, and drove it out of the gate. Twenty-five minutes later, he crossed the boundary of the Rimrock and switched off his headlights. With the November moon just bright enough to show the road, he drove to the bungalow where his daughter had lived.

Ralph's old pickup was still parked outside. It took only a few minutes for Abner to hitch the rear axle to the tow truck, pull out of the driveway and onto the road. What he was doing was illegal as hell and could cost him his job. But as he'd told himself all the way here, this was for the greater good. This was for his daughter and his grandson.

After he'd found the money in the truck, it hadn't taken long for the truth to fall into place. That kind of cash could only have come from one source—the person who hated Will Tyler enough to burn down his barn. She would have needed to pay someone to do the job, someone who worked for the Rimrock and had access to the place. That someone had been Ralph.

The money, mostly new bills, was evidence. It would likely have Stella's prints on it. Here, at last, was something that could link her to a crime.

His duty as sheriff demanded that he follow through and arrest the woman. But arresting Stella could expose the quid pro quo favors she and Abner had done for each other over the years. Worse, it would implicate Ralph, who was being lauded as the hero who'd given his life to rescue the Tylers' horses.

Ralph's baby boy could grow up as the son of a hero or the son of a criminal. The end result could make all the difference in his young life. That difference, here and now, was up to Abner.

Still driving by moonlight, Abner turned the tow truck onto a rutted side road that ended two miles later at a shallow, raw dirt gully, strewn with trash and the remains of before-hunting target practices. After unhitching Ralph's truck, he used the tow truck to push it into the gulley. The rusty old vehicle rolled down the slope and settled into place, right side up, amid the clutter of old bedsprings, empty beer cans, and ancient TVs with their screens shot out.

Abner took the canister of black spray paint he'd brought along and used it to decorate the doors and windows of the truck with known teenage gang symbols. The cash was still inside, stuffed under the driver's seat, where he'd found it. He'd deliberated long and hard about keeping it. The money could go a long way toward helping Vonda raise her son. But the bills had likely come from drug deals. If Stella, who had eyes and ears everywhere, decided to track it down and get it back, his whole family would be in danger.

Battling regret, he backed the tow truck to a safe distance, took a heavy gasoline can out of the bed, hiked down into the gully, and doused the old rustbucket, inside and out. Sooner or later, word would get around that

Ralph's truck had been stolen and burned. When Stella got the news, she would assume, rightly, that the money was gone.

As he climbed back up the slope, Abner poured a thin trail of gasoline behind him. Standing at the gully's edge, he lit the trail with a match and took off at a run. The truck, money and all, exploded in a giant whoosh of flame behind him.

Abner hung around long enough to make sure the fire wasn't going to spread. Then he drove back to town, replaced the tow truck, tossed the paint canister in a handy Dumpster, and went home to his family.

CHAPTER 15

True to his word, Will was at the hospital by eight o'clock the next morning. He found Sky sitting up in bed, drinking a protein shake through a straw, with an oxygen tube clipped to his nose.

"You look like hell," Will said, taking a seat next to the bed.

"I feel like hell." Sky managed a grin. Even so, he didn't look as bad as Will had feared. Where the soaked bandanna had covered his nose and the lower part of his face, there were only a few minor burns. His ears and upper head had suffered worse, his hands, wrapped in special water gel bandages, the worst of all. But the real damage, Will knew, would be from the smoke in his lungs. Sky could be a long time regaining his health.

"Dare I ask how things are on the home front?" Sky's eyes, though slightly glazed from pain medication, had recovered some of their old spark. "I take it the barn's a total loss. Do you think the insurance will cover it?"

"Some, but not all. The devil of it is, we've had three fires this year—the machine shed last spring, the wildfire, and now this! What if the insurance company cancels our policy?" Will shifted the chair closer to Sky's bed. "And the timing's a bitch with winter coming on. We're already salvaging material from the barn to set up storm shelters in the paddock. But by the time supplies come in for the new barn, even with all the hands working, it'll take weeks to get the basics up. They're cowboys, not builders. Beau's been calling around to get construction bids, but with money so tight . . ." He shook his head. "Sorry to burden you with this, Sky. It's a royal mess."

"I've got a pretty good crew working to finish my house. Take them. They can show your cowboys what to do."

"But I thought you and Lauren wanted the house done before Christmas, for your wedding."

"We did. But since we'll be putting the wedding off until I'm in better shape, the house can wait. The outside's weather-tight. It'll be fine."

"That would be a huge help," Will said. "Are you sure it's all right with Lauren?"

"We already talked about it. In fact, lending you the workers was her idea." Sky glanced around as the bathroom door opened and Lauren stepped out.

"Should my ears be burning?" She was making an effort to smile, but she looked totally wrung-out, as if she'd spent the night awake, sitting up in her clothes and worrying, which she probably had.

"Take this woman home, Will," Sky said. "She hasn't stopped fussing over me since she got here, and she was terrorizing the poor nurses all night. She needs to get some sleep and come back later—if they'll let her in."

"I was just making sure you got the attention you needed. Like now—for heaven's sake, you're out of ice." Lauren refilled his water glass from a pitcher on the tray. Sky managed a comic eye-roll.

Will chuckled. "Don't worry, I won't leave here without her. And thanks for looking after him, Lauren. I was worried about leaving him, myself, but I knew he was in good hands."

"I'll be fine," Sky said. "The worst part of all this is having to be here when you need me, Will."

Will knew the words carried double meaning. Whatever happened at the trial, Sky's help would be sorely missed—especially since, until his burnt hands healed, he'd be unable to ride or even drive.

Which brought Will to the news he was dreading to deliver. Sky might not take it well, but it had to be said. Will hardened his resolve. "We're going to have to sell off most of your colts," he said. "We're asking best offer. That'll mean taking a loss on them, but with the money situation being what it is, we can't afford to feed them over the winter. Beau's already sending out sale notices, not just to the Texas ranches but all over the country."

Sky's mouth tightened. Will knew how much work and care he'd put into selecting, breaking, and training the colts. The green young horses had been brought in to shore up the ranch's finances, in case the drought forced a sell-off of the cattle. Most of the cattle were already gone, at a loss. And with other Texas ranches in similar straits, nobody in the state was paying big money for horses.

"Damn." Sky exhaled, wincing with pain. "Some lucky folks are going to get a bargain on some great cow ponies. I know you wouldn't do this if we weren't scraping bottom. But I'd like to ask a favor. There are a couple of those colts I wouldn't mind keeping for myself. Would you let me buy them from the ranch at the going price?"

Will knew Sky must be thinking of Quicksilver, the sharp gray gelding that had become his favorite. And he'd likely want a good filly to breed with one of the Rimrock stallions so he could start his own herd on his land. But with the expenses of his new house, Sky wasn't exactly swimming in money, either. "Tell you what," Will said. "They're yours. Call it a wedding present."

"Not on your life," Sky said. "I know you're going to need every cent to keep the ranch afloat."

"We can talk about that when you're on your feet," Will said. "Meanwhile, let me know your choices. I'll make sure Beau doesn't put them up for sale."

Sky was about to answer when two hospital aides, dressed in scrubs and carrying a stack of folded linens, walked in. "Looks like it's cleanup time," Sky said, clearly trying to sound cheerful. "Get my woman out of here, Will. Take good care of her. See that she eats and rests."

"Don't worry, we'll all look after her," Will said.

Lauren took time to kiss her fingertip and touch it to his lips. "You rest, too," she said. "I'll see you later. Will, I left my car and my purse at the ranch. You can just take me there."

She let Will usher her out the door and down the network of hallways to the parking lot. As they walked to his truck, with his hand resting lightly under her elbow, he could feel her falling apart. She was rigid but shaky, her features braced against the emotion that was threatening to crush her. By the time they reached the truck, and she settled into the seat, her jagged breaths had become dry, racking sobs.

"Go ahead and let it out, girl." Will slipped into the driver's seat and started the engine. "You've been through a hell of a time, and you're worn to a frazzle. You're a strong woman—I've seen it and I know. But you don't have to be strong twenty-four hours a day."

Little by little, Lauren brought herself under control.

"Thanks, Will. It's just, seeing Sky like that, helpless and in pain . . ." She drew a long, tight breath. "Yesterday I didn't know if I could do this. I almost left."

"But you didn't."

"No, I didn't. And today he's doing better. But I was so scared! I never want to be that scared again!"

"Sky needs you, you know," Will said. "He's a tough man, and too proud for his own good, but I don't think he could make it through this time without you."

"I understand," Lauren said. "But that's not the reason I decided to stay. I stayed because I realized how much *I* needed *him*."

"Then all I can say is, he's a damned lucky man."

Will lapsed into silence, thinking about Tori—all the times she'd needed him, when he hadn't been there for her. That last time, when he'd raged at her over the phone, he'd actually been furious at himself for letting her down and leaving her open to another man's attentions. Hell, he'd known she didn't care about Garn Prescott. He'd known she wasn't having an affair. But between the stress of his father's illness and the fear of losing her, he'd just plain lost it. And that had been the end of everything.

Now there was a new man in her life—the sort of fellow who drove a sedan and wore cashmere sweaters and wingtips. Steady and stable, Drew Middleton was probably just what Tori thought she wanted. All Will's instincts urged him to stand up and fight for her. But he had nothing left to fight with. Even without the specter of prison hanging over him, he was flat on his back financially, and on the verge of losing the ranch. He had nothing to offer any woman, let alone a classy lady like Tori.

"You know who was responsible for setting that fire, don't you?" Lauren asked, changing the subject.

"I've got a pretty good idea. But no way to prove it."

"No more than I've got a way to prove Stella ruined my father, or that she tried to have his car rammed, and almost killed me by mistake. She's an evil monster, Will. There's got to be a way to bring her down."

She shifted in the seat, turning toward him. "I asked Sky if he'd seen Ralph inside the barn. He said no, but he'd noticed that some of the stall gates were already unbolted. People are saying Ralph was a hero. But what if he'd been paid to set the fire, and on his way out of the barn, he decided to give the horses a chance to get out—or make himself look like a hero—and then something went wrong, and he didn't make it out?"

"It makes a good story," Will said. "But with Ralph dead and the barn burned to ashes, we may never know for sure. For all we know, he could've seen the fire, run in to help, and passed out from the smoke. The coroner's report should tell us something."

"But you'd given the men the afternoon off. Why wasn't he home? And what about that old truck of his? Why didn't he drive it to the barn, unless he didn't want to be seen? Maybe if we looked inside—"

"The truck's gone," Will said. "When I drove by the bungalow this morning, it wasn't there. I'm guessing maybe the sheriff or his deputies impounded it."

"The sheriff—that's another thing," Lauren persisted. "What if he's on Stella's payroll, or at least owes her a few favors? That could explain a lot, especially about the way he's treated you."

Will shook his head. "Nobody puts much stock in Abner as a sheriff. But does that mean he's crooked? Like I say, there's no proof. For now, all we can do is rebuild and move on."

Lauren sighed, shifted in the seat again, and sank into

silence. Will had to admit her ideas made sense. But he was already dealing with more than he could handle. Somebody else would have to play detective.

He found himself wondering if Lauren had done anything about the transfer of the canyon land. She'd mentioned that she wanted to explore it first, but she and Erin had already spent time up there exploring to their hearts' content. On a stressful day like this, would it be crass of him to mention it again? Maybe so, but he was running out of time.

"I was just thinking about that canyon—" he began, then realized she wasn't hearing him. Lauren's head had sagged against the window. She was fast asleep.

Tori came out onto the porch as Will pulled up. By then the ranch hands, under Beau's supervision, were already clearing away the rubble from the burnt barn. With the aid of the farm-sized backhoe and bulldozer, they were setting aside any salvageable materials and pushing the rest into piles to be hauled off later.

Tori waited until Will had climbed down from the cab. "How's Sky?" she asked.

"Doing better this morning. But he'll be out of action for a while." He strode around the truck and opened the door for a drowsy-looking Lauren. "See that this lady gets some rest, or at least some coffee before she drives back to town," he said. "She's been up all night."

Tori took in her friend's hollow-eyed expression and rumpled clothes. "You look like death warmed over," she said. "Jasper and Erin are eating breakfast now. Come on in and join them—unless you'd rather just lie down."

Lauren gave her a flicker of a smile. "Thanks. Actually, I'm starved."

Tori had ushered Lauren inside and was about to follow her when the sheriff's tan SUV came roaring up the long gravel drive and swung toward the area where the hands were cleaning up the barn debris.

"Here comes trouble," Will muttered, taking off at a fast clip across the ranch yard. After a second's hesitation, Tori followed him. As his lawyer, it was her job to keep any exchange with Abner from getting out of hand.

By the time she got within hearing range, the sheriff was out of his vehicle. She could hear him shouting at Beau. "What do you think you're doing? This place is a crime scene!".

"Since when?" Beau stepped up to face him, looming over the short, chubby sheriff.

"Since the coroner's preliminary report came back this morning. It looks like Ralph Jackson most likely died from a fractured skull. To me, that spells murder. I can't let you disturb the evidence."

Beau's color was rising, and with it, his temper. "Look around, you lamebrain! It's already disturbed! Your deputies were here yesterday. They took photos, picked up a few things that caught their eyes, and left. Your people are done here."

Will was quick to jump into the argument. "Damn it, Sheriff, we need to clear this place to rebuild the barn. Every day—every hour—we lose puts us closer to winter. If you want to look through those trash piles, go ahead. But we can't afford to stop working."

Abner pouted beneath his trooper's hat. "You know, I could have you charged with obstruction of justice for destroying evidence."

"Hell, I'm already charged with that!" Will snapped. "What do you want us to do, put everything back the way it was? You're not even making sense. This is nothing but harassment!"

The situation was becoming a powder keg, about to blow, which could be just what Abner wanted—an excuse to drag Will back to jail. Fearing the worst, Tori stepped forward. "Sheriff," she said in a firm but civil voice, "you're welcome to look around, but this is private property. Unless you have a court order, we have no obligation to stop this work."

Abner puffed his chest, saying nothing.

"*Do* you have a court order?" Tori asked again.

"I can get one."

"Then please don't interfere until you have it." Tori's voice dripped ice.

"I'll guarantee you haven't heard the end of this!" Abner wheeled and stalked back toward his SUV. His oversized tires spat gravel as he drove away.

Beau gazed after him, shaking his head. "Now what the hell do you suppose that was about?" he mused out loud.

"I don't know," Tori said. "But I had the distinct impression that the sheriff was bluffing."

"I've got a pretty good idea who might've put him up to it," Will said. "But what we need right now is to forget Abner Sweeney and get this mess cleared away from the foundation. Let's get the hell back to work."

Feeling like a fool, Abner Sweeney gripped the steering wheel with sweating hands. His pulse was racing, and his prostate was acting up again. If he couldn't hold it till he got back to his office, he'd have to pull off the road and pee in the cold. To make matters worse, his personal cell phone was ringing, a call he knew better than to ignore. Slowing down, he reached for the phone in his pocket.

"Well, how did it go?" Hearing Stella's voice was like feeling a rattlesnake crawl across his foot. "Did you put the fear into those Tylers?"

Abner stifled a groan. "I gave it a shot, but Tori was there. When I threatened to arrest Will for obstruction, she demanded that I show a court order to put the barn site off-limits—something no judge would give me. All I could do was leave."

"That bitch!" Stella muttered, then continued. "But you told them your son-in-law was murdered, didn't you?"

"I told them I suspected it. They'll be wondering about that for a while." *Even though it isn't true,* Abner reminded himself. It had taken the retired surgeon who served as part-time county coroner about five minutes to determine that Ralph had been kicked in the head by a horse. Whether it was the blow that killed him or the smoke he'd inhaled while unconscious would have to be determined by a full autopsy. Either way, as he'd already told Stella, the boy's death hadn't been murder.

"Well, you'd better keep pushing those Tylers," Stella said. "Will Tyler murdered my Nicky. Don't give that bastard a moment's peace."

Abner ended the call, pulled onto the shoulder of the road, and emptied his bladder in the barrow pit. At least, so far, there was no evidence to prove Ralph had started the fire. But he was sick of being Stella's errand boy. When he'd held Vonda's baby son in his arms, he'd realized he needed to be a better man, and a better example to his family. But how could he walk away from Stella when she knew enough to destroy him?

Still thinking about her, he climbed back in the SUV and headed for his office in town. It wasn't like he'd done anything seriously illegal. But in exchange for interest-free loans, which he always paid back, he'd traded department information with the woman. And he'd looked the other way while she carried on her so-called business transactions. That night when he'd met Ralph on the road, he'd suspected his son-in-law might be running drugs for Stella. But he'd played dumb and let the boy go, partly for Vonda's sake, but mostly because he hadn't wanted to get crosswise with Stella. Maybe his sins weren't bad enough to get him sent to prison. But if word got out, his ass would get fired on the spot, and he'd never work in law enforcement again.

Now, with Vonda and her baby in the house, and two more mouths to feed, he needed his job more than ever. But the thought of what Stella would ask for next, and what she'd do if he refused, was keeping him awake nights.

Since her brother's death, Stella was becoming more and more demanding—like today, when she'd ordered him to drive out to the Rimrock and harass the Tylers just to make trouble. It was as if she'd become obsessed with punishing not just Will, but the whole family.

Abner had no love for the Tylers. But enough was enough. If Will's upcoming trial ended in acquittal—which it could, given the true evidence and a fair-minded jury—Abner feared that Stella's fury would push her over the edge. He dreaded what she might do—and what she might demand of him.

Somehow he needed to get clear of this mess. But how? Walk away, or try to arrest her, and the woman would use what she knew to take him down, or worse. Stella had trapped him—just as she'd trapped Hoyt Axelrod, Slade Haskell, Lute Fletcher, Garn Prescott, and poor, stupid Ralph.

All of those names were inscribed on tombstones now, or soon would be.

Was his name destined to be next?

Still unsettled by the clash with Abner, Tori walked back to the house. The dry November breeze bit through her thin cotton shirt, raising goose bumps on her skin. In her race to catch up with Will, she'd left her jacket in the house. Now her teeth were chattering.

Behind her, Will, Beau, and the crew of ranch hands had gone back to clearing away the barn debris. They'd be at it all day, until dark, then back on the job by sunrise.

Will had looked exhausted this morning, she thought. The strain of the ranch's money problems, the coming trial, and now the loss of the barn, all had to be wearing him down. But she knew better than to fuss over the man and insist he rest. Will wouldn't stand for that. He'd be out there pushing till he dropped. Some things never changed.

Natalie's white SUV was parked next to the porch. Seeing it, she remembered that her friend had promised to come by this morning and check Tesoro's shoulder wound.

She found Natalie in the kitchen, drinking coffee while Lauren finished a breakfast of bacon and eggs. Jasper had gone, and Erin was nowhere in sight.

"Your daughter's getting her coat," Natalie said. "Do you want to come out to the shed with us?"

"If it won't take too long." Tori had planned to drive into town to check her house and take care of some legal matters. Even with Will's case pending, there were other clients who needed her. She couldn't fall behind on the work that was her livelihood. "Lauren, you're welcome to go in and rest on my bed."

Lauren rose, gathered up her dishes, and carried them to the sink. "I'll rest better at home after a shower and a change of clothes," she said, loading the dishwasher. "Don't worry, I'll be fine driving back to town."

Erin burst into the kitchen, wearing her fleece-lined denim jacket. "I hope Tesoro's okay. He looked fine when I went out to feed and water him before breakfast."

"Even if he's fine, we'll need to check the wound and change the dressing," Natalie said. "Did you wash your hands, Erin?"

"I did. Let's go."

Tori slipped on the old work coat she wore around the ranch. "Be careful, Lauren, okay?"

"I will." Lauren found her coat and purse and headed for her car. Tori hurried through the back door after Erin and Natalie, who'd brought her black leather medical bag.

Until his shoulder healed, young Tesoro couldn't be allowed in the paddock with his roughhousing friends. A stall-sized enclosure at one end of the hay shed had been blocked off for the palomino foal and his mother, Lupita. The buckskin mare raised her head and nickered at their approach. "I bet she's lonesome," Erin said. "She doesn't understand why she and Tesoro can't be with the other horses."

"Smart thinking, Erin." Natalie set her bag on the ground outside the enclosure. "How did you figure that out?"

"Sky's always telling me to think like a horse, so that's what I try to do," Erin said. "I wish he was here. I really miss him."

"We all miss him," Tori said. "At least your dad said he was doing better this morning."

"Next time somebody goes to see him in the hospital, can I go, too?"

"We'll decide that later." Seeing Sky burned and bandaged could be too much for the girl, Tori thought. But then, her daughter was mature beyond her years. She would probably handle it fine.

"Remember what we talked about in the kitchen, Erin. Are you ready?" Natalie pulled two sets of latex gloves out of a packet in her bag and handed one pair to Erin. "Can you hold the mare out of the way, Tori? She might not understand what we're doing to her baby."

"Got her." Tori didn't have the Tyler touch with horses, but she was confident enough to grasp Lupita's halter and, with pats and reassurance, ease the mare to the far side of the makeshift stall.

Erin had put on the latex gloves Natalie had given her. Tori watched in disbelief as Natalie took Tesoro's head and stepped back to make room for Erin in the stall. "You're the one he trusts, Erin," Natalie said. "Go ahead."

The area around the gash in Tesoro's shoulder had been lightly shaved, and there was a gauze dressing taped in place. Singing softly to her trembling foal—as Tori had known Sky to do—Erin stroked his neck with her left hand, while her right gently peeled away the tape and lifted off the gauze dressing. "What do you think?" she asked, stepping back so Natalie could see.

The eight-inch wound, probably a skin rip from an exposed nail or splintered wood in the barn, didn't look as bad as Tori had feared it would. However, the sight of the torn edge, gleaming with ointment, made her knees go watery. She soothed the nervous mare, her hand gripping the rope halter, her eyes on her daughter. She'd never realized Erin was capable of doing what she was doing now.

"The wound doesn't look infected." Natalie spoke in answer to Erin's question. "But it's still oozing a little. I'd say we should keep the dressing on it at least one more day. Here." She handed Erin a fresh, ointment-coated gauze pad. Erin pressed it gently into place and secured it with lengths of surgical tape. The golden foal quivered, but didn't try to move.

"Good job," Natalie said as Erin stepped back. "It might fall off later. If it does, don't worry. Just let the wound heal in the air."

Tori let go of the mare. "You did great," she told her daughter as they walked back to the house. "I was proud of you. Maybe you should think of becoming a vet, like Natalie, one day."

"I have thought about it." Erin sounded surprisingly grown-up. "I wouldn't mind being a vet, but I'd have to go away for my schooling—for years. I don't want to leave the ranch that long."

"But, surely, you'll want to go to college," Tori said. "The money's there. Your grandpa Bull left it to you in his will."

"Dad never went to college," Erin said. "Neither did Sky. I want to stay right here on the ranch and train horses. I can learn all I need to know right here."

Tori gazed at her daughter, already growing so tall. This was a child speaking, she reminded herself. A child just short of her thirteenth birthday.

"I know the ranch needs money right now," Erin said. "I'm going to tell Dad he can use what Grandpa left me."

"Erin! Your dad would never take that money from you!"

"Not even to help save the ranch?"

"Not for anything," Tori said, knowing she was right. "Do you want to go into town with me this morning? We could get lunch at Burger Shack. You must be getting tired of leftover turkey."

Erin hesitated, then shook her head. "I'll stay here. I want to keep an eye on Tesoro. If I go, I'll be worried about him."

"All right. I'll see you later, then." Tori watched her daughter scamper off toward the coop to gather eggs for Bernice. Maybe by the time she finished high school, Erin would change her mind about college. But she had inherited her father's stubborn nature and his love for the land. Something told Tori that her decision was final. As a mother she could only hope and pray it was the right one.

After changing her jacket and collecting her briefcase, Tori went out to her wagon and headed for town. When had her little girl become such a determined young woman? she wondered as she drove. What would Erin do if the worst happened and the Rimrock was no longer there for her?

Tori remembered Will's request—that if he was sentenced to prison, she and Erin would move back to the ranch. She'd told him she'd have to think it over. But now, after hearing Erin's decision, she knew it would be her only option.

How would that limit Tori's life, especially if things became serious with Drew? But how could she even think about that when Will was facing years behind bars?

The jangle of her cell phone broke into her thoughts.

With her free hand, she fished it out of her purse. The caller was Drew.

"Hi," she said, realizing she'd scarcely given him a thought since the barn fire. "How's Omaha?"

"Boring. I missed my favorite lady, so I drove back early. I know you're busy, but I need to talk to you. How about getting together for lunch?"

CHAPTER 16

Tori had an hour-long appointment with a middle-aged couple, setting up a family trust for their grown children. After they'd left, she spent another hour organizing the paperwork and filling out the formal documents on her computer. The next time she glanced at her watch, it was almost noon—time to meet Drew for a quick lunch at the Burger Shack.

Seeing him again would be good for her, she'd told herself. Drew was easy to be with. He always knew how to make her smile. But anxiety gnawed at her as she drove to Blanco's only restaurant. Drew wouldn't have come home early on a whim. Something had to be weighing on his mind.

Drew had offered to pick her up at home, but she'd told him she had errands to run after lunch, which was true. It was also true that if they were alone in his car or her house, and he wanted to push her to a decision, things could get emotional. Meeting in public would be a safeguard against regrettable words and actions.

His car was parked outside the Burger Shack when she pulled up. He'd be waiting for her inside, maybe expecting some answers about their relationship. But she had none to give him. The past few days had left her more distracted and confused than ever.

The Burger Shack was crowded today, the booths and tables full. Behind the counter a cook was piling up a tower of takeout pizza boxes. *Somebody must've ordered for an army,* Tori thought.

Drew stood next to the booth he was saving. He gave Tori a smile as she walked through the door. He looked like a photo from *GQ,* in a gray sweater, khaki slacks, and a dark brown lambskin jacket. Tori, still in the frayed jeans and plaid shirt she'd worn on the ranch, with her hair raked back in a careless ponytail, looked more like a panhandler he'd invited in off the street.

Always the gentleman, he helped her with her coat before they sat down, facing each other across the red-checked vinyl tablecloth.

"How was your holiday?" she asked.

"Not bad. Eating dinner with my sister, her husband, and three rambunctious kids was better than eating alone. How was yours?"

He wouldn't know about the fire, of course. Tori shook her head. "Awful. It's a long story. Let's order, and I'll tell you."

The waitress had reached their booth. Tori scanned the menu, deciding on a tuna melt and coffee. Drew ordered a burger, fries, and a Coke.

"So tell me," he said. "Was your Thanksgiving really that bad?"

She told him, then, about the fire, the horses that had to be rescued, the injuries to Sky, and the dead man they'd found after the fire was out. Drew listened, his expression sympathetic.

"Good Lord, you weren't kidding, were you? It must've

been terrible, being there and going through that. I'm so sorry."

His hand slid across the tabletop to rest on hers. That was when the restaurant door opened and Will strode in.

He was headed for the counter—and the pizzas he'd evidently ordered for his work crew—when, out of the corner of his eye, he glimpsed the pair holding hands in the booth.

Tori saw him hesitate, as if resolving to ignore them and leave. But knowing Will, she had a feeling that wouldn't happen. Instinctively, she tried to pull her hand free. Drew tightened his clasp in a gesture of possession, pinning her palm firmly against the tabletop.

The two men had never met, but there was little doubt they recognized each other. Will would know Drew because he was with Tori. And Drew, sensing Tori's sudden reaction, would guess that he was looking at her ex-husband.

Jaw set, Will turned and walked toward them, taking his time, like a bull elk sizing up a rival. He was dusty, unshaven, and windburned, his eyes still reddened from smoke as he loomed over the table. "Will Tyler." His voice was a hoarse growl. "Pardon me if I don't shake hands. I've been shoveling ashes most of the morning."

Drew had risen. He was almost as tall as Will, but a few years younger and probably twenty pounds lighter. In a physical fight his only chance would be to run. "Drew Middleton," he introduced himself. "Tori was just telling me that your barn burned. I'm sorry. Nobody deserves that kind of bad luck."

"Something tells me it was more than bad luck," Will said. "But even knowing for sure won't bring the barn back. Sorry I can't stay and visit. I've got a hungry crew

to feed—even got the bunkhouse cook working the line."
He turned away, then glanced back. "You two enjoy your
lunch."

"You're welcome to join us," Drew said needlessly.

"Another time, maybe." Will walked to the counter,
paid with his credit card, and carried the stack of pizza
boxes out the door.

Drew had taken his seat again. He took a sip of the
Coke the waitress had left on the table. "So that's your ex-
husband," he said. "He's pretty, uh . . . formidable."

"Will can be overbearing." Tori stirred creamer into
her coffee. "But he's a good man and a good father. Erin
adores him. If I don't win this case, I don't know what
she'll do."

"And what will *you* do, Tori?" He captured her hand
again. "Something tells me there's more at stake here
than Erin's feelings."

"Of course there is. The charges against Will are
ridiculous, but for some reason the prosecution is out to
get him. I can't let an innocent man go to prison, especially knowing what being there would do to him, and to
his family."

"And to you?" His fingers tightened around hers. "Are
you still in love with him, Tori?"

Her heart gave a thud, like a rock hitting the bottom of
a well. "Of course not. We've stayed friends for Erin's
sake. But when we were married, we drove each other
crazy. Most of the time I can barely tolerate the man."

He released her hand as the waitress brought their
meals and set them on the table, but his light hazel eyes
continued to hold hers. "I'm not a fool," he said. "You're
the woman of my dreams, and I want you for keeps. But
when you're in my arms, I need to know it's me you're

thinking about, not another man. I understand that you have to put this trial behind you. But once it's done, whatever the outcome, I'll need you to give me an answer."

"I understand." Tori poked at the sandwich on her plate, her appetite gone. "You've been an angel of patience, Drew. I promise I won't keep you waiting much longer."

"I'm holding you to that. If you say yes to me, I expect it to be a hundred percent. No hanging on to the past, agreed?"

"Of course. That would be the only way." *And it would,* Tori thought, *but maybe it is time.* For the past eight years, she'd been living in limbo, caught between her work in town and the ranch, never moving beyond that half-life with Will that was more than friendship, yet no longer a marriage.

Now she'd been given a chance to change all that. Drew was a good man—intelligent, sensitive, kind, and patient. She was physically attracted to him—not in love yet, but she could be, once the baggage with Will dropped away. She could almost imagine saying yes to him.

But what about Erin?

Drew picked up a French fry, swirled it in the ketchup on his plate, and put it down again. It appeared he had no more appetite than Tori did.

"What is it?" she asked. "Is there something you haven't told me?"

"You're very perceptive," he said. "As a matter of fact, there is. It's the reason I came back here early—to talk it over with you."

"Tell me," she said.

"I've been offered a new job—assistant principal at a big school in a wealthy district that can afford to pay teachers what they're worth. I'd be making twice what I make here, to say nothing of the chance to move up the ladder. The job would start spring semester."

"So, have you said yes?" Tori spoke calmly, but her head was already spinning with the implications of what she'd just heard.

"I promised them an answer within two weeks," he said. "If I take the job, my assistant could handle things here till they found a replacement. It's short notice, but given what the job could do for my career track, I can't imagine turning it down."

"And where is this educator's paradise?" Tori struggled to ignore the flip-flopping sensation in her stomach.

"Seattle—a great area close to the university. You could find plenty of legal work, or even go back to school if you wanted. You could—" He broke off with a nervous laugh. "Why are you staring at me like that? Don't you know I'm asking you to come with me? With a ring on your finger or without—your choice. This isn't really a proposal, unless . . ." He reached over and captured her hand again "Unless you want it to be." He paused, an uncertain look creeping over his handsome features. "So what do you think?"

Tori found her voice. "I'm just wondering about Erin."

"She'd love it," he said. "Beautiful, green city, lots of culture, friends, and things to do. You could put her in a good private school, take her on trips, give her a chance to learn about the world beyond Blanco Springs . . ." He shook his head. "Sorry. I know I'm rushing you. I know you need to focus on the trial. Just promise me you'll keep it in mind. That's all I ask."

Tori willed herself to breathe. "I will. Don't expect much from me until the trial's over. But when it's done, you'll have my decision."

"I understand, and I won't push you." He released her hand and glanced down at her tuna melt. "Your food's gone cold. Let me order you something else."

"Thanks, but I'm a bit emotional right now." She rose and reached for her coat. "I hope you'll give me a rain check when things calm down."

"Sure. But you'll think about what I said, won't you?" He got up to walk her to her wagon.

"Of course." How could she *not* think about it?

She was still thinking about it as she drove back to the ranch. Drew's proposal—or whatever it had been—had caught her like a flash flood in a narrow draw, leaving her shaken and confused.

She should have turned him down on the spot and saved both of them the pain of uncertainty. So why hadn't she? Maybe there was a reason. Maybe leaving Blanco Springs and going to Seattle with Drew could turn out to be the best decision she'd ever made—for herself, as well as for Erin, who'd never experienced the world outside rural Texas. Or it could turn out to be a disaster for all concerned. Either way, she couldn't make an intelligent choice until after the trial.

As she pulled up to the house, she could see the work crew clearing away the ruins of the barn. Will was with them, looming over the others as he paused to shout directions or stooped to help drag a heavy timber free of the rubble. He would work until he dropped from exhaustion and never say a word about what was bothering him. That was Will's way when he was worried, especially if he happened to be unhappy with *her.*

Seeing her with Drew hadn't sat well with him, she knew. Oh, he'd hidden it, but Tori knew the signs. He'd been too polite, too congenial, too cool. And while he was talking to Drew, he'd scarcely given her a glance.

She'd planned to stay in town overnight, for some needed quiet time. But that had been before Drew called and before Will had shown up at the Burger Shack. Now, although it shouldn't be allowed to matter, she'd felt compelled to come back to the ranch. She needed to let Will know she was here.

Beau's Jeep was gone, and Erin was nowhere in sight. Inside the house Tori found a note on her daughter's closed bedroom door.

In case anybody wonders, I went to the hospital with Beau and Natalie. Natalie had a doctor's appointment. Beau wanted to visit Sky. I did, too, so they let me tag along. See you later.

The house was quiet. Bernice was probably napping, and Tori had seen Jasper on the Kubota yard tractor, hovering around the workers who were clearing the barn. Even if he couldn't work, the old cowboy would want to be part of the action, and maybe do some supervising.

Savoring the silence, Tori sank into the cushions of the well-worn leather sofa. The stress of the past few weeks was getting to her. She'd forgotten the last time she'd had a decent night's sleep. It felt good just to sit here in the familiar stillness and close her eyes for a moment . . . just for a moment . . .

Will had come back to the house to phone the insurance company, submit some forms on line, and order a batch of supplies for the new barn. He was headed down the hall to the ranch office and happened to glance into the living room. Tori was on the couch, fast asleep.

He'd seen her drive up to the house about an hour ago,

but he'd been too preoccupied with the barn work to pay much attention. Now he found himself wondering why she hadn't stayed in town with her new boyfriend.

Giving in to an urge, he walked into the room and stood looking down at her. She was curled on her side, her knees tucked up, her head resting on a cushion. Tangles of spun-gold hair framed her face and spilled over the suede pillow. Shadows of weariness rimmed her closed eyes. Seeing her in her sleep, he realized how tired she must be and how much of herself she'd given to helping him.

As always, Will had counted on her competence and her willingness to do her job, whatever it took. Only today, seeing her holding hands with Drew Middleton, had it hit him how much he'd taken her for granted. Tori was a beautiful, intelligent, sexy woman. He needed her like he needed air to breathe and water to drink. But needing her wasn't enough—not unless he had something she needed in return. And Middleton seemed to be filling her needs just fine.

Seeing her with the man today had damn near killed him. He'd managed to keep a civil tongue, but it had been all he could do to keep from smashing his fist into that smug, pretty-boy face. Drew Middleton was well-educated, as was Tori. He probably had more interesting things to talk about than horses and cattle and the coming weather. The fancy bastard probably knew his way around the bedroom, too.

Will cursed under his breath. Why was he torturing himself like this? He had more pressing worries than holding on to his woman—not that she was his anymore. Legally, she hadn't been his for eight years—and there wasn't a damned thing he could do about that.

His jaw tightened as he gazed down at her, holding back emotions he had no right to feel. He ached to lean down and taste those plum-ripe lips in the secret hope they would soften to his kisses; but no, that wouldn't be smart. If she pushed him away, he wouldn't be able to stand it.

He settled for lifting the woolen afghan off the back of the sofa, unfolding it, and laying it gently over her body. As it settled into place, she whimpered, stirred, and opened her eyes.

Will's heart dropped for an instant. "Sorry, I didn't mean to wake you," he said.

"Did you . . . need something, Will?" Her voice sounded muzzy, the way he remembered from those long-ago mornings when they'd awakened early to make love before starting the day.

He shook his head. "I just wanted you to be warm. Go back to sleep."

"No . . . 's all right," she muttered, sitting up. "I was out cold. What time is it? Is Erin back?"

"It's almost four, and no, she's not back." Will hesitated, knowing he should keep silent, but needing to clear the air. "About today—"

"Drew's a friend. He says he'd like to be more than that, but I've told him I need to focus on the trial for now."

"So you still haven't slept with him?" Will could have bitten his tongue off, but it was too late to take back the question.

Tori raked back her hair, tightening the fabric of her blouse over one breast. Will cursed himself silently for noticing.

"Not that it's any of your business," she said, "but no, I still haven't. This is no time for a heavy relationship, especially since I've got Erin to think about." She stood, tucking her blouse into her jeans. "Trust me on this. Whatever happens, in the end, I'll do what's best for our daughter."

"Does that include moving back to the ranch?"

"Don't push me, Will. I said I'd think about it."

"It's what Erin wants. She told me."

"So you've been lobbying her behind my back?" Annoyance sparked a fire in her eyes.

"You know I wouldn't do that. Erin was the one who brought it up to me."

Tori's shoulders sagged. She shook her head. "Anyway, it isn't going to matter, because I'm going to win your case. When that's behind us, the rest will fall into place."

"With you, me, Erin, and what's-his-name. Right?" Will knew better, but he couldn't resist the jab.

"Don't make this any harder than it is," she said in a flat voice. "Just don't."

Her face was close to his, her gaze coldly defiant. Will fought the urge to seize her in his arms and kiss away all the anger, all the bitterness between them. But something told him it would take a lot more than kissing to accomplish that.

The tension was broken by the sound of footsteps and voices across the porch. An instant later, Natalie, Beau, and Erin burst inside.

"Hi, Mom," Erin said. "I thought you were staying in town."

"I changed my mind," Tori said, causing Will to wonder if she'd changed plans because he would have known she was with Middleton.

"How's Sky?" he asked.

"Mending," Beau said. "But he's not happy about being out of action when he's needed here. I did have some news for him. You'll be interested, too." He'd brought a folded newspaper inside. Laying it on the coffee table, he opened it to the regional news page.

"Right here. I bought a paper in the hospital gift shop and just happened to see this." He pointed to a brief article accompanied by a grainy news photo. The headline read, *WOMAN WANTED FOR ARMED ROBBERY.*

Will scanned the short paragraph that began, *The robber of a Wichita Falls pharmacy has been identified as Marie Fletcher, shown in the above surveillance photo. Anyone knowing this woman's whereabouts . . .*

Will studied the blurred photo. The long-legged figure shown at the pharmacy counter was wearing a hooded sweatshirt and a baseball cap. But she'd happened to glance up at the wrong moment. The camera had caught the long, sharp face, the fierce dark eyes, and the white slash of a scar from temple to chin. It was Marie, all right.

"So Sky's cousin is up to her old tricks," Will muttered, handing the paper back to Beau. "Looks like she might've been a little careless this time. You say you showed this to Sky?"

"I did. Sky said he'd washed his hands of her. Can't say I blame him after the woman shot Jasper, likely murdered her own brother, and damn near killed Lauren. I just hope she ends up behind bars, where she belongs."

"Even with all that, I can't help feeling sorry for her," Natalie said. "What chance did she have, growing up in that horrible family, and then having her ex-husband slash her face?"

"Sky grew up in the same family, and he's got his own scars," Beau said. "Everybody has choices. Marie made hers."

"Hey, I smell something good!" Erin dashed toward the kitchen doorway, where Bernice had just appeared. "Is it brownies?"

"It is, honey," Bernice said. "I just took a batch out of

the oven and iced them. I can already hear Jasper at the back door. He's got a nose like an old coyote! Who else is hungry?"

"Me!" Erin bounded into the kitchen.

"Me too," Beau said. "But I'll have to grab one and eat on the run. I've got to get back to work."

"Count me in," Natalie said, laughing. "After all, I'm eating for two! How about you, Tori?"

"Sure. I . . . didn't eat much lunch." She moved toward the kitchen, paused, then turned back. "Will? Are you coming?"

Will hesitated, then shook his head and turned away. One more memory of the family gathered around the kitchen table, talking and laughing, would be enough to break him. In his mind he was already distancing himself from the things he loved—the things that, days from now, if the trial went badly, would no longer be part of his life.

Ralph Jackson's funeral took place the following Monday afternoon in the Community Church on the outskirts of town. Glancing back from his seat in the front pew, Abner experienced a rare sense of satisfaction. The small chapel was filled to the doors. Bethel's friends in the congregation had come to support her, which was to be expected. But what pleased him most was that the back rows were filled by folks from the Rimrock.

True, Abner wasn't on friendly terms with the Tylers. But according to custom, when a family death occurred, differences were put aside long enough to pay respects. Will Tyler, looking drawn and restless, was seated on the aisle, with his young daughter beside him. No sign of Tori, but someone had mentioned she was in court today. Beau was there with Natalie. Sky, still looking raw

around the edges, had come with the Prescott girl. Even
Jasper was there, wearing a twenty-year-old brown suit
that was too big for his age-shrunken body. The row behind them was filled with cowhands who'd worked with
Ralph.

All in all, it's a nice turnout. Really nice, Abner thought.
And the medical examiner had been thoughtful enough to
release the body for a timely funeral. Ralph's death had
been ruled a tragic accident, a consequence of his trying
to save the Tylers' horses. By now, the burnt truck had
been found. The evidence showed it had been stolen and
vandalized, probably by a teenage gang. Thanks to Abner,
no one would ever know the truth about Ralph—except
maybe Stella, who had every reason to keep it to herself.

Abner's family filled the entire front pew of the little
church. Bethel sat beside him, putting on a good show of
grief for a woman who'd detested her son-in-law. Vonda,
in black, wept quietly as she soothed her baby. She was
still a pretty girl—pretty enough, hopefully, to find a better husband than Ralph had been. Next to Vonda, the other
Sweeney children sat in descending order, like steps.
Even the younger ones were awed into silence by the oc-
casion. They sat with their arms folded, and their feet, in
hand-me-down shoes, dangling from the bench.

The Tylers' insurance had paid for the funeral. It
would also pay out a handsome benefit to Vonda and her
child; and Ralph would go down in memory as the hero
who'd sacrificed his life for his employer's horses. Abner
smiled to himself. *All in all, things could be worse.*

Sometimes the ends really did justify the means.

Will had given the men who'd known Ralph a couple
of hours off to attend the service, but no time to socialize

afterward. The work on the barn couldn't wait any longer. By now, the rubble had been cleared off the foundation, and, with the help of Sky's construction crew, the walls were being framed. So far, the cold, dry weather had held. But nobody had forgotten the norther that had frozen the pastures and paralyzed the ranch for days. Another storm could blow in at any time.

Will had driven his pickup to the funeral, with Jasper riding shotgun and Sky, Lauren, and Erin crowded into the backseat. Now, as they turned off the main road and onto the gravel drive that led up to the house, Will remembered Lauren's invitation. Last night she'd announced that she had a surprise to show him, something that had to be seen by daylight—something that couldn't wait.

There'd been no need to explain. Today was Monday. With the trial on Wednesday, and so many things left undone, Will's time was running out.

Pressed by the need to get the barn up, Will had tried to put her off. But Lauren had been insistent. Sky, newly home from the hospital, had backed her. So had Jasper, who seemed to know more than he was telling. "It's a damned conspiracy," Will groused. But he couldn't help being intrigued. Something was up—and there was only one way to find out what it was.

Half an hour later, they'd changed out of their funeral clothes and met again on the porch, wearing warm coats, gloves, and hats. Jasper was tired after the funeral, and Sky was under doctor's orders to rest, so the two of them wouldn't be going along. But Beau had gotten wind of the adventure and declared himself in. He'd even offered to drive the secondhand Kawasaki four-seater UTV that Will had bought at auction last year, when the ranch was flush. The big, rugged four-wheeler had already been put up for sale. All the more reason to use it while they still could.

Will waited on the porch with his daughter and Lauren while Beau found the open-topped vehicle in the shed, started it up, and brought it around to the front of the house. Minutes later, they'd left the heart of the ranch and were rolling across the scrub-dotted flat toward the foothills that rimmed the escarpment.

Seated next to Beau on the front passenger seat, Will found himself savoring the sunlight on his face, the cold wind biting his skin, the smells of sage and earth, and the faint, distant ring of hammers. The ice storm had blasted the landscape, leaving behind a frost-bleached wilderness. But even here there was life. Clumps of sage and cedar, impervious to the cold, still held their muted autumn colors. Jackrabbits bounded ahead of the massive tires, zigzagging off into the brush when they wearied of the game. A ground squirrel, less bold, flashed across the trail and darted into its hole.

The late-day sun blazed above the caprock. A golden eagle flapped off its kill to circle upward on wings as broad as a tall man's reach. Will's senses embraced all these things, holding them in memory, to keep for when he needed a place for his mind to go.

The vehicle's engine drowned out any attempt at conversation. Only when Beau turned onto a familiar trail did Will realize where they were headed. This was the way to the petroglyph canyon, with its bitterly disputed side-branch and rumored Spanish gold.

His pulse quickened as Beau parked at the mouth of the canyon, where the trail ended. From here the only way to go was on foot. It had occurred to him that Lauren might be planning to deed her land back to the Rimrock. But she could've done that at the ranch. Why drag him clear out here on a frigid and busy day?

They climbed out of the vehicle and trudged single file up the narrow, rocky path. Erin was walking just ahead of him. Will touched her shoulder. "What's this all about?" he asked her. "Did you and Lauren find the Spanish gold?"

"Not really. You'll see." With a toss of her ponytail, she strode ahead, following Beau and Lauren.

In the sheltered petroglyph canyon, the sound of trickling water echoed off the high walls. A covey of quail, drinking at the spring, whirred away at their approach.

Silent now, they turned aside and followed the water's path upward to the level of the smaller canyon. There they stopped. "This is what I wanted to show you," Lauren said.

The canyon, which Will hadn't visited since his boyhood, was much as he remembered. But in one place, where heavy scree had fallen down from the overhead cliff, something was different. In one spot the rocks had been cemented together to form a wall, about four feet wide and just as high. In its center was a marker of polished granite, with an inscription etched into its surface.

COOPER PRESCOTT
March 12, 1940–July 9, 1949
Sleep in the Arms of Angels

"This little boy would have been my great uncle," Lauren said, turning to Will and Beau. "He's the reason my grandfather wanted this canyon. Jasper knows the story. He's agreed to tell you when you get home."

She drew a folded document from under her coat and held it out to Will. "Here's a signed, notarized deed. It's yours on condition that this grave never be disturbed, and that I and my family be allowed to come here and visit it."

"Of course." Will had never considered himself an emotional man, but he felt the welling of tears.

Lauren wiped her own eyes and managed a smile. "Now," she said, "how about that dollar you owe me?"

CHAPTER 17

Clay Drummond's day had been long and tiring, and it wasn't getting any better. He'd just climbed into his white diesel Mercedes and thrust the key into the ignition when his cell phone rang. Even without glancing at the caller ID, he knew it was Stella. *The bitch is probably somewhere nearby, spying on me.* Her timing was too good to be a coincidence.

"What is it?" he muttered.

"Just checking to make sure you're ready. The trial's two days off. I'll be in that courtroom watching you every minute, and I don't want any slipups. If Will Tyler doesn't walk out of there in handcuffs, you know what I've got and what I can do with it."

Clay blinked, struggling to focus his eyes. The sun, a blinding glare through the windshield, was triggering a migraine. "Maybe, Stella, but you can only do it once. Ruined, I won't be any good to you. I'll have nothing left to lose."

"Then it won't be my problem, will it? Just put that

murdering bastard behind bars. Then we can negotiate for the tape."

She was doing it again, dangling that damned surveillance tape in front of him like a carrot on a stick. At times like this, Clay could almost imagine putting his fingers around her throat and squeezing until her breath stopped and her cat-green eyes glazed over.

"Who's the judge?" she asked. "Any leverage there?"

"Sid Henderson. He's a friend, but he's a pretty straight arrow. Anyway, the verdict will be up to the jury."

"How about Abner?" she asked. "Is he on board to do his part?"

"Why don't you ask Abner? You've probably got something on him, too. That's how you operate, isn't it?"

She laughed, a sound that reminded Clay of the villainess in a Disney movie. "Now, now. Play nice. We're on the same team, remember? I'll see you in court."

She ended the call. Grinding his teeth, Clay drove home. He wasn't looking forward to the trial. Yesterday in court Tori had whipped his butt in an assault case that he'd expected to be a slam dunk for the prosecution. The woman was good—damned good. As his onetime junior partner, she knew all his strategies. Clay had taught her well. Now his lessons were coming back to kick him in the face.

The worst of it was, he knew Will, and he knew the man didn't deserve to go to prison. Will had done what any protective father would have done—what Clay himself would have done in a similar situation. But he couldn't let that sway him. All his focus would have to be on doing his job, which was to win.

Clay thought about his career, his children, his marriage, and all the advantages that Louise's money made possible. Everything was hanging on the outcome of Will Tyler's trial.

If he lost this case, his life, as he knew it, would be over.

Stella kept her brother's ashes on a shelf behind the bar, where he'd worked and kept her company for the past two years. The black metal urn was a constant reminder of the childlike man who'd done whatever she asked of him—the only person she'd ever truly cared about.

With Nicky gone, the urge to pull up stakes and leave Blanco Springs was growing stronger every day. Even without selling the bar, she had plenty of money stashed away. All she'd have to do was close the place up, load her car, and head for Mexico.

But she couldn't leave until Nicky's killer paid the full price for what he'd done.

This afternoon she'd taken time to drive to the county parking lot and phone Clay as he was getting off work. She didn't like leaving the bar when it was open. But business wouldn't pick up until later in the evening, and the new waitress she'd hired seemed capable enough to manage without her for a few minutes.

She returned to find the place quiet, the country music low, the new girl polishing the tables. Only one customer was in the bar, a handsome, well-groomed man sitting alone in a booth, sipping Corona from a tall glass. Stella paid him scant attention until it struck her that she'd seen him before. He'd come in late one night with Tori Tyler.

Intrigued, she opened another Corona and sauntered over to the booth. "Howdy, stranger," she said. "You don't look like a cowboy."

"Is there some law against not being a cowboy?" His light hazel eyes took her measure, probably deciding she was too old for him. Damned shame. The man was some looker.

She laughed at his question, leaning over the table to give him a glimpse of her ample cleavage—but only a glimpse. "Stella Rawlins," she said. "I own this place, and I take pride in getting to know my customers. Mind if I sit?"

"Not at all." He extended a hand as she took the seat across from him. "Drew Middleton."

She accepted the handshake. His palm was smooth and cool, not horny with a cowboy's hard-earned calluses. "Well, Drew," she said. "Experience has taught me that a fine-looking man like you doesn't drink alone unless he's got troubles—most likely woman troubles."

A slight twitch of his mouth told Stella she'd hit the bull's-eye. "Not long ago," she continued, "I noticed you in here with a beautiful blond lady. Now I don't see her. Is she the reason for that long face?"

He gazed into his half-empty glass. Stella refilled it from the bottle she'd opened. "On the house, honey," she said. "If you feel like talking, I'm a good listener."

He managed a bitter laugh. "Don't get me started. I could be here all night."

"No problem with that. Talking will make you feel better. And not a word that goes into these ears will ever come out between these lips."

He sipped his beer in silence.

"So the lady dumped you and broke your heart. Am I right?" she asked.

He shook his head. "If she'd dumped me, at least I could get over it and move on. No, what she's doing is keeping me on the back burner till she gets things sorted out with her ex-husband."

"Her ex-husband?" Stella feigned surprise. "My-oh-my, the plot thickens. What's the problem? Do you think she's still in love with him?"

"That's crossed my mind. She's defending him in a trial and—" He broke off, staring at her. "Oh, Lord, I should've realized who you were. It was your brother that Will Tyler shot, wasn't it? I don't know if I should even be talking to you."

"Why not? Will Tyler isn't exactly my favorite person. Something tells me he isn't yours, either." Stella topped off his glass again. "Just curious, mind you. Where were you the night the shooting happened?"

"With Tori. She was in my car when she got the call from Will to come and get their daughter. I offered to drive her, but she insisted on taking her wagon and going alone."

"Why alone? Because she didn't want Will to see her with another man?"

He shrugged. "All I know was that she was in a rush. She wouldn't tell me much, but on the phone, I heard something about an *incident*."

"You say she was in a rush?"

"A big rush. I walked her to the door, pulled out of her driveway, and headed back toward Main Street. A couple minutes later, she roared past me, going at least seventy. She even ran the red light. I'm just glad she didn't have an accident."

He glanced at his watch, a nervous gesture, as if he'd become worried about saying too much. "I'd better be going. I've got someplace to be."

"Sure." Stella rose, slipped out of the booth, and moved

to block his exit for a moment. "Feel free to come back anytime you need a cold Corona and a listening ear, honey. But let me leave you with one thought. If Will Tyler gets off, chances are, your lady will go running right back to him. If he ends up in prison, she'll be alone—and lonesome."

Turning away, she sashayed back toward the bar, giving him a view of her swaying rump. He might or might not be back, but never mind—he'd already made it worth her time.

As his car pulled away, Stella found her cell phone and scrolled to Clay's number. If he was at home, he wouldn't pick up; but right now, that didn't matter. She waited for his voice mail, then spoke.

"I've found another witness for you. His name is Drew Middleton. Call him."

Curled on her couch, with her glasses on her nose and her laptop on her knees, Tori reviewed her opening statement for tomorrow's trial. How many times had she read through her notes—moving a paragraph here, striking a sentence there, arranging and rearranging her ideas? Having it perfect had become an obsession.

The lamp behind her cast an island of light in the house that was otherwise dark. By now, it was after eleven. What she needed was to put the files aside, get some sleep, and look at them with fresh eyes in the morning. But even then, she could miss something vital, something that might make a difference for Will.

For the past few days she'd spent most of her time at the ranch, but today, needing quiet time to prepare, she'd fled to her house in town. Erin had stayed with Will, who'd made it clear that he wanted an ordinary workday with no fuss and no emotion.

Tori wouldn't be seeing either of them again until to-morrow's trial. Beau would be driving Erin and Will into town, leaving Natalie to rest at home. Sky had wanted to support Will at the trial, too, but somebody needed to oversee the ranch work, so he'd offered to stay. Lauren, already in town, would be there and had promised to text him updates as they happened.

Erin was to be a key witness. Tori had hoped to spare her by using the interview she'd taped with Abner, but Clay had insisted on calling her for the prosecution.

Tori lifted away her glasses, cleaned them on the hem of her sweatshirt, and put them on again. She was getting tired, but she had to be sure she was ready. She'd tried hundreds of cases over her career, but none that mattered the way this one did. Will's freedom, Erin's happiness, and the future of the Rimrock were all depending on her performance tomorrow.

Heaven help her, what if she failed?

Will stood alone on the front porch, gazing out across the yard. The house was dark, behind him, and Erin and Bernice long since asleep. Moon shadows, cast by wind-driven clouds, flowed like phantom water across the bare ground. The windmill creaked in the darkness. Coyote calls echoed down from the foothills.

The cold breeze burned his cheeks. If the jury found him guilty, he could be going away for years. Would this be his last night on the ranch before prison gates closed behind him? Would tomorrow morning be the last time he awoke to dawn chores and Bernice's coffee—the last time he forked hay for the horses and cattle, broke the ice on the water troughs, and watched the sky fade from onyx to silver above the eastern plain?

Will's cold hands gripped the porch rail as he pulled himself back to reality. He'd promised himself he wouldn't think about the things he'd miss if he went to prison. The jury would find him innocent—he had to keep believing that. After all, hadn't he done what any good father would do—acted in defense of his child?

Tori would give her all to save him. He could count on that. He could count on *her.* She might not be his wife anymore, but she'd always been there for him and for Erin.

Hadn't she?

A picture rose from his memory—Tori sitting in the booth, holding hands with Drew Middleton. For all he knew, she could be with the man right now, and not just holding hands.

Damn! Will cursed himself. This was no time for jealousy. He had to trust Tori, had to believe she wouldn't let him down. She might be independent to a fault, but she was honest and true to the marrow of her bones and she always gave her best.

The night of the ice storm, their need for each other had broken down the barriers between them. Tonight he needed her again—with a soul-deep ache that had become physical pain. For most of his life, he'd tried to be like his father—tough, closed-off, priding himself on always standing alone. But he wasn't Bull Tyler. He needed the only woman he'd ever loved—needed to see her, touch her, hold her, just one more time.

He could call her. But no, it was late. By now, Tori would be asleep—and if she wasn't alone, he didn't want

to know. He would see her tomorrow, in court, at a polite
distance, when he put his life into her hands.

Will was about to go back inside when his cell phone
rang. His pulse leapt.

"Did I wake you?" Tori's voice washed through him
like a soft spring rain.

"Not even close. Something tells me I won't get much
sleep tonight. What's up?"

There was a beat of silence before she answered.
"Nothing much. I just wanted to make sure you were all
right."

"No need to worry," Will said. "I'm fine."

"Are you? Are you really?" she asked.

"Hell no. I'm scared to death."

"So am I."

Will forced a chuckle. "Glad we got that out of the
way. I might be scared, but I know you'll give this trial
everything you've got."

"And if that isn't enough?"

"We'll cross that bridge when we come to it, sweetheart, like we always have."

The endearment had slipped out, unbidden. On the
other end of the call, there was silence—then, at last, a
muffled whisper. "Oh, Will . . ."

"Don't go anywhere," he said, knowing that if there
was one chance in a million for them, he had to take it
now. Long strides carried him down the steps to where
his pickup was parked. A moment later, the truck was
rocketing down the road toward town.

Tori's porch light was off when Will pulled into her
driveway. The windows were dark except for the faint

glow of a lamp in the living room. Pulse racing, he walked up to her front porch and, instead of ringing the bell, gave a light rap on the front door. If she'd gone to sleep, he wouldn't wake her. But if she was inside, waiting . . .

His heart dropped as she opened the door. She was dressed in her baggy blue sweats, no shoes, her ponytail askew, her eyes set in weary shadows. The bridge of her nose was marked with a red spot where her glasses had rested. To Will, she had never looked more desirable.

Without a word she clasped his arm and drew him inside. He crushed her close, one hand reaching back to shut the door and lock it behind him. Their kisses were hungry, frantic. She moaned as his mouth devoured her, ravishing her lips, her tongue, her face, her throat. Lord, how he needed her—this stubborn, tender, maddeningly sexy woman who set him on fire every time he looked at her.

Her fingers tore at his shirtfront, buttons popping to the floor as she yanked it open. Will's hand found the hem of her sweatshirt and slid upward against her warm skin. She flinched slightly. "You're cold," she whispered.

"Warm me." The words rasped from a deep well of need. His seasoned fingers unhooked her bra, freeing one satin breast to fall against his work-roughened palm. *Heaven in my hand.* He stroked her, thumbed her taut nipple. Little whimpers rose in her throat. She arched against him, her body begging for what they both wanted so desperately.

His erection was rock hard, the jutting pressure threatening to push through his worn jeans. Tori's hand tugged at his belt buckle, her fingers eager but awkward—too slow for what he needed now.

With a half-muttered growl, he swept her toward the

stairs of the split-level house. Fumbling in their frantic haste, they left a trail of clothes along the upstairs hallway—his boots, jeans, and boxers; her sweats, bra, and lovely lace panties—all in a tangle. Naked, they tumbled into the bed, and then he was there, where he'd yearned to be—deep inside her, his swollen sex thrusting into that slick, honey-sweet warmth.

Her long legs wrapped his hips. Her hands clasped his shoulders as he lost himself in the silken feel of her, in the womanly smell and taste of her, and in the sound of her little love cries as he brought her to her climax, once, then again, until he shuddered and burst in a release that shook him like an earthquake.

Spent, he lingered above her, bracing on his arms. She lay with her hair fanned on the pillow, her lips swollen from his kisses. "Can you stay?" she whispered.

"For a little while. But not for long. I'll need to be getting back to the ranch."

"Come here." She pulled him down to her, stretching onto her side so they could lie in each other's arms. Will checked the urge to thank her and to tell her how much he loved her. This was no time for words, or for making promises he might not be able to keep. For now, all he could do was hold her close and be grateful. Whatever tomorrow might bring, at least this night would be his to remember.

Too restless to sleep, Drew Middleton drove slowly up Main Street and turned the corner toward Tori's house. He'd planned on staying clear of Will Tyler's trial, leaving Tori to do her job. But then, out of the blue, the county prosecutor had called him as a witness. Drew had tried to excuse himself, arguing that the only thing he'd witnessed was Tori's end of the conversation with Will. But Clay Drummond had insisted that was enough. Drew would bet a week's salary that Stella Rawlins had had a hand in this. He should never have opened up to the woman.

Tori had asked him not to phone her until the trial was over. Even after Clay Drummond's call, Drew had tried to keep his distance. But tonight he couldn't stop thinking about her. Was she all right? Should he let her know that he'd be testifying for the prosecution?

At least it wouldn't hurt to drive past her house and see if she was awake. It was late, but she might still be up prepping for the trial. If the lights were on, he could phone her. She might even invite him in.

As he neared her house, he could see that the place was dark. Then he noticed something else—Will Tyler's pickup, parked in the driveway.

Drew's hands tightened on the steering wheel as he resisted the urge to stop and do something he might regret. It was after midnight. If Will was here at this hour, it could only mean one thing. Marching up to the door and confronting him, or Tori, would only be an exercise in humiliation.

Tires spat gravel as Drew gunned the engine and roared away. What a fool he'd been, letting Tori string him along while, all this time, she'd still been in love with her ex-husband.

He remembered their dates, their kisses, and the way she'd always seemed to be holding something back. Had she cared for him at all, or was she just hedging her bets in case Will went to prison?

Either way, he was through playing along with Tori's games—and after tomorrow's trial she would know it.

Will eased himself out of Tori's bed and stood looking down at her. She lay in a pool of moonlight, the rumpled sheet framing one perfect breast. Her eyes were closed in sleep, the lips he had kissed softly parted. He checked the impulse to lean down and kiss her one last time. She needed her rest, and it was time he was leaving. When she woke and found him gone, Tori would understand.

The luminous digits on her bedside clock said 3:35. Time to go. If he left now, he'd make it back to the ranch before the cowhands started their day. He would help with the chores and finish in time to grab a bite of breakfast, shower, shave, put on a suit, and catch a ride into town with Beau. No need for him to drive his own truck—especially since, if things went badly, he might not be coming home again.

Following the trail of his boots and clothes, he dressed in the dark hallway, put on his coat, and went outside into the frigid dawn.

The town lay deep in slumber as he drove down Main Street to the highway. Even the cheap neon sign above the Blue Coyote had been turned off. Since Stella would be at the trial, the place would probably be closed for the coming day.

The ranch house was dark as Will pulled up to the porch, shut down the engine, and switched off the head-lights. The bunkhouse, too, was quiet, with no sign of anyone stirring. *Good.* The boys would snicker if they caught their boss sneaking back from a hot night in town.

Going to bed was out of the question. Even if it wasn't too late, he wouldn't be able to sleep. But at least he could make a show of coming out of his bedroom, dressed and ready for chores.

He had mounted the porch, when a voice from the shadows startled him. "I was wonderin' when you were gonna show up, Will Tyler." Jasper was sitting in his customary chair, wrapped in his old sheepskin coat. The dog lay at his feet.

"Reckon I don't have to ask you where you been."

Will was grateful the darkness hid the flush on his face. "What are you doing out here at this hour? It's cold."

"Couldn't sleep. Restless, I guess, just like you. I don't plan to be at your trial. Got an old man's plumbing and it keeps me goin' too much to sit long. But I'll be rootin' for ya. Sky promised he'd pass on everything he hears from Lauren."

"Thanks. I need all the rootin' I can get." Will took the empty chair next to Jasper's. Who knew when he'd have another chance to talk with the old man who'd been like a second father to him over the years? If he went to prison, Jasper might not even be here when he got out.

"Your dad would be right proud of you, defendin' your little girl like you did," Jasper said.

"I'd do it again—but I hope I never have to." Will rocked back far enough to put his boots on the porch rail. "You said Bull shot a couple of rustlers. Did he ever kill anybody else?"

Jasper scratched the dog's head while he pondered the question. "Nobody that didn't need killin'. And he never got arrested for it. Things are different nowadays. The law makes it harder for a man to stand up for his family."

"What do you think Bull would say to me if he was here right now?"

"He'd say, 'Give 'em hell, son. Do the family proud!' Since he's not here, I'll say it for him. Give 'em hell, Will!"

Behind them the front door opened. Erin, barefoot and wrapped in an afghan, pattered out onto the porch. "I heard voices," she said. "Is everything okay?"

"It's fine, honey," Will said. "We were just talking. It's early. You might as well go back to bed and get some more sleep."

"I don't think I can sleep. I haven't slept all night. I'm scared, Daddy. What if I say something wrong at the trial today?"

"Come here." Swinging his feet off the rail, Will indicated his lap. Erin eased herself across his knees and nestled her head against his chest. It had been a long time since Will had held her like this. Her legs dangled almost to the floor of the porch. She was going to be tall like her mother.

"Don't worry about saying anything wrong," he said. "Just tell the truth, like you did with Abner."

"But what if they try to trick me?"

"Your mother will be there. She won't let that happen. Mr. Drummond will be asking questions first. You know him. He used to work with your mother, and they're still friends. He's a nice man."

Will wondered about that last part. Clay Drummond could be a pit bull in court, but he didn't want Erin to go in afraid of him. Tori would be there to object if Drummond went too far, but if he could find a way to trip up a hostile witness's testimony, he would do it—even to a child.

Erin had fallen silent. She lay with her ear against Will's heart, as if memorizing the sound of it. Across the yard the light was on in the bunkhouse kitchen. The smell of fresh coffee drifted on the breeze. The men would be stirring, dressing, grabbing a quick cup before heading out to their chores. In the east the stars had faded, leaving a streak of pewter dawn above the horizon. Reluctantly Will eased Erin off his lap and stood.

His day of reckoning was here.

CHAPTER 18

The jury selection started at 9:00 a.m. and took less than an hour. Tori knew most of the citizens who'd been called. She looked for family men and women who would understand Will's need to protect his daughter. Clay tended to choose people who were new in town and might not know Will, or those who'd patronized the Blue Coyote and might be more sympathetic to Stella's loss.

There were some calls for elimination from both sides, but nothing serious enough to hinder the process from going forward. By 10:00 a.m., the jury of seven men and five women had been impaneled and sworn, and the trial— the *People of Texas* versus *Williston Tyler*—was ready to begin.

Wearing the gray business suit he'd always hated, and a blue silk tie that felt like a noose around his neck, Will took his seat next to Tori at the table for the defense. Today his ex-wife was all business in the black tailored suit and ivory blouse she favored for trial wear. There was no sign of the pliant, needy woman who'd lain naked in his arms last night. She was sharp, edgy, and primed for battle, a warrior queen in black stilettos.

The gallery was filling with spectators. Turning in his seat, Will flashed a thumbs-up sign to Erin in the back row. Dressed in soft blue, the color of truth, with a demure white cardigan that matched the bow in her tawny hair, she sat next to Lauren, who'd promised to take her outside if the proceedings became too intense.

Beau had taken a seat in the row behind the railing, close enough to whisper to Will or Tori if the need arose. The local press was there, as well as a flock of curious townspeople who had nothing better to do than watch what they probably viewed as a live soap opera. *They're like vultures gathering for a feast,* Will thought. *To hell with them all.*

Heads swiveled, almost in unison, as Stella entered the courtroom. She was all in black, her vermilion hair drawn back into a bun, her makeup subdued. She was dressed to play the part of the grieving sister, and Will had no doubt she would give an Oscar-worthy performance.

Every eye was on her, and she was making the most of it. Her dress and makeup might be subdued, but her walk was the familiar Stella strut—hips swaying, butt thrusting, putting on a show from the rear. A murmur went through the spectators as she walked down the center aisle to her seat at the rail behind the prosecutor.

"All rise!" The bailiff—a husky former trooper with a commanding voice—announced the arrival of the judge. Sid Henderson was nearing retirement after more than twenty-five years on the bench. A blocky, humorless man, with a jowly face and a thatch of white hair, he could be counted on to run an efficient court with little tolerance for drama. When it came to handing down sentences, no judge in the county was harder on convicted wrongdoers.

Will could only hope that issue wouldn't have to be faced today.

After everyone was seated and the judge had spoken a few words, Clay Drummond stepped before the jury box and waded into his opening statement like a heavyweight boxer lumbering into the ring. The man was good. Damn good. His claim that Will's reckless shot had killed a harmless man who'd already surrendered his gun was so compelling that Will might have bought it himself, if he hadn't been the one on trial.

But Will, who'd known the prosecutor for years, noticed something else about Clay. He looked as if he hadn't slept in days. His eyes were swollen and bloodshot. His voice was hoarse, his stance slightly wide-legged, as if he had to brace himself to stay erect. There was an air of desperation about the man. The more Will watched him, the more convinced he became that something wasn't right.

When her turn came, Tori was in top form. Will's actions, she argued, had been those of any responsible parent with a child to protect. He'd fired believing the victim to be a dangerous fugitive who wouldn't hesitate to overpower him and take his daughter hostage, or worse. The question before the jury was whether the defendant had acted in a reasonable manner. If so, they would be dutybound to find him innocent.

When she took her seat again, Will had to stop himself from giving her a touch of encouragement. Right now, he mustn't think of himself as her ex-husband, her friend, or her lover. He was her client; and the best thing he could do was leave her alone to do her job.

"The people call Sheriff Abner Sweeney."

Clay began his case as expected. Abner appeared nervous as he took the oath and described what he had found when he'd arrived at the alleged crime scene. At that point Clay introduced the bagged knife, a small switch-blade, as evidence and asked Abner to confirm it was the one that had been found in the victim's hand.

"Sheriff, were any fingerprints found on the knife?"

Abner looked down at his lap. "No. The knife appeared to have been wiped clean."

Will's pulse slammed. Nick Tomescu had been wearing gloves. But, surely, he would have left prints on the knife earlier. What was going on here?

"Sheriff," Clay continued, "why do you suppose the knife had no prints on it? Could Mr. Tyler have taken the knife, wiped it clean, and put it in the victim's hand after shooting him?"

"Objection!" Tori said. "Calls for conjecture."

"Sustained," the judge rumbled. "Please confine your questions to the facts, Mr. Drummond."

"Very well, Your Honor." Clay took a sip from the water bottle on the table. "Sheriff, did you find any evidence that the alleged crime scene might have been tampered with?"

"Yes." Abner was sweating. "A contaminated blanket had been laid over the body, and a key eyewitness, Mr. Tyler's daughter, had been removed from the scene before she could be questioned."

Will swore silently. So that was their game. If they could convince the jury he had something to hide, the implication of guilt was bound to follow.

"Sheriff, what did the defendant tell you when you asked to speak to his daughter?"

"He said she hadn't seen anything, and her mother had taken her home."

"Was it true that the girl hadn't seen anything?"

"No, that was a lie. I found out later that she'd witnessed the whole thing." Abner wiped his forehead with a crumpled handkerchief. "Mr. Tyler said I could speak to her in the morning, with her mother present."

"I take it that meant after the girl had gotten her story straight."

"Objection!" Tori was on her feet.

"Sustained." The judge scowled at Tori. "Sit down, Ms. Tyler. You'll get your turn."

There were more questions about the alleged crime scene and the evidence. Then it was Tori's turn to cross-examine.

"Sheriff, who made the nine-one-one call that summoned you to the scene?"

"The defendant."

"He has a name," Tori said. "Please use it. How did Mr. Tyler behave toward you when you arrived? Was he cooperative?"

"He was fine."

"When you arrived, did he appear to know the identity of the man who was shot?"

"By then, he knew it wasn't the robber. But when we pulled the helmet off the body and saw those tattoos, Will—Mr. Tyler—seemed knocked for a loop, just like I was."

"Thank you, Sheriff. No more questions for now." As Abner stepped down, Tori took her seat and waited for Clay to call his next witness.

"The people call Miss Erin Tyler."

At Mr. Drummond's words, Erin stood. Her legs were shaking, and her mouth tasted like she'd sucked on a penny. For an instant she froze, her feet refusing to move. Then she felt the touch of Lauren's hand on her back. "You can do this," she whispered. "Go on."

As Erin moved into the aisle and walked forward, she could feel every eye in the courtroom on her. Some were friendly, others curious. A few were even hostile. They all watched her as she took her seat in the witness-box and was sworn in by the bailiff.

. . . *Tell the truth, the whole truth, and nothing but the truth.* That's what her parents had told her to do. She could only hope the truth would help her father.

She glanced around the courtroom, feeling small and out of place. In a room full of stern adults, how could the testimony of a twelve-year-old girl make any difference? Then she met her father's blue eyes across the distance and remembered how much he loved and trusted her. The thought gave her courage.

Erin straightened in the chair as Clay Drummond stood and walked toward her. His mouth was smiling, but the expression in his eyes reminded her of a snake closing in on a baby bird. Her father had reminded her that Clay Drummond was a family friend and a nice man. But Erin knew better than to think he would be nice today. That was not his job.

"Do you know who I am, Erin?" he asked.

"Yes, sir."

"I'm just going to ask you a few questions. There's no need to be nervous."

"I'm not nervous, sir."

"Very well. To start, what did your father do after he shot Mr. Tomescu?"

"He got back in the truck and hugged me. Then he got out again. He called my mother and the sheriff and laid a blanket over the dead man."

"So he called your mother first, then the sheriff. He must have been in a big hurry to get you away from there. Did you hear the phone calls?"

"No, he made them outside the truck. But he'd told me what he was going to do."

"Why do you think he covered the body?"

"Objection!" Erin's mother said. "Conjecture."

"Sustained," the judge said.

"Fine. One more question. Did you see the defendant—your father—touch the knife in any way—like maybe pick up the weapon and look at it, or even put it in the man's hand?"

"No. I was watching. He didn't do anything like that."

His posture sagged slightly, as if someone had loosened a string. "Thank you, Erin. No more questions."

"You may cross-examine the witness, Ms. Tyler," the judge said.

Erin's mother stepped forward, looking as slim and polished as a movie star playing a lawyer on TV. "Erin," she began, "did either of your parents or anyone else instruct you in what to tell the court today?"

"They only told me to be honest."

"I'm sure you will be. Please tell the court exactly what you saw happen on the night in question."

Erin related the events, as she remembered them, hearing the radio announcement, hitting something in the road and blowing a tire, her father getting out, then seeing the motorcycle lights.

"Why didn't you get out with him?" Tori asked.

"I wanted to. But he told me to stay in the car. He thought he might've hit an animal."

"Is that why he took his gun, in case he'd hit an animal?"

"I think so."

"When did he tell you to lock the door and get down?"

"When he saw the motorcycle coming. I'm pretty sure he thought it was the robber."

"And did you get down?"

"Not all the way. I wanted to see, so I peeked over the window."

"Tell us what you saw."

Erin told the court what she'd seen happen. She did her best to keep her voice steady, but toward the end her throat began to quiver. Only now did she realize how truly scared she'd been.

"Think carefully, Erin," her mother said, handing Erin a pen. "What exactly did the man do with the knife? Can you show us?"

"It happened really fast. I didn't see where the knife came from, but he went like this." Erin demonstrated with the pen, holding her arm up and back as if she were about to throw it.

"And did he throw the knife?"

"No. That was when my dad shot him."

"Thank you." Her mother took the pen. "Just one more question, Erin. Did your father know you were watching?"

"No. I was afraid he'd be mad, so I didn't tell him. He didn't find out till the next day."

"So, when he told the sheriff you hadn't seen anything, he wasn't really lying. And he wasn't trying to hide anything, was he?"

"No." Erin shook her head. "My dad doesn't lie."

"Thank you, Erin." Her mother gave her a little smile. "No further questions."

Rising, Erin stepped down from the witness chair. As she walked back toward the aisle, she glanced to one side and saw the dead man's sister, Stella Rawlins, staring at her over the rail. A chill crept through her body. The hatred in those fierce green eyes was like icy claws creeping over her skin.

She'd faced the court and made it through the questions without a stumble. But now, for the first time today, Erin felt fear.

"The people call Mr. Drew Middleton."

Will heard Tori gasp. She thumbed through her notes, probably to see if his name had been added to the witness list. If it had, she could've been too busy to notice the update. She was clearly caught off guard.

Her body went rigid as Middleton walked in through the back doors, strode down the aisle, and took the witness stand. Her fingers gripped her pen as the bailiff administered the oath. Will studied her taut profile, unable to read her emotions.

"Mr. Middleton," Clay asked, "please tell the court where you were on the night in question."

"I was with Ms. Tyler." He did not look at Tori. "We'd been to dinner in Lubbock, and I drove her home."

"So it was a date?"

"Yes."

"And how did the date end?"

"We were in my car, in front of her house, when her phone rang. I could only hear one side of the conversation, but it appeared there'd been some kind of accident—an incident, she called it—and she had to go and get her daughter right away."

"Did you get the impression her daughter was hurt or in danger?"

"No. But Tori—Ms. Tyler—was in a big hurry. She rushed into the house, and a couple minutes later, her wagon passed me racing up the road."

"Why didn't you drive her in your car? That would have saved time."

"I offered. But she insisted on going alone, as if she was on a secret mission or something."

"Objection." Tori's voice was icy.

"Sustained," the judge droned. "Strike the part about the secret mission."

Clay cleared his throat. "Mr. Middleton, why do you think she was in such a hurry? Was it because the defendant, Mr. Tyler, wanted his daughter gone before the sheriff arrived on the scene?"

"Objection!" Tori snapped. "Calls for speculation!"

Clay shrugged. "Withdrawn. Your witness, Ms. Tyler."

"No questions." Tori shuffled her papers as the judge excused the witness. Middleton left without ever making eye contact with her. Whatever they'd shared in the past seemed to have gone sour. *One less thing to worry about,* Will told himself.

"Call your next witness, Mr. Drummond," the judge said. "After that, we'll break for lunch."

"The people call Ms. Stella Rawlins."

A murmur swept through the gallery as Stella took her time walking to the witness stand. Every eye was fixed on her. Aside from running the Blue Coyote, she'd kept a low profile in the town. For many of the spectators, this was their first chance to get a good look at the woman. *Damned if she isn't putting on a show,* Will thought.

After she'd taken the oath and stated her name for the record, Clay began his questioning. He looked more harried than ever. A bead of sweat trickled down his temple. His hands seemed unsteady, and his left eye had developed a noticeable tic.

Does Stella have something on him? But how can that be? Will wondered. Clay Drummond was a paragon of integrity, a leading citizen in the town, and the most likely candidate for a judgeship when Sid Henderson retired. Stella had brought down some powerful men, like former sheriff Hoyt Axelrod and Congressman Garn Prescott. But Clay? That didn't seem possible.

"Ms. Rawlins, for the record, the victim, Nikolas Tomescu, was your brother, is that correct?"

"Yes. Nicky was all the family I had." Her voice quavered on the edge of tears. The lady was good.

"And had you ever known him to act in a violent way?"

"Heavens, no! Nicky was slow and sweet, like a little child. I'd never known him to even kick a dog, let alone harm another human being."

"So the defendant and his daughter were in no danger whatsoever on the night in question?"

"No. Poor Nicky wouldn't have hurt either of them. He was most likely scared to . . . to death." She dabbed at her eyes with a lace hanky.

"I see." Clay gave the jury a meaningful glance. "No more questions. Your witness, Ms. Tyler."

Tori stalked toward the witness stand. "My condolences for your brother's loss, Ms. Rawlins." Her voice was level, even cold. "Are you aware that the deputies found a packet of cocaine on your brother's motorcycle?"

Stella's eyes glittered with suppressed rage, but her husky voice betrayed nothing. "That's what I was told. But I don't know anything about it. I'd warned Nicky not to fool around with drugs, but evidently he didn't listen to me."

"The gun he had was registered to you. Did you give it to him?"

"We kept a gun in the drawer below the cash register. He had access to it anytime."

"Were you aware that on the night in question, your brother was riding around on his motorcycle with drugs and a gun?"

"Objection!" Clay Drummond broke in. "The witness isn't on trial here."

"No, I want to answer," Stella said. "Nicky was an adult. I never told him what to do or what not to do. As long as he showed up for work, his personal life was none of my business."

"I see." Tori's tone was skeptical. "But do you agree that if he was carrying drugs, he'd be more likely to act in an aggressive manner—say, by drawing a gun or using a knife?"

Stella shrugged her ample shoulders. "How should I know? I always told Nicky to be nice to people. But I don't know how he might've behaved when I wasn't with him."

"But didn't you just tell the court your brother was harmless and would never hurt anyone?"

"Objection! Badgering the witness!" Clay protested.

"Withdrawn." With a knowing glance at the jury, Tori turned away. "No more questions for now."

"Mr. Drummond?" the judge asked.

"The people rest, Your Honor."

Stella strutted back to her seat, a stormy look on her face as the judge dismissed the court for a lunch break. The prosecution's case had proven little, but the trial was far from over. This afternoon it would be Tori's turn to present her case. And it would be Clay Drummond's job to rip holes in her defense.

Clay had brought a couple of ham sandwiches from home, planning to have lunch in his office. But once there, he realized he was too churned up to eat. Pouring himself two fingers of bourbon in a Dixie cup, he slumped at his desk. He knew better than to return to the courtroom with alcohol on his breath, but what the hell, he needed a drink.

He'd struck a few blows for the prosecution, but he was off his game, too tired and stressed to think straight. He'd hoped to get a few slipups out of the daughter, but Erin had turned out to be almost as poised and cool as her mother. Drew Middleton hadn't been much help, and even Stella had faltered under Tori's sharp cross-examination.

Will would be the afternoon's remaining witness. All along, Clay's best hope of a guilty verdict had been to convince the jury that the defendant had tried to cover up the crime. Now, once Tori had introduced the audiotapes supporting Will's motive, it would be the only remaining hope.

The jangle of his personal cell phone triggered a spasm in Clay's stomach. It was Stella. And he knew better than to let the call go to voice mail.

"You were dead on your feet out there, Clay." She sounded like she was talking through clenched teeth. "You let the Tyler woman ask me too many questions. And that little brat of hers made you look like a fool. You need to up your game. I want that bastard brought to his knees!"

"I'm doing everything I can, Stella."

"Not by me, you aren't."

"I'll get my chance at Will this afternoon. Don't worry, I'll give it all I've got."

"You damned well better. If Will Tyler walks out of that court a free man, you're finished."

The call ended in silence.

The clenching sensation in Clay's gut had become a sharp pain. Maybe he was getting an ulcer. Scrolling down, he punched in Abner's cell phone. The sheriff had gone back to work after his testimony. Now Clay was going to need him again.

"Are you alone?" he asked when Abner answered.

"For now. How's the trial going?"

"Still dicey. I'll want you back here to confirm that the knife was bagged at the scene and found to have been wiped clean of prints."

"No."

"What?" Clay almost dropped the phone. "Why, for God's sake?"

"You know why. I've been doing some soul-searching, Clay. If anybody finds out I wiped that knife myself before it was dusted for prints, and then lied about it under oath, I could go to jail. I've got a new grandson, a fine boy, to raise. I want to be there for him."

"Damn it, Abner." Clay gripped the phone harder. "I could ruin you!"

"That wouldn't be very smart. Evidence tampering, if it came out, would guarantee Will Tyler's acquittal. And I wouldn't be slow to let folks know you were in on the scheme. Call me to the stand, and I'll resign. Then I'll tell the truth. Your choice, Mr. Prosecutor."

With a muttered obscenity Clay ended the call. *What a time for Abner to get noble!* But the little toad was right about one thing. Clay couldn't touch him without incriminating himself.

Clay glanced at his watch. The lunch break was over. It was time to be back in court. And he had nothing left.

Will shifted forward in his chair as Tori introduced two audiotapes into evidence and played them for the jury.

The first was a recording of the radio announcement, describing the fugitive. The second was the tape of Will's urgent call to the 911 dispatcher, when he believed he'd killed the robber. More than any other evidence, these tapes supported Will's reason for shooting the man on the motorcycle and confirmed that he'd truly believed he was facing a dangerous criminal. Now it was time for Tori to call her first, and only, witness.

"The defense calls Will Tyler."

By the time Will told his story on the stand, most of it was old news. When he was finished, Tori had just one question for him.

"Please explain to the court why you covered the body and why you called me first, before you called the sheriff."

"In answer to both questions, I wanted to spare my daughter," Will said. "The sight of a dead man with a bloody hole in his chest would've haunted her for the rest of her life. I didn't want that picture in her mind. As for the call, I didn't know she'd witnessed the shooting. I only wanted to get her away from an upsetting scene to someplace safe and familiar. For me, that was even more urgent than calling in the law. That's all I have to say."

Clay's cross-examination was tepid. And the man looked even more ragged than he had that morning, his eyes sunk in shadows, his speech far from its usual machine-gun delivery. By the time he finished his closing statement, once more pressing the point that Will's impulsive shot had needlessly killed an innocent man, he appeared so exhausted that Will wondered if he might be ill—or maybe trying to garner sympathy.

Tori's performance, in Will's eyes at least, was flawless. As she faced the jury, looking spectacular and pointing out that Will had done what any reasonable father would do, one thought took root in his mind. If he walked out of this courthouse a free man, he wanted Tori back. He wanted her in his home and in his bed, with his ring on her finger. He wanted a normal, loving family life with his wife and daughter. And he wouldn't give up until he'd made it happen.

But right now, everything depended on the outcome of the trial.

So far, Will had reason to be hopeful. But juries could be unpredictable, verdicts surprising. There was no way of knowing what would go on behind those closed doors. A strong case didn't always win. And this one, based more on circumstance than on solid evidence, would be a judgment call. It could go either way.

With his freedom hanging on their decision, Will watched the jury file out of the courtroom, charged with finding on two counts—manslaughter and obstruction of justice. They could be out for an hour. Or they could be arguing into tomorrow.

Will, Tori, Erin, Lauren, and Beau drove the seven blocks to Tori's house to wait. Tori broke out cold sodas and snacks for everyone. Erin and Beau switched on a video game. The action crackled, heightening the tension in the room as they played. Lauren, looking tired, phoned Sky, then wandered into Tori's room to lie down. Tori and Will, too edgy to relax, alternately sat and prowled. Time crawled, minute by anxious minute.

Two hours from the time they'd reached the house, Tori got the call. The jury had a verdict. They piled into her wagon and rode in silence back to the courthouse. Sitting beside Erin in the backseat, Will felt his daughter's hand creep into his. He held on tight as they pulled into the parking lot and stopped at the side entrance to the courthouse. In the foyer they glimpsed Stella, in her tight black dress, hurrying into the courtroom ahead of them.

Pulse racing, Will took his place at the table with Tori. Erin and Lauren had moved forward to sit behind him, next to Beau. They'd scarcely had time to get settled before the jury filed back into the box and "Please rise" signaled the entrance of the judge. As they sat again, Will glanced across the aisle at Clay Drummond. Beads of sweat gleamed on the prosecutor's forehead.

"Ladies and gentlemen of the jury, have you reached a verdict?" the judge asked.

The foreman stood. "We have, Your Honor."

"Will the defendant please rise?"

Will stood, his expression frozen in a stoic mask. Beside him, he could feel Tori trembling.

"On the count of manslaughter, how do you find?" the judge asked.

"We the jury find the defendant, Williston Tyler, not guilty."

Will's knees went slack. He groped for Tori's hand, not finding it.

"And on the count of obstruction of justice? How do you find?"

"We find the defendant not guilty."

Not guilty!

As the words sank in, the courtroom erupted in sound and movement. Erin flung herself over the rail and wrapped her arms around Will's neck. Beau was hugging his shoulders. As if from far away, he heard the judge thanking the jurors and telling him he was free to go. His arm reached for Tori and pulled her close. Quivering, she pressed her face against his jacket.

Looking past her, Will caught a flash of hate-filled green eyes. Facing him from across the aisle, Stella mouthed something he couldn't understand. Then, with a last, venomous look, she turned and stalked out of the courtroom.

CHAPTER 19

A bner got word of the verdict from the bailiff, who'd called to let him know that Will Tyler wouldn't be needing the jail cell he'd reserved. Too bad in a way. Seeing the high-and-mighty Will locked up and headed for prison would have given him some satisfaction. But he'd known all along that the man wasn't guilty. At least now his conscience would be clear.

Damned funny thing, his conscience. He'd almost forgotten he had one until he'd held his newborn grandson in his arms. When he'd looked down into those pure eyes, it was as if they could see all the way into the depths of his corrupted soul. That was when Abner had known he had to become a better man.

Clay Drummond was going to be sore. So was Stella. For now, he knew enough of their secrets to keep them from doing him too much damage. But he was playing a dangerous game—a game that could leave him disgraced or dead, and little Ralphie without a grandfather.

Abner thought of all the times he'd skirted the limits of the law. Evidence tampering, leaking confidential information, looking the other way when Stella did her dirty work—so many small crimes that he'd lost count. He had loved being sheriff, loved the authority, the respect, and the sheer fun of playing detective. But a man with his secret record had no business in a position of public trust. To cleanse his conscience and keep himself safe, he would have to start over.

There was only one way to do that.

Bringing up his computer, he opened a blank document and began typing a letter of resignation.

At home, in a locked drawer of his study desk, Clay kept a loaded .38. Now, alone in his courthouse office, he found himself thinking about that gun and how he might use it to end his life. Even death would be better than what he and his family would face if Stella released that damning surveillance tape.

Through the west window the setting sun cast a blood-red glow into the room, reflecting off the empty bourbon bottle on his desk. He was borderline drunk. But his office door was locked, his staff gone for the night. Nobody was going to walk in on him.

What now? Would Stella warn him first or would she simply leak the tape to her press contacts? Either way, he had no doubt she'd do it. She'd ruined Garn Prescott after he'd let her down. She'd do the same to him.

His ringing cell phone broke the silence. Clay glanced at the caller ID. His stomach clenched.

"You really blew it today, didn't you, honey?" Stella's voice was like the purr of a big, sleek cat toying with a mouse.

"Please, Stella," he begged her, almost blubbering. "I'll do anything! Just don't release that tape!"

"You say you'll do anything?" She laughed, dangling

the bait. "What would you say to a chance to get the tape back?"

Clay's pulse leapt. But he was sober enough to know that whatever Stella had in mind would be illegal and dangerous. Desperate as he was, he had to keep his head.

"Whatever you want, I'll do it on two conditions," he said. "First I want your promise that you'll give me the tape."

"Cross my heart, honey. Do the job and it's yours. What's the other condition?"

"I want to keep my life—my job, my reputation, and my family. If my involvement can be kept secret, I'm on board."

Again she laughed. "That can be arranged—as long as you're not stupid enough to get caught. But once I've told you the plan, you're in. Get cold feet, and you'll be humping an underage girl on the ten o'clock news."

The knot in Clay's gut felt like a tangle of barbed wire. "I'm in," he said. "Tell me what I have to do."

Will had celebrated his acquittal by going home, changing his clothes, and working on the barn until dusk. *Lord, but it feels good to be a free man!* After what he'd survived, even the money troubles seemed surmountable. Now that the specter of prison was gone, he could plan. And he could make the hard decisions it would take to keep the ranch running.

That night the ranch family had celebrated around the dinner table with green salad, fresh garlic bread, and a big pan of Bernice's lasagna. Now it was late, the meal finished, the leftovers put away, and the dishes loaded in the dishwasher. Erin and Bernice, worn out by the day, had gone to bed. Sky, Lauren, Jasper, Beau, and Natalie had left for the night.

Only Tori remained. Wrapped in the afghan, her stocking feet tucked under her, she sat on the front porch with Will in the opposite chair. The night was clear, the stars like the spill of a million diamonds across the sky. The breeze was no more than a whisper.

Will studied her moonlit profile—the chiseled nose, the soft, full lips, the stubborn chin, and the wisps of golden hair framing her face. There was nobody like Tori. He ached to make her his again.

Tonight could be his best chance to tell her what was on his mind. But he'd never been much good with romantic talk. Maybe that had been part of the problem when they were married. He'd been too tough, too macho, to say the words a woman needed to hear.

Could he say them now?

She stirred, untangling her legs. "I suppose I should be going," she said.

"You don't have to go," he said. "You could stay here tonight. We could even do some more celebrating."

"Will—"

As soon as she spoke his name, he knew he'd said the wrong thing. "Sorry," he muttered. "Did I assume too much?"

She shook her head. "Last night we needed each other. But that doesn't mean it's going to happen again."

Her words stung Will like a slap in the face, but he stuck to his guns. "You know it was good for both of us. What's wrong, Tori? Is Middleton still in the picture?"

"No, that's over. There's nobody else. It's just that . . . the woman you were married to doesn't exist anymore. This woman won't answer to any man's beck and call, even yours."

"So I'm supposed to wait around like a hungry dog until you crook your little finger? Damn it, Tori, I want you! I want my family back!"

She stood, clutching the afghan around her. "We've been a family of sorts all along, haven't we? Has that been so bad?"

"It's been tolerable—better than nothing. But sleeping alone and only seeing my daughter when school's out isn't my idea of being a family."

"Will." Her voice was flat with strain. "Half the single women in the county would jump at the chance to be your wife. You could get married again, even have more children."

"Damn it, if that was what I wanted, I'd have remarried a long time ago!" Frustrated, he turned away from her and glared across the moon-shadowed yard. "Never mind. This is going nowhere. If you need to go home, just go."

"Fine. As soon as I get my things." She crossed the porch, then paused at the front door. "I'll be here on Sunday to get Erin. She misses her friends. She wants to go back to school in town."

The news jolted him. "Are you sure that's safe?"

"It's what she wants. I already promised her."

"I wish you'd talked it over with me before you promised."

"The trial's over," Tori said. "You were judged innocent. We need to move on. Even Erin needs to move on—with her school, with her friends. She needs to put this ordeal behind her and get back to normal."

"But does it have to be so soon?"

There was no reply. Tori had gone inside.

* * *

Minutes later, Tori swung her station wagon away from the house. Tires spat gravel as she headed down the lane toward the main road. Will had been gone when she'd come back outside with her shoes, jacket, and purse. There'd been no chance to make things right, or even give him a conciliatory smile. He'd opened up to her, and she had wounded him.

Will was a proud man. The next time she saw him, his behavior toward her would be that of a polite, cold stranger.

Welling tears blurred the road in her headlights. Why couldn't she have said yes to Will? It would have made him happy. Erin would have been overjoyed, and the whole ranch family would have celebrated her return.

But she knew why. The sad, hard truth was that she was scared. Will was the love of her life. There would never be another man like him. But being his wife had crushed her spirit in a way she would never tolerate again. Over the past eight years, they'd become different people—she was stronger; Will, perhaps less like his father. But some things never changed. Going back to him would be like picking up where they'd left off, with all the old hurts coming to the surface.

They could end up hating each other.

Out of the darkness a buck deer flashed into the road, leaping high in her headlights. Tori slammed the brake. The wagon screeched to a stop, missing the animal by the barest inch as it bounded away. Pulse hammering, she slumped over the wheel. Another split second and she might have hit it in midair, sending its heavy body smashing into her windshield. Or she might have swerved and rolled the vehicle off the road's steep shoulder.

Still shaking, she drove on. If the timing had been off

by a sliver, she could have died back there—without saying good-bye to Erin, and without ever letting Will know she loved him. Life was fragile, and no one was ever truly safe. A heartbeat could change everything.

As the lights of Blanco Springs came into sight, she tried to shake off the dark mood. She'd had an exhausting day, she reminded herself. With the trial behind her, all she needed was a good night's rest. Tomorrow everything would be back to normal.

Everything was going to be fine.

Stella double-checked the locks on her apartment door and windows before she settled onto the sofa, poured herself a brandy, and opened the newspaper she'd brought home from work. Every night she scanned the pages, hoping for news of Marie's arrest. So far, she'd found nothing. Either the hoped-for story hadn't been worth a mention in the press, or the woman was still out there somewhere, hiding from the law and plotting her revenge.

Nothing again tonight. Stella shoved the paper aside, lit a Marlboro, and hoisted her aching feet to the coffee table. Days from now, she'd be safe, where nobody, not even Marie, would ever find her.

A week had passed since the trial. Will Tyler's acquittal had left a bitter taste in her mouth. But never mind. She had a backup plan, one that would guarantee her a comfortable retirement and devastate the whole Tyler family.

All that remained was to carry it out.

She took a drag on the cigarette and laid it in the ashtray. It was almost midnight, time to check in with her Mexican friend Don Ramon, who'd be waiting for her call in the bedroom of his stately hacienda, south of Piedras Negras.

He picked up on the first ring. "Is everything ready?" His English was accented but passable.

"Almost. Can you guarantee the border crossing?"

"*Como no.* Of course. As long as I know when you'll be there."

"I'll call you when I'm on my way. Have you found a buyer?"

"More than one. The bids are still going up. Forty percent of the final price for me, yes?"

"Fine." The rascal would probably hold out for even more, but never mind. She couldn't do this without him.

"It would help to have a photo," he said.

"I don't have one, but I promise you, the girl's a beauty. Blue eyes, blond hair. And very young. Your friends always go for that type."

"You're sure she's a virgin?"

"You'll have her checked, of course, but I'd stake my life on it. She's from a good family. Very protected."

"So it will be tomorrow, you think?"

"Tomorrow after school, if all goes well," Stella said, trying not to think of how many things could go wrong. "I'll be crossing the border at night. Wait for my call. If I'm not coming, I'll let you know."

"*Buena suerte,*" he said, wishing her good luck.

"*Adiós, amigo.*" Stella ended the call. Now everything depended on luck—and on Clay Drummond. She would give him a call tomorrow to make sure everything was on. When she knew he had the girl, it would be time for the rest of her plan.

By 3:00 p.m., Clay was sweating bullets. Kidnapping was a federal offense. Get caught, and he could be put away for life. But even that couldn't be any worse than what would happen if Stella released that surveillance tape.

Anyway, he wouldn't really be kidnapping, he told himself as he cruised past the middle school and pulled onto a side street. He'd only be giving the kid a ride. What happened after that would be out of his hands. He could only hope Stella would keep her promise and give him the tape.

For the past few days, he'd kept an eye on Erin Tyler. She usually left school at 3:15 p.m., walking with a girlfriend. When they reached the top of her street, the two would separate. Erin would walk the rest of the way alone, let herself into the house, and wait for her mother to come home.

This afternoon Tori was in court on a civil case—Clay had checked to make sure. If her daughter followed her customary routine, he would put the plan in motion. What he was setting out to do would be the most despicable thing he'd ever done. But he mustn't think of that now. Instead he would focus on getting the tape back and freeing himself to move on with his life.

Now, from where he'd parked, he could see students pouring out of the school. It took him only a moment to spot Erin. Dressed in jeans and boots, with her backpack slung over one shoulder, she was heading down the sidewalk with her dark-haired friend. Clay hung back, keeping his distance until the two separated and Erin turned the corner for home.

He took a moment to call Stella and tell her the plan was on. Then, stepping on the gas, he sped around the corner after Erin and screeched to a halt, short of the house. With a worried look on his face, he pulled up to the curb and rolled down the window. Erin had stopped and turned to look at him.

"Thank goodness I've found you, Erin!" he said. "Your mother passed out in court. She's been taken to the hospital. Your dad's on his way there. He asked me to find you and bring you."

Fear flashed in her eyes. "What's the matter with her? Is she all right?"

He reached across the seat and opened the passenger door. "Get in. We can talk on the way."

She ran around the car, tossed her backpack into the rear seat, and buckled herself in beside him. "Let's go," she said.

Clay swung the Mercedes back into the street and headed for the road out of town. Stella would be waiting in an isolated spot off the freeway. The transfer would've been safer at night, but they'd agreed there was little chance of catching the girl alone, outside, after dark.

"Tell me about my mother," she said. "What's wrong with her?"

"The paramedics weren't sure. She was still unconscious when they put her in the ambulance. A stroke, maybe, they said."

Such brutal lies, and the girl looked so worried, so trusting. It was all Clay could do not to tell her it was all a mistake and shove her out of the car. But he'd long since passed the point of no return. He had to do this.

"Let me call my dad." She twisted to reach for the backpack she'd thrown behind the seat. "Maybe he can tell us more."

"No!" Clay tried to hide a surge of panic. If she got her hands on her phone, he'd be in big trouble. "Either your dad will be speeding to the hospital or he'll be in the ER with your mother—not a good time to take a call. You can talk to him when we get there."

"Oh—okay. But hurry." She settled back, agitated fingers gripping the seat belt. Clay could smell the stink of his own sweat as he swung onto the freeway. His heart was pounding so hard, he feared he might burst a blood vessel.

Take the second exit, onto the old ranch road. That was what Stella had told him. *Drive till you see some cottonwoods and a tumbledown shed. I'll meet you there.*

The exit was already coming up. Clay swung the Mercedes onto the off-ramp.

"Where are you going?" Erin grabbed his sleeve. "This isn't the way to the hospital!"

"I heard there was a big wreck up ahead. A semitruck rollover, blocking traffic. This road will get us around it." Clay could see the trees in the distance. The asphalt pavement had ended in a weathered farm road. What the hell would he do if Stella wasn't there?

"How do you know there was a wreck? Who told you?" She was getting suspicious, Clay could tell. He stomped the gas pedal. The Mercedes shot forward, rocketing down the rutted road. He thought of the chloroform-soaked rag, sealed in a plastic bag, which he'd put in his pocket. He was going to need it.

"Stop!" she said. "Stop right now! I want to call my father!"

"Fine. Go ahead." Clay eased the car to a stop. One hand reached into his pocket and unsealed the ziplock on the bag. Hampered by the seat belt, she turned to reach for her pack.

"I'm sorry, Erin," Clay said, and he clapped the cloth over her face. The girl barely had time to resist before the chloroform took effect and her body went limp.

Leaving her sagging against the shoulder strap, Clay started the car again and sped toward the trees. Now he could see the dilapidated shed and the back end of Stella's Buick parked behind it. She was here. Soon this nightmare would be over, and he could start living his life again.

As he pulled up to the shed and climbed out of the car, she stepped into sight. "You've got the girl?" she demanded.

"Right here. Fast asleep." He opened the passenger door to reveal Erin, still slumped in the seat.

"Good. Give me a hand with her." She raised the lid of her trunk, which was lined with a dirty-looking quilt. Clay unfastened Erin's seat belt, lifted her in his arms, and laid her on her side. He'd hoped he was finished, but Stella handed him a roll of duct tape. "Wrists, ankles, and mouth, then fold the blanket over her," she said. "Be quick about it."

Clay did as he was told, trying not to make the tape too tight. "You won't want to tape her mouth. If she gets sick to her stomach in the trunk, she could choke to death."

"Fine. But I'll need to keep her quiet. Give me the chloroform in case she wakes up."

Clay resealed the washcloth in the bag and gave it to Stella. She tucked it into her red leather purse and closed the trunk.

"Aren't you forgetting something?" Clay asked.

Stella raised an eyebrow.

"The tape. You promised it to me if I delivered the girl."

"So I did." With a smile she reached into her purse and handed him the cassette from the surveillance camera.

"Can you swear this is the one?"

"Don't worry. It's the real deal, and it's all yours. I

won't need it where I'm going." She turned back toward her Buick. "I believe this concludes our business. Have a happy life, Mr. Prosecutor."

Clay felt an unaccustomed lightness as he walked back toward his car, clutching the tape. He had just done the unthinkable. But he'd salvaged everything that mattered to him. He was free to pursue his ambitions—become a judge, maybe go into politics. Nothing would be out of reach now.

He'd just opened the driver's-side door when the bullet slammed into his skull, passing from back to front and knocking him forward across the seat. His body twitched once and lay still.

Will had come inside to read his mail when Tori called. "Will?" She sounded worried. "Did you pick up Erin after school? She's not in the house, and she's not answering her cell phone."

Dread clutched him like a cold steel vise. "No. I haven't heard from her. Did you call her friend?"

"I'll do that next. But if she was at Allison's, she'd have let me know, and she would've had her phone on. Will, I'm scared."

"Call the sheriff's office—now. Tell them to check the Blue Coyote."

"Dear God, you don't think—"

"Until we find Erin, we've got to assume the worst. Call them. I'll get Beau on this."

The acting sheriff since Abner's resignation was his young deputy, Rafe Sanchez. The kid was sharp, had the makings of a good lawman, but he lacked the experience to handle a life-or-death emergency. As a former DEA agent, Beau was a seasoned crime fighter with contacts in the FBI. If Stella, or somebody in her pay, had taken Erin, every minute's delay could make a difference.

Beau had been outside, supervising work on the newly erected barn. Seconds after Will's call he burst into the house, out of breath. "You're sure she's been taken?"

"Not yet, but if she has, we can't afford to waste time."

"Stella?"

"Until we know more, that's my best guess."

"The first thing we need to do is put out an AMBER alert. I'll make some calls."

While Beau was on the phone, Will got another call from Tori. His pulse skipped. Maybe she'd heard from Erin. Maybe all this panic was nothing but a false alarm.

But no, as soon as he heard her voice, he knew the news would be bad. "The dispatcher put me through to the sheriff," she said. "He was out by that ranch exit off the freeway, checking something the Life Flight pilot had spotted from . . . the air." Her voice quavered, then broke.

Will's throat jerked. "Was it Erin?" he asked.

"No." Her breath caught. "It was Clay Drummond's car. Clay was inside, shot dead. And Erin . . . Oh, Lord, Will. They found her backpack, with her phone in it, behind the seat. But Erin was gone."

CHAPTER 20

At last the sun was going down. Stella slipped off her sunglasses and massaged the bridge of her nose. While the daylight lasted, she'd kept to the back roads, doing her best to stay out of sight. Soon it would be dark enough to pull onto the freeway and make a beeline for Eagle Pass, where she would cross the border into Mexico.

She'd already called Don Ramon on her burner phone to let him know she had the package and was on her way. He'd assured her that the car wouldn't be searched. Not that there was much chance of that. The Mexicans weren't too fussy about what crossed into their country, especially when there was a *mordida* involved.

One of Don Ramon's trusted agents would be waiting in Piedras Negras to give her the cash and take the girl off her hands. With the little bitch gone, she could finally get some rest.

Her passenger was awake and stirring. Stella could hear thumping, kicking, and cries of fear and rage from the trunk. At least the girl seemed to be in decent condition. But the car was running low on gas and Stella had to pee. If she stopped at a service station, the commotion in the back might draw attention. She would have to open the trunk and use the chloroform to knock the girl out again.

Now was as good a time as any. She glanced at the ski mask lying on the seat beside her. She hadn't wanted the girl to see her face. But why bother? Erin Tyler wasn't stupid. Mask or no mask, she'd know who had her.

The road was deserted. Deciding not to wait for a service station, Stella pulled onto the shoulder, climbed out of the car, and squatted behind a clump of sagebrush to relieve herself. The wind was blowing in hard from the northwest, bringing with it a bank of roiling black clouds. A storm was moving in. If she wanted to make the border before the weather hit, she'd have to step on it.

Unzipping the plastic bag with the chloroform-soaked washcloth in it, she slipped it in her pocket and opened the Buick's spacious trunk. The girl, her wrists and ankles taped, her clothes twisted and rumpled, was glaring up at her like a wounded hawk, as much in fury as in fear.

"Where are you taking me?" she demanded.

Stella chuckled. "That's for me to know and you to find out, honey. Let's just say I'm planning to retire, and you're going to fund my pension."

Fear flashed across Erin's pretty face, but the look hardened into something else. The girl had fight in her. "So you need to keep me alive," she said.

"Alive and pretty. That's the plan."

"I could use a bathroom break," she said.

"That's your problem." No way was Stella letting her out of the trunk and freeing those long legs. She'd probably take off like a jackrabbit.

"At least give me some water," she said. "My throat's really dry."

"Oh . . . what the hell. Just a sip. I've got a bottle up front." Stella walked around to the car's front door, opened it, and found the plastic bottle she'd tossed onto the passenger seat. She was out of sight for no more than a few seconds, but she walked back to find that the girl had rolled, dropped her bound legs over the rear bumper, and was almost out of the trunk.

Time for a little education.

Stella tossed down the water bottle and grabbed the girl's arm. "Where d'you think you're going, you little spoiled shit?" She backhanded her hard across the face. "You think you can hop all the way home to your daddy, eh?" She hit her again, so hard that Erin's head snapped to one side. "Don't mess with me, princess, or you'll be sorry!"

She clamped the washcloth over the girl's face and held it there until the slender body went limp. Then she shoved her prisoner back in the trunk, took her shoes for good measure, and slammed the lid shut. She'd never liked kids, and this one could turn out to be more trouble than she was worth. Only the thought of the money the girl would bring kept her from dumping the little twit on the road and leaving her there to freeze.

Climbing back in the car, Stella drove on. If the weather held, she could be over the border in a couple of hours. The idea of a warm bath and a soft bed in Piedras Negras was sounding more and more like heaven.

How could anything be harder than waiting?

Will, Tori, and Beau huddled in Tori's living room, all of them silently praying for good news. Until they had some word of Erin, there was nothing they could do except be here, and be available.

Tori's cell phone rang. The caller was Natalie, who was waiting back at the ranch with the rest of the family. She'd called Tori because Beau wanted to keep his phone free for police or FBI calls. "Any news?" she asked.

"Nothing yet." Tori forced herself to use her lawyer voice. She was crumbling inside, but this was no time to break down.

"They're sure it was Stella who took her—and shot Clay?"

"Positive. The sheriff's men matched up the boot prints and tire tracks. Plus, the waitress at the Blue Coyote hadn't seen her boss all afternoon. The best guess is that she's headed for Mexico. The highway patrol has an all-points bulletin out, but no one's spotted her car. She may have switched vehicles."

"Oh, Tori . . . ," Natalie whispered.

"Don't," Tori said. "Sympathy can wait."

"They must be doing more than that to find her," Natalie said.

"There's a statewide AMBER alert out for her. And the police will be checking every car that leaves the country through Eagle Pass. If all Stella wanted was revenge, she could've killed Erin when she killed Clay. If she's keeping her alive, and taking her over the border, it's for one . . . reason." Tori choked on the last words.

"I'll let you go," Natalie said. "Tell Beau I called. We're all praying."

"Thanks." Tori ended the call, struggling to get a grip on her emotions. It was all she could do to keep from dashing outside, jumping into her station wagon, and rushing off in the night to find her daughter. But that would be useless. All she could do was stay here and endure the agony of minutes crawling past with no word.

Will was sitting next to her on the couch. Tori reached

for his hand and felt his big, rough palm close around hers. They held each other in silence, seeking comfort, drawing strength, and sharing the pain that only parents of a loved child could know.

A light rap on the door jerked them all to attention. Beau opened it to find Sheriff Rafe Sanchez on the porch. Just twenty-two, the son of an unmarried Mexican mother, he'd stepped into Abner's job barely a week ago. Now he was in charge of investigating the scene of Erin's kidnapping and the murder of Clay Drummond.

"Any news?" His dark eyes took in their stricken faces. "No, I guess not. I just wanted to give you an update on what we found at the scene. I don't know if I'm supposed to share it, but . . ." He shook his head. "What the hell, you deserve to know."

"Come in." Beau stepped aside and ushered him into the living room. "Have a chair. Can we get you something to drink?"

"Thanks, but I can't stay." He remained standing, a tall young man, his lean body still filling out. "We're pretty sure Stella was blackmailing Clay. We found a surveillance tape in his hand—something that would've ruined him if it had gone public."

"That's no surprise," Beau said. "Blackmail was Stella's stock in trade. We know better than to ask you what was on the tape."

Sanchez nodded. "For now, we're not telling the family. Stella's prints were on the cassette. She could've offered it to Clay in exchange for delivering Erin."

"Erin would've trusted Clay." Tori felt a wave of staggering rage. "It couldn't have been too hard for him to get her in his car."

"So Stella gave him the tape and then killed him." Will

was on his feet. "The woman who's got our daughter isn't just a kidnapper. She's a cold-blooded murderer—but I guess we already knew that."

"Yes." Sanchez's English was measured, as if he'd learned most of it in school. "She's capable of anything. But if she went to that much trouble, she must want to keep Erin alive, most likely to sell her. At least that buys us some time."

But how much time? Will and Beau exchanged glances. In a kidnapping the odds of a safe recovery dropped exponentially with every hour that passed. Time, they knew, was swiftly running out.

Erin stirred and opened her eyes. She was still in the trunk of Stella's car, bound hand and foot by duct tape. Her neck was sore, her face bruised and tender where Stella had hit her. Her throat felt as if she'd eaten a fistful of sawdust. Her limbs were cramped, and her shoes, she realized, were gone.

The darkness smelled of cigarette smoke, mildew, and dirty carpet. Being in the trunk was like being inside a coffin. But she couldn't give in to panic. She'd already worn herself out with useless struggling. She had to stay calm and alert, to think from moment to moment. Whatever happened, she had to survive until she could find a way to escape.

Shifting and wiggling, she used her bare feet to explore her prison. If she could find some kind of tool, or anything with a sharp edge, she might be able to slice through the duct tape. But there was nothing. Stella must have cleared out the trunk ahead of time. Erin had seen a movie where a person trapped in a car trunk had knocked out a taillight from the inside to attract attention. Her toes probed the corners where the taillights would be, but she couldn't find any way to break one.

The trunk was cold and getting colder. She shivered in her light jacket. Through the metal trunk lid, she could hear wind whistling around the car. A heavy patter, like tacks spilling into a tin bucket, filled the dark space around her. It had to be hail. The car was still moving, but its speed felt slower, as if the road surface might be slippery. Maybe the car would slide off the road. Maybe then a patrolman would come by and rescue her. But that was just a fantasy. For now, all she could do was pull the blanket over her as best she could, curl into a ball, and try to keep from freezing. That, and pray.

Driving through the storm on the ice-slicked freeway had been a hellish experience, but at least it had lessened the chance of her car being spotted. Now the weather was clearing. Ahead, in the distance, Stella could see the lights of Eagle Pass. Soon she'd be safely over the border, with the money in her purse and Will Tyler's precious daughter on her way to some Mexican drug lord's bed.

Reaching for the burner phone, she called Don Ramon's number. He answered at once.

"Is everything ready?" she asked.

"Unfortunately, *querida,* there has been a slight change of plans."

Something clenched in Stella's empty stomach. "Did you get the money?"

"The money? Yes. *No problema.* But I just got word that the police on the American side are checking every car, looking for you and the girl. You will never get through."

"Both crossings?" There were two border bridges in Eagle Pass, a large one and a smaller one.

"Yes, both. But don't worry. My man is in Piedras Negras with the money. Find a motel in Eagle Pass, someplace cheap and quiet. Check in and call me. He will find you, pay you the cash, and take the girl. *Entiendes?*"

"Yes," Stella said. "But—"

"Let me finish. The police will be looking for your car. Tomorrow you can leave it somewhere to be stolen and walk across the bridge with the foot traffic. No police will stop you. You will be safe. But one more thing."

"What?" Stella was liking this less and less.

"My man will need a truck or a van to smuggle the girl across the border. To arrange this may take time."

Stella mouthed a curse on the man's ancestors. "How much time?"

"Who knows? Not long. Perhaps a few hours. Maybe less. You can rest and wait."

"I don't like this," Stella said.

"What else can we do? The police are everywhere."

"Fine. I'll phone you." Stella ended the call and pulled off at the first exit. Too bad she hadn't switched cars, but she'd been in a hurry, and it was too late now. She had little choice except to follow Don Ramon's directions.

Eagle Pass was a fair-sized town. But with the police on the lookout, she didn't want to drive in very far. Anyway, the older, cheaper motels would likely be found on the run-down outskirts.

Fifteen minutes from the freeway, she found a place that might do. The El Camino was a row of clapboard units, set back from the quiet street and overhung by a sagging willow tree. Two battered-looking pickups were parked outside. At one end a sign in the window said *VACANCY*.

Parking the car at a safe distance, Stella climbed out. The night air was frigid, the ground coated with icy hail. She would have to bring the girl inside, a bother, but she'd promised to deliver the little bitch in good condition.

A bell rang when she opened the door of the office. The Mexican woman who came to the desk was wearing a ratty fleece bathrobe. From somewhere out of sight, a TV was blaring.

"Just one of you?" the woman asked.

"No, my daughter's with me. She's sick. I'm taking her to the doctor in the morning." Stella thrust a wad of small bills across the desk. "Here's an extra ten for keeping things quiet."

Stella was given a key to the unit on the far end. She backed the car up to the door and got out to open it. Before unlocking the trunk she took the Smith and Wesson .38, the gun she'd used to kill Clay, out of her purse. Before today, when someone needed killing, she'd always paid or manipulated others to do the job. Until she'd fired at the man and seen him fall dead, she hadn't known what a powerful rush it could be. She wouldn't mind feeling that rush again, maybe soon.

The girl was alert but quiet. Stella thrust the pistol toward her face. "Behave yourself and you can come inside. But no tricks, understand?"

She nodded. Stella had parked at an angle to keep the inside of the trunk out of the office woman's line of sight. It took some maneuvering, with the back door open, to make it appear that she was getting someone out of the backseat. She blocked the view with the blanket while

Erin got out of the trunk. Then, without freeing the girl's ankles, Stella wrapped her in the blanket, jump-walked her inside, and shoved her onto the bed. "Stay," she ordered, taking a moment to step out and close the trunk, then lock the door. "I'll cut your legs loose so you can use the bathroom, but you'll have to do it with your arms taped. And the door stays open. I'm not taking my eyes off you, hear? And don't you make a sound. Right now, I've got a phone call to make."

It was coming up on midnight when Beau got the call. Will and Tori were on their feet at once, crowding close as they tried to make sense of the half-heard dialogue. Only after he'd ended the call did they get the full story.

"They've found where Erin is," Beau said. "This woman in Eagle Pass, who checked them into a motel, saw the AMBER alert on TV and called it in."

"They're sure it's Erin?" Tori felt faint.

"She said the woman gave a different name, but she had red hair and claimed to have her daughter with her. The girl went inside wrapped in a blanket, so she wasn't seen. But the license plate on the car is a match to Stella's. It's got to be her!"

"Have they got Erin yet?" Will demanded. "What's happening down there?"

"The local police have the place surrounded, but they're holding off, waiting for the FBI hostage negotiator to show up before they move in. They're all hoping the situation won't turn into a shoot-out."

"Lord, we can't just sit here and wait!" Will paced as he talked, his hands clenching into fists. "If we can get there, we might be able to help, or at least let Erin know we're there!"

"But the border's hours away," Tori said. "If we have to drive . . ." She shook her head.

"I know," Beau said. "That's why my friends from the FBI are stopping by to pick us up in the chopper. Get your coats on. We're meeting them at the school athletic field in twenty minutes."

Using the toilet with her hands taped behind her back was tricky, but after two hours in the motel room, Erin was getting the knack of it, even in the dark. She sat with the bathroom door open, in full view of Stella, who was sitting in a chair with her back to the door and the pistol resting in her lap. Through the drawn curtains the street-lamp outside cast long shadows into the unlit room.

Erin's hopes that the woman would fall asleep, so she could carry out her escape plan, were fading. It was a good plan, she thought—lock the bathroom door, break the water glass, and use one sharp edge to cut through the tape, then unlatch the bathroom window and climb out. She'd seen it done in the movies. There was no reason it couldn't work in real life. But Stella, watching her every move with those cold green eyes, showed no signs of nodding off.

Erin tried not to think about how scared she was. Stella would enjoy seeing her fall apart and cry. But she wouldn't give the red-haired witch the satisfaction. She wouldn't let the woman see the terror that lay like a coiled reptile in the pit of her stomach.

"Aren't you getting hungry?" she asked, sitting on the bed. "Maybe there's a vending machine outside. We could at least get a couple of candy bars."

"Shut up, you little bitch!" Stella snapped. "Nobody's going anywhere till my friend comes to pick you up.

After that, you won't be my problem anymore." She stiffened, as if hearing something. One hand moved the window drape aside far enough to see out. "Maybe that's him now. It's—*Shit!*" She dropped the curtain and sprang to her feet. "It's the cops. One peep out of you, girl, and you're dead." She pointed the gun at Erin. "Lie down on the floor—over there, on the far side of the bed!"

Erin did as she was told, trembling in spite of herself as Stella bound her ankles again, then taped her mouth. Through the curtain she glimpsed headlights moving beyond the window, then nothing. Unable to cry out or get up, she could only lie still and wait.

Tori clutched her shoulder bag as the helicopter swooped in over the lights of Eagle Pass. FBI agent Forbes, an experienced hostage negotiator, had told them not to bring any weapons. But until now, Tori had forgotten about the nine-millimeter Kel-Tec Will had given her to carry. Her fingertips traced the small pistol's outline through the purse's leather folds. She didn't plan to use it, of course. But it gave her a measure of comfort to know it was there, loaded and ready.

Will sat silent beside her. She could feel the tension in his body, see the determination in his face, and she knew he would do anything to get their daughter back. But he was afraid, too, just as she was. Anything could happen down there, in the dangerous dark.

The helicopter touched down in an empty parking lot, where a local police car was waiting for them. Agent Forbes climbed in front with the driver, leaving Tori, Will, and Beau to crowd into the backseat. They listened while the driver gave Forbes an update.

"It's not looking good. Somebody made a move too soon and the woman got wind of the police. She's threatening to kill the girl if we don't back off."

"Just get me there." Forbes spoke calmly, but Tori could feel her heart in her throat. How many times on the news had she seen hostage situations where both the kidnapper and the hostage ended up dead? Right now, it appeared that Stella was using Erin as a bargaining chip. But if the woman was facing certain capture or death, it would be like her to kill her enemy's daughter as a final act of revenge.

Lights flashing and siren blaring, the police car sped to the scene. They found three other black-and-whites parked with headlights glaring on the door and curtained window of the end motel room. The officer in charge ushered Tori into the backseat of one of the cars, while Will and Beau were given bulletproof vests to wear. No doubt in the officer's mind, a mere woman was best kept out of the way.

Seething with anxiety, Tori rolled down the window and strained to see what was happening. Forbes was speaking through a bullhorn, evidently trying to set up communication with Stella. An officer in protective gear walked to the door and laid a phone on the stoop. As he backed away, the door opened a few inches and the phone disappeared.

Somewhere beyond that door, helpless and terrified, was Erin. It was all Tori could do to keep from leaping out of the car, rushing to the door, and screaming to be let in.

A young policeman, perhaps assigned to keep an eye on her, stood nearby. Tori caught his attention. "What's going on?" she demanded. "That's my daughter in there."

He stepped forward to listen, then reported back. "The woman's demanding half a million dollars in cash and

safe passage to the border. Once she's across, she'll release the girl."

"She won't do it," Tori said. "I know her. She'll kill
Erin before she lets her go. Tell them that."

"Don't worry, Agent Forbes knows his job," the
young officer said. "I've worked with him before. If anybody can get your daughter back, he can."

If anybody can . . . Lord, what if nobody could?

Through the open window she could hear Will arguing vehemently with Forbes. His words tore at her heart.

"Listen to me, damn it! I'm the one Stella wants. Let
me go in. Maybe I can trade places with Erin, or at least
be inside to protect her."

"That's not the way we do things, Mr. Tyler," Forbes
said. "Now stand back and let us do our job."

"Stand back, hell!" Will growled. "I'm going in. If
you don't back me, damn it, I'll do it without your help."

As Forbes relented, Tori forced herself to breathe.
Will would lay down his life to save Erin. Right now, she
had no choice except to let him—even if it meant she
could lose them both.

Her frantic hands twisted in her lap. How could she just
sit here and wait? There had to be something she could do.
Will would be unarmed. But she had a gun. She barely
knew how to shoot, but if she could make a difference she
had to act—and act now.

With everyone's eyes on Will, Tori took the small pistol out of her purse and pulled back the slide to chamber a
bullet. Then she slipped out the far side of the police car.
Ducking low and keeping to the shadows, she cut around
through the darkness, heading for the back of the motel.

* * *

Erin had rolled onto her belly and managed to inch-worm her way across the linoleum floor. Now she was just a few feet short of the door. Stella, gripping her pistol and intent on the danger out front, had yet to notice her. What now? She couldn't use her hands or her feet. She couldn't cry out. But if the chance came to make her move—any move she could—she had to be ready.

As she lay there, tense and waiting, she heard a voice outside—her father's voice.

"Stella! I'm unarmed and I'm coming in! I'm the one you want, not an innocent girl! Take me and let Erin go!"

Stella opened the door a few inches. Lying behind her, Erin could see her father standing in the bright light with his hands up. He was wearing a bulletproof vest, but his head was unprotected. As Stella raised the pistol, Erin knew that was where she would aim. At close range it would be an easy, and fatal, shot.

Erin had to do something.

As Stella tensed to fire, Erin flung the last of her strength into a lightning-fast tuck-and-roll that slammed her curled body into the back of Stella's legs. The pistol roared. Through the partly open doorway, Erin saw her father reel and drop to his knees. A red stain flowed down the sleeve of his jacket.

Stella staggered to one side, caught off balance. Pushing to her knees, Erin head-butted her out of the way, shouldered the door open, and tumbled out onto the stoop.

As the police rushed forward, she heard the door bang shut behind her and the *click* of the lock. Stella was still inside, but now she was alone.

Tori had heard the gunshot from the rear of the motel. As she made her way through the overgrown oleander bushes, she could only pray that the single bullet hadn't struck any of her loved ones.

She'd guessed that in an old motel like this one, there would be a bathroom window in the back of each unit. If she could get in that way, she might be able to catch Stella by surprise and rescue Erin. Now she saw that she'd been right about the window. But it was high and appeared to be latched from the inside. Never mind, this plan was her only option. Somehow she would make it work.

She was glancing around for something to climb on when the window slid open. Tori raised her pistol as a dark shape, barely lit by the moon, squeezed out through the opening and dropped five feet to the ground, landing with a grunt of pain.

As the figure pushed to a crouch, the moonlight fell on an upturned face. Eyes as fierce as a cornered puma's glared at Tori. It was Stella.

She'd dropped her pistol as she hit the ground. Keeping her own gun leveled at the woman, Tori kicked the heavy .38 into the bushes, out of reach. Blind rage swept through Tori as she leveled her weapon. "Hands up, Stella!" she snarled. "You don't know how much I'd enjoy pulling this trigger right in your ugly face."

Stella's laugh was pure evil. "You don't have the guts to shoot me, lawyer lady. As soon as I can get my legs under me, I'm going to get up and walk away." She pushed partway to her feet, grimaced, and lowered herself to the ground again. She'd landed hard. Tori guessed that she might have broken something—her ankle or even her leg—but despite the pain Stella kept that cruel smile on her face.

"Too bad about your daughter. She was a pretty little thing. She'd have fetched a good price if she'd lived, but she was dead by the time you showed up. Too bad about your ex-husband, too. One shot, and he went down like a load of bricks. At least you can have the pleasure of giving them both a nice funeral."

Shock and rage blotted out Tori's grief for the moment. It didn't matter what she did now. Without both Erin and Will, her life was over. She'd have nothing to live for. At least killing this evil monster of a woman would give her some satisfaction.

Stella was still grinning when Tori raised the pistol. White-hot fury blurred her vision as her shaking finger tightened on the trigger.

"Stop, Tori!" Beau's arms clasped her from behind, forcing her gun hand down. She struggled, fighting against him, wanting nothing more than to destroy the she-devil who'd taken her loved ones. "Let me go!" she muttered. "She killed Will and Erin! I want to make sure she never hurts anybody again!"

"It's all right, Tori!" Beau's grip tightened. "Stella's lying! Will's only wounded and Erin is free! They're waiting for you out front now."

The pistol dropped from Tori's fingers. Too drained to speak, she began to tremble. Beau, her lifelong friend, laid an arm around her shoulders and guided her away as the police closed in to arrest Stella.

"It's over, Tori," he said. "Will and Erin are waiting for us. Let's go home."

Together they came around to the front of the motel. There, in the glare of headlights, she saw Will sitting up on an ambulance stretcher while a paramedic tended his shoulder wound. Bruised and disheveled, Erin stood in the clasp of his free arm, sobbing as she clung to her father.

Breaking loose from Beau, Tori ran toward them. An instant later, she was holding them close—the two people she loved most in the world. Her family. Whatever happened, she never wanted to be separated from them again.

EPILOGUE I

Tori would remember that Christmas on the ranch as the happiest ever. There hadn't been time or money to put many presents under the tree. But just having the ranch family together had been reason enough for joyous celebration.

The best part of it had been waking up next to Will and seeing his sleepy face on the pillow beside her. They'd been married a few days earlier in a small, private ceremony. This time everything felt right. For Tori, it had taken almost losing her precious daughter and the man she loved to realize that they needed to be a family again. They would be a family forever.

That morning they'd looked outside to find the land blanketed with soft, gently falling snow. While the men trooped out to do chores, the women had gathered to start preparations for Christmas dinner—dressing the turkey, mixing the rolls, and setting the table with the elegant china and silver that had belonged to Will and Beau's mother. They chatted and laughed, enjoying the time together. Lauren, her pregnancy no longer a secret, was planning her wedding. Now that she and Natalie were both expectant mothers, they'd become fast friends.

The exterior of the barn was finished, and there was other good news for the ranch as well. Days ago, a big outfit in Montana, the Triple C, run by the Calder family, had made a generous offer on twenty of the best young colts. The money would pay off the bank loan with enough left over to buy all the winter hay they needed.

When they sat down for dinner, Tori looked around the table, thinking how much she loved everyone there—crusty old Jasper and patient Bernice, Beau and Natalie, Sky and Lauren, her own dear husband, Will, and the daughter they shared. Lives would change as the years wore on. But this day was one to hold and remember for always.

EPILOGUE II

Three months later
Gatesville Women's State Prison, Gatesville, Texas

Dressed in an orange jumpsuit, her hair fading from red to gray, Stella walked into the prison lunchroom, where she would likely be eating for the rest of her life. It wasn't the Ritz. But, thanks to a good lawyer, at least she wasn't spending her days on death row.

She missed the old times, especially the Blue Coyote, which she'd sold to Abner Sweeney at a bargain price to pay for her defense. It tickled her to imagine Abner running the bar. His straightlaced wife had probably thrown a fit. But at least the bar made good money—better than a county lawman's pay.

As a new prisoner here, she was still finding her place in the pecking order. She would keep her head down at first. But once she knew the ropes, she'd be on her way up the food chain, all the way to the top.

Goading Tori Tyler into killing her would have been a mistake. She enjoyed taking on life's challenges, and even here, behind bars, there would be opportunities to win. Stella knew human nature, and she knew how to make her way. Another six months here, and she'd be running the place.

After going through the line, she took her tray, filled with the slop that passed for food, to an empty table and sat down to eat and watch. You could learn a lot about people from who they sat with and the way they ate. She was learning more every day.

She had nearly finished when she heard a footstep behind her. A tall, familiar shadow fell across the table. Stella's pulse jerked. Her gaze traveled upward to the stringy black hair, and the narrow face with its slashing scar.

The crooked mouth smiled. "Hello, Stella," said Marie Fletcher.

*Don't miss the next exciting Tylers of Texas novel
from Janet Dailey, coming soon!*

TEXAS FIERCE

He's the prodigal son ready to claim his legacy . . .

He came home to sell his family's failing ranch, but
once twenty-year-old Bull Tyler sets foot on the Rimrock, he's determined to tame the rugged land and
make it his own. First he'll have to take on the powerful Prescott clan, who'll do anything to get their hands
on the Tylers' holding—even murder. Then Bull sets
eyes on the breathtaking woman earmarked to be Ferg
Prescott's bride. Now nothing will stop Bull from taking the land—or the lady who stirs his blood like no
other—and building a dynasty worthy of both . . .

She's the pampered beauty he won't let get away . . .

She was born to privilege, and raised to do the right
thing. But Susan Rutledge has never felt anything like
the fire she feels for Bull Tyler. Yet can she defy her
father's strong will and leave her secure life for a
ramblin' rodeo man? She'd have to be crazy—or
crazy in love . . .

Connect with

U s

Visit us online at
KensingtonBooks.com
to read more from your favorite authors, see books
by series, view reading group guides, and more.

Join us on social media

for sneak peeks, chances to win books and prize packs,
and to share your thoughts with other readers.

facebook.com/kensingtonpublishing
twitter.com/kensingtonbooks

Tell us what you think!

To share your thoughts, submit a review,
or sign up for our eNewsletters, please visit:
KensingtonBooks.com/TellUs.

More from Bestselling Author
JANET DAILEY

Calder Storm	0-8217-7543-X	$7.99US/$10.99CAN
Close to You	1-4201-1714-9	$5.99US/$6.99CAN
Crazy in Love	1-4201-0303-2	$4.99US/$5.99CAN
Dance With Me	1-4201-2213-4	$5.99US/$6.99CAN
Everything	1-4201-2214-2	$5.99US/$6.99CAN
Forever	1-4201-2215-0	$5.99US/$6.99CAN
Green Calder Grass	0-8217-7222-8	$7.99US/$10.99CAN
Heiress	1-4201-0002-5	$6.99US/$7.99CAN
Lone Calder Star	0-8217-7542-1	$7.99US/$10.99CAN
Lover Man	1-4201-0666-X	$4.99US/$5.99CAN
Masquerade	1-4201-0005-X	$6.99US/$8.99CAN
Mistletoe and Molly	1-4201-0041-6	$6.99US/$9.99CAN
Rivals	1-4201-0003-3	$6.99US/$7.99CAN
Santa in a Stetson	1-4201-0664-3	$6.99US/$9.99CAN
Santa in Montana	1-4201-1474-3	$7.99US/$9.99CAN
Searching for Santa	1-4201-0306-7	$6.99US/$9.99CAN
Something More	0-8217-7544-8	$7.99US/$9.99CAN
Stealing Kisses	1-4201-0304-0	$4.99US/$5.99CAN
Tangled Vines	1-4201-0004-1	$6.99US/$8.99CAN
Texas Kiss	1-4201-0665-1	$4.99US/$5.99CAN
That Loving Feeling	1-4201-1713-0	$5.99US/$6.99CAN
To Santa With Love	1-4201-2073-5	$6.99US/$7.99CAN
When You Kiss Me	1-4201-0667-8	$4.99US/$5.99CAN
Yes, I Do	1-4201-0305-9	$4.99US/$5.99CAN

Available Wherever Books Are Sold!

Check out our website at www.kensingtonbooks.com.

Books by Bestselling Author
Fern Michaels

___The Jury	0-8217-7878-1	$6.99US/$9.99CAN
___Sweet Revenge	0-8217-7879-X	$6.99US/$9.99CAN
___Lethal Justice	0-8217-7880-3	$6.99US/$9.99CAN
___Free Fall	0-8217-7881-1	$6.99US/$9.99CAN
___Fool Me Once	0-8217-8071-9	$7.99US/$10.99CAN
___Vegas Rich	0-8217-8112-X	$7.99US/$10.99CAN
___Hide and Seek	1-4201-0184-6	$6.99US/$9.99CAN
___Hokus Pokus	1-4201-0185-4	$6.99US/$9.99CAN
___Fast Track	1-4201-0186-2	$6.99US/$9.99CAN
___Collateral Damage	1-4201-0187-0	$6.99US/$9.99CAN
___Final Justice	1-4201-0188-9	$6.99US/$9.99CAN
___Up Close and Personal	0-8217-7956-7	$7.99US/$9.99CAN
___Under the Radar	1-4201-0683-X	$6.99US/$9.99CAN
___Razor Sharp	1-4201-0684-8	$7.99US/$10.99CAN
___Yesterday	1-4201-1494-8	$5.99US/$6.99CAN
___Vanishing Act	1-4201-0685-6	$7.99US/$10.99CAN
___Sara's Song	1-4201-1493-X	$5.99US/$6.99CAN
___Deadly Deals	1-4201-0686-4	$7.99US/$10.99CAN
___Game Over	1-4201-0687-2	$7.99US/$10.99CAN
___Sins of Omission	1-4201-1153-1	$7.99US/$10.99CAN
___Sins of the Flesh	1-4201-1154-X	$7.99US/$10.99CAN
___Cross Roads	1-4201-1192-2	$7.99US/$10.99CAN

Available Wherever Books Are Sold!
Check out our website at **www.kensingtonbooks.com**